CREATURES OF WANT...

"Tanzer's charming, confident follow-up to *Creatures of Will and Temper* continues the conceit of drawing on famous literary source texts for character and plot material; here, *The Great Gatsby* crashes into the works of H. P. Lovecraft, with, of course, chaotic results . . ."

—*Publishers Weekly,* starred review

"Tanzer expertly weaves an authentic historical setting into a tense, engrossing supernatural frame with lush descriptions and a steadily building pace."

—*Booklist*

"This is a measured, atmospheric novel, with compelling characters and a deeply disturbing undercurrent of horror."

—Tor.com

"Tanzer has a deft hand with characterization [and] every page is compelling."

—*Locus*

"Profound and enthralling. This book is a delicate dream, mixing its own internal mythology with a brutal tale of prejudice and human frailty . . . Tanzer is absolutely one to watch."

—Seanan McGuire, best-selling, award-winning
author of *In an Absent Dream*

CREATURES OF WILL AND TEMPER

"Gorgeously portrayed three-dimensional characters and sensual prose propel this smoothly entertaining story to an emotionally affecting end."

—*Publishers Weekly*, starred review

"An artful, witty, Oscar Wilde pastiche with the heart of a paranormal thriller."

—Diana Gabaldon, best-selling author of *Outlander*

"A delightful, dark, and entertaining romp with serious intent behind it . . . Molly Tanzer is at the top of her form in this beautifully constructed novel."

—Jeff VanderMeer, best-selling author
of the Southern Reach trilogy

"Extraordinary, peculiar, odd and compelling . . . The atmosphere breathes life. It has a generosity of spirit, beneath the dark bits."

—Tor.com

"There has never been a better time for a spirited, feminist reinvention of *The Picture of Dorian Gray* . . . *Creatures of Will and Temper* is a wild ride from start to finish, beautifully and boldly written, and a most worthy successor to Oscar Wilde's scandalous novel."

—Amy Stewart, author of *Girl Waits with Gun*

"Decadent Victorians clash with dueling demon-hunters in this page-turning reinvention of Oscar Wilde's classic tale."

—Charles Stross, award-winning author of *The Delirium Brief*

CREATURES OF CHARM AND HUNGER

CREATURES
OF
CHARM

HUNGER

Molly Tanzer

A John Joseph Adams Book

MARINER BOOKS

HOUGHTON MIFFLIN HARCOURT

BOSTON   NEW YORK

2020

389 3528

For information about permission to reproduce selections from this book,
write to trade.permissions@hmhco.com or to Permissions,
Houghton Mifflin Harcourt Publishing Company,
3 Park Avenue, 19th Floor, New York, New York 10016.

hmhbooks.com

Library of Congress Cataloging-in-Publication Data
Names: Tanzer, Molly, author.
Title: Creatures of charm and hunger / Molly Tanzer.
Description: Boston : Mariner Books/Houghton Mifflin Harcourt, 2020. |
Series: The diabolist's library
Identifiers: LCCN 2019039872 (print) | LCCN 2019039873 (ebook) |
ISBN 9780358065210 (trade paperback) | ISBN 9780358066729 (ebook)
Subjects: GSAFD: Occult fiction.
Classification: LCC PS3620.A7254 C65 2020 (print) | LCC PS3620.A7254 (ebook) |
DDC 813/.6—dc23
LC record available at https://lccn.loc.gov/2019039872
LC ebook record available at https://lccn.loc.gov/2019039873

Printed in the United States of America
DOC 10 9 8 7 6 5 4 3 2 1

PROLOGUE

EDITH BLACKWOOD CAREFULLY SELECTED ONE of the cut-crystal perfume atomizers from the narrow table by her front door. Holding it in her palm for a long moment warmed the pink fluid within — just a touch; just as she needed.

I hate London, complained the demon Mercurialis in a voice only Edith could hear. Decades of familiarity with her constant, invisible companion meant she understood it in words, but its speech registered more to her mind as a series of plucks and whirs and chirps, as well as the occasional chime.

"I know," she said aloud to the silence of her Paris flat. "I don't like England either, but go we must. Jane Blackwood is my only niece, and I will not miss her Test. Nor could I! I agreed to give it to her and to her friend Miriam. But even more than that, I want to be there to see her progress beyond her apprenticeship. She'll celebrate in style even if it means I must sojourn to the northern wilds of England. Otherwise, my sister will likely just let Jane stay up half an hour late as a treat. She deserves more for taking such an important step along the path to becoming a Master diabolist." Edith's demon agreed wholeheartedly with all of this. "And it will be good to be somewhere quiet for a few days. It's been months since we went out without always looking over our shoulder."

Mercurialis conceded this point too. The Occupation might be over, but the war was not; the streets of Paris were not yet safe. They hadn't won until they'd won — and they hadn't won. Not yet.

Edith misted herself with a few spritzes from the warmed bottle, then set it aside, picking up a long silver needle. She pricked her finger with it. As the blood beaded up, she took hold of her valise in her other hand and stepped within a slate circle set into the marble floor of her foyer. She let the welling blood drip down, and as soon as it hit the floor, pale blue electricity began to crackle all along her body, currents of lightning running up her legs, encasing her like bright vines. After a moment, they receded, save for a few extra flashes along the jet beadwork of her black dress and the black fur collar of her cape ...

And she was somewhere else entirely: a disused kitchen in a shabby London boarding house, standing upon a slate circle similar to the one in her own apartment. The morning sunlight filtering through the dirty windows was dreary and watery, wintery and unmistakably English.

The demonic sigh in Edith's mind sounded more like the twittering of a distant bird, but its point was clear and inarguable.

Edith was surrounded by a column of woven golden mesh that ran from floor to ceiling. Through the fine holes she could see the shape of a man sitting in a chair. She could also see the glint of the gun he had trained on her.

She had come here expecting such a welcome. Edith was a spy, and this was a spy's gate into the UK. Protecting it was of utmost importance.

"Swift wings, swift victory," said Edith.

"Swifter wings, swifter victory," said the man with the gun.

Edith stepped through the door of the mesh cage, set down her valise, and rucked up the sleeve of her dress to reveal a tattoo on her forearm: a stark white equilateral triangle and, within that, a talaria—the winged sandal of Hermes. The brightness of the white ink against her black skin was itself evidence of the mark's diabolic nature, but the group she was part of—the Young Talarians—hadn't gotten as far as they had by cutting corners when it came to security.

The man with the gun used his teeth to pull the cork out of a phial and dribbled an oily fluid upon her tattoo. It fizzed and popped and sizzled away into silver smoke, at which point he curtly nodded once.

Edith, like most diabolists, was also a member of an international organization known as the Société des Éclairées. While the Société had long ago denounced the Nazis, their sympathizers, and their ideology, due to its worldwide nature it could not be aggressively political without causing internal problems. The Young Talarians—the group to which Edith belonged—were technically independent ... but not forbidden from using the Société's resources.

It was impossible to say how much the Young Talarians had done for the Allies over the course of the war. Their help had been as invisible as it was invaluable. The Nazis, of course, had their own diabolists.

Edith had been a founding member of the Young Talarians, along with a few of her closest friends—Maja Znidarcic, Zelda Lizman, and Saul Zeitz. She could not sit idly by, not being who she was. Edith had been a small child when the Blackwoods adopted her, taking her from her West African homeland after her parents had died, to travel the world with them and their daughter, Nancy—but Edith had never forgotten her roots.

"Welcome to London, Edith," said George, lowering his Webley and holstering it. "You're right on time."

"Is my car waiting for me?" she asked, readjusting her sleeve. She wasn't late, but she'd need to get moving if she wanted to arrive in Hawkshead by the afternoon, given the distance and uncertain state of the roads.

"At the garage on St. Mark's," he said. And then, with a complete shift in his manners, he grinned. "Good luck to the young hopefuls, too."

Edith cocked a manicured eyebrow at George. "Young hopefuls?" she asked, conveying with her tone that it was an improper thing for him to have said. "To whom are you referring?"

George straightened up. "Sorry. It's only that Monsieur Durand had mentioned Jane and Miriam were to undergo their Test."

Of course it had been Patrice Durand who had blabbed! Edith frowned at George as Mercurialis quietly chuckled to itself over her consternation. When an apprentice diabolist underwent their Test, it was supposed to be a private affair. Patrice Durand and his former lover, Edith's sister Nancy Blackwood, were estranged, yes, but he knew that Nancy had always been a stickler for the rules.

"What else did Patrice have to say about my niece, my sister, and her ward?" asked Edith, her tone icier than the streets beyond the windows of the kitchen.

"Nothing," said George, blushing now. All his earlier cool had left him. Edith sighed—new recruits were always a bit jumpy.

"Let's forget we had this conversation," she said. This new evidence that Patrice had not changed, in spite of his claims to the contrary, cast quite a shadow over another reason for Edith's visit: Edith had finally resolved to at last tell Jane who her father was, even though this was explicitly against her mother's wishes. Jane had always longed to know, and as she had just turned sixteen a month ago, Edith had thought to give this knowledge to her as a belated birthday gift. Now, she was even less certain this was a good idea.

"If you'll excuse me, I'll just use the ladies' before I depart," said Edith. George nodded and Edith swished by him, her heels clicking on the tile.

In the washroom she opened up her makeup bag and applied a light dusting of powder to her cheeks and some mascara to her dark lashes. Both cosmetics were specially formulated with diabolic essences to conceal her appearance. Glamour, indeed! Now, anyone who looked at Edith would see a white woman . . . unless they took a careful second look. For anyone who did, she put on a black hat with a little veil. No one wanted to look at a widow for too long—at least not here in England.

If she'd needed a better disguise, she would have drawn on the power of her demon. Mercurialis lent its host unusual power over many amusing types of illusion, changing one's appearance being one of them. But for just a short walk along busy streets, Edith did not need to tax her resources in that manner.

George looked a bit surprised when she emerged, but then quickly recovered. "When will you be returning?"

"Within a week. Do you need a specific date and time?"

"No, ma'am. I'll be here."

"I promise to be in at a decent hour." She favored him with a smile.

He returned it. "It's not that; the gate just takes a moment or two to set up, and I wouldn't like to make you wait."

"It's still faster than the Night Ferry!"

Edith was in a good mood. She was pleased to have a little shopping to do and then a nice long unbroken drive ahead of her, two things almost impossible in Paris.

Edith peeked out the door to find a light drizzle falling upon the gray paving stones of the street. She claimed an umbrella, black of course, from the umbrella stand.

"I promise I'll return it," she said, before stepping out into the morning gloom. Her foot immediately found a puddle.

Mercurialis sighed.

CREATURES OF CHARM AND HUNGER

1

IT WAS A COLD MORNING in early February, but outside the windows of the old farmhouse, the world was still cloaked in blackest night. Not even the sliver of a moon silvered the frost and snow crusting the yard and the rock-strewn hills beyond. Only the pale starlight showed Miriam Cantor the barn where she must go to feed the geese and the ducks.

She hesitated before opening the back door and venturing forth into the profound stillness only found just before the dawn in deep winter. But it was not the silence that made her hesitate, nor the darkness, nor the chill—nor was it fear of what predators might be between her and the barn. At least, not animal ones. Foxes and weasels did not frighten her; it was the threat of *who* might be out there, not *what,* that caused sweat to prick at her neck and under her arms even in the raw predawn.

Her worry was absurd, she knew it was. There were no Nazis prowling through the frigid gloom. There were no Nazis anywhere nearby, not down the lane in the picturesque village of Hawkshead, not in the houses of their distant neighbors. Here in the north of England, she was safe—and yet every morning, Miriam had to remind herself of that before she could pick her way along the path that wound its way through the hoary remains of last year's victory garden.

"Who's the real goose here?" muttered Miriam as she let herself into the barn. The truth was, if Nazis ever *did* intrude upon their privacy, her "aunt" Nancy, whose treasured flock impatiently pecked at Miriam's shoes, would know. Mrs. Nancy Blackwood was no mere widow living quietly with her daughter and ward on a farm in England. Nancy Blackwood was a diabolist—a natural scientist who had summoned a demon and worked with it and its essences rather than more traditional chemicals or creatures. Her demon lent her certain unusual abilities in exchange for sharing her experiences and her body.

Nancy was also the official Librarian for the Société des Éclairées, the current worldwide organization of diabolists. The Société formally oversaw the education of individuals interested in working with demons—or rather, the powerful, ineffable beings they called demons. That meant Nancy had more methods of protecting herself than the average widow—more than the average diabolist, even—to protect her home and the books within the Library beneath it.

It was also true that Miriam, as Nancy's apprentice, was not entirely helpless. Even so, she was only fifteen and had not yet passed her Test.

Miriam rubbed at her numb and dripping nose before starting to scoop grain onto the ground. She, like most apprentices, spent a lot of time pondering demons and their abilities, but actually summoning one was something only Master diabolists were allowed to do. As an apprentice, she was limited to minor works of diablerie, such as concocting armamentaria—the diabolical potions, pills, and powders that were the essence of the Art. Before she advanced beyond that, Miriam would need to pass her Test, and then submit the results of her Practical for judgment by the Société before she would be deemed qualified.

Even an apprentice diabolist could do much without actually summoning a demon, however. For instance, by using diabolic essences culled from plants and minerals, Miriam had created a potion that let her assess an opponent's weaknesses if she had to strike out with fist or knife, and a pastille that granted her increased strength and speed. Keeping a phial of the former and a small tin of the latter in her pocket helped Miriam stay calm when she needed to venture into the village.

The trouble was that the effects of apprentice armamentaria did not last long. Creating them was a process intended to educate, not endure. But once Miriam had summoned her own demon, she, like Nancy, would be a powerful diabolist, capable of ever so much more.

As she scattered grain on the ground, Miriam's mind strayed to a different farm, in a different country, where she'd fed different ducks. Her aunt—a real aunt, her father's sister Rivka, whose farm outside of Weimar had been seized by the Nazis—had also kept poultry, and goats too.

They'd stopped visiting her long before that, when the laws had made it difficult for their family to do much of anything without being harassed. The last time they all went out as a family, a boy had thrown a stone. A policeman had laughed when it hit Miriam's father in the back. That was when Miriam's mother and father had written to Nancy to ask if their daughter could live with her, in England . . .

No—she could not think on that now. Miriam pushed the memories away, shoving them down inside a shadowed place deep within her that served as a repository for her fear, her rage, and her disappointment. That silent shadowed hollow never judged, never rejected, never asked questions—it just took what she offered it, and absorbed it, and made it go away.

"All that happened a long time ago," Miriam said to the ducks and the geese as they nibbled at the grain. She couldn't let her mind wander away down those unpleasant paths—there was too much to do today in anticipation of the arrival of another "aunt": Aunt Edith.

Edith was Nancy's sister. She, too, was part of the Société, though, unlike Nancy, she was not an elected official. The position of Librarian meant living in the Library, which was here, in rural Hawkshead. Why the Library was in Hawkshead no one knew, but it had been there in various forms since the Middle Ages—

long before the Société formed in Paris, a hundred years ago—
and there it would remain after the Société gave way to some new
organization, whenever it inevitably did.

Once she had finished feeding the poultry, Miriam returned to
the farmhouse. Nancy was awake and in the kitchen, frying a bit of
their weekly ration of bacon in a skillet on the cooktop of her ancient beloved AGA. The smell of it was mouthwatering and, even
after all this time, a little guilt-inducing. But hunger was hunger,
and rationing was rationing.

"How are they this morning?" asked Nancy, as Miriam shrugged
out of her coat.

"Snug and warm and fed." Miriam tied her apron around her
waist with a satisfied tug. It was a relief to once again be within
four walls and under a sturdy roof.

"I wish I could say the same," said Nancy's daughter, Jane, as she
bustled into the kitchen to put on her own apron. "I'm starving!"

Miriam's "cousin" had obviously gotten up early to set herself
to rights. Jane's hair was coiffed and shining, and she was already
dressed, nicely, in a dark gray skirt and a fashionably stark white
blouse. The cardigan she wore over it was also gray, but the color
of smoke rather than charcoal.

Miriam unconsciously glanced down at her tweedy ankle-
length skirt. It was one of Nancy's hemmed and patched-up hand-
me-downs, lumpy and too large but suitable for keeping her calves
free of muck when she went out to the barns or her legs warm as
she worked in the lab and Library. She'd not thought of dressing
for Edith's arrival; perhaps she should have.

"Is it ready?" asked Jane, reaching for the tea before she even really sat down. "I think I shall starve to death if I have to wait any
longer!"

"Must you be so dramatic?" said Nancy, turning around with a
tray full of bacon and toast, which she set down in the center of
the scarred wooden kitchen table alongside the small pat of but-

ter they must share. Jane scowled at the word *dramatic* and slurped her tea.

"A lady is as a lady does," remarked Nancy airily, as if this wisdom had just come to her mind unprovoked. At last she sat down and poured herself a cup of tea. Then, from a pocket in her apron, she withdrew a little dropper bottle of smoked glass. She squeezed a bit of clear fluid into her tea before taking her first sip, doctoring the beverage not with milk and sugar, as Miriam liked it, but with a distillate of the essence of her demon, the Patron of Curiosity.

In order for diabolists to comfortably maintain contact with their demons, they had to regularly consume their essences. Every diabolist had their preferred way of doing so, some more elaborate or decadent than others. Nancy, being a no-muss, no-fuss sort of woman, produced a tincture from the unusually beautiful and robust chives she cultivated in pots on her sunniest windowsill.

"And speaking of dressing nicely," said Nancy, after taking a sip, "I don't know why you've done that so early. You still have to dust and sweep, you know! I won't have you begging off smartening up the house just because you've already smartened up yourself."

"But I dusted and swept yesterday!" cried Jane.

"It could do with another going-over. This time, use the dust rag on the woodwork instead of talking to it like it's Clark Gable."

For a while now it had been Jane's joy to go see every picture she could at the theatre in Ambleside. She talked endlessly to Miriam about the sophistication and beauty of the women on the silver screen, but Miriam had only Jane's word for how wonderful they were. She had never gone. It was five miles to Ambleside, and the thought of the bus made Miriam dizzy. In a way, though, she felt she'd seen *Meet Me in St. Louis, Cover Girl,* and other films; Jane liked to talk over the plots after she got back, doing impressions of the actresses Miriam knew only from still photographs in Jane's magazines.

Jane was good at impressions—so good she'd managed to incorporate a few little turns of speech and gestures into her everyday manners. And as they were at that age where it was common for girls to quickly become young ladies, only Miriam was pained by her friend growing up.

Nancy, for her part, seemed to find it amusing.

"Edith won't arrive until around two, so you've plenty of time to do your chores *and* reapply that lipstick before we leave if it gets smudged. Yes, I noticed," said Nancy, who disapproved of cosmetics. Miriam thought that a bit funny, given that Nancy was a Master diabolist; most people would likely see trafficking with demons as a far greater offense against nature than a bit of mascara.

Jane looked like a little girl as she sullenly poked at her breakfast.

"You'll trip over that lip if you don't pick it up," said Nancy, but her teasing did little to mollify her daughter. "Oh, come now. What would your beloved Edith have to say if she saw you like that?"

"Mother!"

That was another change—Jane had always called her mother "Mum" until lately.

"Oh, come now. If you'd known Edie as long as I have, you wouldn't feel there was some great need to make yourself up for her," said Nancy. "She was once your age, you know—and a lot wilder and more scabby-kneed than either of you."

"Scabby-kneed!"

Miriam was now the sullen one as she stared at her plate. Jane's affected horror at this information exasperated her. Why should it surprise Jane that Edith had had to put away childish things, just like anyone else? Did Jane really believe her aunt had sprung forth into the world as a stylish adult?

And anyway, squeamishness was not for the ambitious when

it came to the Art. Master diabolists saved their hair trimmings, their nail clippings, their scabs, sometimes even their menstrual fluid—anything that could become infused with the essences that diabolists regularly consumed to maintain their connection with their demons. Some diabolists had been known to harvest permanent parts of their own bodies in the service of empowering a particularly powerful preparation—such things could be rendered down to enhance the overall potency of diabolic armamentaria. *Scabby knees* weren't a patch on, say, extracting one's own perfectly healthy molar.

But Miriam didn't say any of this. She took a discreet, calming breath and pushed her annoyance and anger down inside her, where the shadow within her welcomed her feelings with open arms.

"Edie played rugby with our brothers until the day she moved away," said Nancy.

"And yet she seems so civilized. I suppose there's hope for me yet," said Jane, before finally stabbing a piece of bacon with her fork.

"Oh, no," said Nancy, with an appraising look at her daughter. "There's no hope for you—or there won't be if you don't finish your breakfast and your chores."

Jane's childish, long-suffering sigh made Miriam smile to herself, but she quickly sobered when her aunt turned her attention to her.

"Aren't you excited about Edith's visit, Miriam?"

Nancy's question caught her off guard.

"Of course I'm excited," she said, but when that sounded a bit flabby even to her own ears, Miriam added, "I've been wanting to ask Edith about her research into diabolically enhanced cosmetics. I think it might help me understand the theory behind the Fifth Transmutation."

This was all true. The only lie was in what she'd omitted.

"Oh, I'd like to hear that too." Jane wasn't pouting now. She was bright, alert, and focused: the Jane that Miriam liked.

Jane was also an apprentice diabolist. They'd learned side by side since Miriam had come to stay, but they couldn't be more different. Where Miriam was pleased to think through the theoretical aspects of an act of diablerie before attempting it, Jane jumped right in to learn how deep the water was.

"The Fifth Transmutation is necessary when attempting Campanella's Substantive Exchange," said Jane. Jane was currently working her way through the Twelve Transmutations, a set of practical exercises. "I can't quite parse it, and I'd like to see a practical demonstration. The *Grimoire Italien* says that demonic vapors and their impure properties are *beneficial,* but it's not clear if it means for the demon or the diabolist."

"The *Grimoire Italien*? Are you using the French translation of *Trasformazioni della Materia*?" asked Miriam. Jane nodded. "Oh!" said Miriam. "In the original medieval Italian, that passage is a bit clearer. The demon benefits, but there's also a chance that . . ." Miriam trailed off as she saw Jane blushing angrily.

Miriam winced. The learning of ancient languages was not among Jane's talents—which was nothing to be ashamed of, in Miriam's opinion. Still, she should have remembered how sensitive Jane was about it.

"Miriam, as usual you're not only correct, but your scholarship is impressively thorough," said Nancy.

Nancy's notice always thrilled Miriam, but it was hard for her to accept the compliment with Jane looking so unhappy and embarrassed.

"I wish I'd known you were reading that," said Miriam. "The modern Italian translation is better, and I have it in my room to compare with the medieval, since the medieval is a bother to read. It's barely even Italian, really—just a dog's breakfast of medieval Venetian vernacular mixed with Latin."

"Thank you," said Jane, with the sort of formality and poise she usually reserved for impressions of her favorite actresses. "I'd be pleased to look at it when you can spare it."

"*Later,*" said Nancy, with a tone that conveyed exactly what the girls ought to be doing just then.

Miriam began to clear the dishes, as keeping the kitchen tidy was one of her responsibilities. Jane, too, stood up from the table, but as she did, a great yowl split the air and a soft gray blur of wounded dignity streaked out the kitchen, the bell of his collar jangling merrily.

"Poor Smudge!" Jane, dismayed, hurried after the cat to check on him.

"You'd think one day he'd learn that sitting behind Jane's chair will only get him a pinched tail," said Miriam.

"Perhaps he enjoys the attention," said Nancy, as she wrapped the remaining bread in a cloth. "I'm off to the stacks, my dear."

"All right."

"I hope you'll join us when we walk into the village? I think it'll be a lovely day in spite of the cold, and a merry party once Edie arrives."

Miriam managed a smile even as her stomach churned at the thought of the long walk away from their safe, quiet home into the relative chaos that was Hawkshead. But she loved Nancy very much and wanted to please her—no, more than that: she wanted to be the sort of person who pleased Nancy.

"Of course!"

Miriam was rewarded with a smile. "I'm very glad," said Nancy. "Now, I must see to a few things before my sister takes up all my waking hours. Ciao!" And with that, Nancy swept out of the room with more flair than was strictly necessary.

For all she was hard on Jane for being "dramatic," Nancy, too, had a bit of the theatrical about her. And as with Jane, it came out even more when Edith visited.

2

SMUDGE WAS FINE, OF COURSE. The large gray tomcat just liked to make a scene. Jane knew that, but running after him had been a good excuse to get out of the kitchen so she could fume alone, in peace.

She was cross with her mother for being her mother, and she was cross at herself for being angry at Miriam. Miriam hadn't meant to embarrass her, Jane knew that, but she had been embarrassed just the same.

Miriam and Nancy might not be related by blood, but they were more similar for that lack, as far as Jane could tell. While Jane might *look* like her mother (albeit a plainer version), Miriam *thought* like her. They came at problems in the same way; enjoyed the learning of languages and the quiet rustle of the turning page. They even shared a middle name: Cornelia, after the sixteenth-century diabolist Cornelius Agrippa.

Jane was glad for it. Mostly. She wanted Miriam to feel like a real part of their family, and of course that was helped by her having a real connection to Nancy. It was just hard, being the odd one out—and it was especially hard knowing Nancy wished her daughter was a little bit more like her ward.

But Jane could only be who she was—and she was someone who felt a healthy respect for the *how* and the *why* of the Art . . . but when it came down to it, Jane would really rather just *do*.

Jane's mother always said that "doing" was too dangerous a method of learning many of the skills diabolists regularly relied upon. That was for "wild" diabolists, as her mother called them—practitioners of the Art who learned it without the safe and effective teachings of the Société.

Jane had no desire to be a wild diabolist—she wanted to be a Master, with all its attendant privileges. But there was no rule in the Société's criteria for Mastery that said Jane had to *enjoy* the theoretical part.

Nor was there any rule about the way an aspiring Master had to think through certain diabolical problems, as far as Jane could tell. While it might please her mother and Miriam to come at every question like two scientists in a laboratory, Jane was free to think of herself as a wielder of arcane powers—as long as the results of her efforts were successful, it shouldn't matter. So much of the Art was about imagination, and about using one's will to change what was possible. But every time Jane used the language of the occult to explain her reasoning, her mother would try to weed it out of her like an obsessed gardener.

"We're not *witches,* Jane," her mother had said to her, time and again.

And that was true. But it was also true that neither were they scientists.

While it was possible that Nancy wasn't as disappointed by Jane as Jane sometimes thought, it was also true that she rarely praised her daughter often or lavishly. Indeed, it was almost better at times not to hear how her mother thought her efforts *good,* said in that earnest but unenthusiastic way that managed to convey that perhaps if Jane tried a wee bit harder, Nancy might think her efforts *very good* or even *excellent.*

Jane had once been able to talk to Miriam about these sorts of feelings, but no longer—not since she realized that in many ways Miriam agreed with Nancy about Jane's study habits and methods, and also about Jane's eagerness to begin the process of transforming into the distinctive young lady she'd like to one day become.

She found Smudge by the front stairs, sitting on a middle step. She plunked down next to him, and the cat crawled, purring, into her lap, a sure sign that all was forgiven. The feel of his silky fur under her fingers was soothing, and when she scratched him behind the ears and under the chin, his eyes closed in feline bliss.

"Oh, Smudge," she sighed. "You understand, don't you?"

Smudge cracked open one yellow eye as if acknowledging her words. She ruffled his ears, and he nipped her on the hand hard enough to leave a wine-colored indentation in her skin before dashing upstairs as if the devil—or more probably, a demon—were after him.

She needed to get to dusting anyway.

Her mother had been right; Jane had made a hash of her chores the day before. But not because she was thinking about Clark Gable—or anyone else, for that matter.

Talking aloud through a problem often helped Jane figure out the answer, and yesterday Jane had been muttering over her latest unsuccessful attempt to make a broomstick fly. Not just any broomstick, either—the fancy one she'd bought in London with Edith last year with the polished black handle and black stitching keeping the bristles secured. Beautiful as it was, it had been unaffected by an armamentarium of flight Jane had made from a bit of dried lemon peel infused with the essence of a demon colloquially called Seven Clouds. An Egyptian diabolist, renowned for her ability to levitate, had sent it to her via a tricky little piece of diablerie involving a simulacrum of a seagull. When it had landed on Jane's windowsill, reeking of fish and salt, it was so lifelike—but after it vomited up a wooden box, it had dissolved into smoke that smelled of autumn's first wood fire.

It hurt that Nancy assumed her daughter's thoughts were so frivolous, especially given the ambitious undertaking Jane was attempting—so ambitious it might, in fact, be impossible.

Magical items like the fairy dust of *Peter Pan*, the flying carpet of *One Thousand and One Nights*, or—Jane's favorite—the witch's broomstick had captured the public imagination since time immemorial. But actually getting objects—let alone people—to fly was seemingly impossible, even for a Master diabolist.

Therefore, to do so as an apprentice would be quite a feather in Jane's cap, if she could manage it.

Most diabolists who wished to fly made the Pact with a demon that granted such an ability. But Jane had looked at the *Bilinen Şeytanların Kitabı—The Book of Known Demons*—and none of those demons seemed like her idea of a life's companion. *Especially* Seven Clouds; beyond granting levitation, all it did for its diabolist was "calm the nerves," and Jane could make herself a cup of tea for that.

And anyway, she didn't want to *levitate*. She wanted to *fly*. Diabolists were like unto gods and goddesses; why should they not have the powers of such?

As she rinsed out her dust rag in the kitchen sink, Jane blushed, her eyes tracking nervously toward the door to the stairs of the Library. Her mother would not like to know that such a thought had crossed Jane's mind. Nancy was always quick to remind them that diabolists were *not* gods; they were *not* kings and queens.

Fine with Jane. She didn't want to rule anyone. Plenty of gods didn't seem to care a fig for the struggles of men. They just wanted to have a good time, and that was Jane's goal too. She longed to escape Hawkshead and Cumbria altogether so she might go on adventures in the deserts of Egypt wearing gauzy white; attend parties in fabulous flats in Paris wearing scandalous, alluring black, a color currently forbidden to her by her mother because, well . . .

We're not witches, *Jane.*

Jane sincerely hoped her mother would enjoy the taste of her own words when Jane was zooming about the countryside on a broomstick like Margaret Hamilton in *The Wizard of Oz*.

Jane didn't have her own looking glass, much to her chagrin, and the bathroom's tin mirror revealed what could be only charitably described as an Impressionist interpretation of her face. For her final inspection, only her mother's vanity would do, so just before noon, Jane took off her apron and went upstairs to see if she was at all mussed from her labors. But when she entered Nancy's rooms, she found the vanity already occupied.

"I don't know why braiding my hair makes me fly to pieces when I can create a potion of binding from memory," snarled Miriam.

Jane felt an overwhelming rush of affection for her friend that did much to dispel her earlier pique.

"Let's see what we can do," she said, coming up behind Miriam. She freed Nancy's comb from where her friend held it twisted in her fingers and then set to detangling the mess before her. There was no salvaging any of whatever Miriam had been trying to do; they'd have to start over entirely. Jane began by trying to find all the pins in Miriam's hair with her nimble fingers.

Jane envied the dark waves that cascaded over Miriam's shoulders. Her own mousy-brown tresses were so thin and fine that there were few fashionable styles that looked well on her—oh, to have Hedy Lamarr's mane to start out with!

"Let's do a few pinned rolls and then use a ribbon," she said, running the brush through Miriam's hair. A bit of blue would accentuate her friend's dark hair and high color.

"I trust you," said Miriam.

"You'll look beautiful," said Jane. It was true, she would, with her big dark eyes and her thick brows that would make Miriam really stand out if only she'd let Jane tame them a bit.

But, of course, the last thing Miriam wanted was to stand out.

"You manage it so easily," sighed Miriam, as her hair began to take on an actual shape and style.

"I find it fun," said Jane. "A harmless distraction from the war, if a bit pointless when one lives in a tiny village. Why, the only person around our age who lives within ten miles and seems remotely thoughtful is the blacksmith's son—hey!"

Miriam had lurched around, her elbow narrowly missing the box of hairpins Jane had set upon the vanity. "*Sam?*" she asked, mouth hanging open in childish astonishment. "Do you fancy him?"

"Goodness no!" Jane put her hand on the top of Miriam's head and physically turned it back to face the looking glass. "I just admire his ability to speak in complete sentences."

"I see," said Miriam.

The truth was, Jane had never fancied anyone, ever, and she didn't think she ever would. In spite of what her mother might think, she felt nothing for Clark Gable or any other star of the silver screen. Jane's interest in the cinema was academic, not romantic. Where else in Cumbria would she learn to act like a lady? The romance plots of films, for Jane, were always just a distraction from the tensions of a drawing room or the currents of a party sequence.

"But if you *did* fancy him . . ." said Miriam.

"Why, Miriam!" Jane pantomimed surprise. "Do *you* fancy Sam Nibley?"

Miriam blushed. "No!"

Jane leaned in, a shark's smile on her lips.

"Are you *sure?*" she drawled.

"Yes!" Miriam was now pale as a sheet. Jane genuinely couldn't tell if her friend was feeling upset at being found out, or was mortified to be accused of something she did not feel. Either was possible, so Jane let the matter drop and turned her attention to the last few pins Miriam's hair needed to stay in place.

When she was done, she stepped back and looked Miriam over with an exaggerated critical gaze, hand on her chin.

"I think you look marvelous," Jane declared, "but how do *you* like it?"

Miriam finally looked up from her twisting hands. "Oh! I barely recognize myself. It's far too glamorous!"

"Oh, stop. You look lovely." The hairstyle wasn't "glamorous" at all—it just showed off Miriam's face rather than hiding it. "Now budge up and let me put myself together."

Jane spent an enjoyable half hour making herself ready anew. A very fidgety Miriam hung about as she did so. She was anxious and doing a poor job of pretending not to be.

"All right," said Jane, with a satisfied pat of her hair. "I think that's all I can do."

"Let's go down to the Library, then!"

Miriam truly loved the Library—she would live down there if she could, Jane suspected. In fact, Jane was amazed Miriam had made small talk with her that afternoon instead of leaving her for the more solitary pleasures of its shelves and aisles.

Jane, on the other hand, couldn't bear the darkness or the quiet for very long. In summer, she wanted to be under a tree, a tatty blanket under her bottom and a picnic basket by her side; in winter, feeding the wood burner in the kitchen with a kettle singing in the background. That wasn't to say she didn't love the Library —she did. She'd been nursed within its walls, taken her first steps across its floor, and said her first words to the sigils and guardians that were some of the cavern's oldest protections.

Not for the first time, Jane wondered what the other residents of Hawkshead would think about this place. Most of them would simply be amazed to know a cave like this existed near them; nature enthusiasts would be a bit more unsettled to note that the curiously squared-off walls had been carved from no local slate or granite, but rather some decidedly imported tufa. The carvings were all authentic Etruscan, but it was a mystery whether its presence here, in Cumbria, was due to the efforts of ancient diabolists or more modern ones. They had records of its existence dating back to the fifteenth century but no further; no one knew how it had gotten there, but there it was, and the climate within always perfect for the preservation of the written word whether it be recorded upon paper, skin, or materials stranger yet. Not only that, but all attempts to move the Library had failed, and those few who had sought to destroy it had met with terrible fates—indeed, that had been the end of the diabolists' organization previous to the Société.

The Library also seemed to expand to accommodate new works, though interestingly its measurements remained the same whenever anyone tried to calculate its size. It was an astonishing work of diablerie, and Jane never failed to be moved by it. She just knew that there were other astonishing wonders out there in the world, and she wanted to see them, too.

"Ah, girls!" Jane's mother was in the process of receiving an ancient scroll through the Library's Basque Lens, a tool used by every diabolist in the Société to send written messages over distances. The Basque Lens lay flat upon Nancy's large oaken desk, and while it would indeed reflect the viewer's face, it did so much more than that. Its surface had been infused with various diabolic essences and coated with layers of specific armamentaria, and once a Master made theirs, they could send written requests for chapters of books, or even entire volumes—from the Library, or from their fellow Masters. Merely press a scrap of paper bearing a message to a Basque Lens's surface, and a perfect copy would appear upon the addressee's.

It was Nancy's duty to keep up with fulfilling what requests came to the Library. It wasn't as onerous a task as one might think, given most diabolists' penchant for owning their own collection of rare volumes, but it still occupied the majority of her working hours.

Miriam raced up to take a look at the pile of Library materials Nancy had been sending along to their recipients. Jane chose instead to wait patiently, though in truth she was just as full of nervous energy and longed to be already walking toward the village.

Her patience was tested as everyone fumbled their way into their coats and their hats and mittens and scarves. No one was dawdling—not even Miriam, who tended to delay leaving the house as long as possible. Regardless, Jane was in agonies by the time they left, and barely able to keep herself from skipping ahead when the white cottages and the spire of the village church came into sight.

"Here we are at last," said Nancy, as they walked up to the low wooden doorway of the Queen's Head, "and now you can relax, Jane! Next time, just put on a collar and bark at us the whole way if you're going to herd us so ruthlessly!"

Jane blushed. "I just thought we should be here when Edith arrives, not out of breath from rushing up at the last minute."

"We're certainly not late," remarked Nancy.

"We could always pop over to the Lion and have a cup of tea," said Miriam, her eyes angled longingly to the neighboring coaching inn.

Nancy peered at Miriam. "They have tea at the Queen's Head, and that is where we are to meet Edith. Does their tea not suit you?"

Miriam shook her head. "No! I just thought it looked . . . a bit warmer, is all."

Jane managed to pretend her snort was just a cough. The village forge was behind the Red Lion, and that, of course, was where Sam worked. Miriam's attempts to hide her interest in him were so clumsy, poor thing. Jane was just about to try to help her out by coming up with some reason, any reason, to amble past the forge, when Sam did them the favor by just appearing from the alley. He was carrying what looked to be, judging from the way his muscles were straining against the sleeves of his jumper, a very heavy box.

Miriam startled like a colt when she saw him. Poor Miriam!

"All right, ladies?" he said, with a smile that showed off his good teeth. "Are you in need of assistance?"

"Hello, Sam," said Nancy. "I can see why you would think we

might be, what with us just standing in the street like three fools. I believe we were discussing whether the Lion would be warmer than the Queen's Head. Have you an opinion on the matter?"

Miriam could not look more miserable and humiliated as she stared at the tips of her muddy boots—which was why it was Jane who noticed that Sam's eyes slid toward Miriam as he spoke.

"The *Lion* is always a bit warmer," he answered, confirming Jane's suspicions; he said it to Miriam, not any of the rest of them. "At least, so it seems to me."

He trailed off as Nancy shrugged elaborately; Miriam still said nothing. Jane was just mulling over how to help out her friend when the rattle of her aunt's stylish but finicky Citroën reached her ears.

"There's Edith!" she cried. A distraction would be the best possible thing for all of them at that point.

"I must be off," said Sam, excusing himself as he walked on with his box, much to Miriam's obvious relief.

Edith *halloo*ed at them, waving wildly with one hand as she steered with the other, much to the dismay of several villagers who were out and about on their various errands. Jane sighed to herself in envy; how she would love to be so noticed as she went through the world!

"Why on earth are you all standing in the street!" cried Edith as she killed the engine and leaped out of the automobile. A very confused stable boy wandered out to accept her gloves when she handed them off to him.

"I wish I knew," said Nancy, embracing her sister. "Were we strange children? I can't remember."

"The strangest!" declared Edith. "And you know it!"

Edith stood out in any crowd, but today she looked the part of the glamorous Continental even more than usual. Her dark skin was set off beautifully by a black suit that looked very much like something a stylish recent widow might wear, complete with black hat and black lace veil. Jane almost moaned, looking at the jet beadwork.

It was likely true what Nancy said—that given their rural location, it was a bad idea for any of them to "look like a witch." Diabolists might not use magic, but they could be prosecuted for it, given the unusual and unchristian nature of the Art. But that was just another reason Jane had for wanting to leave the village. No one in a city would bat an eye to see a smartly dressed young woman attending a party all in black. At least, so it seemed from Edith's accounts—and the movies Jane loved so much.

"You girls can't stop growing up, can you?" said Edith. Jane's heart soared when Edith caught her eye and gave her a private, approving nod.

"They won't slow down even though I beg them," said Nancy.

There was no road to the old farmhouse, just a path, so Edith supervised the loading of her luggage into the mule cart and passed the driver a pound coin. He looked pleased and promised prompt delivery.

"*Brr*, it's cold," she complained, as they began to walk. It was two miles from the village to their farm in the lonely countryside, over muddy paths dotted with frozen puddles. "How *do* you manage?"

"It's not so bad," said Miriam, the picture of loyalty. "The house is very snug."

"It's the Library I'm more worried about," said Edith, shivering inside a long black greatcoat she'd pulled from somewhere; its dramatic collar and cinched waist gave her a silhouette that would not be out of place in an Erté. "It's not exactly warm down there even if it's dry. I'll have to borrow some slippers so my toes don't freeze during your Test!"

"Test?" asked Miriam. She sounded as shocked as Jane felt. "*Whose* Test?"

Edith pulled a bag of what looked like fancy sweets from her purse and popped one into her mouth. They were her method of keeping in touch with her demon Mercurialis, but to any non-diabolist it looked like nothing more than a woman indulging in a bit of candy.

"Yours," said Edith, matter-of-factly. "It's time, according to Nance—but she couldn't test you herself. She'd be too easy on you." Edith's dark eyes flashed wickedly as she took Jane's hand and beckoned for Miriam to come along. "That's why I'm here at this dreadful time of year. Don't look so *surprised,* my dears, or at least don't *act* so surprised. It slows you down, and I'm perishing for want of a hot cup of tea."

"Oh, of course we'll have tea before you begin," said Jane's mother. "I even made a Victoria sandwich yesterday."

"I can't imagine having enough eggs for cake!" Edith sighed happily, but as she looked from Jane to Miriam, she sobered somewhat. "Such long faces! And with cake awaiting us! Don't worry, girls. You'll do just fine! You're ready!"

"Ready for what, though?" asked Miriam.

Jane had a different question, directed at both her mother and her aunt. "Why didn't you tell us?"

"Tradition," said her mother.

Jane scowled. *Tradition* was her least favorite reason for anything.

"Think about it this way—we've saved you the trouble of worrying about it!" said Edith.

Jane wasn't so sure about all that. They still had the entire walk home before them, after all.

And tea.

3

Nancy Blackwood's Victoria sandwich had won a prize three years in a row at the Hawkshead village fête—and it might have won more if Nancy hadn't stopped entering for the sake of the other bakers. War rationing meant Nancy baked less often these days, much to everyone's regret, so a slice was always a treat. Today, however, the perfectly delicate sponge was like ashes in Jane's mouth and the jam a cloying paste too sweet on her tongue. She could barely manage three bites.

Edith was having no such troubles; she had already polished off a second helping and was just washing it down with the last of her tea.

"If I can fit into any of my dresses by the end of this visit, it'll be a miracle," she said.

"Nobody's forcing you to have so much," said Nancy.

"*You* are," said Edith, pressing the pad of her manicured forefinger into the crumbs. "There's no cake like this in London—no cake like this in Paris, even. I think it has to be baked in the country to taste this good."

"Flatterer." Nancy shooed her sister's hand away from her plate. "Stop that and take these girls down to the Library. They both look like they'll shed their skins if we put this off a moment longer."

Jane looked at Miriam, but there was nothing she could think to say. It was time.

"Bring your tea," said Edith.

Jane's had long ago gone cold. She shook her head; she'd had enough—but to her surprise, her mother poured her a fresh cup, and Miriam too.

"Bring your tea," said Nancy, and there was a bit of sternness to her tone.

Jane took her cup and saucer. Miriam did too, similarly mystified.

"Now, let's get comfortable and talk about this Test," said Edith, as she led them down the stairs to the Library. "No need to keep you in suspense any longer."

"Why keep us in suspense at all?" asked Jane.

Edith's sympathetic expression did little to mollify her when the reason was, of course: "Tradition, Jane. If anything important having to do with the Société ever seems byzantine or unnecessary or even just plain silly, just think to yourself, *This is probably a tradition.*"

"I know! But—"

"Questions later. For now, sit."

They stopped at a little reading area with comfortable chairs that surrounded a low table. Edith flung herself into a wingback and produced an eyedropper from somewhere upon her person. When Jane and Miriam set down their tea, she put a few drops in both cups.

"Drink up," she said. "Mandatory, sorry. It's part of the Test."

"What is it?" asked Miriam, before Jane could even open her mouth.

"Truth serum," said Edith smoothly.

"So we can't cheat?" asked Miriam.

"So that you cannot cheat yourself." Edith's response was irritatingly cryptic. Jane took the cup and drank it all in one swallow.

Edith gave her an approving smile as Miriam rushed to catch up.

"Now," said Edith, "the Test is nothing like what you may have

experienced in school. It's not going to be me testing your knowledge of the Art. Instead, it will be a test you give yourself; or rather,
you will be tested on your own willingness to become a diabolist."

"How?" asked Miriam.

Edith didn't reply. After a moment, Jane felt her stomach lurch
—Edith wasn't being coy, she wasn't moving at all. She'd frozen
in place, her darkly rouged lips parted to reveal straight teeth as
she leaned against the left arm of the leather wingback chair. She
didn't blink, and when Jane stood to investigate, she didn't appear
to be breathing.

"Miriam," said Jane, but Miriam didn't answer.

Miriam wasn't there. She was gone as if she'd never been, and
when Jane put her hand on the seat of the chair, it was cold.

"Miriam?"

She isn't here.

The answer came from somewhere inside Jane. It wasn't a voice
—she felt it, rather than hearing it; the words weren't articulated
so much as conveyed.

She screamed.

It's all right. Please don't worry.

Jane's wildly beating heart did not slow at this request. She felt
faint as the tea sloshed gently in her heaving stomach and she
fell to her knees. It wasn't just the shocking sudden presence of
whatever it was that now occupied her mind; it was how much
of her mind it felt free to occupy. It was not only speaking to her
with an expectation of a response—it was looking her over, paw-
ing through her memories, her feelings, invading everything that
made her Jane Blackwood. It was the most intimate thing she'd
ever experienced, and she hated it so much. She felt she would
rather die than endure it a moment longer.

"Stop!" she cried. It was embarrassing, to be so exposed before
someone, or rather some*thing*, she hadn't given permission to look
at her. How could her beloved aunt have betrayed her so utterly?

Stop? But you invited me.

"I didn't!"

You did. You summoned me; we made the Pact. Forever shall I be a part of you, Jane Blackwood, and you, me. Be not afraid! We shall work wondrous acts of diablerie together.

Jane looked up, hoping her aunt might have come back to herself, but Edith was now gone, as was the chair she'd been sitting in. Jane was amazed to find herself in, of all places, a flat. A flat in a city Jane could not immediately identify from the bright skyline beyond her windows. She looked down and saw she was in a black dress that pulled across her breasts and her hips in a way that somehow gave her the illusion of curves. She was standing before a table with a black cloth softening its edges. Beakers and phials and bowls of powders had been set out—whoever was missing from this scene had been in the midst of some sort of diablerie.

Shall we finish up?

Jane's opinion of the presence in her mind did not improve as it persisted.

"Finish?" asked Jane.

You said you wanted to finish up before you went to the Admiral's party. And if we don't get started, we'll be more than fashionably late.

"But—"

They'll find you irresistible, said the voice. *The perfume will befuddle their senses, bewitch their minds, hold their attention!*

"Why?" asked Jane.

Because that is your will. Your desire. Jane didn't think that sounded like her at all, and she began to suspect something odd was going on with this entire experience. *You want them to notice you, to see you, admire you. You want to be at the center of their lives, don't you?*

Jane felt greasy and unsettled. "I *do* want that," said Jane—why lie; it could read her thoughts!—"but I want to win that on my own, not through a perfume . . ."

You are a diabolist, Jane! It sounded almost annoyed, as if she were betraying some sort of previous agreement between them. *Jane!*

"But—"

"Jane," someone said. "Jane!"

It was her mother. Jane startled up in her chair as Nancy squeezed her hand with a deep and reassuring pressure. This rare motherly gesture brought Jane back to herself.

Better still, the presence in her mind was completely, totally gone.

"There you are." Nancy's smile was tense and worried.

"What's wrong?" she asked. "Is it Miriam?"

"No, no. Miriam's been awake for a while — she's upstairs, with Edith."

"She disappeared . . ."

Jane's mother squeezed her hand again. "She was here the whole time. So was Edith. It's the nature of the serum; it takes you into your own mind, but sometimes in surprising ways."

Jane's head began to clear. "I didn't really speak with a demon today, did I?"

"No," said her mother. "You didn't. It was a diabolic hallucination. It was meant to show you your own mind about how you'd act if you had made the Pact."

Jane felt an enormous sense of relief. "I passed, then. I said I didn't want to control anyone or make them bend to my will or something."

"That's good to know!" Nancy looked extremely, almost disproportionally relieved. Then she said: "But your reaction to the actual experience of sharing yourself so fully with a demon was what was being tested."

"My reaction?"

"It can be . . . unnerving, sharing one's self so closely with another," said Nancy. "A lover could never be so intimate. And it doesn't tend to get *less* intense. There's no privacy to be had after you summon a demon. They know everything; they're a part of you forever."

She peered at Jane. "I only mention this because, usually, the longer the Test takes, the less successful the encounter."

"Is that so?" Jane made sure to convey only the mildest of interest in this as she yawned and stretched, but in reality she was starting to feel very uncomfortable.

She couldn't have *failed* the Test. That was impossible! She'd always been destined for Mastery. It was the only thing she'd ever wanted.

"The truth is"—Nancy still seemed anxious, as if Jane hadn't said the right word or phrase that would end this nightmare for them both—"the Société has found that those who do not enjoy their experience during the Test rarely go on to enjoy having a demon companion. We'd rather just not have them among our ranks—for their sake. The Test allows us to weed them out early, before it's too late."

"Of course." Jane would not let herself be *weeded out*. She deserved to be here as much as anyone.

She forced herself to smile. Nancy visibly relaxed. "Why would they want to continue anyway?" she asked, a decoy inquiry.

"You'd be surprised." Nancy still had that aura of anxiousness. "Sometimes the *idea* of being a diabolist is so appealing that people ignore their reason and dive in when they're not suited for it. It rarely works out for them," she said with a sad smile.

Jane knew she had to distract her mother, and quickly. She decided to try a new tack. "I was dressed so fabulously in my dream, or whatever it was," she said. "I hope that *also* bodes well!"

That was what Nancy had wanted to hear, apparently. "That's my Jane," she said, visibly relieved. "A black dress, I assume?"

"Oh, yes!"

"Come along upstairs, then," said Nancy, standing and helping Jane to her unsteady feet. "Let's go see Edith and Miriam. We have to celebrate!"

"Miriam passed too, I take it?"

"Oh, of course she did," said Nancy. Jane cringed inwardly at this; *of course* Miriam had passed, but her mother had been clearly quite worried about her own daughter.

And the worst part was she was right to be so.

"Oh, Jane!" said Nancy. "I'm so proud of you." And with that she embraced her daughter, a rare though coveted occurrence — and in this case, an entirely undeserved reward.

4

J ANE HAD HAD QUITE ENOUGH tea for the day, but she politely accepted a cup after Edith welcomed her into the farmhouse's kitchen with embraces and tears of joy that were agonizing to endure. Worse, however, was Miriam's reaction—she
was, as always, reserved, but the emotion in her eyes was sincere.
Under other circumstances, Jane would have been truly moved by
the support and enthusiasm of these women, but receiving it when
she didn't deserve it was a kind of torture.

Nancy was not talented at idleness; not long after their return,
she was up and making some hot water crust pastry for the raised
meat pie that would be their celebration dinner.

"The Test wasn't always a test of one's self," said Edith, answering some question Miriam had asked. Jane had only been half
listening as she mulled over in her mind what had happened in
her dream. "It's only since the last, oh, fifty years or so that they
changed it, right, Nance?" Nancy nodded. "The Société felt that
studying for a proper examination was pointless. Only apprentices
with the aptitude necessary for the Art ever make it far in their
studies. We needed to test whether they had the *disposition* for it."

"I never even thought about that," said Miriam, as Jane kept her
expression studiously neutral. "I imagine it might go poorly for
the Société—and others—if someone violent or dangerous became a Master."

"Oh, it doesn't stop *that*," said Nancy. "It's more . . . if diabolic
possession isn't going to make someone happy, then it's just all
such a waste, isn't it?"

"A waste?" asked Jane, and then cursed herself for prying.

"A waste of time, a waste of resources . . . and for what?"

"Oh, come now, Nancy, you know what it's for." Edith reached into her bag and took out a silver compact mirror. Dipping her finger into the powder, she tapped it along her brow line and looked up at them out of big blue eyes that had been dark brown a moment before. "There are other professions that are more lucrative, or that put one more in the spotlight . . . but none so *powerful* as ours. We take the world, Nancy, and we remake it to our will!"

"Only temporarily," said Nancy. Indeed, Edith's eyes were already darkening. "It is not good to get too cocky about what we can do, sister mine."

"Pardon me for implying diabolism might be fun!"

"What's not fun about spending all day, every day in a dark library under the earth, all alone, in silence?" Nancy smiled archly down at her pastry as she worked on shaping little vines and leaves for the top of the pie.

Edith's eyes rolled to meet Jane's, and for the first time since she'd realized how poorly things had gone during her Test, Jane's smile was genuine.

Diabolism was her birthright. A test couldn't tell her she was ill suited for it. She was just a bit different from the average diabolist. There had to be room for a range of experiences, surely; otherwise, all diabolists would be the same, and that just wasn't the case.

"Ah, girls," said Edith. "I'm ever so glad you passed. Why, if you hadn't . . ."

Jane's smile faltered.

"Edith!" Jane and Miriam both snapped to attention at the tone in Nancy's voice. She was *angry* for some reason Jane could not perceive.

"What?" Now Miriam was the one asking unnecessary follow-up questions. "What would have happened?"

Nancy answered, speaking over Edith. "Not that it's important, given you both passed, but when apprentices fail, it can be a bit of a problem. By then, they have intimate knowledge of our organization and our ways and even the locations of our members. Sometimes stern measures have to be taken."

As this sank in, Jane's eyes found Miriam's. The revelation was just as shocking to her, given her pale face and pinched expression, though she of course had no reason to fear for her personal safety.

Jane, on the other hand . . .

Edith, who was never one to read a room, elaborated on her sister's point. "Nobody's ever *thrilled* for it to happen, but it does. We try to make the best of it, but sometimes failed apprentices are deemed to be more useful as their physical components. There are, as you know, more arcane armamentaria that use bits of *people*. The Société tries to keep a stockpile on hand, so that people don't have to run the risk of obtaining what they need through baser means."

Everything about the Société had always seemed so *civilized* to Jane. It had never occurred to her that the Art's more outré practitioners might to this day be accepted within its ranks.

"Oh, stop looking at me like that," said Edith, as Nancy continued to glare. "They passed, didn't they? And now they're on to the next phase in their education, which means their understanding of the Art will only increase."

Jane willed herself to stop sweating. She could not betray herself now—not ever.

"No need for them to learn it all in one day, much less the same day as their Test," said Nancy. "Besides which, I'm sure neither of you girls would have been rendered for parts. Your family connection to the Société makes you an ideal candidate for a number of jobs that Master diabolists aren't able to do, for one reason or another. Being amenable to that sort of employment has spared many a failed apprentice." Nancy paused, and after looking from Jane's face to Miriam's, seemed to realize she hadn't made either of them feel any better. "What I'm trying to say is that we're not bloodthirsty monsters; we are, after all, a society. But of course it's for the best that you both passed!"

Jane nodded on instinct; a purely animal sense of self-preservation.

So, a failure like her wasn't seen as useful for merely her organs and bone fragments. Her labor could also be made use of. And *that* was considered mercy!

Jane knew in that moment she'd need to find a way to hide her failure, and hide it perfectly, hide it forever. She wouldn't let the Société consign her to the scrap heap, nor would she be their grateful servant.

She would become a phenomenal diabolist, no matter what anyone else thought.

There was her answer: *no matter what anyone else thought.* If they all thought she was phenomenal, her position would be secure. The best and the brightest always received the least supervision. So, she'd just have to fool them all.

Edith had finished her tea—and, incredibly, another slice of cake. She now reached for a red-cheeked apple that sat in a low wicker basket on the table. "So, you've passed your Test, and Nancy says you both have strong ideas for your Practical—really, I'm quite astonished at your ambition. But I wonder, have you given much thought to what you'll do afterward?" She bit deeply into the fruit, as if she hadn't eaten for hours.

"They have plenty of time to think about that," said Nancy, and Jane perceived a note of warning in her mother's voice.

She suspected that Edith would ignore it.

The subject of "the future" had always been a sore one in the Blackwood household. Nancy would only say, "We'll just have to see what life holds for us all, won't we?" whenever either girl had mentioned the question of "what's next"—and the way she said it invited no further remarks. Thus, Jane had always felt a vague sense of shame surrounding her desire to go beyond Hawkshead and see the world. She knew it would not please her mother.

"Plenty of time?" said Edith, after swallowing. "Not at the rate they're going! Really, they can't start any sooner. They may not come away from their studies certain which demon they want to summon, or what they want to do with their lives. An internship could provide some helpful guidance, but they have to apply for those, and that means researching what's available. But it's something that could really broaden their horizons."

"They have every book on diabolism ever written below their feet." Nancy had paused in her adorning of the top of their dinner pie with a magnificent pastry bird. "Their horizons are sufficiently broad."

The mood in the room had changed, the warm kitchen now downright icy. Jane looked from one woman to the other, and then to Miriam, who looked as unhappy as Jane felt about suddenly being the subject of bickering.

"I'm not saying their education has been neglected or that they're ignorant little beasts, Nance," said Edith. "I'm just saying that it seems the world will be ours again, *soon,* and they might want to experience a bit of it. We did at their age—and they've been cooped up here for years now."

"Cooped up! They're not chickens."

"No, but you're being a goose! There's no harm in them thinking about what they want to do with their lives."

"Yes, but—"

"I'd like to do an internship. Abroad." Jane interrupted her elders—rude, yes, but she couldn't bear their sniping at one another a moment longer. Usually something like this happened once or twice during Edith's visits, but Jane really didn't want to be the cause of a fight—not after everything that had already happened.

"See?" said Edith, but Jane cringed at the triumphant tone in her aunt's voice.

"Well!" said Nancy. Her mother was very obviously offended, so it didn't quite ring true when she said, "That's fine. Where would you like to go?"

Jane didn't know what to say, given the uncertain results of her Test, and how upset her mother was about this turn the conversation had taken.

"Go on, Jane," said Edith. "What were you thinking?"

"I'd like to travel," said Jane, almost whispering it. "I want to study more, but I also want to see big cities and ancient ruins and other countries. What's left of them, at least."

"Oh, Jane!" cried Edith. "I know the reports from the front have been terrible—and it's true, the devastation is heartbreaking. The world will never be the same. But there's still so much out there!"

"A big city. Very ambitious." Nancy's mouth was an inscrutable line. "Those internships are always highly competitive. It can be difficult to get exactly the one you want unless you've *really* impressed the Société with your work."

Under ordinary circumstances, it would have been hard to swallow Nancy's words, her tone, *and* her apparent belief that Jane might fail to sufficiently impress the Société. But coming on the heels of Jane failing her Test, it was almost too much to be endured. Jane felt her face go red, in spite of her best efforts to keep it and herself under control.

"There are always plenty of opportunities for those who want them." Edith had noticed Jane's distress but was pretending not to.

Nancy hadn't noticed or didn't care. "Yes, but included in that 'plenty' are internships in some rural town, even if it *is* a town in another country."

"While all that's true, I'm certain you will excel in your studies and be able to have your pick of opportunities when the time comes, Jane," said Edith.

At the crispness in her sister's tone, Nancy finally glanced up at Edith and then her own daughter.

"I've always believed my daughter is capable of achieving anything she wants," she said. Jane knew that was Nancy's way of apologizing, but what Jane felt wasn't relief. It was something she couldn't quite name: part anger, part self-loathing, part resentment.

"What have you to say about all this, Miriam?" asked Nancy, changing the subject.

Miriam stared at the dregs of her tea for a moment. When she looked up, Jane was horrified to see her friend's eyes were red and her lower lip was trembling. Jane realized in that horrible moment that she hadn't just upset her mother by speaking her mind, she'd upset her friend, too.

She'd ruined their evening by trying to save it.

Jane's earlier warm feelings for Miriam went cold. It hadn't been her intention to hurt anyone. In her haste to stop what had seemed like an impending row between sisters, she'd caused other, worse problems. She'd been trying to help—and just like her Test, she'd failed.

"I ... I ..." Miriam had gotten sufficient control of herself to speak, but she seemed nervous for some reason. Jane was beyond caring, though she maintained an expression of polite interest.

"Go on," said Nancy, in a more kindly manner than she'd spoken to Jane.

"I don't have expectations," said Miriam, so softly they all leaned in to hear, "but if ... if there was an internship *here* ... I really love the Library—the books, I mean, and the Library itself, too. I wouldn't mind learning more about it, not that I'm after your job, I mean, I just—"

"Miriam, first things first, there will *always* be a place for you here, as long as you want it," said Nancy. "This is your home! How could you think otherwise, after all this time?"

"Yes, but internships have to be approved by the Société," said Edith, as she inspected her apple for any bits of flesh still clinging to the core. "You know Markus's apprentice Lieke has her heart set on coming here, and she's highly promising."

"I wasn't talking about an internship," said Nancy.

"I wouldn't want to impose," said Miriam. "I know I'll have to work hard; I wouldn't want it to seem like you were playing favorites."

Jane resisted the urge to punctuate this remark with an ironic snort.

"Everyone knows how hard you work," said Nancy warmly. "You're a brilliant apprentice, and you'll be a brilliant Master. My colleagues are already discussing your potential."

"How would they even know of me?" Miriam looked downright panicked now.

"Oh, I've often spoken of your abilities," said Nancy.

Jane experienced an uncomfortable mix of feelings as she listened to this exchange. She knew Miriam often felt like she was intruding, but this entire conversation was evidence that she was as much a part of the Blackwood family as if she'd been born into it — *more, even,* said a small mean voice in Jane's head. So, while Jane was glad to see her friend relax upon hearing she'd always have a home in the little farmhouse outside Hawkshead, it upset her deeply to hear her mother come out so strongly in favor of Miriam's abilities after expressing doubt over her own.

That the doubt was apparently reasonable was the injury added to the insult.

"I just don't want to leave before I've learned everything I can," said Miriam, almost stumbling over the words, "because that's what I love. I love learning, and I need to be here to do it!"

"No one could doubt it," said Nancy.

Jane "loved learning" too — she just wanted to do it while learning things other than those inside books. After all, apprentices in more cosmopolitan areas often socialized with one another as companions and associates; they weren't judged as frivolous for doing so.

Jane sat up a bit straighter. She had more to worry about than approval from her mother or her friend. If they didn't recognize her dedication for what it was, telling them wouldn't make them see.

The kitchen had gone very quiet for a celebration. After an awkward moment, Edith rose to put her apple core in the compost bin, and Nancy went back to her pie, prodding at scraps of pastry with her fingertips.

"I don't know about you, but I couldn't eat another bite," said Edith, but her lighthearted joke felt leaden. "I'll just clear away the tea things."

Jane looked up to find that Miriam was staring at her, her expression inscrutable. Jane, cross and disinclined to be generous, tossed her hair as she turned to her aunt.

"I'm finished, thank you," she said, meaning more than just the tea.

Miriam winced and seemed to shrink into herself a little. Though she was usually not so good at reading people as she was her beloved books, she'd apparently managed to perfectly divine Jane's meaning.

5

HOURS PASSED WITH EACH WOMAN in whatever corner of the house best suited her. For Miriam, that was down in the Library, though it was not long before she gave up reading for idly scanning the shelves for any titles that happened to catch her eye. Eventually, the savory smell of the pie brought them all back to the kitchen in a better mood than they'd left it, and a bottle of Nancy's homemade sparkling cider dispelled the remaining tensions. Miriam and Jane also had a goodly share of it, more than Nancy would ever pour them save perhaps on Christmas Eve.

"It's a celebration," she said, but her tone was not exactly celebratory.

The cider was good, sweet with a tart note from the tough-fleshed apples that grew at the northern edge of Nancy's property. It was very strong; Miriam felt it sliding down her throat, intruding into her stomach, forcibly relaxing her muscles and her mind.

It had been a long day of confusing emotions. When Edith announced her intention to examine them, Miriam hadn't been afraid; she was confident in her abilities. But she had been unhappy to feel caught short at a time when she was most vulnerable —out-of-doors where anyone might see her.

Then the Test had been far more bizarre than anything she could have predicted. She had quickly realized she'd been drugged, which had not done anything to further endear Edith to her. She had perceived there must be some reason for the experience, however.

The presence of a demon inside her mind had confirmed that. There was no way Edith would have slipped them both real diabolic essence; they hadn't yet made the Pact, hadn't yet chosen a demon to petition. Realizing all this had helped her negotiate with the hallucination as the dream played out a scenario where she had to escape a house when enemies knocked at the door. She'd done so quickly and efficiently; there had been nothing to fear, not really, so it had actually been fun.

A lot of fun. Dream-Miriam had been so much more able, more powerful, more capable than Miriam was in her everyday life. She'd evaded her pursuers with minimal effort. And having a demon with her, helping her, had felt *right*—like it was *her* right to be part of such a partnership, her *birthright* as her father might say. It was almost as if that shadow-place she sometimes imagined as existing within her had come to life to serve her differently.

She'd felt pleased, deeply so, when Edith told her she'd passed, and Nancy's praise was, as always, Miriam's favorite reward. Miriam felt a bit guilty, actually, over just how much Nancy's regard meant to her. She felt more of a connection to her surrogate mother-figure than she ever had to the mother she'd left behind.

But there were also Jane's feelings to be considered. Miriam didn't want to supplant Jane in her mother's heart, of course she didn't. She wanted Nancy to regard them equally. That's why Miriam's pride had quickly turned to dread when Jane had lagged behind. She didn't know what that meant, but Nancy and Edith started exchanging looks when ten minutes became twenty, then thirty . . . That's when Nancy had gone down to the Library, only to come back with a strangely quiet Jane in tow. She'd passed but didn't seem pleased.

And as if that wasn't enough to worry about, Nancy then announced her intention to cook a special dinner.

Miriam's mood had plummeted. Celebratory meals were the favored battleground of the Blackwood women; having one was a surefire way to guarantee the evening would be marred by an argument. Miriam had known something would happen, because something *always* happened—like the time Jane and Miriam had huddled together in Jane's bed, listening to the Blackwood sisters' raised voices after Edith had asked Jane if she would like to come to London for a few days, and Jane had accepted without asking permission. Or the time Nancy had alluded to some romantic feelings Edith held for someone, and Edith had been furious for some obviously very important reason that the girls never learned but had speculated upon endlessly.

At least it was easy enough to plead exhaustion once they'd finished the cider and the dessert. After the long walk to Hawkshead and back and the ensuing excitement, it was natural for her and Jane to want to retire early. Miriam supposed it was also natural for them to retire *separately;* Jane didn't speak a word as they went upstairs together and then said nothing but a pale yet sincere "Congratulations, Miriam" before slipping inside her room. Well, Miriam had made an ass of herself, getting upset over Jane's disclosures—and as usual she found it too difficult to begin any of the conversations it would take to patch things up.

Compared to Jane's room, with its second wallpapering of movie star glamour shots and shelves thick with natural curiosities, Miriam's was very plain. She'd arrived in England with little more than her clothes. Her mother had been so afraid that she'd demanded Miriam leave behind anything that might indicate her Jewish heritage—but her father had insisted she be allowed to go with *something.*

Miriam had first thought to take the family's mezuzah, but in the end she'd selected her father's antique "devil-trap," a clay bowl used by ancient Jews to capture spirits who might be a nuisance to the household. Her father had been amused by the irony of the object, given his profession, but Miriam had always loved the hypnotic lines of the spiral inscription as well as the warm feel of the ancient clay in her hands.

It had soothed Miriam to hold the bowl even before it became her only connection to her former life. But, like all childhood comforts, she'd largely set it aside as she'd gotten older. That night, however, she took it carefully in hand and sat with it on her bed.

A knock at the door startled her. Miriam had been so lost in thought that she nearly dropped her bowl. She set it carefully aside before calling, "Come in!"

She'd hoped it would be Jane. It was Edith.

"Hullo there," she said, and Miriam summoned a smile in an attempt to make her ersatz aunt feel welcome. She wasn't exactly craving more of Edith's company, but the woman had an air about her that made Miriam suspect she had something important to relate.

"I'm here to apologize for introducing a contentious topic of conversation at the dinner table," she said, standing in the center of Miriam's room like a child instructed to atone for bad behavior. She had, for some reason, her handbag, and clutched it in front of her like Eve with her fig leaf. "I didn't realize it would spoil the mood, but as you know, divining the right time for a discussion is not a talent of mine."

To say "yes" would be an insult, to say "no" would be a lie, so Miriam simply shrugged.

"I'm also here to talk with you about something sensitive. And I'm not so good at delivering sensitive information, as I'm learning."

Edith's expression revealed nothing as she perched on the edge of Miriam's desk. Miriam felt the backs of her knees start to sweat where they were tucked under her. She wished Edith would just get on with whatever she had to say. There was only one topic that Miriam would have considered "sensitive": the fate of her parents.

For the first four or so years of Miriam's stay in England, she had received letters from her mother, at first through the Basque Lens and then, later, through the mail, their postmarks and addresses forged diabolically. They'd never been long letters, nor regularly sent, but they'd come. Miriam had kept them all, of course, but the last of them she was especially careful with. It had clearly been written in haste and arrived very dirty. They'd given her their love and told her not to worry about them, but that had been impossible.

"Your parents . . ." Edith hesitated again, maddeningly.

"Are they dead?" asked Miriam, keeping her voice as emotionless as possible.

Edith's dark eyes went wide. "Oh, Miriam!"

Miriam's stomach dropped. "I wondered," she said. "I haven't had a letter in . . . I'm sure you know exactly how long."

"The truth is, we don't know." Edith looked very serious, indeed. "We do know they were taken."

"Taken where?"

Miriam's parents hadn't told her anything about being spies; Edith had been the one to answer Miriam's questions. She had always been good to Miriam in that way, believing as she did that Miriam was a young woman who had a right to know what was going on with her family.

"I can't tell you," said Edith, and Miriam nodded. Of course Edith couldn't say. "I can only tell you it's happening, we're aware of it, and we're responding as we can."

Miriam thought for a moment. "Can you tell me if you, personally, are worried about them?"

"I am."

Miriam trembled; this feeling was too big to hand off to her shadow-self. "But I will also tell you that I'm doing my best to make sure we find them, and that the truth is discovered."

"The truth?"

"There are what I can only describe as *troubling rumors* about your parents, Miriam."

"Rumors of what?"

Edith was not usually a fidgeter, but as she spoke, her long fingers toyed with her black scarf. "The Nazis have their own diabolists. That's always been the case, but lately their efforts have gotten much more effective. It's as if they had help from one of us."

Miriam's confusion quickly turned to rage. "You think my parents—"

"I don't think your parents are traitors," said Edith. "But the timing of their disappearance has some tongues wagging."

Miriam got control of herself, slowing her breathing deliberately, pushing her fury down, down, down until the shadow claimed it.

"It's not just them," said Edith. "Every member of their cell is a suspect until we find out what happened. What they were up to . . . Miriam, it was hugely important to the war effort, and it seems like it's all come to nothing at the worst possible time."

"I see," said Miriam. She had been prepared to receive devastating news about her parents—or, at least, she had been prepared to accept that there was some. She had not thought to steel herself against the accusation of treachery. "Thank you for letting me know."

"You don't have to . . ." Edith trailed off. "I don't know what to say, honestly."

"You don't have to say anything." In reality, what could be said? Miriam was now not only a German expatriate and Jew in hiding, but the child of suspected traitors. Her shoulders were tired from carrying the pity of others; that soft sympathy weighed on her as much as any tangible burden. Maybe she wouldn't be so opposed to being social if people saw *her*, and not some girl-shaped bag of tragedies.

Edith talked a bit more, but Miriam wasn't really listening. She had been so certain about the thrust of her Practical, but now it all seemed so unimportant. What really mattered was—

"All right?"

"Hmm?" Miriam realized she had completely lost the thread of their conversation.

Edith peered at her. "The higher-ups at the Société didn't want me to tell you. They were afraid you were at a delicate stage in your education, one where it was possible to make some serious mistakes out of anger. But I vouched for your temper and your character. You've always taken everything in stride."

"I know, I thank you," said Miriam. "I owe you a great debt."

Edith sighed. "Does that mean you won't do anything foolish?"

"I won't," said Miriam. After all, foolish was in the eye of the beholder.

"I'm very glad to hear it," said Edith. "I know you've had a long day, and I'm sorry to have made it longer. I just didn't think it was right to keep it from you."

"I appreciate it," said Miriam.

Edith still seemed uneasy, and Miriam wondered what she needed to do to get her aunt out of her room.

She tried a smile. That seemed to work.

"Thank you," she said, with as much enthusiasm as she could muster. "It's not what I wanted to hear, but it's something."

This reply seemed to satisfy Edith.

"I'm on your side, Miriam," said Edith. "Just know that. I love you, and I love both your parents. I won't be sitting idly by. Now, I know it doesn't make up for all my bad news, but I did bring you something—a present of sorts. I know how private you are, so I saved it until now, when we were alone."

Miriam was startled by this courtesy—she hadn't known Edith was capable of such sensitivity. She was doubly startled when Edith withdrew a small grease-stained paper box from her purse.

"I saw them in a bakery," said Edith, "and I thought perhaps they'd be a treat for you—a taste of home."

Miriam was completely mystified until she opened the lid to see two perfect hamantashen, the three-cornered pastry traditionally eaten by Jews at Purim. From the look of them, one was poppy-seed-filled; the other, prune. The fragrance brought back memories of her childhood—but also a sense of shame. When, she wondered, was the last time she'd thought about Purim? Her family had never fully embraced the rhythms of a Jewish household, what with them being mixed-faith and diabolists, but they'd always given a passing nod to the holidays. Now, away from her community, her aunts and uncles and family friends who came by to remind her father, Egon, of his duty, she'd forgotten everything so entirely that she'd even forgotten to miss it ... Miriam once again felt the terrifying absurdity of it all: her exile, the possible death of her parents, the actual death of no one knew how many more Jews, the war itself. She had relatively little relationship with the faith that had made her and her family a target for unspeakable violence. And she was only a Jew according to the Nazis! Miriam's mother had not converted. But that didn't matter.

Not that proper Jews deserved what they had received. Of course they did not. No one did. It was simply the Nazi way to force the mind to have that conversation with itself about who was what—and what that "meant." Their philosophy was death, and because of it, no matter *who* she was, *here* she was—and there her parents were. Forces more powerful than any diablerie had torn her family asunder, forever it seemed.

"Do you like them?" asked Edith, and Miriam realized she'd been staring at the cookies for a long time without speaking.

"So thoughtful," she managed to say, and Edith smiled in relief. "Really, thank you so much."

"It was my pleasure," said Edith.

Then Edith gave Miriam an even better gift than the hamantashen by saying good night. After she'd gone, Miriam set the pastries aside without tasting them. She waited in her room for a bit, pacing, and then peeked out into the hallway. All was dark, except for lights under everyone's bedroom doors, including Nancy's.

Miriam took extra care to make no sound as she tiptoed down the hallway. Edith was right; it had been a long day—and Miriam didn't want to answer any questions about why, after everything, she'd be heading down into the Library at this hour.

6

MIRIAM WISHED SHE WAS THE SORT of person to run off in the dead of night, secure passage across the Channel, and make her way through enemy lines to hunt down her parents, but she wasn't. She could barely walk to the village without a mental rehearsal of the ways it wasn't a dangerous thing to do.

But lacking the courage of a soldier didn't mean Miriam's hands were tied. What she might lack in valor, Miriam felt she more than made up for in ambition.

Edith had as good as said she was doing something to try to help Miriam's parents. Probably several members of the Société would involve themselves, both those who believed in Miriam's family's innocence and those who believed they could prove the reverse.

But they didn't have every known text on diabolism at their fingertips.

Miriam did.

Furthermore, this was personal for her; a passion project. As much as Edith might care for Miriam's parents, it couldn't ever be the same for her. Miriam loved her mother and her father, not because of the secrets they carried or their role in the fate of the war effort, but because of who they were, and what they meant to her.

She had to clear their names.

Usually, Miriam was able to fold her anger into little neat packages, but this rage was too big, too messy for that. How could anyone dare accuse them? Her mother hadn't been sad about Hitler's election, she'd been *furious;* her father had become withdrawn and started going to services at his synagogue again, after years of intermittent attendance at best.

He'd brought Miriam with him, too. When she'd asked why she had to go, her father had replied, almost sharply: "If they hate us for being Jews, we'll be as Jewish as we can be!"

She refused to believe that either of them had become collaborators.

Miriam was never one to put off work, but in order to avert suspicion on Edith's part, she made sure to be at least reasonably social the rest of her aunt's visit. She even walked with Edith and Jane into Hawkshead to look at what was in the few shop windows, though the trip didn't seem to afford any of them much pleasure.

Jane was usually at her brightest when Edith visited, but she had been in a strangely dour mood ever since the night of their Test. In better days, Miriam would have intruded into Jane's room to winkle out of her what weighed so heavily upon her mind, but the truth was Miriam was too afraid of what might be said if she did.

"You're up to something," said Jane, the last morning of their aunt's visit, when the two girls passed on the stairs.

"What?" Even to her own ears, Miriam sounded startled, not innocent. "I mean, why do you say that?"

Jane leaned back like a movie star, head tilted, arms crossed; if she'd been smoking a forbidden cigarette, the look would have been complete. Miriam just stood there, right foot on the stair above, her hand gripping the railing for strength.

"You've had your nose in a book even more than usual."

Miriam winced. "I didn't mean to be so obvious."

"Did Edith say something to you? After their fight, I mean?"

Miriam wasn't sure she wanted to discuss Edith's disclosures with Jane *at all*, but certainly not in the stairwell. "Just that she was sorry for everything."

"She apologized to me, too."

Miriam tried to throw Jane off her scent with what she thought would be the blandest possible explanation. "It's just that, well . . . we passed our Test. It's time to get to work on our Practical."

"Oh!" Jane blushed. "Yes, of course. Me, too. I mean, I feel the same! I've just been a bit distracted." Her eyes flickered to the kitchen, where Nancy and Edith were talking.

"She'll be gone soon enough," said Miriam, and then realizing how that sounded, added, "and you'll be able to focus more easily on your endeavors. The two of you enjoy one another's company so much, and get it so infrequently . . . no one could blame you for wanting to take advantage of it while you can."

Miriam was surprised by Jane's annoyed shrug.

"It's interesting, isn't it? They say we're growing up so fast, but how would they know? They're still children themselves."

Miriam realized Jane was disappointed by something, but it felt presumptuous to ask what it might be. "True enough," she replied, "but I'm only sometimes able to be an adult about things. Maybe growing up is just about adjusting the percentages."

Jane laughed. "That's as good an explanation as any. Just the same, I wish they hadn't quarreled like that. It was so *embarrassing.*" She said all this very rapidly, almost whispering it. "It's an old argument between them, I guess."

"Old argument?"

"Edith didn't want Mother to become the Librarian." Miriam wondered how Jane knew all this, but also didn't want to interrupt to ask. "She thought Mother was too young to bury herself in the country for the sake of a bunch of books."

Miriam couldn't hold back any longer. "Did she tell you this?"

"No!" Jane grinned. "After their fight, I hid in the hall and listened to them."

"Eavesdropping!"

"Oh, go on! But that seems to be it. When Mother was pregnant with me"—Jane's face went all funny for a moment; Nancy would never tell Jane anything about her father, much to Jane's chagrin—"she put her name forward for Librarian and was accepted. Up until then she and Edith had been traveling around together. Edith said, 'You loved these books more than you loved me—you jumped at the chance to come here and leave me to deal with the world on my own.' And Mother said, 'You're still jealous of this place?' And they went on from there. Anyway, then Edith said, 'You took away Jane's chance at having the life she deserves.'"

"No wonder they've been so polite to one another," said Miriam. "This was quite a fight. What did Nancy say to that?"

Jane's mood shifted slightly, her smile going from rueful to wry. "She said, 'Perhaps, but I'm glad to have been able to offer Miriam a safe place to grow up when she needed it.'"

Miriam didn't know what to say.

"I'm glad too," added Jane.

Miriam looked up, wondering if Jane might be attempting to traverse the rift between them, but then Nancy called them to breakfast.

Jane's expression soured. "Shall we? Last one of these for a while, thank goodness. And they're always perky on the last morning of a visit."

They were indeed, and, even better, Nancy suggested the girls might like to ride in the back of the mule cart when it came to collect Edith's luggage. A bumpy cart ride was one of the few outdoor activities Miriam really loved; she scrambled right up. Jane hesitated, but after Edith declared her intention to walk, Jane planted herself beside Miriam.

"See you there!" called Jane, and the two of them bid the boy, "Drive on, drive on!" just as they'd used to do when they were younger.

The cart jolted over the winter-rough road, and more than once the girls squealed as they knocked into one another. The weather had turned colder again, and their breath puffed out in white clouds that disappeared against the gray sky.

Even on a dreary day like this one, Miriam thought this the most beautiful countryside she'd ever seen. While at times she still missed the low, flat German landscape, Cumbria's rolling, rock-strewn hills and rushing culverts had claimed her heart.

Since coming here she'd learned that Beatrix Potter's sweet lit-tle depictions of ducks and rabbits weren't inaccurate — but Cum-bria was also a wild place, lonely and remote with as many black and mysterious pinewoods as it had sunny farmyards.

They arrived in Hawkshead well before Edith and Nancy, of course. Jane bemoaned the lack of ice cream, for she *desperately* wanted one — if Jane wanted something these days, she wanted it *desperately*. For her part, Miriam wanted a cup of tea at the Red Lion, but she could not speak this desire aloud.

Once Nancy and Edith arrived, there was the usual snippy fuss-ing that went into loading all her luggage into her too-small car. Then Edith said her farewells.

"I don't know when I'll be back again, so please try not to grow up too, too much before I return?" she said, gazing fondly upon them both.

"No promises," muttered Jane. Miriam said nothing at all.

Edith looked rather annoyed as she got into her car. "Upon sec-ond thought, perhaps you might both use my time away to push through this awkward stage you seem to be in. Ta!"

And with that, she roared away in her Citroën.

"I'm surprised at you, Jane," said Nancy. "Usually you're one step away from stowing away in Edith's boot."

"We're all very busy," said Jane, "and it will be nice to get back into a routine."

Miriam's spirits sank further as they returned to the old farm-house one Blackwood fewer. The rain-washed slate roof and white walls made her feel strangely ill at ease. Miriam usually considered the first sight of home to be the best part of a journey, but to-day it filled her with dread. She wondered if she and Jane would ever again ride to the village together in the back of a cart — if they would ever speak again in hushed whispers about the ways in which a family visit had gone wrong.

It wasn't just Jane who was changing, not anymore. With this new quest before her, Miriam sensed she'd started down a path that led away from childhood — and that she would never be able to retrace her steps.

7

Edith had indeed paid a visit to Jane on the night of the Test—but she hadn't merely stopped in to apologize, as Jane had told Miriam. Edith had had another, more shocking purpose for intruding upon Jane's privacy.

"I think it's time you learned something about your father, Jane."

That wasn't the first thing Edith had said. No, she'd asked for "permission to come aboard," with a little salute that Jane didn't acknowledge, made herself comfortable, and then sighed deeply.

"I see now why Nancy has always been so scrupulous about not playing favorites."

Jane bit back her urge to say, "She has?" Her own wounds were known to her; Edith's point was not.

Edith continued. "It seems that by declaring for you early on, I've alienated my sister and hurt Miriam. Not to mention made your own mother a little more suspicious of your dedication to the Art than she ought to be."

"Do you blame yourself for that?" Jane didn't offer even a token protest in defense of Nancy's fairness. She just wanted to know why Edith felt the way she did.

Instead of answering, Edith said, "Nancy asked me to come with her, when she took this job."

Jane was amazed. Edith always seemed to enjoy the novelty of country living during her visits, but it should have been obvious to anyone that she would not have thrived here, miles away from anything and anyone.

Edith, too, seemed to be contemplating the life she might have led. She was gazing into the flame of a candle Jane had burning on her desk, and for the thousandth time Jane was struck by her aunt's sublime poise and grace. The dipping of her head was elegant, almost swanlike. How could Nancy have even asked Edith to bury herself here?

"I declined," said Edith, "obviously. And I think we both came away feeling betrayed. She didn't have to take this job; we had plenty of money from Mother and Father. We could have kept on traveling the world, going to parties, and doing fabulous works of diablerie—yes, even with an infant in tow! Especially *you*, given how you turned out." Edith favored her with a smile.

Jane had heard all this from eavesdropping, but she played along anyway, sensing there was something yet to be revealed.

"People change. They end up wanting different things. For a long time, I felt Nancy had chosen these books over me. Now, I see how much she loves her work." Edith shrugged. "Sadly, I don't think Nancy's ever been able to understand why I couldn't give up the world for her ... and for better or for worse, I think your mother looks at you and sees me."

How Jane wished it were so! Or at least, that it were due in part to some physical resemblance, not just their shared bits of character. Edith's beauty was shocking—the smooth darkness of her skin, her birdlike throat, her perfect posture. Jane would have sold her soul for a share of her aunt's poise and grace.

"She also sees *him*." Jane held very still, and after a moment, Edith said, "I think it's time you learned something about your father, Jane. I know it's a forbidden subject. Nancy would probably burst in here to strangle me if she knew what I was about."

Nancy had never been willing to tell Jane even the smallest detail about the man who had sired her. She stuck firmly to the story she told everyone—that she was a widow who'd moved to the countryside. Little things here and there had made Jane wonder whether that was true, and after listening to that argument between her mother and aunt, she was sure there was more to the story.

"Your father is alive," said Edith, and Jane went perfectly still. "His name is Patrice Durand. He lives in Paris, though before the war he used to spend half the year in Indonesia."

A French father! This seemed unexpectedly glamorous to Jane, even if she suddenly felt rather less English.

But also exhilarating. She knew his *name*. With his name, she could learn more about him. She could send him a message through the Basque Lens in the Library. They might even meet one day!

Though it made her feel a bit silly, Jane asked the one thing she'd always most wanted to know:

"How did they meet?"

"The Société, naturally. Patrice also works directly for the organization, but his role is rather different. He's currently the Société's Evaluator . . . something in between an officer of the law and a judge. He investigates alleged violations of our codes and our laws and decides what should be done about them . . . anything from appointing investigative committees to dispensing justice."

Jane didn't have ask if "dispensing justice" meant what she thought it did; Edith offered the information freely.

"I was picking at your mother, earlier," she admitted. "Neither of you girls would have been at risk of such dire repercussions, had you failed, but part of the Evaluator's duties include deciding what's to be done with those who don't pass their Test."

"How droll," said Jane. Edith had recoiled from her waspish tone, but Jane didn't care. It was awful in every way to finally—*finally*—learn who her father was, only to find out he would be the one to decide her fate if it were ever discovered she'd failed her Test. "That's a perfectly ghastly thing to joke about, in my opinion."

Edith looked surprised. "I—I suppose it is. Forgive me, Jane, I didn't mean to upset you. I was just feeling so merry after you both passed . . ." Jane was not mollified by this. "I forget how isolated you've been here. In a city, apprentices often swap information and tales, so when the realities of the Art are revealed, it isn't quite so shocking." Edith looked really worried. "You've learned a lot tonight, and that after an ordeal. Perhaps I should have held off on telling you all this."

"I've waited long enough to hear it, I think." *And be disappointed by it,* she thought. Jane knew she was acting like a spoiled and tired child, but she was, frankly, appalled to realize the entire dreadful conversation she'd endured earlier at the kitchen table was due to Edith trying to needle Nancy—and it had been about her father.

Never in a million years would Jane have believed that she'd find out her father was alive and not wish to contact him! But how could she? He would be the one holding the knife to her throat.

"I can see I've made a misstep somewhere, so I'll just say this information was meant for your ears only. In fact, I ask you to swear to me that you'll not contact your father until you're no longer living under Nancy's roof."

"Why?" Jane felt her interest in contacting her father increase as a result of this demand for a promise, rather than the reverse.

"It's not my story to tell, but your mother's affair with Patrice ended badly. He loved her so much; he wanted her to stay, wanted to raise you together. But he has a temper, and when Nancy said she would not, he declared he wanted nothing to do with either of you, and didn't even say goodbye when she left for England. But, Jane," said Edith, registering some of the very real hurt Jane was feeling, "as you can see, time changes all things."

"Not my mother."

Edith acknowledged Jane's point. "No, not your mother."

Jane had one more question. "Why did you tell me this now? Why not tell me later instead of asking me to wait?"

Edith hesitated. "That's a fair question. I did it at the request of your father." She had the air of someone choosing her words very carefully. "The losses in this war have been heavy and far-reaching.

Patrice may not be on the front lines, but he has seen his share of sorrow. He is eager to make up for lost time."

"Then—"

"Do not think this is a step that can be untaken," said Edith, so sharply that Jane jumped. Her aunt had never spoken to her like that before; Edith, too, seemed surprised at herself, and when she spoke again, it was more gently. "There's nothing I can think of that would do more to damage your relationship with your mother."

But of course there were things Jane could learn about her father that didn't require contacting him. She couldn't see the harm in looking up certain information, and so she did: his address in Paris, his service record, his birthday, his parents' names and their occupations (famous diabolists in their day, it turned out—he, and therefore she, had quite the pedigree). Jane read these tidbits as she could, when she could, even before Edith had departed, sneaking looks when her mother wasn't in the Library and Miriam was lost in her studies.

Jane didn't feel like she was violating her promise to her aunt, and yet she did feel vaguely guilty about her secret researches. But she wasn't doing anything with the information—she was merely finding out the facts. And the facts were Patrice Durand was two years younger than her mother, he lived in a flat in the heart of Paris, and Jane could contact him if she wanted to.

But she didn't want to. All that had changed was that the *option* was now at her fingertips.

It felt frivolous, thinking about her father at all, really. Jane had many more pressing concerns.

While Jane could accept that she'd failed her Test, she would not accept that she was done as a diabolist. Rationally speaking, she knew there was a slim chance that the Société would decide she warranted divvying up to those individuals who might enjoy the use of her liver or eyeballs, but neither would she bow and scrape before them, begging for whatever dreadful jobs they saved for the disappointments.

She needed a plan, and fear being the excellent motivator it was, she came up with one quickly. It was simple, at least relatively so: she would just have to be the very best diabolist the Société had ever seen. She would need to demonstrate her abilities beyond the shadow of a doubt so that no one would ever suspect she was not ideally suited for practicing the Art. Because *of course* she'd practice it; of course she'd summon a demon. She had to. There was no other choice, even if the thought of again sharing herself in that way made her shiver with revulsion.

Before that, however, she had to complete her Practical—no, she had to excel at it, impressing everyone with her results.

She had to figure out a way to make her broomstick fly.

8

EDITH HAD PLANNED TO SPEND an extra night or two in London doing a little shopping and calling on Société acquaintances, but Jane's ungrateful farewell had put her nose so very out of joint that she stepped off the slate circle in the foyer of her Paris apartment not twenty minutes after parking her Citroën at the Société garage in London.

Mercurialis was thrilled by this; Edith, less so, but her mood improved as she took a deep breath. The air of her foyer smelled like home; it had a crispness she found wonderful after the wretched soggy chill of northern England.

See?

Edith laughed at what felt almost like childishness from Mercurialis. "You were right," she said. "Coming home was the right choice."

It was true, Edith could not have spent another moment in England. What a brat Jane was! Edith kicked off her shoes and stomped her way angrily into her flat. A continent was not enough distance. Maybe there had been more merit to Nancy's complaints about Jane's moody ways than Edith had previously assumed.

Would you be so angry if you didn't think of your niece as an ally in the war you're still waging against your sister?

Edith often appreciated her demon's insights, but not this time. "Oh, what do you know about it?" she snapped.

Mercurialis said, *Much,* to her annoyance.

Jane had inherited a bit of her mother's cool haughtiness, but she was, in general, a pleasant and even-tempered girl eager to make herself distinct from her peers. Edith had therefore expected Jane to swan about the house, making bold statements about passing her Test. Instead, Jane had spent the proper amount of time with her aunt and everyone else, no more, no less, being almost suspiciously modest and amiable.

Jane had put up a wall, emotionally speaking—even after Edith told her what she'd always longed to know about her father! It was absurd, and it was a little bit annoying too. What more could she have done? Why, she had even left a *dress* for Jane.

Edith knew her niece well enough to know exactly what dress Jane would want as a present for passing her Test, so Edith had had it made for her in Paris, and by her own dressmaker no less. It was similar to the one that Jane had practically *drooled* over when Edith had arrived in Hawkshead—similar enough that when it was discovered in the armoire of the guest room, she hoped Nancy would assume she'd simply forgotten it there in the haste of packing. Jane, of course, would try it on, and find the note pinned into the inner lining.

It was an arcane method of gifting, but Edith had learned caution after the time she'd given Jane that stylish black cloche and Nancy had been so cross because of some silly "no black clothing" rule. But if she was going to give Jane a dress, it would be one her niece would actually want.

Contemplating these matters did little to enhance Edith's mood. She didn't wish to be alone. The house was too quiet. She needed company after being sequestered in the country for too long.

It was later in Paris than in London, and the sun had already set, but that was all right. For a diabolist, the nighttime streets of Paris were substantially less dangerous, though not without their perils. There were others out there with agendas—and abilities. She would be taking precautions.

One did not need a demon to effect a disguise, but Mercurialis gave Edith's illusions an unparalleled verisimilitude. At night, she usually chose to appear as a young university student with light brown hair, tall and lean as he slouched through the streets in his too-large coat. He was not handsome enough to attract attention from women or from men, not wealthy-looking enough to attract thieves or bawds, not poor enough to make the police wish to hassle him. Edith didn't use her cosmetics to create him, she had a mask she'd altered diabolically. It disappeared on her face when she applied it with a glue she made from the diabolically altered roses she grew in pots in her atrium. The other illusions— her height, her distinctive and yet wholly generic gait—were the combination of her use of her body and Mercurialis's gifts.

That night, her destination was the Société headquarters. While it might not be Paris's most fashionable venue, it was always open to any diabolist, at any hour of the day or night. There were rooms for socializing, a library, a kitchen, and even a few bedrooms for those who needed them, as well as offices and official meeting spaces. Furthermore, only there would she find people who *understood*.

The Société was located in what appeared to be one of those always-closed restaurants that are part of the Parisian landscape. She let herself in through the alley door with her key.

"Ah, Mademoiselle Blackwood," said François, as she walked in the door, even before she'd shed her mask. Shrugging out of her coat, Edith approached the manicured man standing behind the desk. No one knew whether it was through diablerie or just phenomenal organization that François managed the Société's front and back of house while also greeting everyone at the door, but he did.

No one knew his surname, either.

"Bon soir, François. Who's about tonight?"

"Of your set?"

At one time, François would have meant the Young Talarians. Now, sadly, he meant only those who still believed in the innocence of Egon and Sofia Cantor—Miriam's missing parents.

While their debated innocence or guilt hadn't exactly caused a schism in the ranks, there was understandably less friendly socializing these days between those of differing opinions.

Edith signed her name in the register with a quill dipped in diabolic ink that always formed the user's real signature.

"Yes, of my set," she said, finishing up the signature with her typical flourish.

"You'll find Mademoiselle Znidarcic, Monsieur Yellowhorse, and Madame Lizman in the Red Room, playing cards."

A faint blush came to Edith's cheeks at the mention of Graham Yellowhorse. François did not comment if he noticed. but Mercurialis, for its part, teased her in a voice that sounded of crickets chirping and the first drops of summer rain on hot cobblestones.

Some diabolists—likely those without such chatty companions as Edith—deluded themselves into thinking they and their demon were of one mind. Edith knew that was not the case, no matter how delightful the fantasy might sound. Smart diabolists knew demons always had their own ideas, their own agendas. Demons honored the Pact because they had to; that was the very most one could say about their motivations with any certainty. The truth of the matter was they were not of the same world as humans, and it was foolishness to assume they could be comprehended, instead of bribed, cajoled, or commanded.

Mercurialis agreed with her thoughts, the sensation of their mingled awareness as familiar as a lover's touch, and as alien, too.

François coughed, distracting Edith from these thoughts. "And if you don't mind my saying . . ."

"Hm? Yes, François?"

"I thought you might like to know that Monsieur Durand is still here. If you had any news for him, I mean."

Had Patrice told *everyone* about Jane's Test? Edith looked at François in exasperation.

"He is in his office, mademoiselle," said François, his eyes twinkling.

"Thank you," she said, and handed him her coat for safekeeping.

She kept her mask. It rolled up and fit into her purse.

The exterior of the Société was shabby for necessity's sake, but inside it was quite grand. The marble of the floors was rose mottled with ivory, warm in the light from the gold sconces. The wallpaper was a pale pink damask, there was framed artwork on the walls and beautiful furniture set about in nooks, and everything smelled wonderful.

This was what Edith needed, after the claustrophobia of the old farmhouse and life in Hawkshead in general. She needed to remember that she was a diabolist. Not that she ever forgot it, with Mercurialis intruding upon her thoughts every moment of the day, but it was more than that. She was a link in a rare and precious chain stretching back thousands of years. To be a diabolist was to know the truth of the universe. She was more than just a wounded sister or a beleaguered aunt. She was exceptional in every way.

Edith, like Jane, enjoyed being distinct from her peers.

Patrice Durand was still at his desk, his bald pate hanging low over stacks of papers like a small moon. His jacket was off, tossed carelessly over a chair. He did not look like he was finishing out his evening.

"Bon soir, Patrice," said Edith, and she smiled as he looked up in surprise. "Long night ahead of you?"

"Edith!" He was up in a moment and rushing toward her to kiss her hand. "Don't keep me in suspense!"

"Jane did fine," she said, summoning a smile as she had once summoned a demon—through determination, know-how, and force of will. "Miriam, too. But did you have to tell everyone in the Société?"

"Oh, well!" he said, embracing her warmly before ushering her to an empty chair. "I knew she would excel. My Jane! Passed her Test! How could she fail, given her pedigree?"

"Everyone knew that but her, of course."

Edith knew Patrice was expecting other news, too. "I talked to her," she said. "She was, I think, pleased to learn that you exist, and that you have a name, and live somewhere, and so on and so forth."

"Will she be in touch?"

Edith glared at him. "I told her she must wait until she's out of the house, as I told you I would."

Patrice looked disappointed. "I've already missed so much," he muttered. "It's wrong for Nancy to deny me this!"

"You both made choices that led to this situation." Willing as she was to help introduce Patrice to his daughter, it was because she knew Jane longed to know something of him. In other matters Edith stalwartly refused to take sides. "It's just a bit longer. Jane is yearning to leave home. I assure you she will apply herself to her Practical and be out on her own as soon as she can. Then the two of you can decide what relationship you wish to have."

"It is not fair," said Patrice. "Jane is sixteen—she should be able to speak to her father if she wishes."

Edith felt herself start to become annoyed. Of course it would not occur to Patrice that pushing ahead to forge a new relationship with his daughter might do much to endanger the other, more established ones in Jane's life.

Mercurialis reminded Edith that she had known Patrice for more than two decades, and thus she had known he was self-centered and obtuse before she agreed to tell Jane about him. Edith agreed—but just the same, the stakes were higher now.

"Life isn't fair," said Edith, rising from her chair. Patrice looked surprised, but Edith did not relent; she had other matters that demanded her attention. "Think of Miriam and her relationship with her parents." Patrice had the decency to look abashed, but Edith did not relent. "You know you invoked them while begging me to carry your water, and you also know my price was that you do nothing to contact Jane until she has left home."

"I remember," said Patrice sourly.

Edith was unimpressed by Patrice's adult pouting. Apparently Jane's apple hadn't fallen far from this particular tree.

"Good. See that you continue to remember," she said. "Au revoir." She'd said her piece, and anyhow he'd turned back to his work. Gone was the gallant Frenchman who'd kissed her hand. Only Patrice was left.

Edith wasn't surprised—not really. While Nancy's decision to sequester herself in the country was as puzzling to her today as it had been sixteen years ago, she'd always known why Patrice and her sister had never been able to really, truly work it out. Nancy was as proud as they came, but Patrice somehow was prouder. No matter what Edith might say to Nancy in the heat of an argument, she understood her decision to separate their lives. Maybe not so dramatically as the distance between Hawkshead and Paris, but some amount, *absolutely*.

Edith entered the Red Room, called such due to the common theme of the furniture's upholstery. Her heart skipped a beat at the sight of Graham Yellowhorse—but she was glad to see all of her friends still pretending to play at French tarot. The cards lay upon the table, untouched; being that no one else was in the room, they had abandoned the pretense and were whispering to one another in hushed tones. As Edith approached, she felt the grumbling tingle of Mercurialis alerting her that she'd just triggered a diabolic ward. Edith was glad they were using them, as was right and proper, and anyway it was only to let them know when someone approached, which is what, indeed, she was doing.

"Edith!" Maja Znidarcic rose from her chair and rushed over

with surprising agility for someone so short and so stout. Edith embraced her warmly. "We didn't want to bother you while you were away, but . . ."

"Tell me everything," said Edith. "I'm back early and eager for news. And yes," she said, exasperated by the eager looks of her colleagues, "they both did *fine*."

"The news isn't good," said Graham. He was an American diabolist who had come over to fight on the front lines, as it were.

"What? What is it?" Edith perched on the arm of Zelda Lizman's chair, hoping genuine dismay covered the excessive sensations she experienced when she heard the deep and dulcet tones of his voice. His demon, Zlovid, granted him exceptional insight, and she was wary of its roving eye. If Graham ever found out how she felt, she wanted it to be from her lips, not from his demon's. "What's happened?"

"We intercepted a transmission," said Zelda. "It might be a trap —and we know that—but it seems like something we need to take seriously. Some of the things they're saying sound like they might be about Egon and Sofia."

"It was sent from Dr. Braune to Dr. Querner," said Graham. "And for the first time, it wasn't sent over diabolic channels. They used a *homing pigeon*. It took a while, but Saul Zeitz cracked the code."

It was concerning, suspicious news. Edith thought back to her conversation with Miriam, hoping she would not need to deliver yet more bad news to the poor girl.

Miriam's parents had disappeared while investigating the small, dilapidated castle that Dr. Wolfram Braune had repurposed as a diabolic research facility. It was known that he and Dr. Karl Querner of the notorious Dark Lab were attempting to develop a powerful diabolic weapon; what was unknown was how close they might be to success.

"What did the message say?"

"There had been another failed *extraction attempt* by Braune on a prisoner—we're not sure what that means," said Graham, "and the request for a copy of a prisoner's file. Their roundabout description sounded a lot like Egon."

"I don't like it," said Graham.

"Intuition?" asked Zelda, peering keenly at him.

"No," said Graham. "Not exactly. I just mean ... they're losing. Everybody knows it. So why do they need notes? What are they doing? I don't need a demon to suggest to me that this is very probably a trap."

"Or they're close enough to success that it's still worth trying," said Maja.

Graham conceded the point by holding up his broad, scarred hands. Oh, how Edith adored him ... but he'd never given her any indication that he returned her feelings. Ordinarily, Edith would forge ahead and make her case, especially these days, when every mission might be her last. But the Young Talarians who'd remained loyal to the Cantors needed to stick together—and a romance would disrupt their operation as surely as a rejection.

"I say we make a run on Braune's château," said Zelda. Edith looked at her in surprise; Zelda was the most martially inclined of any of them, but an all-out assault on a highly protected Nazi laboratory staffed by diabolists and housed in a castle was a bit much—even for one who had summoned the demon known as the General. Edith had seen Zelda punch through brick, leap over walls, dislocate her joints to fit through small crevasses, lift enormous objects—but that still would not be enough. "I'm perfectly serious. Why else have we gathered all this intelligence?"

Maja considered this, to Edith's surprise. "You may be right. But something so direct ... we might lose much to gain little, with the war ending, too."

"If they develop this weapon ..." Zelda shrugged in a philosophical manner. "We can't know the future. They do say the war will end any day now, but what if it doesn't? What if it takes longer? What if something changes?"

"The reports from several locations are appalling," said Edith. As much as she liked Graham, Zelda had won her over. "Losing has only increased the Nazis' savagery."

Graham frowned—not at her, just thoughtfully—and looked down at his hands. Edith didn't need demonic insight to tell that he was mightily unhappy. Edith understood his reservations, but she agreed it was time to act. Zelda and Maja immediately began to discuss the trip to the south of Germany, where the castle squatted on some ghastly sounding plain, but Edith held up her hand for silence. There was something she needed to know.

"Before we start to consider *what* we ought to do, we need to ascertain *who* will be with us," she said, trying not to look at Graham. "Our numbers will determine our strategy."

"Oh, I'm with you." Graham, on the other hand, did have demonic insight. He knew to whom she spoke. "I just can't help but think this won't end well for us."

Edith shrugged. "The more important thing," she said, "is making sure it doesn't end well for *them*."

9

J ANE HAD ALREADY DONE ENOUGH preliminary research on the subject of flight to know that every book that so much as touched on the matter seemed written to confuse rather than educate. Once she began to read in earnest, however, she came to truly hate the diabolists who had put quill to parchment only to waste a lot of both for no reason. For example, the one she'd selected one rainy afternoon had this to say on the subject of flying:

> It might be that natural laws such as gravity may not be broken, being that they are both natural and law. Better and safer to manipulate changeable things, like the desires of man, or the weather of the world.

Jane was unimpressed by this eleventh-century Portuguese windbag, and she questioned his decision to title his treatise *On Flying*, given that it contained no information whatsoever about flying. Instead, he'd written about why it was "utterly impossible," which felt to Jane like he'd tried until he was tired of failing, and then given up in a huff.

"What do you think, Smudge?" she whispered to the cat, who currently sat on her lap as she sprawled across the chaise lounge, perusing page after worthless page. "How would *you* do it?"

The cat declined to comment, but at the sound of his name, he did flick his tail from side to side. Jane went back to her book, but a moment later a volley of rain struck the farmhouse's windows and drummed across the roof as the weather moved through the valley. Jane looked up, and so did her mother, who was knitting on a shawl the same color as the storm outside in a rare moment away from her desk of requests. Her hands did not pause as she surveyed the wet weather, and as her mother worked, Jane guiltily remembered her own neglected knitting project: a wine-colored hat she'd planned to give to Miriam for her birthday.

It had only been a week since Edith's visit, but it felt more like a lifetime ago that Jane had had time to do such things as work with her hands to create something, rather than to have them be empty of much beyond books, pens, and paper.

Nancy chuckled. "I remember when a stormy afternoon filled me with dread—there never seemed to be enough to keep you girls occupied! These days you're so deep in your researches, I can barely get a word out of either of you."

Jane didn't know what to say. She detected the sort of verbal trap that failing to navigate correctly would earn her a teasing remark for her troubles. If only it didn't fall to her to reply ... but of course Miriam was no help. She didn't even lift her nose from her book.

"It behooves me to spend my time wisely now that I've passed my Test," said Jane, appealing to responsibility—and the absolute legitimacy of her continued efforts. "My Practical won't complete itself."

"I see. Just remember, it's easy to keep up with a good habit right after a success," said Nancy. She sounded amused. "It gets harder as the days and weeks wear on."

For the millionth time, Jane found herself wondering what in the world motivated her mother when she said things like that —those piercing remarks that were sharper than any knife, went deeper than any needle. This one was especially pointed, and still the question remained of why she would wish to hurt her daughter at all.

Some long-forgotten impulse claimed Jane then, and she looked to Miriam for support as she once would have done. In the past, Jane's almost-sister and best friend would step in and do her best to distract Nancy from these sorts of situations. Today, however, Miriam remained silent—though her expression spoke volumes. She did not like this one bit. But that didn't make her an ally.

Jane was on her own here.

"Of course you're right, Mother," said Jane, keeping her tone as bland as possible. Even so, it seemed as if her mother and her friend picked up on her skepticism just fine. Miriam even looked up from her book, which Jane chose to view as a triumph.

The mood in the room had indeed shifted. The fire in the wood burner no longer seemed as warm, and the rain made everything dreary, rather than cozy.

"Why, Jane!" exclaimed Nancy. "Don't tell me you're cross!"

Jane was all too pleased to respect her mother's wishes. "Fine, I won't," she said, standing suddenly and sending Smudge leaping away with a reproachful *mrowl* and an indignant jingle of his collar bell. The cat stalked off with tail held high; Jane planned to quickly follow suit. "I needed a change of scene anyway!"

"Jane Blackwood! I'm surprised at you. The fact is, passing your Test is only one crucial step to achieving true Mastery. People fail at every stage of the process. I'm sorry if the truth annoys you, but I can't pretend otherwise, even to spare my own daughter's feelings."

Jane went very red in the face as her cool slipped from her face like the mask it was. "If you think I'll fail, Mother, then I'll just have to prove you wrong."

"I never said I thought you'd fail," said Nancy, finally setting aside her knitting. "You mustn't be so *dramatic* all the time."

Miriam was almost squirming in her seat; she had turned back to her book, her eyes studiously on the page as Jane and her mother quarreled. On one hand, Jane understood the position Miriam was in; on the other, she could say *something* as Jane was forced to endure this assault.

Jane stuck her nose in the air, channeling her inner Katharine

Hepburn. "*Dramatic,* is it?" she asked softly. "Is it *dramatic* to wish to be left alone while I'm working instead of being the subject of unfair and unprovoked attacks?"

"Unfair attacks! Is that what you consider a bit of mild teasing to be?" Nancy shook her head. "You mustn't be so sensitive, Jane. The world won't pet you for doing the right thing."

"Don't worry," said Jane. "You've taught me that lesson *very* well."

Nancy's expression was priceless, but Jane knew the cost of seeing it would be very high.

"Please excuse me," said Miriam, shutting her book and getting to her feet in one motion. "I need to get something from my room." And then she dashed out the door.

Jane took advantage of the distraction, turning on her heel and following Miriam out into the hall.

She was furious. It wasn't fair—none of it. She should have passed her Test—she was smart enough, *capable* enough to be a diabolist. She deserved it, after all her hard work—and what's more, she wanted it. Shouldn't her conscious will, her self-knowledge, matter more than some induced hallucination?

And it also wasn't fair, the way her mother picked at her scabs and then faulted her for bleeding. Not for the first time did Jane wonder how different life would be had her father been a part of it. Would he have intervened? Would he have noticed his daughter's discomfort and spoken to her mother about it, in private, during those brief precious hours parents had to speak to one another without their children present?

Jane's gaze was suddenly, unconsciously upon the stairs to the Library. There, the answer to her questions awaited her. She just had to decide if she was going to take it.

"She was being unkind," said Miriam.

Jane shrieked. She hadn't seen Miriam standing a few steps up the big staircase, and she felt a mix of annoyance—over being startled—and guilt, as if Miriam might know she'd been thinking wicked thoughts.

"Sorry," said Miriam, stepping awkwardly down and closer.

Jane recovered enough to pat her hair back into place with some dignity. "No need to apologize. I just didn't see you."

"Jane," said Miriam, "back there, I wanted to say something. But I'm afraid."

"Afraid of *what?*" Jane wasn't interested in any apologies from Miriam. "You'd have to fall a long way before you'd be even with me in my mother's opinion."

Miriam looked hurt, which made Jane savage.

"I can't wait to leave," she said loftily.

"I don't blame you."

Jane was surprised. "I wish I understood what she wants! Before, she'd scold me for not sufficiently applying myself. Now I'm applying myself, and she's cutting me down for trying."

"You've been working very hard," said Miriam.

So Miriam *had* noticed. Jane felt a bit better to have her diligence observed, and thawed enough to crack a joke. "Maybe she just knows how little progress I've made."

"It's been tough going for me too," said Miriam, with a rueful smile. Hearing that was like a warm sunbeam hitting Jane's shoulders on a cloudy afternoon. It wasn't just her who was struggling! Jane smiled back, but the moment passed too quickly. "I just had a breakthrough though—at least, I think did. I might have solved something that's been troubling me; at least, I hope I have. I just need to . . ." Miriam trailed off uneasily.

Miriam was always one step ahead of Jane, and always, it seemed, eager to remind Jane of that.

But Jane's annoyance quickly turned to fear. Maybe that was because Miriam really was better at all this than she was.

Maybe she didn't deserve to be a diabolist.

No—she couldn't think like that. Not now that she knew the

consequences of failure. She would be neither harvested by her greedy colleagues nor told she should smile while sweeping up after them.

"Please don't let me keep you from your pursuits," said Jane. "My own Practical puts many demands on my attention, of course."

And with that, she headed for the stairs down to the Library.

She, too, had had a breakthrough. But it wasn't about her project—it was about her situation.

There was no way she was going to be able to impress the Société enough to convince them she absolutely, unequivocally belonged there. Not on her own merits. Not without a leg up. Not without an edge.

It was time to contact her father.

10

M IRIAM HADN'T BEEN SPEAKING OF her Practical when she'd mentioned her breakthrough. In fact, she'd been surprised when Jane mentioned it. Her path to Mastery within the Société had been utterly absent from her mind since the night Edith had told her of her parents' disgrace. More important was proving their innocence by finding them, or discovering what had happened to them.

They'd stayed in danger to fight. Miriam had left to live in safety. She hadn't had a choice in the matter then; she did now. She would not let her brave parents disappear and become infamous. Even if all she could do for them was find out the truth, she'd do that—no matter what.

To that end, Miriam had researched how to see without being seen—to search without being present. There were quite a few ways for diabolists to do so, but Miriam's specific needs narrowed the scope. She was, for instance, substantially limited by not being a Master; any solutions involving diabolic partnerships were therefore unworkable. She also suspected she would need some mobility to stage an investigation. The ability to interact with matter would also be a good thing.

Neither astral projection nor outright body-snatching would do, the former because her range would be limited as an apprentice, and the latter because not only was it frowned upon by the Société, but it was permanent, and it involved hollowing out one's victim on a spiritual level in order to make enough room for the invader's consciousness and will. None of that sounded right to Miriam.

Thankfully, there was a third option, in the form of a technique she discovered in, of all places, a tenth-century manuscript simply called *Badgerskin;* it was unclear if that was the title of the book or the author's name. The best Miriam could translate the obscure Gaelic word for the technique was *cleave,* with its double meaning in English of both separating and sticking together; with it, a diabolist could temporarily ride along with another body. And while the book was angled at possession of animals, the author indicated the process could be used for humans, too.

Miriam was strongly reminded of a story her father had used to tell her of the dybbuk, a Jewish ghost that could possess the living by "sticking" to them. Sticking, clinging, *cleaving*—the association was powerful, and Miriam didn't like it coming up in this context at all.

But now was not the time to be frightened by folktales—and, anyway, a dybbuk was a spirit of the dead who clung to the living. Miriam wasn't dead.

As she read on, Miriam was surprised that she'd never heard of the practice of cleaving. It seemed so useful. One would think that *someone* among the Société's ranks must have tried this technique in, oh, the past few hundred years. But then again, after she read all the warnings that misusing this technique, or even just using it too often, could cause a decline of her health—physical *and* spiritual—Miriam understood better. The author's warning about the "intrusion of the shadow-soul," an ill-defined possibility that might be a flowery way of saying catatonia or might not be, was substantially off-putting by itself, and that wasn't the only thing that could go wrong.

The shadow-soul … it was either that, or *the shadow cast by a soul,* according to how she translated the Gaelic. She was intrigued by it regardless, given her fancy of having something similar within her.

The book was quite a find. The author, a self-professed "pagan follower of Christ," seemed more honest than most ancient diabolists. While still vague at times, she—Miriam was convinced it was a she—was never deliberately misleading; in fact, she detailed the two main risks of what Miriam set out to do. In the days before the Société and other such organizations, diabolists would often be false in their instructions, caught in a bizarre fugue of wanting to document their accomplishments but wanting no one to be able to duplicate their results. Thus, Miriam felt grateful to this ancient diabolist for being so open as to note things like how, apparently, the flesh aged more quickly when separated from even a tiny piece of the spirit. That was really good to know.

There was no denying it was a risky technique. She was afraid —genuinely so. But Miriam knew her parents had likely felt the same about staying to fight in the war. They'd still done it, in the end, and she would too.

THE MATERIALS MIRIAM NEEDED to begin to learn to cleave were almost deceptively simple: a veil knife, general diabolic essence, and a way to separate her soul from her body.

The last was, interestingly enough, the easiest, as it required no subterfuge, just diablerie. There were plenty of recipes for something that would temporarily detach Miriam's spirit from her physical body. She settled on an easy sublingual tablet.

A veil knife was just an iron blade infused with diabolic residue that gave it spiritual mass. This allowed it to be wielded both by a person of flesh and blood—or a soul freed from it. Nancy had one among the Library's collection of tools. While she had never granted the girls permission to use it, neither had she ever explicitly said they couldn't.

With the veil knife, Miriam could shave off a portion of her detached spirit and use it to cleave to another creature. But of course, her goal was not simply to experience life as a beetle or a bird. Miriam needed to be able to control them, too.

The ancient Gaelic diabolist but briefly touched upon the idea that one might master the will of another creature, but it was clear she didn't approve of the idea. Still, she acknowledged that obviously many diabolists would wish to learn how to use animals for some purpose or another, thus it was better to reveal how to do so as safely as possible—for animal and human alike.

Basically, controlling a creature required sacrificing more of her soul each time. It also required more diabolic essence.

Diabolic essence was, essentially, the gasoline of all diablerie. It made the Art *go*. That's why diabolic essence was such a closely guarded resource among all diabolists.

There were two types:

Specific diabolic essence came from those plants into which diabolists had summoned demons. It could be turned into the food or tinctures diabolists consumed to keep themselves in touch with their demonic companion, or it could be processed into other components to power armamentaria. Specific essence could only be used in, well, specific ways, for specific armamentaria—which is why organizations such as the Société existed, at least in part. It made it much easier to share and share alike.

General diabolic essence was created from diabolists themselves. The process of communing with a demon infused the body with diabolic essence. Thus, a diabolist's nail clippings, hair, lost teeth, or other byproducts could be collected and rendered down for what excess diabolic residue they still contained.

Long ago, diabolists had realized that diabolic essence was changed by the body. It was just raw power, and could thus be used to fuel any pills, potions, and powders that a diabolist might wish to create.

Nancy could afford to be generous with her stores of general diabolic essence. She really didn't do too much diablerie—her interests were fulfilled by the more mundane aspects of the Art. Even so, there was a necessarily limited supply of it, so Miriam had to be careful not to take too much.

The day of Miriam's second attempt, she woke up a bit early to dig through the compost heap before feeding the ducks and geese. Finding three worms, she put them in some earth in a jar, and then left it in the barn for after Nancy went down to the Library and Jane went off to do whatever Jane did with herself ever since Edith's visit.

Out of sight of the house, Miriam studied the simple creatures in the shadowed late winter light behind the potting shed. Their bodies glistened as they squirmed.

Miriam knew what she had to do. Her first successful attempt had been on one of Nancy's ducks—but while it had seemed like a simple beast, it had proven too complex for a novice. She'd managed to cleave to the bird, but she could only endure the experience for a moment before it became too overwhelming.

Putting the jar on a rock, Miriam took the veil knife out of her pocket along with the tin of tablets she'd created and a blue glass eye-dropper bottle of liquid general diabolic essence.

Settling cross-legged on the bare cold ground, Miriam put the pastille beneath her tongue. She gradually became aware of the sensation of distance, though in a different way than perceiving how far or near something external to herself was. Looking down, she saw her body, still on the earth. She raised her hands, but the hands that moved were not solid flesh, but rather ones made of mist or something yet more insubstantial. She flexed her fingers, watching them move with her spirit's eyes.

Just as her body waited below her, the physical knife rested on the earth. When she picked it up, however, the blade's spiritual double came away in her hand. She raised it to her arm, contemplating steel and flesh.

By her wrist was a small indentation in her spirit-flesh, where she'd shaved off a sliver of spiritual skin on her first try. The area looked raw, like a healing wound, and oddly some pale charcoal-colored smoke could occasionally be seen drifting from it. She wondered if that was the shadow-soul the book had mentioned. She hoped not; it seemed to be dissipating, and she felt anything soul-related really ought to stay inside of her.

Surely it would heal. Disturbing as it might look, the book had said that souls regenerated over time.

To a point. What that point was, it hadn't said.

Miriam felt the bite of the blade as she sliced into her spirit-arm—not as pain, but neither did she enjoy the sensation. Thankfully, she didn't need to take off much.

Miriam took a deep breath. The bit of her spirit she'd sliced was turning to vapor. She inhaled it, concentrated on one of the earth-worms—and instead of exhaling, her whole world *changed.*

Miriam spent a few bizarre but incredible moments tunneling through the compost, seeking, consuming, wriggling, eliminating. When she felt her hold on the creature weakening, she allowed herself to withdraw.

The cut she'd made on her arm was weeping more of that odd smoke. Miriam watched it, a bit mesmerized, until the pastille wore off and her spirit settled back down into her flesh.

Her success was exhilarating, but she couldn't celebrate too much. Literally—she was too exhausted to do much of anything. She was so tired, in fact, that she fell asleep reading in her favorite chair in the Library. She had gone down there to get a book, just a little light reading before bed, and the chair had just looked so *nice.*

She awoke thinking it was morning, but after a moment she realized it was still the middle of the night, and that whatever she was hearing was not bacon frying in the pan. A message was materializing over the Basque Lens Nancy used to receive Library requests and to send pages and passages out in turn, burning into the stack of paper left on its surface just for that purpose.

As much as she didn't want to, Miriam knew she needed to get up and go to bed properly. She stood, wincing as she stretched her neck left and right. Her left leg was a bit tingly, so she ambled over to the desk. It was tidy, just like everything else about Nancy and the old farmhouse.

Miriam's eyes fell upon the paper atop the Basque Lens.

Dear Jane,

That was how it began.

Miriam found out how the letter ended, too.

Dear Jane,

As always, I was filled with indescribable joy upon receiving your letter. Long ago I gave up the dream of being any part of your life as you grew up, so it is always a delight to hear from you. I am also pleased to hear Nancy is well. Edith naturally passed along news of you both, but I'm elated to have more frequent updates.

I am sorry to hear you are still feeling frustrated with your Practical. I know we have been dealing with one another as equals, but you must let me play the father here when I say that these things take time, Jane! You are neither expected nor encouraged to hurry your way through this part of your training. Diabolism is an art, and art is a slow thing. The point is not to hurry. But if I may be so bold, I sense you are not hurrying away from childhood and your apprenticeship so much as other things. This I understand, but I must caution you: it will be hard for you to give up one without the other.

As I write these things to you, my Jane, I detect a hesitation in my hand. I am afraid of being misunderstood. I wonder, would you consider a more direct form of communication?

It would not be difficult for us to arrange a face-to-face meeting through this very Basque Lens. Consider it—if you would look in Modern Mirror Methods *by J. Bunnell, you will find a recipe for a wax that, if you rub it onto the glass, will allow us to see one another and converse as if we were sitting in a café together. It is more work for you, I know, but the materials are easily obtained. Selfishly, I hope you say yes—I have only seen photographs of you, after all, and the last one was not so recent. And I might be more helpful when it comes to your Practical if we could really converse, instead of in this remote and stilted manner.*

Your affectionate father,
Patrice Durand

Miriam had been groggy before she started the letter, but she was wide awake by the time she finished it. Jane's father was alive —and they had a secret relationship!

Surely this was the hand of Edith at work. That woman would not rest until she'd stirred every pot.

But Edith's attempt to upend the status quo at the old farm-house—however justified it might be—wasn't the only thing occupying Miriam's mind. Far from it. Buried within this letter was not merely this shocking revelation about Jane's personal life, but also very possibly the solution to her problems.

Cleaving to another creature required being able to *see* that creature—not, as far as Miriam could tell, being *near* it.

That wax might be the answer to her troubles. She needed that book . . .

Nancy was an early riser, though she did not usually go down to the Library before making breakfast for the girls. That meant Jane would likely steal down here soon, in order to retrieve her secret message before her mother spied it.

Knowing she had no time to delay, Miriam slipped off her shoes and padded in her stocking feet to the card catalogue. It was but the work of a moment to locate the listing and a moment more to scurry to the location of the book. There it was, bound in black leather with silver lettering on the spine: *Modern Mirror Methods*.

Miriam took it down from the shelf.

She felt badly, stealing upstairs with it, knowing Jane would soon be looking for it. But Jane only needed the book to talk to her long-lost parent more conveniently. Miriam's need was genuinely urgent. She was trying to discover whether either of her parents were still alive at all.

11

THANKFULLY, THE PASSAGE MIRIAM NEEDED was short and easily copied. The book was back on the shelf not a day after she'd removed it, and as far as she could tell, Jane had never missed it.

A few days later Miriam looked for it again, just to see. The book was gone, so clearly Jane had ended up wanting it—but Jane seemed intent on doing whatever she would do without ever whispering a word about it to Miriam.

She wasn't whispering *any* words about it at all, come to think of it. Jane had a habit of always muttering to herself about her work, and sometimes going so far as to ask Miriam's opinion or her mother's advice to work through difficult concepts. But not anymore.

It made Miriam wonder just what Jane was up to these days—beyond speaking with her father. Was her friend truly preoccupied with work in the wake of her Test? Perhaps something the Société would frown upon?

Miriam wished they could talk about it, but that was impossible. Intimacy required balance, and she couldn't tell Jane about any of her own plans.

That's why Miriam was alone when she took it upon herself to trek to Hawkshead on the next fine day—specifically to the forge at the Red Lion. She was glad when no one batted an eye when she mentioned it; her out-of-doors experiments with a duck, worms, and most recently a fish had made it less remarkable when she made the announcement that she needed some air.

"I think I might go all the way to Tarn Hows," she said, a lie that was an excellent excuse for being gone as long as she would be. The lake was quite a ways off, so Miriam tucked an apple in her pocket for verisimilitude. "There's not a cloud in the sky, but the good weather won't hold for more than a day or two this time of year." Her voice felt strained and uneasy to her ears, but Nancy didn't seem to notice.

"It's quite cold," said Nancy. "Are you sure?"

"I can always turn around."

"Just make sure to bundle up."

Jane's only reaction was to look away when Miriam caught her staring with that curious but also suspicious expression in her eyes.

Miriam had many reasons to wish the silence between her and Jane wasn't so oppressive, but that day her concern came admittedly from a vain and selfish source: she would have liked to ask Jane to do her hair the same way as she had the day of Edith's arrival. She settled for tying back her waves with the bright blue ribbon Jane had used, consoling herself that any further change would likely make it too obvious that she had an interest beyond the professional in talking to Sam.

The kiss of sunlight upon Miriam's face was warm and welcome, but the wind was still wintery, and the damp was not the sort that encouraged things to grow. She set out across the field toward Tarn Hows, but once she was out of sight of the farmhouse, she doubled back to intersect with the road to Hawkshead, also avoiding their gossipy neighbor, Mrs. Fielding. Whenever a car or cart passed her by, Miriam pulled up her hood, worried a neighbor would remark to Nancy if she was seen walking alone into the village that day, but it was a risk she had to take.

From *Modern Mirror Methods*, Miriam had learned that a "magic mirror" like the Basque Lens in the Library was not silvered glass set in a frame—it was a series of layered armamentaria that mimicked a mirror's reflective surface. Miriam had been disappointed but unsurprised to find that she could not simply go into town to buy herself a mirror. She'd have to get one specially made and ensure various dried and powdered diabolic substances were forged into the metal.

Good thing she knew a blacksmith . . .

Miriam cut around the edge of town to come at the forge on the bias. Lost in her thoughts, she shrieked when she almost ran into Sam as he pushed a wheelbarrow around the side of the building.

"Why, Miriam!" he exclaimed. "What did you want to do that for?"

"Do *wh-what* for?" she stammered.

"Scare me like that!"

Miriam blushed, to her horror. "I didn't mean to scare you."

"Hmm," said Sam. He seemed skeptical—but he was just teasing. "What are you doing, then, if you're not trying to scare me?"

"I—I need something made, at the forge I mean, but it was such a fine day I walked around and—"

It occurred to Miriam that she'd never spoken this much with Sam ever, and definitely never alone, as they were now. It was thrilling—not just because she was talking with the handsomest boy she'd ever seen in her life, with his fawn-colored hair and his soft beard that had just started to really come in; it was also a welcome respite from thinking only about her project or the simmering tensions of the old farmhouse.

Sam smiled at her kindly, and though beforehand she'd been shivering from her walk, now she felt warm.

"Is that so? Let me load up this wood, and you can come inside and tell me all about it."

"Want help?"

"With the wood?" Sam grinned. "Surely these logs are too heavy for you."

"No, they're not!"

"Pssht. How could you pick up anything with those scrawny arms!"

Outraged, Miriam set to helping him load up his wheelbarrow with split logs, their breath puffing in the thin sunlight.

When they'd finished, Sam surveyed their effort with a critical eye. "Not bad," he said. "I'm impressed."

Miriam realized he'd been teasing her again, and she stuck out her tongue.

Sam stuck his own tongue out at her, and she giggled. "Come on, let's warm up with a cup of tea. Tell me what you need so badly that you came into town on a cold day like today to get it."

"I need a mirror," said Miriam, as they entered the forge. It was blessedly warmer in there. She liked the smell, too, of hot things —metal and wood, warm sawdust and water.

"A mirror?" Sam shook his head as he began to unload the wood. "That I can't make for you. You have to have a special kind of glass."

"Oh, I have the glass," lied Miriam, wishing she'd come up with some other way to describe what she needed. She didn't need a mirror per se, just something slightly concave, with a handle. "It's the frame that broke."

"Odd," said Sam. "Usually it's the opposite."

"It was a very old frame," said Miriam hastily. "Anyway, the glass is a circle, six inches around, and it's about a quarter of an inch thick, so I'd need a rim around the edge that deep."

"Did you bring the glass with you?"

"No, I didn't want to take it out of the house."

Sam nodded. "I wish I could see it myself though. It was six inches exactly?"

"Exactly," said Miriam. This was a lot harder than she'd antici-pated. "I measured it across in several places."

"You always struck me as a careful sort," said Sam. He wiped his brow now that they'd finished up. "You know I can't really do any-thing too fancy, right?"

"It doesn't need to be fancy, just functional."

"Ah, so it's for you!" he crowed, as if in triumph. "I've been puzzling over whether you wanted it for yourself or as a gift for Jane. At first I thought it must be for Jane, as of the two of you, I'd say she's the one to spend her time staring into a looking glass, but she'd also want something finer than I could make her."

It felt bad, being compared to Jane and judged the sloppier, even if it was true.

"I mostly make horseshoes, you know," said Sam after a moment. "But if you really don't care how the piece would look—"

"I don't!"

"Then I'll do it."

"Good." Now came the hard part. Miriam took the bag of powder out of her pocket and set it on the table. "I need you to put this into the, ah, hot—molten—metal you'll use."

"What is it?"

Miriam had forgotten to come up with an excuse, but Sam took her pause as embarrassment.

"It's not my business," he said. "It might weaken or discolor the metal is all."

"That's okay," said Miriam. She was certain it would not, but of course she didn't tell him that.

"I'll make sure it gets in there," Sam said. He picked up the bag and hefted it in his palm. "All of it?"

Miriam nodded.

Task completed, body warmed, Miriam had no need to tarry longer—but she also had no idea how to take her leave of Sam. She was saved by the return of his father.

Mr. Nibley was not much like his son—their hair was of a color, but he was a stern man with big muscles and a big beard and a big frown. He came in through the door clearly expecting to find his son at work, not sitting and talking with a girl.

"Where are we at with those nails, son?" he asked.

"Very nearly finished," said Sam, after tucking the bag into his apron pocket. He was flushed, but whether it was from embarrassment over not being done with his work, or his father's failure to greet their guest, Miriam could not say.

"We'll settle up later," said Sam, as he showed her out. "I'll get it done as quick as I can, I promise."

"I'm sorry if I got you in trouble," she whispered, as she stepped outside.

He winked at her. "Don't you worry about me. I'll be all right." And after rolling his eyes back toward where his father waited, he shut the door.

Miriam turned away, but she paused when she heard a raised voice from within—Sam's father. The window of the forge was cracked to let in a little fresh air, and from that sliver of space she heard exactly what Mr. Nibley said so loudly:

"If you're going to trifle with the local girls in my place of business, I'd prefer if it wasn't with the village Jew."

The village Jew.

How stupid of her, to think that she could ever truly escape the prejudice that had brought her here to begin with. She'd mistaken her neighbors' silence on the obviousness of her identity as a lack of interest in it; now she knew that it was quite the reverse. They had just been too polite to mention their true sentiments toward Nancy Blackwood's ward.

She stumbled as she took a step back. When her foot came down not on the stoop but empty air, she yelped. When she recovered, through the window she saw Sam's face. He was mortified to see her still there.

Upset for a number of reasons, Miriam took off at a brisk pace toward her home, heedless of who might see her, her shoes squelching in the muddy ruts she was in too much of a hurry to avoid. She did not slow her pace until she was well beyond Hawkshead; her lungs, too full of cold air, screamed silently at her to consider them.

She knew there was no reason to be terrified, but still she was. If they came — *they would not come* — but if they did, if they asked questions . . . If the Nazis won, she would be taken away, or killed right there in her own home — and Nancy and Jane too, for harboring her. Collapsing against a fence post, Miriam wheezed and choked as she recovered her breath.

"Miriam!"

Sam was flushed from rapid walking — and from anger, too, given his expression.

"He's an old fool," said Sam. "I'm sorry you heard that. Most people don't care."

Then he did something incredible, he took one of her hands in his and raised it to his lips.

"*I* certainly don't care," he said.

"Oh," she gasped, confused to feel so good after feeling so afraid. She gasped again when he took her in his arms and kissed her — not on the hand this time.

"Miriam," he said softly, fondly. "I always thought I saw you looking at me, but until today I didn't know for sure if you really *fancied* me."

"I didn't say I did . . ."

"You didn't have to. I know what I saw."

"I have to go," said Miriam, her heart a wild and feral creature desperate to escape the cage of her ribs. "My aunt is expecting me."

"Go," said Sam, and kissed her a final time. Miriam tore herself away from him, cutting overland so that she would come back to the farmhouse from the right direction, but before she'd gotten far, she turned back and waved at him.

"Hey!" she called. "I still want the mirror! It wasn't a ruse!"

"Of course!" he cried back to her, and she took off running again, but this time because she was happier than she could ever remember being in all of her life.

12

JANE SNUCK DOWN TO THE LIBRARY just before the clock struck one in the morning. Smudge trotted along behind her, the cat intrigued by her late-night jaunt.

Nancy had been pregnant when she'd accepted the position of Librarian, which meant that Jane had never before beheld the face of her father, even as a wide-eyed infant. Her mother had denied her this, as she had denied Jane so many things that ought to be hers, like a proper social life, or the agency to select her own clothes, or even the words Jane would choose to use to describe her style of diablerie.

Jane's candle threw off a golden glow as she descended the steps. When she was halfway down, Smudge bounded ahead of her all of a sudden, as was his pleasure. His fluffy tail threw weird shadows everywhere as he raced to the bottom to wait, impatiently pacing, for Jane to join him.

Jane knew that given her precarious situation, it was a substantial risk to contact her father *at all,* but she had to. She was getting nowhere with her research. It hadn't been that long, she knew that —no one expected results so soon. But Jane also knew that if she wanted to create the appearance of being exceptional, she would need to outpace Miriam. Fair or not, they'd be judged against one another as well as on their own merits. This meant that to be complete, the illusion needed to contain Jane beating Miriam to the finish line.

JANE KNEW SHE COULDN'T ASK her father about making her broomstick fly, not specifically. If she was truly unable to succeed, she didn't want him — or anyone — to know.

Charming as he seemed to be, Patrice Durand had not yet fully earned Jane's trust. How could he? While it was true that the man who wrote Jane back seemed intelligent, avuncular rather than paternal, and deeply pleased that Jane had sought him out, he was still the Société's Evaluator—and Jane could not let herself forget that.

That said, her father was right. Jane *was* smart. Maybe she wasn't a genius at languages or the fastest reader, but she knew how the world worked—in spite of the best efforts of her mother. It gave her a bit of savage pleasure to think how the films and popular novels she enjoyed (and her mother so disdained) had given her the sort of context she needed to keep herself from being manipulated.

She was the one doing the manipulating here. Not for sinister purposes, but out of a desire to keep her life together. Or perhaps to keep her life, period.

All she was doing was showing her father how respectful and charming she was, how mature, and how eager she was to make up for all the years they'd lost. She wasn't lying about any of that; she was just also making sure that if ever a question arose about her legitimacy within the ranks of the Société, her father would have to consider not only the rules, but also his feelings for his daughter.

Usually, Jane wanted to turn on every available light in the Library when she was down there, especially at night, but tonight she did not. She needed to be able to conceal herself and what she was doing in an instant should she be discovered.

It still seemed odd to her that *Modern Mirror Methods* should be gone from the Library's shelf the moment she received a letter suggesting she read it, but it had reappeared so quickly that Jane assumed her mother had pulled it at someone's request. It was just that her mother was meticulous about always following her own rules for checking out Library books . . .

Miriam was, too, which was what made it even odder.

That sliver of doubt kept Jane peering into the darkness as she scurried along the main corridor of the Library, the muted yellow light spilling over the mosaic tiles of the floor and flashing against the wooden ends of the bookshelves. Smudge padded along beside her; Jane kept an eye on him — not out of fear of bad behavior, but to take advantage of his superior senses; whenever he stopped and sniffed, she'd flash the candle around to see if he had detected anyone in the shadows.

The desk upon which the Library's Basque Lens lay looked oddly imposing with the candlelight making the hollows in the carvings and scrolls so much darker. Jane approached slowly and was pleased to see no new messages atop the mirror, like little telegrams atop a salver.

She was worried a message would come in while she and her father spoke — the book hadn't said what would happen in that case — but it was a risk she had to take. In one decisive movement, she pulled a small flat jar from her pocket and with a rag began to apply the waxy contents to the surface with circular movements. The glass went milk-white wherever she spread the wax, until the whole surface was covered. It glowed gently in the darkness, like a little moon.

The last thing Jane had to do was set her father's simulacra on the mirror. The Library had one on file for every member of the Société, in order to receive requests and send out research materials. Individual diabolists might share them, too, as a way to stay connected — they were most commonly small glass phials with a bit of skin or blood or fingernail clippings inside, something to mark it as their own for the purposes of direct communication. Thankfully, Patrice Durand's was nothing more troubling than a bit of gray hair in a tube sealed with the brightest purple wax Jane had ever seen. It was beautiful, flecked with gold, and stamped with a seal that looked like some sort of elaborate tropical beetle.

"Patrice Durand," said Jane, and the white glow began to swirl. Eventually it resolved and she saw an ornate plaster ceiling.

Her father's ceiling!

Only in that moment did Jane appreciate the enormity of what she'd done. She'd violated her mother's trust, disregarded her promises to her aunt, and voluntarily solicited the attention of the man who would be in charge of meting out justice if she was ever found out.

She'd better make it worth it.

"Jane?" The voice was French, but Jane could tell immediately from the way he said her name that he spoke fluent English. A bald head poked over the edge of the mirror into view, then came a wrinkled forehead, and then two large, black-fringed eyes with large dark gray brows, and below those an enormous nose. So that's where she got it, she thought ruefully. Her father's mouth was also large, as were the teeth within it. She saw them when he smiled.

"Jane!" This time it was no question, he clearly saw himself in her features. Jane smiled too, with her own large teeth.

"Wait," she said, and pulled up a chair. By kneeling on it, she could lean over the mirror and see much better. She was too afraid to pick it up, lest it break.

"Ah, yes, yes!" Jane's father gazed at her admiringly. "That is much better!"

His Basque Lens was a hand mirror, and he was holding it out fairly far; he was sitting in a wingback chair in a lavishly appointed room that looked exactly like Jane had imagined a chic Parisian diabolist's workroom might look, though she knew the blackout curtains were not for privacy. She was thrilled, not just because she was seeing how her father lived after being told for so long that he did not live at all—but because it was evidence that she came honestly by her love of fashionable things.

And that a love of fashionable things was not actually a sign that she was frivolous, inattentive to her studies, or even unusual.

Her father, as she'd learned, was a respected diabolist—an elected official within the Société!—and yet he did not seem to feel there was any conflict in working hard and excelling while being surrounded by beauty.

He had noticed her looking on in wonder and was smiling at her as she stared. Jane blushed and filled the awkward silence with the first thing that came to mind: a question about a curious item just behind him.

"Is that an astrolabe?" she asked.

"Ah! Similar—but no. It is infinitely more fabulous!" He stood, and Jane grinned as the mirror showed her his trousers—neatly pressed—and his Turkish carpet as he walked over to the desk. "I beg your pardon," he said, righting the mirror again. He moved it closer so Jane could see all the intricacies of the splendid brass object, with its layers of working parts. Her father moved a small lever with his thumb, and it began to spin, slowly. To her delight, some areas lit up as the object moved within itself and others disappeared; some areas rose, and some fell more delightfully than any carousel. "This device is somewhat like an astrolabe but also like a globe—based on *An Atlas of the Diabolic Continents,* by Usman Khan; it is a representation of our best understanding of the . . . geography—that word will just have to do—of the diabolic realm. But, of course, the diabolic realm is much different than our own."

The diabolic realm! Jane was intrigued; she wanted to pepper him with about a thousand questions, but she kept her focus. She wanted to show her father her best self—calm, collected. Brilliant, perhaps. Why, she'd even styled her hair and put on a bit of makeup. First impressions and all that.

"What is its function?" she asked.

"Sometimes it can be useful for a diabolist to know where a demon resides when it's at home," said her father. "Demon-summoning—all diablerie, really—is trial and error; it's seeing what works and hoping that at some later date you can duplicate your results. If there's one thing that's consistent, however, it's that the more information you have, the better." Jane's father shrugged at her visible dismay. "If you want specific results, the more knowledge you have, the better. So, if you know the demon you seek lives here within the Cloud Kingdom"—he touched something, and the device whirled to reveal clouds the same impossible coral color of a summer sunrise—"or the Breathing Sea"—he turned it and, somehow, tiny blades of grass sprouted, grew, and then withered —"or the Vale of Tears"—he turned it and revealed a crevasse that glowed with a color Jane could not name—"then you have a better chance of success."

Jane considered this as she rubbed at her watering eyes. "A summoning can go badly?"

"The risk is very low," said her father, but they both knew that was not a *no*. "*The Book of Known Demons* helps us, and the one you have at the Library is the most up-to-date of all of them, naturally. And you will have ample help when you are ready to pursue your summoning."

This was it. This was her opportunity.

"I'm eager for that," said Jane. "The sooner the better, as far as I'm concerned."

"Oh, Jane. Many apprentices feel so." Patrice veered into the paternal with his tone. "Just remember: it's not a race. You have the rest of your life to be a Master, with all its attendant demands and difficulties. No young person ever understands when the old speak wistfully of childhood, but you will one day, my dear."

Jane might love wit and charm and cunning, but artifice was never her delight—not until recently, at least. But the time had come.

"You're right," said Jane. "It is not that I wish to be done with my apprenticeship—not necessarily. The Library is endlessly fascinating, but I've spent sixteen years here. I'm ready to go to new places, meet new people. I just want to be done with my Practical so I can see what the world is like!"

"Ah, Jane!" said Patrice. "What a fool I was not to insist on my father's rights. Travel is highly restricted these days, but before the war I could have shown you Paris, Jakarta . . ."

This story didn't quite match up with Edith's account of Patrice's paternal sentiments toward his daughter, but now was not the time to interrogate further.

"Mother doesn't understand," said Jane, knowing very well that Nancy understood perfectly — she just disapproved. "She's happy here, and she feels I should be too."

"Much of Nancy's character was shaped by her youth spent traipsing about the globe — she ought to see that yours, too, will be formed at least in part by your isolation."

"Exactly!" No duplicity tinged Jane's passionate reply, but she recalled herself after and spoke more calmly. "I know for a fact that Mother won't let me out of her sight until I've completed my Practical, so I'm working as hard and as quickly as possible. But I'm just *stuck*."

Patrice nodded. "It is something we all encounter. Be patient, my Jane. It's been but a handful of weeks since your Test — some apprentices take years to complete their Practical. Oh, I know that's not for *you*, but it's perfectly fine for any apprentice to take things at the pace that suits them."

Not any apprentice — not Jane. "I'm not averse to hard work, I just wish I could speed things along. Find what I needed sooner. Even with the indices and catalogues, I'm still spending so much time looking at books that just don't have anything helpful in them. It's agonizing sometimes!"

Patrice's thoughtful expression gave Jane a bit of hope. "It is a pity you're so isolated. Other apprentices have the advantage of gossiping with one another. They hear of tricks and tips that may be, ah, technically against the rules, if one applies the strictest of standards, and yet are unlikely to be noticed by anyone—for example, how could anyone know if an apprentice employed a skimmer or a strike chain in pursuit of their aims?"

Jane had never heard of a skimmer, a strike chain, or any other sort of research aid. That such things might exist was itself a surprise, though she felt silly for not assuming that someone, somewhere, might have felt the same frustrations she felt and looked for a shortcut.

"I suppose that's true," said Jane, making a mental note to look these things up as soon as possible. After all, that's likely what her father was giving her permission, if not urging her, to do.

"Even I used a skimmer in my day," said Patrice, with a casual air that was clearly not at all casual. "Everyone did. And I still use it—their use is not forbidden to Masters, of course. It is for that reason that I, as well as many other members—not your mother—feel it's a bit silly to deny apprentices little tricks of the trade like that. I certainly don't see the need to be so medieval about things in a world where we're dropping bombs onto one another out of airplanes."

Jane shrugged. "That's for the Masters to decide," she said. It was the most neutral reply she could think of before redirecting the conversation toward something she could profit from. "Please don't think I'm lazy for wishing I could proceed at a more rapid rate. I'm just frustrated as I'm researching a lot of new material while being forced to invent new theory."

This was true. Jane's research had provided her with several ideas and avenues of thinking—just before coming down to the Library, she had been contemplating how two unrelated and seemingly oppositional remarks about diabolic buoyancy might actually provide a crucial insight when considered together.

"New theory?" Patrice seemed thrilled. "My brilliant daughter!"

Unused to compliments, Jane was suspicious of everything that seemed like flattery. She punted. "Thank you for saying so . . . you know, I don't know how to address you. Patrice? Monsieur Durand? Father?"

"*Father* has a nice ring, I think?" He looked nervous as he said this. "If you're comfortable calling me that?"

Jane nodded. "Thank you, Father."

The title seemed to please him, as she'd hoped it would. "Ah, Jane! I wish to help you. Is there nothing I can do?"

Jane could think of many things, but she didn't like to ask. He'd already done so much; asking for more might give her the appearance of a greedy child . . .

"Knowing I have your support and your confidence is enormous," said Jane. "It seems to me that the burden of an apprentice is to perform as proficiently as a Master under artificially arduous circumstances. I cannot use research aids; I am constrained by the resources allotted to me. But if the Société has worked this way for so long, and works well, there must be a reason for it. It also falls to an apprentice to submit to the wisdom of the Masters."

"The resources allotted to you . . ." Her father's expression became calculating.

"Mother is generous," Jane said quickly.

"Of course she is—I'm certain she's as generous as she can be! I know it is technically against the rules, and enforcing the rules is technically my responsibility within the Société"—Jane leaned in, intrigued—"but it's not so uncommon for students at your stage to get a bit of help here and there. All I am saying is that if you ever need, say, an extra source of diabolic essence—oh, hello!"

With a mighty *mrow,* Smudge had jumped up onto the desk where Jane was still perched, rudely walking across the glass on his silent paws to bonk Jane's chin with his forehead. Jane shooed the cat off the Basque Lens and adjusted her position so that she could gather Smudge into her arms and hold him still.

"Ah, and this must be Smudge—your familiar!" Her father

chuckled at Jane's look of surprise, but she was astonished that he would joke about such a thing as a diabolic familiar. Familiars were no joking matter.

As a girl, Jane had often daydreamed about having her very own witch's familiar. Nancy had put a stop to it, forbidding Jane to even play at having one. *It's not appropriate,* she'd said — and when Jane had asked *why,* her mother had told her in no uncertain terms that summoning a demon into an animal was one of the only things absolutely, explicitly, and *completely* forbidden by the Société.

She'd explained that while summoning demons into plants was the foundation of modern diablerie, summoning demons into animals was too absurdly risky to be allowed. While it was true that pollen or seeds could spread, greenhouses and indoor cultivation substantially reduced the risk. Not having legs or a conscious will that could be taken over by an enterprising and curious demon, plants had limited ability to wreak havoc.

An animal, however, could never be completely controlled. These days, only an untrained, uninformed, wild diabolist would be so brazen as to attempt it.

"I see Nancy has instilled in you her dislike of magical notions and terms," said Patrice.

"She's attempted to," replied Jane, her tone dry as old leaves.

"My Jane! How delightful you are! I expected you to be thoughtful and intelligent, but I did not think you would end up with style, hidden away from the world like Rapunzel."

Patrice's smile was so admiring that Jane felt her control slipping. Thankfully, Smudge saved her by leaping away over the mirror and scooting into the darkness.

"What a cat!" said her father. "I didn't mean to shock you by calling him a familiar — Edith calls him that, is all. She says you're almost inseparable. And given her description of your *style,* Jane — it seemed fitting."

"Do you really think I have style?" It slipped out before Jane recalled she was supposed to be cool and calm.

Patrice looked astonished. "But of course! Just look at you! The cut of your blouse might be plain, but the way you wear it—the way you do your hair, your poise. And really, how could you not, being my daughter?"

Jane glanced up—not because she heard something, but because she had too much on her mind to concentrate on impressing her father any longer. "I think I should go," she said quietly.

Patrice looked concerned. "Is all well?"

"Yes, just being cautious," said Jane. "Father . . ."

"Yes?"

"Thank you for talking with me."

Patrice looked very moved, and his voice was a bit thick as they said their good-nights. Jane tidied up quickly but carefully and then chased down Smudge so that she could get out of the Library and into bed. As Jane carried her beloved cat up the stairs, her fingers toying thoughtfully with his fluff, she thought over her night. Patrice Durand had given her quite a lot to think about.

Jane frowned in the quiet darkness of the old farmhouse, taking comfort in Smudge's bulk and warmth. If only she'd passed her Test! She felt terrible for deceiving her father, but it was nothing compared to the guilt she felt over what she was going to do with the information he'd knowingly—and also unknowingly—just given her.

THE SKIMMER HER FATHER HAD spoken of ended up being a clever bit of diablerie that employed a diabolically altered jeweler's loupe that allowed the eye to more quickly assess written passages. It was indeed just the sort of thing a cosmopolitan apprentice might hear about, and easily obtain, but Jane was not a cosmopolitan apprentice.

Creating a strike chain presented different problems, though they were more easily surmounted, at least for Jane. A strike chain was just a pendant a diabolist could hold over a text to determine whether it contained something useful to the diabolist's will. Easy enough, save that the pendant itself had to be created from a part of the diabolist. And not only that, but a part sturdy enough to stand up to several applications of some pretty nasty pastes and solutions.

The book claimed the easiest to sacrifice was a tooth; Jane wasn't so sure about that, though in the end that was her choice too. A bit of gauze soaked in diabolically infused clove oil packed the wound and healed it quickly enough that all she had to do was pretend to have a sore belly to cover her unwillingness to chew and swallow for a day, but there was no way around taking a pair of pliers and yanking it out to begin with.

There are no shortcuts to becoming a diabolist—only sacrifices. Her mother had said that to her many, many times over the years.

Now Jane knew, in reality, there were both.

It was worth it though. It was always worth it. All diablerie, from the simplest armamentarium to her new strike chain, gave Jane a sense of boundless, unceasing delight. It was the act of creating a miracle, and she never tired of it.

While the skimmer might have let Jane assess individual passages more rapidly, the strike chain let her know if her reading at any pace would be worthwhile. All she had to do was focus her will while holding the strike chain over a text; a clockwise spin of the tooth meant yes, counterclockwise no. Watching it start to shudder for the first time didn't lessen the dull ache in Jane's jaw, but it did make her feel as though all the pain and blood had been worth it.

In half an hour, Jane had a stack of books comprised of new titles, some she hadn't seen yet, some that she'd already perused. But at least she knew they deserved her time, and she guessed — correctly, as it turned out — that once she got her thoughts more organized regarding what she wanted to achieve, she could use the strike chain to narrow her reading even further; even within a text.

The strike chain couldn't invent new theory for her, nor could it assure her that what she wanted was possible for an apprentice to achieve. Regardless, for the first time since even before her disastrous Test, Jane was going to bed at night knowing she was finally making some real progress.

13

EDITH HAD CROSSED INTO ENEMY territory several times over the course of her years as a spy, but this was her first experience with something even more nerve-racking: *camping.*

It amused Mercurialis how little she enjoyed it. Of course it did. More than once the demon tested her patience by noting how the three hardy Young Talarians who manned the outpost seemed invigorated by living so closely with nature. That was all well and good, but any charms the experience held for them were lost on Edith. First and foremost, the sight of Braune's castle disturbed her. It clung to the horizon like a tumor, black and rotting—but there were plenty of other reasons to dislike the place, from the coldness of the stream by their camp, to the dampness of her tent, to the earliness of the sunrise.

She hadn't expected to enjoy herself. Edith knew people liked wildernesses and went to them voluntarily—just look at her sister and where she'd ended up! Not Edith; she was not one to be moved by the cold splendor of the starry night sky, nor for the first joyous smatter of birdsong before dawn. She found natural places inconvenient more than she found them beautiful, and this one had the additional detriment of being genuinely dangerous.

They'd been three nights in this dreadful field, three nights without a hot bath or a comfortable bed. The camp had only the most basic of amenities, but Edith was grateful for the few reminders of her lost humanity; she found it difficult to stay cheerful when all she had to sit upon was a damp log, and every cup of tea seemed to go cold immediately after brewing.

The only person more miserable than Edith was Graham Yellowhorse. Edith's eye was upon him frequently as he huddled in a big red woolly cap with earflaps and an oversize pea coat, sitting so close to the fire, his boots were in danger of catching. The cold did not agree with him, nor did their camp food. And he barely said a word—not that he ever spoke much to begin with.

Graham noticed her gaze; Edith had been letting her eyes linger too long. She averted them and sipped her latest cup of quickly cooling tea.

Say something, said Mercurialis. *Hop on over to his log like a friendly toad. There's no time like the present. And who knows how much present we have left, you and I?*

"This is hardly the time or the place," Edith muttered under her breath. Graham looked up at her curiously.

She blushed, apologized, and after a long quiet moment got up from the fire and walked off. Mercurialis laughed and laughed in her mind.

"I'm glad *you're* entertained, at least," said Edith.

A copse of thin trees marked the boundary of their camp— or rather, the boundary was marked by red yarn knotted through the branches like an enormous cat's cradle. A simple trick but an effective one. Their location had not yet been discovered by any wide-reaching patrols from Braune's facility or even the occasional planes that flew overhead. It was the sort of diablerie Edith loved, elegant, beautiful, and effective: only someone with what amounted to a specially attuned diabolic compass could locate this place.

And there were other things protecting them, too.

She was jumpy. Sitting and waiting was not her style, and yet sit and wait she must.

Right now, Maja and Zelda were currently out with one of the diabolists who manned this outpost; they weren't late coming back, not really, but Edith was eager to hear from them. The faint birdsong and the ceaseless rustle of the wind in the grass was wearing on her nerves.

At last, a flurry of activity—someone was scuttling down from the lookout platform. It was Amina Hadžić, and she greeted Edith with a brisk "They're here." As Graham got to his feet, Amina set to unhooking the woven door to the yarn structure that kept them all out of sight. A few moments later three people crested a depression in the rolling hills and then were safely inside the boundary. It was Zelda, Maja, and their guide—a Swiss named Luca Müller.

"How did it go?" asked Edith.

Zelda looked a bit tired. "I think it's doable, but we'll need to act quickly. *Something* is happening. They've increased the patrols around the castle—the frequency of them, I mean, not the volume. They actually seem short-staffed, harried."

"It's a recent change," said Luca. "A few days before you arrived, a caravan left with what seemed like the nonessential personnel. The remaining staff seem harder at work than ever. If you would come with me"—Luca gestured at the office tent—"we can start formulating a plan of attack."

"I'm ready," said Zelda. "Are you ready, Maja?"

Maja spat on the ground.

"I couldn't have put it better if I'd tried," said Edith.

Mercurialis, too, agreed with the stout Croatian's earthy rejoinder. This surprised Edith. The demon had always supported her ambitions as regarded the war effort, but it didn't *care* about human politics. It couldn't; at least, not in any way that a human could care. Being intrigued by a possible outcome or even rooting for the home team was not the same as being emotionally invested in a cause, and diabolists who forgot that were the ones who generally found themselves in a good bit of trouble eventually.

And yet Mercurialis hadn't just been amused by Maja; it concurred.

Even a demon can have a heart, it said, answering the question she hadn't been able to formulate. *At least, the sort of heart humans mean when they speak of having hearts.*

Edith wondered if that was really true or not; Mercurialis sent a wave of song through her mind that, roughly translated, meant it admired her skepticism. Mercurial, indeed . . . but she had too many other things to think about in that moment to consider it for long.

MERCURIALIS DIDN'T JUST APPROVE OF their intentions—it admired their plan.

Not that it mattered what the demon thought. Its interest had nothing to do with tactical soundness or their likelihood of success. It was simply glad that Edith would assuredly need to draw upon its powers several times. It enjoyed that sort of thing. Mischief was part of its nature, and while infiltrating Dr. Braune's castle was not exactly a caper, it did require sneaking, deceit, and trickery.

Edith was less sure she approved. Not only did she have reservations about the way they'd get inside the facility; she also had mixed feelings about their goals.

The Young Talarians had done much over the years, but they'd never been able to locate the Dark Lab of Dr. Querner, nor ascertain fully what horrors he and Dr. Braune were collaborating upon. Discovering both was now paramount.

The problem was that Dr. Braune and Dr. Querner were both diabolists; a few of their staff were, too. They'd have wards, they'd have traps, they'd have the advantage of home turf. All things considered, Edith would have preferred instead to go in there with a Valentine tank and a section of infantry. Using diabolism to thwart a diabolist was always unpredictable, fighting fire with fire and all that . . .

To all these ends, they'd done a lot of brainstorming and contingency planning, but in the end their plan came down to finding someone and getting them to reveal what they wanted to know. Whether it fell to Zelda to beat it out of them or Edith to use subtlety and subterfuge, that didn't matter. It just had to be done.

Edith caught Graham looking at her as they checked over their packs and tied their boots—German issue, just like the uniforms they wore. If he perceived her doubts, he didn't remark upon them.

Perhaps he perceives something else, said Mercurialis, unhelpfully.

Edith silently denied this. Graham hadn't had much to say as they talked over their plan for hours, looking over Luca's maps, listening to Amina's descriptions of the castle grounds, and discussing intricacies with an Englishman by the name of George Stuart and a Roma diabolist who simply went by Grizelda.

Everyone but Grizelda had come along; she had remained behind to watch, so that someone could report back if they failed.

If they failed . . . at least Edith had said what she needed to say to Jane on her last trip. And she'd given her the dress. That comforted her, as did knowing she'd told Miriam the truth so that it could not be denied to her by others.

She'd put her affairs in order.

Largely. She hadn't had the conversation she truly wanted with her sister, Nancy. Dearest, impossible Nancy—the calmest woman Edith had ever known and yet the least equipped to deal with upheaval in her life. How it rankled that she presented herself as the sensible one who had the good head on her shoulders when what she did most with that head was stick it deep, deep into the sand.

She'd just have to make it back. Clearly, she still had a piece of her mind with a big *N* branded upon it. She couldn't die until she'd given it to Nancy, gift-wrapped with a big bow on it, if possible.

The fate of the war might be at hand, and you're thinking about telling off your sister . . .

Mercurialis was right to recall her to the present, but Edith felt it didn't have to sound so *smug* about it.

THEY TREKKED TOWARD BRAUNE'S CASTLE that same afternoon—single file, keeping to the lengthening shadows, and all holding links of a chain clutched in their hands. Another interesting use of the Art, of Luca's own design: the illusion was stronger the more people were included.

Edith had wanted to ask a lot of questions about it, and about Luca's demon, but there hadn't been time.

It was just before dusk when the castle hove into view, looking as it always did: like it should be swaddled by fog, with jagged lightning bolts illuminating it from above. The few windows were ablaze with light; those inside were working well into the evening.

Edith caught Zelda's eye and nodded. Their hope had been to sneak inside as people were eagerly going about their final few tasks and not paying much mind to who might be poking around. Indeed, a few trucks were still out front of the portcullis, and uniformed men were loading and sometimes unloading crates, but at a leisurely pace instead of the efficient clip of rested soldiers first thing in the morning.

Luca had a map of the castle that he'd made not long after the Talarians had discovered it two months ago. Edith had helped with that raid, too, though remotely. She'd supplied a bit of her special foundation that had allowed Luca to seamlessly blend in among the officers. He'd only had the one shot; what with rationing, Edith had barely enough for herself, but the war effort meant making sacrifices of many sorts.

Resources were always the biggest limitation on feats of diablerie, and their resources had never been lower.

They all had a few tricks up their sleeves that afternoon. Edith wasn't the only Société member who donated to the cause. George Stuart had given Edith two phials, one with sand that would stick someone to the ground on the spot; the other would soften nearly any surface enough that Edith could push her way through it. Luca had a sack of pebbles that bounced like rubber balls; Maja had an egg that when cracked filled a room with the sound of twittering birds. They had weapons less arcane, as well; Edith had her Astra 300 nestled in her pocket alongside a few armamentaria.

And me!

And, of course, she had Mercurialis.

They were close to the castle. Edith waved to get everyone's attention. She got out her compact mirror and dusted everyone's faces with her special powder, dear as it was to her these days. While it wouldn't fully transform anyone's appearance, it would make most people see a familiar face instead of a strange one if they didn't look too hard.

Edith had more on than just powder. She had downed a potion to increase her uptake of the diabolic material in her bespoke sweets, as well as applying several other cosmetics to mask her decidedly non-Aryan features. She'd dabbed a bit here and there on Amina, too—and for a few exhilarating moments, on Graham.

The plan was to divide into two groups so that they could enact a simultaneous infiltration of both entrances of the castle, for there was a modern rear gate as well as the original. Edith wished Zelda was coming with her; alas, she was taking Maja and George Stuart in the side entrance to better access the Records Department. There were more guards that way.

Edith was taking Luca, Amina, and Graham through the front. Except for the inevitable sentries posted at the gate and at the door, the route to Braune's medical facility in the great hall was circuitous and largely unobserved—only one checkpoint.

Edith caught Maja's eye. She looked determined and unhappy; Edith felt about the same.

Graham's eye she did not seek.

A few hand signals were exchanged between Edith and her team, and then they settled in to wait for a patrol or a truck to come by. They'd slip past the gates by marching with a company, and then disperse into the crowd.

Edith, who so hated waiting, was grateful when the sound of a vehicle reached her ears not too long after they'd settled in for their uneasy vigil. They fanned out after the twilight-bright head-lights had passed them by, sliding into formation behind the rear-guard as the truck passed.

Edith was wary of the guards, but they didn't so much as blink. That didn't mean much, however. Dr. Braune was a diabolist, and diabolists didn't need guards to protect themselves.

Luca reached into his pocket and slid out a clockwork dragon-fly. He fiddled with it for a moment, and it buzzed off toward the portcullis. There it did something Edith couldn't quite perceive before returning to Luca's outstretched palm.

Luca noticed Edith's attention and nodded in satisfaction. When they marched through the gate, it seemed they triggered no wards.

Edith reached inside her uniform pocket to fish out one of her sweets. She'd need all her power soon enough.

Mercurialis had many wry remarks to make about the castle's dark and dismal interior, but Edith was in no mood to listen. Things were going fairly well, considering—Edith had gotten them past all the guards and a nurse who became interested in their party, and Luca was sure of himself as they threaded through the dank stone halls. Graham's insight more than once led them to hold when moving forward would have meant detection. Amina was excellent at spying traps, diabolic and otherwise, but had otherwise yet to use her Art.

The trouble began when they finally made it to the servants' entrance to the great hall. Amina had used a dart on the guard, and Graham had known exactly where to be to catch him and let him down easy. But as Edith peered in through the watery glass of the ancient window set into the wooden door, she was surprised to see that it was fairly bustling inside. They hadn't expected to come upon anything major happening at this hour of the evening, but as they looked on from the doorway, several nurses were at work fetching tools or washing beakers—there was even one dabbing at the forehead of a powerfully built older man with thick glasses and a bushy, gray-threaded beard. He looked in need of it—he was laboring under bright lights, doing something with a magnifying glass and a long, gold, seven-tined fork to a woman strapped to a wheeled metal table. Tubes were coming in and going out of her. Some fluids were more recognizable than others.

Her feet were twitching. She was awake.

Braune said something to the nurse; she dabbed at his forehead one final time before turning to a sort of drinks cart full of implements with more occult purposes than a bottle of gin and a cocktail shaker.

The nurse picked up a pair of tongs and selected a pyramid-shaped purple crystal. It glowed faintly as Braune took it and held it over the woman. He had pulled on thick leather gloves to protect his hands; the woman on the table was not so fortunate. She was nude, and when Braune placed the magnet on her stomach, her skin began to bubble and let off clouds of yellow steam.

The woman screamed, loud enough that Edith heard it through the closed door. She convulsed in pain, sitting up as much as she could while restrained. It was Sofia Cantor.

As Edith watched in mute horror, Sofia's body began to expand and then ooze in flowing gooey puddles off of the table. The once-purple pyramid was now glowing red and hot; it went crashing to the floor as she liquefied entirely.

Edith had seen some bizarre and terrible things over the past few years, and it had hardened her in ways she felt were useful; others, not so much. This tableau, however, took her so utterly by surprise that she could not think of what to do.

"Let's get in there," said Graham.

Edith was grateful for this reminder of her duty.

"What's the plan?" said Luca, but Edith was already pushing open the heavy door, disregarding his question and Mercurialis's simultaneous yelp informing her that she'd triggered about a dozen wards at once.

She immediately realized something was amiss. It was dark in the great hall, for one—then all the lights came on at once, bright white electric bulbs that emanated some sort of non-light energy that weakened Edith's connection to Mercurialis.

The door behind them slammed shut.

"Shit, shit, shit," said Amina.

This place clearly was Braune's lab—all the equipment was there, just none of the people.

"How could it be a trap?" said Graham, sounding confused and devastated. "Zlovid said—"

The double doors at the bottom of the hall opened, and through them came the man from the scene they'd watched in the window. He was wearing a different outfit—no apron—but he had the same glasses. His beard, if anything, was bushier.

"A lovely bit of diablerie, don't you think?" His German was loud and thick and uncouth to Edith's ears. "Perfection. The treated glass captures everything about the scene. Even *presence.*"

Dr. Braune was not alone. There were a half-dozen guards standing by the open doors, armed, watching.

"It was a trap," said Dr. Braune, and chuckled ghoulishly. "And don't think you'll be rescued by that squad of bruisers you sent to the Records Department. We got them, too. Froze them," he said, as if that explained everything.

"We lured you here to make sure you couldn't make a run on the Dark Lab," he continued. "We're closing down things here, have been for some time. In three days, I am scheduled to depart to join my colleague Dr. Querner in the north. I am ever so glad you stopped by before I left. The frozen bodies of so many diabolists will mean quite a lot of raw materials for our further experimentation. We're so close . . . what you saw with the Cantor woman, that was indeed a failure, but we've substantially improved upon the process and hope to have a successful run soon."

"You'll have to catch us first," said Graham.

Edith turned to Graham and grinned at him. He'd broken Braune's thrall with his bravado.

To her surprise, he grinned back.

"Not an issue," said Braune. "I can't imagine you'll put up more fight than that small one I froze a little while ago. She was quite the spitfire."

"Perhaps not," said Edith. "Then again, we might not need to."

As she'd spoken, Edith had reached into her pocket and grabbed the stoppered tube of sand that lay nestled there. She opened it with her thumb and then cast it in front of them in a wide arc.

"I'll get the door," said Luca.

"I want them alive!" shouted Braune.

The first guard who ran over the sand got stuck, falling to his knees with a horrible crack, as did the second. The rest figured it out after that, but it slowed them down as they cast about for a broom. Even a single grain would be enough to cause some issues for them.

Edith used the confusion to take aim at one of the stuck guards with her trusty Astra. The bullet struck the first one in the neck, and he slumped and went still as a gout of dark blood spilled over the floor. The second she missed as he thrashed, then hit in the stomach. Edith winced; she'd been aiming for his head.

"Never mind—kill them!" shouted Braune.

Edith ran for cover. Graham and Amina were already out of sight.

"Let's see if we can't thin them out further," said Graham, sliding beside her from where he'd been hiding. He used his teeth to pull the pin on some sort of narrow porcelain-colored grenade. He hurled it into the cluster of guards who were trying to sweep up the sand as Braune shouted at them.

They dived away from it, but it didn't explode. It didn't do anything that Edith could tell. She turned away to see if she could help Luca as he fiddled with the door, but Amina was there, guarding him as he worked.

That's when the screaming began.

"Spiders!" cried a guard, and ran for the exit. He was brushing at himself in horror. "Spiders!"

Mercurialis cackled in Edith's mind.

The final three guards had gained their feet. They fanned out, looking for Graham and herself.

She readied her Astra. Five bullets left. She'd make them count.

Graham put his hand on her shoulder and pointed at a guard rounding the corner of a long metal table. Edith nodded, then screwed up her courage as Mercurialis urged her on.

She put her hand atop Graham's and squeezed.

Graham looked surprised, then pleased. But they both knew that getting out of there was paramount, and just as quickly were back to back, ready to fight.

"Move away from the door," said Braune.

Braune's voice seemed to come from everywhere and nowhere, a clever parlor trick. Edith didn't like this—weak as her connection to her demon might be, she decided it was time to use a bit of the Art.

Reaching into a pocket of her coat, Edith got out a small phial of light green fluid. She pulled the cork out with her teeth and swallowed the whole thing. Tossing it aside, she grabbed for her cigarette lighter. Exhaling an anise-flavored mist, Edith flicked her lighter and held it to the cloud.

It didn't ignite, it coagulated. As she stepped inside it, Edith disappeared, even to her own eyes.

It was a powerful armamentarium, but it didn't last long. Edith made the most of it.

Amina was in a standoff with two guards; another was about to encounter Graham. As for Braune, he was traversing the room by walking atop the tables, peering here and there for signs of his quarry. He carried a thick metal rod in his hand, the purpose of which Edith could not guess.

Edith took aim, hoping to end this quickly, but she dropped her Astra when what felt like a burning-hot spiderweb struck her face. Dizzy, Edith fell to her knees as every joint in her body thrilled with terrible pain. Her skin felt as if ants were crawling all over her, inside her clothes, on her ears and everywhere.

"Got her!"

She opened her bleary eyes to see someone enormous standing above her—a giant the likes of which she hadn't seen since she was six years old and all adults were impossibly, unachievably tall. He was a muscular man with a strong chin and close-cropped blond hair, and he was reaching for her with black-gloved hands.

Move! Mercurialis urged her to her feet, but she couldn't—she felt too sick and she couldn't catch her breath. Something was very wrong with her vision, not just the blurriness. Everything in the room looked different to her, larger and farther away.

The man grabbed her with his huge, powerful hands, dragging her to her feet. Edith had never felt so helpless, and she actually screamed. There was something terrifying about how big he was —but as her vision cleared a bit, Edith saw that it wasn't him who was huge.

We're small, said Mercurialis, a moment before Edith realized it.

The report of rapid gunfire caused her assailant to spring away, releasing her. Edith ran for it, putting as much distance and equipment as she could between herself and her attacker given her short legs and the pain in her joints. She couldn't quite catch her breath, either—

Edith realized she had the bends.

She'd never even heard of an armamentarium like this, but she had no time to worry if somehow this diabolist had managed to shrink the size of her atoms or reduce the space between them. Or if the effect was temporary or permanent . . .

She peeked out from behind a table. Luca and Amina were still alive; the guards were all down, it seemed. Amina was just standing up, her hand smoking vaguely; behind her, one of the guards' faces was melted like a candle. Perhaps Edith's armamentarium of softening was Amina's creation.

Braune drew a sigil in the air with his metal rod and uttered some nightmarish word as he finished with a flourish. The air condensed where he'd traced the lines, the light bending in unusual ways. Then through the center of the pattern stepped something vaguely human-shaped and made of copper-colored mist.

Braune pointed at Amina and Luca. Edith realized she'd just been watching, transfixed by this, failing utterly to pay attention to what was directly behind her.

Look out!

Thankfully, Mercurialis was less amazed by this ghastly, unknowable creature. Edith turned and dodged the grabbing hands of the blond man with the leather gloves.

"You're losing," he said, smiling down at her with even teeth. "Surrender and save us all the trouble! Dr. Braune's mist golem will—"

A man's scream made them both pause. The copper-colored being was not attacking Luca and Amina; it had turned on Braune and sprang upon him like a jaguar. They all watched in horror as the creature overwhelmed Braune and began to tear out his throat.

"Mein Gott," said the blond man. "It's—"

The mist golem glanced up at his words, looking his way out of its featureless face.

"No!" he cried, and raced for the open double doors. Edith chased after but couldn't catch up with him, she was half her usual size and still couldn't breathe very well. As she limped along, Graham overtook her—but as her friend passed her, his long legs pumping, the mist golem leaped on him from across the room, sinking its spectral claws into his back.

"Graham!" she cried, as he screamed and fell to the floor.

"Edith!"

Amina was gesturing at her; what could she do but obey? She couldn't fight this being, not in her state—maybe not ever. Mercurialis also goaded her to back away and retreat; she did, but not before noticing that the blond man had not retreated. He was messing about with a metal box on the wall; getting it open, he hit a button inside and then fled.

The double doors slammed behind him as metal shutters slid down, covering the few windows. Fluorescent lights flickered on, gradually intensifying as Edith began to feel hot and uncomfortable.

"I can't get this door open," said Luca.

"What on . . ." Amina squinted up at the lights. "Are they . . ."

The mist golem left off with her beloved Graham's limp and bloodied body and uttered an indescribable sound before collapsing. Edith felt it too—the lights were doing something to her, making her feel even worse somehow.

She couldn't feel Mercurialis for the first time in over two decades.

"We have to get out of here," she said, really panicking for the first time. "It's doing something to our diabolic material, it's—"

But Luca was on the ground, shuddering in a terrible seizure.

Amina, too, was close to fainting. Edith resisted the urge to sit down and thought hard on what to do.

The armamentarium Luca had given her! The one that would soften anything! Edith got it out, hoping against hope that it still might work even under these bright hot lights. She carefully uncorked it; it was thick and viscous. She drizzled it on the door.

She gave it a moment and then grabbed Amina's pistol so she could poke at the softening metal with the handle. It gave a bit but not enough. Edith used the rest of the potion as her body fizzled and cracked under the lights, until finally the door was malleable. With an apology to her fallen friend, Edith took his wool jacket and used it to push.

The hole she eventually achieved was just big enough for her tiny body.

As soon as she was through, Edith shook out her bag of sweets and ate three. Mercurialis surged back into her mind, yapping and crying at her like a dog too long separated from its master.

"We have to get out of here," gasped Edith. Mercurialis agreed.

Edith thought of Graham—poor Graham! She would never hear his warm voice again, nor thrill at eliciting a smile from his serious mouth, nor look with interest upon his weather-beaten hands. She thought of Luca and Amina ... the Englishman George Stuart and her friends, Maja and Zelda, "frozen" elsewhere in the castle; she thought of their failed mission.

All she'd learned was that Sofia Cantor was dead. She still didn't know where Querner was; he was still safe in his Dark Lab. And she still didn't know the nature of his weapon.

But in her weakened, shrunken state, Edith couldn't imagine what she could do about any of it.

Instead, with a heavy heart, Edith selected the snuffbox secreted in her pocket. She opened it; sprinkling a pinch on the back of her hand, Edith snorted it, and then plucked a hair from the head of the dead guard they'd left outside the door. Holding that under her tongue, she would take on his appearance for a time.

After her exposure to those dreadful lights, Edith had no idea how long the armamentarium would last. She would just have to trust that it would allow her to escape the castle. The alternative was too terrible to contemplate.

14

I T CAME TO JANE ONE MORNING as the first sunlight of the day leaked through a gap in her curtains to spill over her eyes, rousing her from dreams of dubious pleasantness. As she was turning over, her sleep-blinking eyes saw the title of the book she'd fallen asleep reading — *Ceremonial Practices of the Puritan Witches* — and two thoughts about the problem of flight came together in her mind as eagerly as Katharine Hepburn and Cary Grant.

Odd how after weeks of reading and note-taking and theoretical maths, it was but the work of a moment to write down what Jane was certain would result in a diabolic formula capable of making an object fly. Her object was, naturally, her broom, so she worked out the equations for a liniment she could rub onto the handle and over the twigs of the brush. As she wrote it down, she felt a surge of fascinating energy filling her, a sense of contentment and fulfilled purpose she'd never before experienced.

This would work. She didn't know how she knew, but she knew. She felt it like she felt the coming of spring.

The problem was, she couldn't do it. Not as an apprentice — not even an apprentice who had an outside source of diabolic essence. In fact, looking at the formula, Jane wasn't sure how many Masters would willingly sacrifice so much of their resources for something so frivolous as a flying broom. Eccentrics abounded within the Société, but most diabolists were fairly practical. They had to be.

A vanity item that took more than a year's worth of resources would not tempt many.

But she'd done it. She'd worked it out. She couldn't prove it — which was rather the point of the Practical — but she'd done it.

Despair claimed Jane, consuming her joy as a storm cloud swallows the afternoon's sunlight. She couldn't move. She could barely breathe. She didn't want to do either; she wanted to bury herself in the earth for a hundred years like a grub, only emerging when she had metamorphosed into someone who could make sense of the world.

"Jane!"

Jane startled to hear her name called up the stairs, but looking at the time, it was indeed the hour of breakfast. A bit past it, actually.

"Jane Blackwood, breakfast is on the table and will be consumed by those not lolling about in bed!"

"Coming!" she called, throwing a dressing gown around herself and running down the stairs like it was Christmas morning. Her robe tie trailed behind her, sloppy and undone, but as she reached the foot of the stairs and went to grab it, a large gray cat pounced from the shadows. Before she'd turned around, Smudge had gotten three paws' worth of claws into the fabric, and a few teeth too.

"Smudge, no!" cried Jane, almost stumbling and then really coming down on her rear end as she fought with the obstinate, surprisingly powerful beast. "Let go!"

"My goodness." Nancy stood over them both, but only Jane felt embarrassed to be caught in such a compromising position. "What happened here?"

Jane had gotten one of Smudge's paws free only to have him snag the robe tie again as well as a bit of her finger. With a yelp of pain, Jane relinquished the coveted item and stood without it, cinching her robe about her with as much dignity as she could muster. Of course, the cat lost interest after that, and scooted away into the parlor.

"If you're done making a scene, we're ready to eat" was Nancy's only remark, and Jane was blushing furiously as she entered the kitchen to see wheat toast and oat porridge set out. Miriam had already tucked in.

"Good morning," said Jane, as she reached for the tea. "I guess I must have needed the sleep!"

Miriam glanced up from her breakfast. If either of them needed extra sleep, it was Miriam. There were circles under her eyes— perhaps the puffiness that comes after a lost night's rest, but it seemed like more than that to Jane.

She had her own concerns. As Jane chewed her way through her breakfast, she contemplated what to do about her problem of power.

At best it would mean more nights lost in the Library, dowsing for knowledge like a hopeful farmer dowses for water; at worst, there was no solution for an apprentice such as herself. Even if through careful study she was able to wring every possible bit of efficiency out of her equations, it might *still* be unworkable without an additional, renewable source of diabolic essence.

A renewable source ... Jane watched Smudge slink into the kitchen, utterly remorseless and keen to see if there was a bit of milk left for him to lick. The waving of his voluminous fur was like a wheat field in high summer, a languid bounce of plenty.

Even if Jane could, somehow, temporarily summon a demon into herself, she would never produce so much raw material to render into diabolic essence. Smudge had a seemingly unending supply of fur, to say nothing of his nails and whiskers.

The audacity of the idea taking hold in Jane's mind also took away her breath. But her father had suggested this too—hadn't he? Perhaps not so directly as he'd suggested the strike chain, but Patrice had put the idea of a familiar into Jane's mind during a conversation where they'd discussed the ways people got around the rules, why that was all right, and also how the rules weren't as strict as some might insist ...

There are no shortcuts to becoming a diabolist—only sacrifices.

Creating a familiar wasn't a shortcut. Far from it. It meant *more* work for Jane, and a lot of it, but it seemed exciting. And it was secret, witchy work too, just as Jane liked.

Maybe those who practiced the Art weren't witches, but when Jane was astride her broomstick, her diabolic familiar by her side, she guessed it would be all but impossible for a layperson to tell the difference.

Smudge jumped into her lap with a soft chirp, and Jane forgave him as always as he butted her chin with his forehead. But as she buried her fingers in his fur, she gazed at the copious fluff at his neck and his long tail with a more calculating gaze than usual.

Though Jane felt certain of her father's sanction, she was curious about the official consequences of making a familiar. The next time Jane was sure she was alone in the Library, she grabbed a copy of the Société handbook and bylaws. She was shocked by what she discovered.

Execution.

Jane stared at the word and then shut the book.

The stakes were what they were. To hear Edith and her mother discuss it, as a failed apprentice Jane might have faced the same fate—and frankly, she'd rather die than become one of the Société's drudges.

She'd just have to be very careful. It was ambitious, yes, but preliminary research made it seem doable. She would simply banish the demon within Smudge after she'd taken what she needed from him. No one would be the wiser.

Jane's furtive perusing of an early modern German tome entitled *Familiars and Their Uses* indicated that the more obedient the animal, the more obedient the familiar. Too bad Jane didn't have some loyal mastiff to recruit instead—Smudge was a cat in his prime, which meant he bit, and scratched, and made as much mischief as pleased him. The cat sometimes seemed already possessed, when he ran around the farmhouse chasing things no one else could see, every hair standing out from his body.

But after reading about a Dutch diabolist who had caused a fatal flood when her crested grebe familiar got loose and built a nest that fouled a windmill's pump, and a West African practitioner of the Art who had been torn apart by his baboon familiar, Jane felt Smudge would probably work out just fine.

Reading those stories—as well as less dramatic incidents involving familiars wreaking low-grade havoc—Jane understood better why the practice was so very taboo. Forget any part of the summoning or binding: give it too slack or too tight a rein, provide less than explicit commands, and the results gave new meaning to all hell breaking loose.

The successes, though—oh, the successes! History was written by the victors, this Jane knew, but at the same time it was curiously exhilarating to read about diabolists all over the world who had achieved some truly astonishing feats with the help of their familiars. It seemed that over time, a real and potent bond might grow between diabolist and familiar; there were reports of diabolists' armamentaria and other projects inexplicably increasing in strength and power once a trusting relationship between diabolist and familiar had been established. It seemed so different from the relationship between a diabolist and a demon summoned in the traditional method—and to Jane, at least, it was preferable. To get the same results as a Master diabolist, but without the mandatory intimacy of the Pact! If only it had been an acceptable path to Mastery, Jane would have skipped down it without a second thought.

"But which demon?" she muttered to Smudge as he slept on the back of a high-backed chair. He had once again sauntered down to the Library with her, as if he knew her plans and wanted to be a part of them.

The Book of Known Demons was the most comprehensive guide

the Société had to summoning forth those beings that dwelt in the realm beyond. It was enormous, a giant tome of thick parchment pages bound in ancient but well-cared-for leather braced with burnished metal fittings. In the Library, it stood alone on a marble pedestal table, illuminated by its own lamp—one with an uncanny yellow flame that would only burn fragrant, diabolical palo santo wood. It was the best-known book in the Library, as it had been perused by nearly every aspiring Master diabolist in the Société, and it had perhaps the most contributors. Any diabolist who discovered the name and properties of a new demon was required by Société rules to make a pilgrimage to the Library and record it. Extra pages had been sewn in many times over the centuries, by diabolists who had practiced the Art long before the Société—and after the Société changed into something else, as it inevitably would one day, it would be studied and added to by the ones who came after. Jane had once called it their "unholy book" as a joke and received a lecture from her mother about "respect"—*that* was what it meant to the Masters.

And now, more than ever, Jane understood why.

Well over a thousand entries had been recorded in *The Book of Known Demons,* some more detailed than others—entries ranged from pages upon pages to a brief paragraph. And then, of course, there were the appendices, where vigilant diabolists had recorded their findings if they went beyond what the initial listing revealed. These were also crucial, as sometimes those discoveries made it clear a demon was unsuitable as a human companion for this reason or that, or could be channeled for other purposes than previously described, and so on.

The encyclopedia-like entries were a nice break from reading and comparing various methods for creating demonic familiars. Jane knew she had to make an intelligent, informed choice and was therefore taking her time about it. She even asked her mother, after spending quite a while coming up with a script that would neither make Nancy suspicious nor leave Jane open to some bizarre critique.

"Mother," she said one afternoon, when Miriam was off on one of her mysterious jaunts. "I don't mean to get ahead of myself, but some of the reading I've been doing for my Practical has made me curious. How did you choose your demon?"

Nancy seemed surprised. "Why, Jane, you know that story! It was your favorite when you were a girl."

"I know *why* you chose the Patron," said Jane. "Now I'm asking *how*."

"How," said Nancy thoughtfully. "That *is* a different question. I suppose it began when I started paging through the abridged copy of *Known Demons* that belonged to your grandparents, but even that small catalogue felt overwhelming. I started looking over what I could about diabolists who had similar careers to what I envisioned for myself. Even back then, I wanted to be if not *the* Librarian than at least *a* librarian—a librarian-at-large, you know, like Akane or Diego—and I found out that most librarians had summoned the Patron of Curiosity. That helped me make my choice, though I still took my time before I made my final decision. There were a few others I fancied—the Eye of the Hawk and the One Who Whispers—but the Patron of Curiosity won out in the end. Ultimately, it was its gentleness that was the deciding factor, but of course you know the rest."

Ironically, the Patron of Curiosity would have been an ideal demon for Jane's purposes specifically because of that gentleness. But to call upon a demon was to be seen by it, and she really didn't want to be seen by her mother's demon. When on good terms with their hosts, demons would often offer up information they thought would be of interest, and while they were mercurial and unpredictable, Jane felt safe assuming that summoning a fragment of its consciousness into the family house cat would be "of interest" to both it and Nancy.

Back to the Library, then, but with more direction. Recalling her mother's admiration for the Patron of Curiosity's amiability toward humans, she began to scan entries for the idea of inquisitiveness.

Not for the first time did Jane wish that *The Book of Known Demons* had an index.

Eventually her efforts were rewarded. After passing over a few entries that seemed less than promising—the Rampant Divine, Seven Hanging Lanterns, and Vindáss were all unsuitable upon further inspection—Jane finally settled upon a demon that she found in an entry beautifully illustrated with rococo embellishments that would not look out of place in a painting by Boucher or Fragonard:

The Ceaseless Connoisseur.

Two things made the Connoisseur ideal for Jane's purposes: One, it was such a popular demon that its summoning was extremely specific, even including its location within the diabolic realm; two, it had never displayed any sort of malice toward humankind. Even the occasional fictional depictions of the Connoisseur were positive—save for one.

"The Ginger-Eaters," a modern epic poem, had been written by the disgruntled child of a "wild" diabolist. It was a work as hyperbolic as it was evocative, and after reading a review of it in volume 29 of the *Journal of Diabolic Studies*, Jane felt fairly confident about disregarding the poet's middle-class moralizing.

At its core, the Ceaseless Connoisseur was a demon that hungered for *experiences*, be they sensual, spiritual, or intellectual. It was pleased to enhance the pleasures of its host almost like an aesthetic aphrodisiac.

Like all cats, Smudge was a hedonist at heart. Jane hoped that meant this demon would be a good fit for him. She wanted that. It was not lost on her that she was taking a big risk with the only member of the household who seemed to genuinely like her, so she wanted to make the experience as pleasant as possible for him.

As pleasant as possible. What that meant, Jane couldn't articulate, not even to herself. She was making a choice for her companion, a big one. She made choices for him all the time, true, but this one was different. It might change him forever, even if she planned to banish the demon as soon as possible.

The guilt didn't stop her, though. She wouldn't let it, not now, not when she was so close. As she gathered her ingredients, some of which were more esoteric than others, she labored in her mind to make this betrayal of her beloved cat feel righteous — or at least acceptable.

NAMES LIKE THE CEASELESS CONNOISSEUR or the Patron of Curiosity were just appellations invented by humans. A demon's true name was something individual, and rarely pronounceable. Calling the Connoisseur by name for a summoning required charred beechwood, a lead pencil, a pearl, a red brick (red specifically for some reason), and "irregular pattering," among other things. Its location within the diabolic realm, a place called the Quarry of Sensation, required other sounds and sacrifices in order to invoke it, but Jane wasn't about to attempt summoning a demonic familiar with a more general invocation. She would call it properly, or not at all.

And really, in the end, it didn't take so very much effort to obtain everything she needed. The worst part was pilfering her mother's jewel box for a pearl; Jane worried about Nancy noticing the scratches on her teardrop earring that would surely occur when Jane scraped it across the bit of red brick, but there was no real reason for her to suspect Jane if she ever noticed.

At least, Jane hoped that would prove the case.

15

A LIGHT BUT STEADY RAIN HAD been drumming against the windowpanes all day. As Jane ate her midday meal of bread and butter, she wondered whether that sound constituted the sort of "irregular pattering" that her summoning demanded.

She was so lost in thought, she nearly jumped out of her skin when Miriam cleared her throat.

"Someone will be stopping by this afternoon," she said.

Jane stared in surprise at her almost-sister. It was a miserable day—not one on which any reasonable person would expect visitors, especially to their remote house on the outskirts of the village.

"*Who?*"

Jane and her mother asked it at the same time. Jane apparently wasn't the only one surprised by this information.

"I ordered something. For my research," said Miriam, staring at a nibbled bit of crust that lay hardening upon her plate. "From the —the blacksmith."

Jane stared at Miriam in astonishment. *From the blacksmith,* indeed! More like from the blacksmith's handsome young son, given the glow blooming like a rose in summer across Miriam's nose and cheekbones.

"I see," said Nancy, to cover the awkward silence.

"It wasn't ready last week, when we went into the village," Miriam began, looking as if she might burst, "but he'd said he was going to take the truck out today to make deliveries, and offered to bring it by." Jane couldn't help the sly smile she wore as Miriam said all this. Miriam had claimed she'd forgotten her gloves at the pub during that sojourn; now she knew what her friend had really gone to get.

"Well!" said Jane's mother. She was obviously experiencing a whole host of emotions. "What a day for it! If you'd like to invite him in for a cup of tea . . ."

"What? Why would I do that?" asked Miriam, looking absolutely horrified by the idea of tea.

"He'll want to come in and warm up, won't he?" said Nancy.

Cruel as it might be, Jane was enjoying the awkwardness. It was nice to have it not centered on her, at any rate.

"He's just making a delivery." Miriam's blush deepened dramatically. "I'm sure he won't want to stay. Others will be waiting for him."

"Of course," said Nancy, and did not press the issue further.

Jane was intrigued by Miriam's caginess, but in truth she was more curious about what Sam would be dropping off than about what might be between the two of them. Regardless, she had other matters to contemplate.

She found Smudge curled up in the lumpy blankets of her unmade bed. He looked so peaceful and warm as the cold rain lashed the old farmhouse.

Jane decided in that moment that if the storm continued into the evening, she'd do the summoning that night. It was time.

She sat down beside her beloved cat, trailing her hands through his fur. Smudge deigned to crack open one eye as she rubbed beneath his ears and under his chin. He began to purr, softly at first but then butting his head into the palm of her hand and writhing to expose the paler fur of his belly. Jane gazed upon it, resisting the urge to touch it—for Smudge, showing his tummy was a sign of trust rather than an invitation.

Even so, Jane would often chance it, knowing she risked tooth or claw sunk into the meat of her hand as a consequence of stroking the downy tufts that stood up in soft peaks reminiscent of her mother's meringues. Sometimes, she even petted his belly not in the hopes of getting away with it, but the reverse—to see Smudge's outraged reaction.

She was not disappointed when he latched on like a bear trap, sinking his teeth into the fleshy side of her hand and grabbing on to her wrist with his front paws.

"Smudge!" cried Jane, though really she was delighted by his ferocity. Naughty as her cat might be, Jane didn't enjoy the idea that soon he'd no longer be the cat she'd always known. Not entirely.

But also not for long. She'd banish the demon as soon as she could.

It would be interesting to see how it all worked out. Jane planned to command her diabolic servant to be as catlike—no, as specifically *Smudge*-like—as it could manage. That said, if there was one thing everyone agreed upon, it was that expecting a familiar to indefinitely pass as a pet was foolish arrogance. They could not conceal their true nature for long.

No one could.

Jane left the cat to his nap and returned to the kitchen to pass the afternoon reading in the perpetual warmth of the AGA. Not long after she settled in with a cup of tea and a book called *The Natural, the Supernatural, and the Unnatural*, Miriam came down to join her, and then Nancy did as well.

The distant rumble of a pickup truck made Jane look not to the window, but to Miriam. Miriam looked everywhere but at anyone, seemingly terrified rather than pleased, and Jane felt a warm sympathy for her friend that she had not felt in a long time.

"Let's go meet him," said Nancy.

Jane had never felt any sort of romantic inclination toward anyone, man or woman, nor was she interested in seeking out the experience. Frankly, she felt those who dabbled in love deserved the ensuing headaches it seemed to cause. But even so, when Miriam looked yet more panicked, Jane did her best to help.

"Mother, let's let Miriam have her secrets," she said.

"It's not a *secret*," snapped Miriam. Jane recoiled a bit and saw Miriam repent immediately. Her reaction had been from nerves, not anger. "I'm sorry—it's just . . ."

"It's private. That's completely fine," Jane assured her, having plenty of her own secrets these days. "If you'd rather go out on your own—"

"No!"

Jane suppressed a smile. Poor Miriam. "I'll get my coat."

Miriam didn't seem over-pleased, but neither did she screech in protest. Sometimes all anyone could do was seize upon the best of two bad options.

"I'll stay in and fix some tea," said Nancy. "For you girls when you get back," she added, when Miriam turned her wild and panicked gaze her way, "but enough for Sam if he does fancy a cup."

Bundled up in coats, hats, scarves, boots, and mittens, for it was still quite cold as well as wet, Jane and Miriam squelched their way up the hill, last year's dead leaves hopping in the breeze around their feet like a flock of small strange birds. Sam was standing beside his truck, looking handsome and manly and unbothered by the foul weather.

The idea of commissioning an outsider to make an item crucial to her diabolic work was bizarre to Jane—but probably Miriam would likewise fault her for attempting to turn Smudge into her familiar. To each their own.

"Hello!" called Sam, as they approached. "I've got your mirror!"

A mirror.

Jane didn't stop walking, but she did pause mentally. Interesting, that she and Miriam were both using mirrors for their diabolic Practicals.

A sidelong glance at her friend told Jane that it had been no mere coincidence that *Modern Mirror Methods* had been missing from the Library just after her father had mentioned it. Somehow Miriam had read that letter and had gleaned something from it that had led her to retrieve the same book for her own purposes.

Which meant Miriam knew Jane was in touch with her father.

"You little—"

"I'm sorry!"

"All this time—you've known!" said Jane. She didn't have to say *about my father.* Miriam knew very well what she was talking about.

"Yes," said Miriam, "but I haven't said anything to anyone about it, I promise! I would never, Jane, I just—"

"You just *what?*" It came out more harshly than Jane intended, but her blood was up. "You *just* read my letter and then—"

"I did read it," said Miriam, folding into herself in the face of Jane's rage like candy floss in the rain. "I took the book, but I brought it back as quickly as I could! Something your—"

"Don't you dare!" Jane wasn't sure what she was saying Miriam ought not dare to do—it might have been acknowledging the existence of Jane's father, it might have been explaining her treachery as if it were reasonable, it might have been just speaking to Jane at all in that moment. For some time now, Jane had borne the word *Miriam* writ in jagged bloody letters upon her heart, and this knowledge opened up many of the older wounds at once. "You—you—you little beast! Knowing what it meant to me, you still—"

"You don't know why I did what I did, Jane Blackwood!"

Miriam did not often raise her voice like that, or call Jane by her full name. In spite of her righteous anger, Jane cringed.

"You're not the only one who uses the Library, and you're not the only one for whom this is all very high stakes." Miriam had lowered her voice, but the intensity was still there. "I needed the book, so I took it, and then I returned it. It's not fair to yell at me for that!"

"What would it be fair to yell at you for?" snapped Jane. "How about snooping?"

Miriam crossed her arms. "Clearly I can keep a secret!"

"That's not the point!"

"Girls, girls!"

Jane had forgotten Sam was there at all.

"*You* stay out of this!" said Jane, sounding exactly like her mother.

"Something I said was the cause of all this," he said. "I didn't mean to. I didn't realize the mirror was a secret."

"Oh, Miriam *loves* her secrets," said Jane, with a level of venom that felt good to express, even if she knew it to be unfair. "And the best thing is, the more you get to know her, the more secrets you'll discover she has!"

And with that, Jane stalked off toward the old farmhouse with such determined footfalls that her heels didn't even slip in the mud. She burst in upon her mother as Nancy was just setting the teapot upon the table.

"What happened?" said Nancy, chasing after Jane as she headed for the stairs and the privacy of her room.

"Nothing!" snarled Jane, not even trying to hide the lie of her words.

"Where's Miriam?"

"How should I know!"

"Jane, wait!"

Jane did not obey her mother. She stormed straight up to her room, more hurt in that moment than she could ever remember being. She wanted to collapse upon her bed to cry, but Smudge was still there, half-buried in the bedclothes, so she flung herself into her chair.

She found it was just as easy to cry there, so she did — copiously and angrily, until Smudge jumped onto her lap to twine around himself in anxious figure eights. Though usually Smudge's solid weight calmed her, today it just made Jane cry all the harder. The irregular pattering of the rain on her bedroom window reminded Jane that this might very well be the last time she would ever experience her beloved companion's pure and instinctive concern for her.

Maybe her mother had been right, and there really were no shortcuts to becoming a diabolist.

Only sacrifices.

16

S
o," said sam, as he ran his fingers along the once-silver trim of the once-blue pickup. When some mud came away on his fingertips, he hastily produced a big gray handkerchief and wiped them off.

"I'm sorry," said Miriam.

"For what?"

"For you having to see that."

Sam shook his head as he tucked the soiled rag into his back pocket. "You and I have both seen worse." He coughed awkwardly into his hand. "I'm sorry I mentioned the mirror."

Miriam didn't say anything as the rain kicked up again and the fat cold drops struck her face and rolled down her hair into her collar. She had indeed betrayed Jane; felt the shame of it keenly. Jane's reaction, however, had been a bit much considering the nature of the crime and its nonexistent repercussions.

Maybe Jane really was up to something. Something beyond speaking with her father. Something against the rules. Something that could get her into a lot of trouble if Miriam knew about it and exposed her . . .

Miriam would never tell on Jane, of course. It was just an intriguing idea.

"Er," said Sam, interrupting her thoughts, "want to go for a ride? In my truck, I mean. You could come along on my last delivery and then I could drop you back here. You wouldn't be away more than an hour."

Miriam looked back at the old farmhouse. Nancy stood in the doorway, watching them.

Miriam didn't know what to do. She didn't want to ask permission to go. She just wanted to go. For perhaps the first time since arriving in Hawkshead, Miriam couldn't stand the thought of being indoors.

She yanked open the cab door. It was heavier than she thought and banged open with a horrifying clatter as she clambered inside awkwardly. Halfway through her scrambling, it occurred to her that her bottom was up in the air, and she slid all the way over, blushing terribly as she gathered her skirts and got them underneath her where they belonged.

"What are you waiting for?" she called to Sam. "Are we going or not?"

Sam glanced back to the house, then climbed in after. "Going," he said, his smile all the sunshine she needed to make this feel like a picnic.

Miriam was glad the truck's rumbling engine was so loud; they couldn't really carry on much conversation as they bounced over the narrow, twisting roads canopied by the mossy dripping branches of old trees. Sam took one curve a little quickly, and Miriam slid across the seat into his side. She started to apologize until he put his arm around her and held her there. Miriam wondered if that had been his plan the whole time; his sly expression answered her question before she could ask it.

Bold as a sparrow, she kissed him on the cheek. It was warmer next to him, and more pleasant. She blushed as she settled back into her seat, but he seemed extremely pleased.

Miriam waited in the cab while Sam dropped off his final delivery. Her breath puffed in the cold air, fogging the windows, which was fine. She didn't really want anyone seeing her, but once they got moving again, she rubbed herself a little porthole with her sleeve so she could see where they were going. It didn't seem like they were headed back home, and indeed they were not.

She felt a flutter of nervousness when Sam turned off the road and headed overland toward a bit of woodland in the distance. She didn't say anything, instead waiting for him to announce his intentions.

"There's a nice spot just up ahead," he said. "Pretty when it rains."

From within, the wood was deeper and darker than it appeared from beyond its border. Sam maneuvered the truck between the trunks and then killed the motor. Suddenly, there was only blessed, terrifying silence broken only by the rain that struck the roof of the cab in staccato bursts.

"Are you still thinking about Jane?" asked Sam as the windows began to fog again and the temperature to drop.

Miriam shrugged. She was not interested in explaining. She was more interested in the way he seemed to be tightening his hold on her, drawing her into the warmth of his bulk. When he took her chin into his callused hand and angled her face up for a real kiss, a proper first kiss, it was easy to relax into that, too.

"Miriam," he said. She liked to hear him say her name; it sounded good in his mouth. He said it again— "Miriam," in a helpless, urgent way that made her body warm up in spite of the rapidly chilling air.

She wasn't sure what he was asking for until his hands found the button at the top of her coat. Feeling strangely calm, Miriam nodded and let him undo it, and undo the buttons of her blouse, too. She blushed for him to see her modest undergarment and the gooseflesh above and below it, but he did not seem displeased with her appearance. In fact, when he pushed her gently down onto the cold leather of the seat, she felt something indicating his enthusiasm as they shifted.

The cab of a pickup truck was hardly the place she'd thought she'd be when first revealing herself to a lover, but, really, the fogged-over windows provided complete privacy. But as Sam pushed her skirt up above her knees, revealing two fuzzy thighs, she realized she ought to have come up with a plan for this sort of situation.

"You're such a beautiful girl," Sam said, gazing at her as she lay there, limbs akimbo, clothing mussed. "And so smart, so passionate."

Miriam knew she was smart, but as for passionate or beautiful — that was an unconvincing compliment. Maybe passionate about her work . . .

His hands were roving more freely now.

"So sensitive," he whispered, when she shivered, but that wasn't it, not really.

Miriam was enjoying his attentions, but wasn't entirely certain how to respond to them. Mostly she was just cold, and when it occurred to her how long she'd been gone, she couldn't keep her mind on what he was doing to her body.

She cleared her throat like an impatient customer waiting to be noticed at a shop. "Sam," she said, and he froze. "I'm not—I mean, rather, it's not that I don't—"

"Let's stop," he said, pulling away from her. "We don't have to do anything right now."

"It's a little cold," she admitted, as she buttoned herself back up. "And I'm worried about getting back."

"Of course," he said, starting up the truck—but before he threw it into gear, he smiled at her shyly. "Did you have fun, though? I did."

"Yes!" said Miriam. It had been fun, even if the conditions hadn't been ideal.

"Good. I'd got the sense you'd be all right," he said. "Not all girls would be."

Miriam had been considering what Nancy might say to a courtship, but something about Sam's words gave her pause.

"All right with what?" she asked.

"You know," he said, returning his hand to her now-covered

thigh and squeezing it affectionately. "Enjoying ourselves together, when we have the time to get away. Appreciating what we can have with one another, not worrying about what we can't."

Miriam finally understood what he was saying. Sam wasn't interested in pursuing her for anything beyond what brief connections they could manage for the moment.

Her uncertainty in the face of this realization must have shown upon her face, because Sam blushed and pulled his hand away.

"I wouldn't want to treat you dishonestly." He threw the pickup into reverse, backing out of the forest slowly. His tone, his expression, his body language were all chillier; he wasn't making love to her now, he was being conscientious and precise. "I can't offer you more."

The idea of a casual arrangement didn't offend her—they were young and barely knew one another beyond their mutual attraction—but just the same, it felt strange to hear that he'd already decided that this was all it could ever be.

"What did you expect?" he asked, pulling farther away.

She hadn't intended for her silence to convey displeasure—she was just a bit confused and needed to think before she spoke.

"I'm not sure what I expected," Miriam said, in order to say *something*. "I suppose I expected that if we were here, doing this, that you liked me as I liked you—which to me means giving you a chance."

"I do like you, Miriam," he said, increasingly matter-of-fact in a way that didn't set her at ease. "But what else could this be, given who we are?"

Miriam realized that Sam wasn't talking about the improbable match of a blacksmith's boy with a diabolist's niece. He was talking about something much more personal. Something Miriam couldn't change—and wouldn't, even if she had the chance.

All she wanted was to be who she was without it being worthy of comment.

"I see," she said, her tone as icy as the landscape beyond the windshield as they rambled overland toward the road.

"Surely you'd want to settle down with, you know. One of your own kind," said Sam, increasingly defensive.

"My own kind." The bitterness in Miriam's voice was not all due to Sam's attitude. He was not the only one to have expressed anxiety over the idea of where Miriam *belonged*. "Who are my own kind, I wonder?"

"You know what I mean!"

Miriam shrugged; it was more that *he* didn't understand what *she* meant.

"To be completely honest," she said, "I haven't contemplated settling down at all. There have been moments over the past few years when I've experienced some considerable doubt as to whether *my own kind* will survive the conflict that brought me to Hawkshead."

"That's nothing to do with me!" said Sam.

"I didn't say it was." Miriam once again used her sleeve to wipe the passenger's side window free of steam. The rolling, gray-green hills beyond now looked dreary and waterlogged rather than romantic and intriguing; she wondered when they'd be back at the old farmhouse and she could get away from him. "I'm sorry you feel insulted, but you've insulted me too."

"I was just being honest. I didn't want you getting attached."

Sam, too, had lost much of his glamour. His upper lip was beaded with moisture, though it wasn't warm in the cab, and his frown made his full lips look petulant rather than kissable.

"My friends, they all said I was crazy for even talking to you," he said. "I told them they were wrong, that you were a sweet girl. That you weren't anything like other—I mean …" Sam had the decency to stammer as Miriam sat there, holding herself completely still, staring at him in disbelief. There was no other word for what she was experiencing—Sam clearly thought he was offering a *defense* of his words and deeds when in fact he was damning himself further. If only he would just stop talking! "Frank, he asked if you'd tried to haggle me down on the price of your mirror, and I said you wouldn't do that. I *defended* you."

Miriam was used to being considered different; she *was* different. After all, back in Germany they had decided there needed to be a word for what she was: *Mischling*. Mixed, a mutt, one who was neither this nor that—but even before that, she'd known she wasn't Jewish to the Jews nor was she properly German to the Gentiles. As proud as she had always been of her family and their ways, the nature of who they were had meant she never fit in anywhere, not even at home.

Then things had changed, and it had become very important to know on some broader level who fit in and who did not. Miriam had suddenly become Jewish, whether she actually *felt* Jewish or otherwise. This in turn meant she'd started feeling a kinship with her father's side of the family that she had never felt before—and she started to feel grateful to Gentiles who didn't treat her with suspicion.

That gratitude had stuck with her even after escaping to England, but something changed for Miriam in that moment. To hear that the other boys in the village—Frank, by name, so probably also Rob and John—had not only *also* known she was Jewish, but, in spite of being friendly with her in the shops and on the streets, had secretly made jokes about her being miserly and whatever else. It broke something inside Miriam; put a crack in the wall that she'd built up around the shadowed place where she kept all her inconvenient feelings. The darkness she kept pressed down deep inside her seemed to well up from the wound and spoke for her.

"When will we be back? Nancy will be worrying, and I need to pay you for the mirror. It'll be dark soon, and I know you'll want to count it twice."

"That's not fair!"

"Then I apologize," said Miriam, not bothering to conceal her insincerity.

The afternoon gloom was turning to evening gloom as they pulled up at the old farmhouse. The kitchen window was bright if not especially cheery in the twilight. Miriam felt as though years had passed and she was far, far older than she had been when she jumped into Sam's cab a few hours before.

Miriam had her little coin purse ready. "How much for the mirror?"

"Just take it," said Sam, taking the mirror out of his pocket and putting it down on the seat between them, not into her hand. Huffy as he might be, she would not yield.

"No, I'll pay you for your work," she said firmly, but after a long silence she accepted the package and replaced it with a few coins —more than she thought he would ask to be paid, just to be sure he couldn't accuse her of cheating him—and climbed out of the truck.

She left the door hanging open behind her.

Nancy had clearly been waiting at the kitchen table; she jumped up at Miriam's sudden intrusion.

"I didn't intend to be gone so long," said Miriam.

"Are you all right?" asked Nancy. There was so much worry and care in her voice, but it did little to warm Miriam's heart.

"Yes. We just talked." That was mostly true.

Nancy's eyes filled with tears. "I knew you girls would grow up one day, but—"

"I was just upset," said Miriam.

"Edith and I quarreled a good deal more than you and Jane ever do, you know. It's hard, sometimes, being sisters."

The word took Miriam aback. When they were small, Miriam and Jane had agreed that no matter what anyone else might say, they were *sisters*—no other term could possibly express the depth of their sentiments for one another.

It had been a long time since she'd thought of Jane that way.

Miriam shrugged. "We all say things when we're upset."

Nancy looked surprised at Miriam's calm chilliness, but Miriam didn't want to discuss the matter further. That would invite questions, and the fewer of those asked the better.

"Are you hungry?"

Miriam's fingers clutched at the paper-wrapped mirror in her lap. She knew she ought to eat. Her tea was long gone . . . but she was eager to get upstairs.

"I'm just very tired," she said.

"All right," said Nancy.

Her adopted aunt stood and started to clear the table. Miriam waited a moment or two, then headed for the stairs.

"Miriam," said Nancy.

"Yes?" She paused in the doorway.

"Like I said, I knew you girls would grow up one day," she repeated, sounding nothing like the calm authority figure Miriam was used to. "It's possible I didn't prepare you properly for the choices you'll have to make now that you're a young lady. When you're a child, time moves so slowly, and then as you grow up, you never know what will happen at any moment. Emotions run high, and decisions—"

"We didn't," said Miriam. She saw no reason to make Nancy worry even if it wasn't any of her business.

Nancy looked like she might faint. Under other circumstances, it might have been amusing. "Oh! All right. I didn't mean to pry."

"Please don't worry about me," said Miriam, and then she told a lie, given what she was about to do: "There's really no need."

Nancy's smile was sad. "I can promise you anything but that," she said.

17

MIRIAM LOCKED HERSELF INTO HER room that night, which was not her custom. She also set up diabolic wards similar to those that protected the farmhouse, some to alert her if she were to be observed physically or diabolically—and others that would hopefully prevent any observation to begin with.

She was ready. She had the mirror-frame Sam had made waiting for her on her desk, and she'd gotten good at not just inhabiting but controlling the ducks and geese of Nancy's flock. Though she knew success might mean getting bad news as easily as good, she was excited to finally learn *something* of what had happened to her parents.

Modern Mirror Methods had been an invaluable find, no matter how she'd found it. The author's method of creating a scrying glass had been easily done, save for requiring a bit of something belonging to the person one wished to scry.

Her only real option had been her father's devil-trap. The book promised that the item would be "returned unharmed," which begged the question of why it needed to be "returned" to begin with—but that was just the way of diablerie.

Whatever Miriam might think of Sam now, he had done a good job with the mirror. It was exactly what Miriam needed, almost uncannily so. It wasn't beautiful, but it was appropriate for its task—and the handle of the mirror fit in her hand as if he'd measured her for it. The well he'd left for her "glass" was unpolished, and the metal grabbed light like a predator. Though Sam could not have known it, he had made an implement destined to be used for the Art.

Miriam startled at the sound of thunder. The storm had picked up a bit; she'd been too occupied to notice. She listened to the howling wind for a moment and then startled again when a piercing shriek reached her ears.

Dashing from her desk, Miriam stuck her head out into the hallway, listening, but nothing more sinister than withering gusts of wind reached her ears. Sometimes the winter wind did seem to scream — it was just that for a moment Miriam thought it had sounded a bit like an animal. Or maybe Jane.

After once again locking the door behind her and resetting her wards, Miriam squared her shoulders, took a deep breath, and popped a tablet into her mouth. Then she poured the potion she'd prepared into the mirror-well. It fizzed as it struck the metal only to become smooth and flowing, almost mercury-like. Quickly but carefully, Miriam set aside the phial and picked up her father's devil-trap.

The clay bowl sat momentarily atop the glassy surface of the potion, reflected in it, before sinking in. Another sizzle, like bacon fat, and it was gone. Miriam hoped it really would be returned unharmed.

Miriam picked up the mirror. If she'd done it right, the liquid would hold its shape.

It undulated slightly but did not spill no matter which way she turned it. She played with it for a moment or two before admonishing herself for acting like a child. This wasn't a toy, and it was hardly the time for play.

"Show me my father," said Miriam, adding, "Egon Cantor," before polishing off a bottle of liquid diabolic essence.

By the time she started to feel that sensation of double-presence, something was beginning to resolve in the rippling surface of the mirror. At first she couldn't understand what she was seeing. The description of the process in *Modern Mirror Methods* had said she would see the person, but all Miriam saw was a quiet forest floor. This year's fragile new grass and last year's leaves were silvered by what moonlight spilled through the pine boughs. It was night, or maybe very early morning—but it was a clear night, though very cold given the frost on the ground.

This was wrong. It was supposed to show Miriam her father, not wherever *this* was. Was this bit of grass, windswept and lonely and cold, where her poor father had been laid to rest? Did that mean whatever had happened had happened so long ago that the earth no longer looked as though it had ever been disturbed?

She noticed a shape in the grass, white as the moon above and similarly curved. She couldn't quite make sense of it.

The tablet was really hitting her now; her soul had peeled away from her body like a scab. While her body's hand held the mirror, her spirit's hand grabbed the veil knife. A strip of spirit-skin and spirit-flesh came away when she used it on her arm—more than she had yet taken, but now was the time. And anyway, while her previous spiritual wounds weren't healed yet, she had observed some spiritual regrowth and thus wasn't particularly worried about it.

Miriam watched her flesh turn to vapor. She emptied her lungs, then inhaled it all.

A passing night-flying insect winged into her line of sight through the mirror, and quick as the blink of an eye she was inside of it.

It *worked.*

Miriam had to keep her elation in check as she felt the whir of her own wings and the night air sliding along her carapace; saw through eyes that were distinct from her own, compound, both more and less accurate to a purpose.

She'd done it. She was inside another living creature somewhere —she assumed—within Germany.

Now, to find her father.

Miriam's wings moved impossibly fast as she asserted her will, forcing the insect to spiral down to where the mysterious pale object waited to be identified. She glided along the length of the white crescent, still wondering what on earth it might be and why the mirror had shown her this. Then she swerved out of the way to avoid a protuberance and almost lost her hold on her host when she realized what it was.

It was a tooth. A jawbone.

Her father's jawbone.

Miriam was back in her room but not her body. She screamed with lungs that had no air, through a throat that could issue forth no sound. She had thought herself prepared; she hadn't been.

Her father was dead in a forest.

Miriam reeled, but she was isolated from the physical sensations of shock. Her spirit's palms did not sweat, could not sweat; her spirit's heart could not pound; she could not cry. There was only the terrible knowledge that she would never hear her father's voice again. She would never see his slow, uncertain smile, nor smell his shaving soap.

How had Egon Cantor gone from a living man reading in his shabby wingback chair in their house in Weimar to a corpse lying silent upon the loam of this frost-rimed forest?

Where was that forest?

Who had left him there?

She'd lost the insect, but not her need for answers.

Miriam knew from experience that she wouldn't return to her body until she had processed the armamentaria. The grief would be there for the rest of her life; for now, she might as well make effective use of her time. She had to get control of herself, push her pain down to that dark and secret place within her. Miriam ruefully considered how this process of cleaving to another being was yet another aspect of her life requiring absolute composure, but it was ever her fate to be restrained in situations utterly beyond her control.

She could manage it, though. Rage was a resource, just like diabolic essence.

She turned her spirit's eyes back to the mirror, waiting for another insect. But what she saw, instead, was a surprisingly plump fox, loping out from behind a tree on some urgent errand. Miriam drew on the power still coursing within her, and then it was her loping over the fields.

She'd never cleaved to such a large, complex creature. At first, she couldn't control it and was merely along for the ride as it found another corpse in the forest and began to make a ghastly meal of it. That had explained how sleek and well-fed it had looked . . .

It took all of Miriam's strength to compel the fox to do as she wished. It wanted its dinner, whereas Miriam wanted to explore.

When she finally asserted control, first Miriam explored the rest of her father's remains. With the fox's keener eyes, she was able to see some white bone flashing through where winter's mud had slithered over him. They had left his tattered shirt and pants on him, and what hadn't rotted away clung but loosely to his remains.

That was all her father could tell her. Miriam looked around through the fox's eyes. The question now was where had he—and the other bodies—come from?

Miriam tested the fox's own feelings, and then made it run toward the place it wanted least to go. She assumed that would be man's habitat instead of its own. In the end, after a brief struggle of wills, the fox broke through the tree line to lope toward a large brick structure. Walls erupted from the earth, bleak and foreboding; Miriam's host had good enough vision for her to see barbed wire lining the top and a man walking the perimeter.

The guard hadn't spotted her. His attention was not on what small creatures might be creeping through the shadows. Miriam took a deep breath through the animal's lungs and trotted forward.

She could see the iron bars of the gate had been twisted into some-thing—a stylized, angular blossom.

"Ey!" The guard on the high wall had noticed her staring. He was pointing his rifle at her. "Verzieh dich!"

The fox wanted nothing more than to "bugger off." Part of Miriam did too, until the Nazi guard lowered his rifle and laughed.

The sound of his merry chuckling only served to stoke Miriam's dangerous fury. How dare he laugh while standing guard at this terrible place!

The fox's hair bristled and its tail puffed. On instinct Miriam leaned forward into an angry stance and issued a high—and truth be told a rather silly-sounding—bark. This just made the guard laugh more, which in turn robbed her of yet more precious control.

Her animal's senses noticed an owl winging its way close. *Bad-gerskin* had been unclear about whether a diabolist could cleave from one host to another. Miriam had inferred that the author was saying that it was inadvisable, but not impossible.

But desperate times and all that.

Miriam sent herself into the bird. The connection was weaker —she herself was weaker, she could feel it—but she still managed to steer it toward the guard as she felt the exhilaration of flight. She was vaguely aware of the fox dashing back into the shadows, but Miriam kept her focus on the guard. He hadn't yet noticed her as she flew toward him on silent wings.

Heedless of her safety, Miriam dived, drawing on the bird's muscle memory. Extending her talons at the last moment, she hit the back of the guard's head, raking it with her claws.

"Scheiße!" The guard staggered away from the unexpected at-tack, dropping his rifle as Miriam wheeled around. The rifle went off when it hit his beetle-black boot, a crack that echoed her scream as she swooped a second time.

He saw her, and his eyes were wide as she caught him in the

face, digging her claws into his flesh and eyes. He screamed now, and swatted at her with his hands as she beat his head with her wings. Back and back he stumbled, and then it felt to Miriam like they were flying again—but really they were hurtling several stories to the earth below. She braced for impact and then realized she and the owl both stood a better chance of surviving if she left this body and returned to her own.

The mirror clattered to her desk from her trembling hand as Miriam gasped her way back into her body. Every muscle hurt, every bone and inch of skin felt tired and worn out. She was pleased to see her father's devil-trap emerge safely—"unharmed"—from the mirror like a pirate ship though mist, but otherwise Miriam was wholly occupied by just getting to her bed and falling upon it. There, she gazed limply up at her ceiling, thinking about what she'd done.

If the guard had died, that meant she'd killed him.

She'd let her feelings get the better of her when she'd been spiritually abroad, and the consequence had been a man's life. Not only that, but she'd jumped two more times than the book had informed her was safe. Now here she was, lying on the floor, exhausted and sick to her stomach.

Very sick to her stomach, it turned out—Miriam didn't think she'd make it to the bathroom, so she scrambled for the wastebasket. She vomited copiously, choking on half-digested rotten meat that Miriam knew had been the fox's dinner.

That thought made her throw up again. It was a long time before the heaving stopped, and longer still before she felt strong enough to crawl shakily into bed.

Daylight on her face woke her the next morning. She'd slept late. She was too exhausted to be horrified over missing her chore of feeding the poultry, too woozy to be more than passively confused that no one had woken her.

Her vomit had turned rank in the night, so she scurried to

the bathroom to pour it down the upstairs loo. She thoroughly rinsed out the bin afterward to rid it of the smell of sick. Eventually she found her way downstairs, an apology for failing to wake up on time on her lips, but it died there when she found mother and daughter sitting quietly at the kitchen table together, hands clasped. Jane especially looked upset. Her eyes were red and she bit at her lower lip. Nancy just looked dazed.

"What's wrong?" asked Miriam.

"Last night something got into the barn," said Nancy. "I heard it, and I got up to go look. It didn't get all of them, but it got some."

"*It* what? *Some* what?"

"Some ducks," said Jane. "As to whatever it was, we don't know."

Miriam felt a chill that she suspected was not from a draft. Odd, that this should happen the very night of her first attempt to send her spirit so far beyond her body. She didn't think it could be possible that her shadow-soul had already grown strong enough to incur those "unintended consequences" hinted about in *Badgerskin* . . .

This was just a strange occurrence, a coincidence.

Miriam enjoyed caring for the birds as an act of service to the family that had taken her in, but, really, these dead fowl meant little to her, not with her father's pale tooth and jawbone fresh in her mind—not to mention the yet-unknown fate of her mother. Regardless, she was grateful that the ducks had provided her with an acceptable cover story for seeming upset.

However long ago her father had died, the loss was fresh to Miriam, and it was a loss she and the shadow-self within her had to endure in silence, alone. Sadness battled with Miriam's exhaustion and won; she sat down with the Blackwoods as they stared into the middle distance together, each alone with her own thoughts.

18

S MUDGE FOLLOWED JANE OUT TO the barn when she went to clean up the mess.

It *was* Smudge. She was sure of it. She'd held him in her arms when he'd been a squirmy mewling kitten; she knew his ways like she knew her own. Currently, Smudge was walking as he usually did, tail swishing from side to side like a fuzzy rudder, his posture alert and focused. A confident tomcat out for a stroll.

Things weren't any different now.

Except they were.

The storm the previous night had raged like Jane's emotions as she'd summoned forth the Ceaseless Connoisseur from its home in the Quarry of Sensation. The demon had answered, Smudge had awoken from his induced sleep within a circle made of crushed coca leaves and rose petals, and Jane had bound them together with words and a bit of virgin white yarn she'd soaked in a solution of mercury, diabolic essence, and single-malt Scotch whisky. After she'd said the final words, the yarn had glowed an eye-watering shade of azure before disappearing into flesh and fur.

After that, the cat had stepped delicately out of the circle, headbutted her chin with the chirp that meant he would like to be petted, and then herded her to bed, as Smudge often did when she was late at her work. Today Smudge trotted his same trot, cocked his tail back and forth with the same jaunty confidence, and looked over at her with his inscrutable yellow eyes the same way he always had when she called his name. And yet she knew he was not really himself. There was something within her cat making his motions a bit swifter, a bit keener. A bit more consciously attuned to her.

Smudge had slept soundly, curled beside Jane's feet all night.

She had been the restless one, tossing and turning after everything she had done. Normally Jane wouldn't think twice of something so normal as the cat sleeping on her feet, but there were the ducks to be considered. Three ducks with their bellies split and their entrails strewn about the barn. Whatever had done it had dragged them around and around, effectively trapping the remaining birds in a circle of feathers, guts, and blood.

Jane knew that foxes and other predators sometimes liked to play with their food; it was just the timing of this gruesome attack that gave her pause. That, and when she looked at the carcasses in the dim light of the barn—Nancy's country pragmatism had made her save the bodies for stock at the very least—she'd noticed their necks were snapped.

Cleanly, not messily. And there were no bite marks.

It was uncanny, and she'd done something uncanny the night before. Uncanny, illegal, dangerous ... whether her actions were ambitious or insane would be for history to decide.

But even a demon couldn't be in two places at once—and they could not exist beyond their host. There simply hadn't been time for Smudge to slip away and murder birds for sport, pleasure, or weirder reasons. The coincidence was just that—coincidence.

Anyway, why on earth would a demon want to kill a few ducks? What reason could it have to do something so petty and disgusting? *Especially* the Ceaseless Connoisseur—it was attracted to sensation, most especially blithe sensation. Not violence or destruction. As Jane considered this, it occurred to her that she didn't need to wonder. The cat was under her control—more so than it had ever been.

"Smudge," said Jane, as she swept entrails into a dustpan.

The cat stared at her from where it sat in a ray of sunshine, its shadow stretched long upon the floor. "Did you do this?"

The cat blinked slowly, once, and then to her absolute horror, it shook its head *no*.

The previous night, as the rain had pattered on the roof and Jane had crushed a lead pencil with some wood while scraping a pearl along a bit of red brick, she hadn't felt afraid. She'd felt confident and in control as she'd spoken the final words — her own addition, and a clever one, in her opinion: "And thou mayest depart for thine own realm when I give thee leave to do so, or upon the very moment of my death, which if it is caused by thy hand or intention, shall result in thine own demise."

The rest of it had been good stuff, too, cobbled together from several different summoning spells from several different books — courtesy of the strike chain — along with some ideas of her own. She'd especially liked the line that read: "Thou mayest not lie to me with either thy voice or thy body," given how reliant every pet owner was on reading nonverbal communication from their animals. Likewise, she was very pleased by "no part of thy flesh, bone, or blood may disobey me, nor mayest thou obey thine own will if it should depart from mine."

It had all gone exactly as described, so to Jane, that seemed to indicate it had gone well.

Jane finished plucking and cleaning the dead birds and scattered fresh sawdust over the blood stains on the barn floor. The surviving poultry relaxed a bit, spreading out from their huddled flock to nibble at some grain. Smudge was still lit from behind by the morning sunshine. The bright light caught the tips of his fluffy mane and the tufts on his ears and around his feline shoulders.

The ducks and geese did not go near him.

Of course, they didn't *usually* go near Smudge, Jane reminded herself. They typically gave him a wide berth. Even a familiar predator was still a predator.

She was just trussing the duck carcasses so they could hang for a bit when a shadow darkened the door of the barn. Jane uttered a squawk of surprise that echoed those of the ducks and the geese.

She'd been so lost in her own thoughts, she hadn't heard Miriam's approach.

"Sorry," said Miriam, stepping inside. "I didn't mean to startle you."

"I know," said Jane.

She wasn't angry anymore, and she knew she ought to say so — but she couldn't make herself. There was something other than anger stoppering her throat — pride, perhaps, or resentment.

"Jane," said Miriam, "about yesterday . . ."

"I'm sorry I yelled," said Jane.

"I'm sorry I read your letter," said Miriam. "And I'm sorry I took the book when you needed it."

An awkward silence descended until Miriam asked, "So . . . are you done here?"

"I am," said Jane.

"I should have offered to help, but I really wasn't feeling well this morning."

"No?"

"It was a long night."

Jane felt the flutter of alarm. She hadn't heard Miriam come home — had she stayed out with Sam? Had they actually *done something?*

Would Miriam confide in Jane if they had?

A strained silence descended as the girls stood together in the warm barn. Sunlight streamed in at the cracks, and the dust from the hay and the grain swirled in the air between them like fairy lights, blinking out when they fell into shadow and then glowing again as they reentered the pale gold of the faint sunshine.

What had they used to talk about? It seemed incredible how easily they had once chatted away their time as they worked and played, covering seemingly infinite topics of conversation. Now, five minutes of awkward apologies left them with nothing more to say to each other.

Miriam was clearly at a loss, too. The girl fidgeted like a child as she stood there, biting her lower lip as if to remind herself to keep it stationary.

Smudge stalked over to rub his face on Miriam's ankle, as he had always enjoyed doing. Miriam squatted down to pet him; he flopped over onto his back, writhing a bit before getting to his feet and flopping over again.

Jane just watched, her neck prickling as her best friend ran her fingers over Smudge's arched spine. The entire interaction was as typical as could be . . . except it wasn't.

That was when something odd happened. As Smudge squirmed and wriggled under Miriam's gentle touch, to Jane it looked as if the cat's shadow *wasn't*. It remained relatively still—and then, for just a moment, two eyes opened up, almond-shaped and empty, revealing the sawdusty floor of the barn.

They blinked, disappearing and reappearing, before swiveling to alight on Jane. Every hair on her neck rose as the eyes narrowed—

"Wicked thing!" cried Miriam, pulling her hand back in annoyance. "Why do I fall for that act of yours every time?"

Smudge had nipped her fingers for his own inscrutable reasons, and now looked pleased with himself as he twisted about in the sawdust.

His shadow followed him, as shadows ought to do.

"So," said Miriam, as she stood, "I suppose I'd better, you know, go and . . . Jane?"

Jane's heartbeat was slowing as Smudge's shadow continued to behave in an entirely mundane fashion. It must have been a trick of the light, or the strain of her shocking morning following a sleepless night.

"Of course," said Jane. "I'll be along shortly. Is it all going well for you?" She surprised herself by asking that last part. She wasn't sure if she really wanted to know.

Miriam looked momentarily pained. "I suppose so," she said. "It's odd, isn't it? Everything's changed so much in such a short time."

Jane bit her tongue—the change had started long before that. If anything, their Practical had simply shone a light on it. That seemed like the wrong thing to say, however.

"It's good to practice taking things a little more seriously," she said. "Once we're Masters, the stakes will be even higher."

"Once we're Masters . . ." Miriam said it like it wasn't a concept she had been thinking much about—which was odd, given her devotion to her studies. "I suppose you're right." She hesitated for a moment and then said, "Goodbye, Jane," and left.

Smudge kicked his paws a few more times before sitting up and stretching. Jane watched him carefully, but there was nothing amiss. Nothing except a strange absence on his collar . . .

"Smudge, where's your bell got to?"

Odd that it should have fallen off; it never had before.

"Let's go get you another one," said Jane. She was certain she had one in her sewing kit. "I wonder if you'll even want to chase birds anymore."

Jane recalled why she was in the barn to begin with and grew quiet. Smudge licked his paw, shook it a few times, and licked it again, like any cat might.

THERE WAS NO WAY TO PREDICT how quickly Smudge's claws, fur, and whiskers would begin to register diabolic essence, and there would be no outward indicator that the change had occurred. Thus, patience was not the only thing required for this next stage in Jane's efforts.

The strike chain had helped Jane locate a clever little candle whose flame would turn bright pink when diabolic material was burning. It was such a helpful, clever bit of diablerie that Jane was eager to try it out—so that afternoon she nipped down to the storeroom within the Library to get what she needed.

Smudge trotted along at her heels by her command. She wasn't about to let the cat out of her sight. Not yet.

Nancy was sitting at her desk, as usual. There were a few slips bearing requests by one of her elbows and books to go out by the other. She was so completely absorbed by what she was looking at that Jane wasn't sure if her mother had heard her approach.

She stood there for an awkward moment, and then another, before coughing delicately into her hand.

Nancy looked up. "All right, Jane?"

"Yes, Mother," said Jane.

Jane hesitated. She didn't know how to ask for what she needed, because what she needed was to be a normal sixteen-year-old girl who'd seen something incredibly strange and wanted to talk to her mother about it.

Jane, however, was anything but.

"Need a book?"

"A component," said Jane.

Nancy hadn't seemed to notice Smudge, who was at that moment sitting up straight, his tail politely curved over his toes.

Jane checked to make sure her cat's shadow was acting like a shadow. It was.

Maybe she could at least try to be a normal sixteen-year-old, just for a moment.

"Mother . . . the ducks . . ."

"Hmm?"

"The ducks. I hung them."

Her mother smiled. "Oh, good, thank you, Jane. That was very thoughtful."

Jane didn't quite know how to respond to that; it wasn't the sort of thing she was used to her mother saying. "But . . ."

"Yes?"

"It wasn't just that they'd been disemboweled." Jane began to sweat, thinking back to the sight of it. "Their necks had been snapped."

Nancy stared at her serenely, as if expecting something more.

"It didn't look like something a fox could have done," said Jane, explaining further. "No teeth, no claws. Just a clean break."

"Oh." Her mother mulled this over for a moment, and then smiled. "Foxes are notoriously wily. It's upsetting, but don't let it worry you. These things will happen."

Jane wasn't satisfied by this answer at all, but she also got the sense it was the best she would get. Her mother wasn't really paying attention.

Then Nancy winked, to Jane's additional surprise. "Now run along and find your book."

"Component," said Jane.

Nancy nodded in agreement.

THE NEXT NIGHT, WHEN THE candles were dry and ready, Jane burned a single hair from Smudge's coat. Nothing happened, as she expected, and nothing happened the second night, either.

Jane had anticipated this, but waiting still wasn't easy. She could only check and recheck her equations so many times before her eyes began to cross. But with her mother suddenly at her desk every moment of the day, and Miriam seeming so tired, withdrawn, and distant, Jane was left with no other diversion but work.

And chores, of course . . .

The three women had always shared the duties that kept the farmhouse a pleasant place to live. While the girls had both been known to shirk their duties, Nancy never did, which is why it came as a shock when Jane's mother's sudden preoccupation with work meant she stopped cleaning, tidying, or cooking.

The first night when dinner had gone unprepared, a shocked Jane had asked if her mother was in need of some help. Nancy had serenely replied that she would be delighted for Jane to step up and take the initiative, which hadn't been what Jane was saying at all.

Not that she minded, not necessarily; she was just concerned and shocked that first night, as she'd prepared a hasty baked savory pudding out of a few early eggs, some stale bread, and their ration of cheese, and she continued to be perturbed when she noticed that Miriam's chore load remained unchanged.

Then again, she never would have found Edith's dress if she hadn't been newly tasked with dusting the guest room.

It was a rainy day—but warmer, with the promise of spring. As the rain pattered on the awakening earth beyond the windowsill, Jane decided she need not get through the cleaning quickly. Her eyes were tired from her morning's reading, the day's bread—a lumpy, misshapen loaf that Jane hoped would at least taste good —was cooling in the kitchen, and the day before she'd gone to the village to shop, so there was already food in the house for dinner. She had hours before she'd need to even think about cooking anything, so she elected to pass the time by making sure the guest room had been really and truly set to rights.

When she opened the closet door, she gasped. It had been a month almost to the day since Edith's visit, and she'd written them two letters, neither of which had mentioned leaving behind a dress. It was blackest black, with tasteful bits of black lace and some jet beading at the collar and wrists. The buttons up the front were fashioned from a shiny material, formed, or perhaps carved, into the shape of little stars.

Jane rubbed the wool crepe between her fingers, luxuriating in the sensation, but she stopped when a bit of it snagged on a callus. This wasn't hers to ruin with her work-rough hands—or was it?

There, pinned in the dress, was a note. Feeling as though she were doing something illicit, Jane opened the small envelope and gasped in delight.

> *Dearest Jane,*
>
> *Don't think I haven't noticed how you look at my wardrobe. Well, you always have been discerning. Here's one of your own, from me. Wear it in good health, but wear it in secret until you're out of the house.*
>
> *Congratulations on passing your Test, Jane—I always knew you would!*
>
> > *Your affectionate aunt,*
> > *Edith Blackwood*

Jane experienced a number of feelings while reading this short missive. How well her aunt understood her—and how little, too! Jane wished they'd parted on better terms . . .

She wished, too, that she'd actually passed her Test.

But that wasn't all the letter said. Beneath, in a hastier scrawl, she read:

> *I hope you're not annoyed at yet another thing that must wait until you leave home, Jane. I do think both will prove worth it.*

It was true that Jane had not passed her Test, and thus did not deserve this dress . . . but it was also true that to maintain the illusion that she had, Jane would need to wear it with pride. The first easy sacrifice of her journey!

And Jane didn't have to wait just to try it on for fit, so after looking both ways down the hall, Jane shed her apron and her everyday dress. Her bare flesh prickled in the cool air of the guest bedroom as she quickly slipped into the gown.

It fit perfectly. She couldn't risk looking at herself in her mother's mirror, but gazing down at her wrists framed by black lace and feeling the deliciously snug silk slithering over her waist, she'd never felt more like herself. While she was a bit ashamed of her bare white legs and common, knobby feet in their homemade socks, she knew exactly the shoes and stockings she'd pair with this, once she got the chance. She noticed such things when she looked at the stills of her favorite movie stars, and firmly believed she'd managed to cultivate excellent taste even if she'd had limited opportunities to prove it in a shop with money in her hand.

Jane allowed herself a twirl and then, offering silent, sincere thanks to Edith, she took it off and hung it back up in the closet. She gave it one last, regretful stroke with her fingertips before closing the door.

Edith had gotten her the perfect dress. If only Jane deserved it!

As she left her bedroom, she nearly ran in to Miriam, who had been walking down the hall with an armload of books. The girl shrieked and dropped two of the tomes she carried; Jane startled too, and stammered an apology as she helped pick them up.

"What were you doing in there?" asked Miriam, peering in the open doorway as Smudge strolled out of it, tail high in the air. Jane hadn't known he had been in there with her.

"Cleaning," answered Jane. "Dusting mostly. Making sure all is to rights."

Miriam looked confused. "You don't usually do that, do you?"

Jane shook her head. "No, but . . ."

"But what?"

"Mother hasn't been as interested in chores recently. Surely you've noticed she's been preoccupied with work?"

"Is that why you made dinner last night?"

Jane refrained from adding, "And the night before that, too." Instead she nodded. "Someone had to. I'll cook again tonight."

"Thank you," said Miriam. She meant it sincerely, and Jane appreciated it. She also appreciated it when Miriam offered to do the dishes that evening. After dinner, Nancy had wandered back down to the Library, having neither said nor eaten much.

"Do you think she's ill?" asked Jane, as she wiped the dishes dry. Miriam had insisted that she would be happy to do both washing and drying, but it was actually quite pleasant to work together. It had been a long time since they had.

"She doesn't look sick," said Miriam. "Maybe it's just a project. Remember when she was trying to reorder the fiction titles in the Library? We barely saw her for three months!"

That was true. But then, she'd asked Jane and Miriam to take over a few of her more taxing errands for a while, and had otherwise seemed mostly her normal self. She hadn't just let things slide until someone took over. This was different.

"Perhaps so," said Jane, without much confidence.

Jane's worries left her mind that night when she held one of Smudge's freshly plucked hairs in her candle flame and it burned a brilliant pink—pinker than anything Jane had ever imagined, even after browsing Ambleside's hat shop, or that one fancy candy shop in London with Edith, or even when braving Smudge's ire to mess with the pads of his toes. The flame positively *fizzled* pink, and Jane grabbed Smudge into her arms in glee.

The cat allowed it. Before, he would have thrashed and struggled his way out of her grasp, perhaps giving her a taste of his teeth or claws to remind her that it was not his preference to be cuddled like a baby. His limp, passive body felt almost dead, a weight both familiar and not.

And strangest yet, he was *purring*.

"Well," said Jane, feeling a bit unsettled as she replaced him carefully on the bed, "I guess now we can start collecting your fur."

Using her own nail clippers, Jane trimmed the cat's nails, setting the bits aside in a jar, down to the very last fragments of nail that she was only able to get by pressing the pad of her finger into the wood of her desk. Then she set to brushing him with the fine-toothed comb. It took off a goodly amount of Smudge's fluff, and he sat still for that too, even letting her comb his belly and tail. She collected an impressive pile before stopping, though it was not nearly enough for her needs, of course; it would take many such brushings for that.

That's when Smudge stuck out one gray foot and touched Jane's hand. For the first time since she'd summoned the demon into him, he stuck his claws into her, the points digging, kneading into her flesh — gentle, though surprisingly sharp.

Jane glanced over at the jar, where the tips of Smudge's nails yet lay. She hadn't imagined doing it; she had indeed just clipped them.

Jane took his paw in her fingertips, pressing on the pads. Wicked claws poked out, the points long and bright in the light of her bedroom lamp.

Smudge purred more intensely as Jane gasped aloud in wonder, finally understanding. She could gather more of what she needed to make her liniment! It was a kingly gift, even for a demon like the Connoisseur, known for its generosity.

What she didn't understand was how it was possible.

It was two hours later when Jane stopped her efforts. She'd trimmed her cat's nails several times over, and the volume of fur she'd combed off him would have been impossible for ten Smudges to produce.

She would need to render it into its pure diabolic essence to make use of it, but that would have to wait for another night. Now she was too tired and frankly too disconcerted to attempt anything more complex than undressing and getting into bed.

Jane didn't think she'd be able to sleep, but after turning off the light, she fell into a deep, dreamless, and restful slumber.

19

I NEED TO USE THE LAB TODAY," Jane said over breakfast
the next morning, as Miriam picked at her toast and Nancy
ate nothing at all. Her mother's presence at the table was becoming largely a formality.

"Of course," said Nancy, without looking up. "Have fun, dear."

Have fun, dear was such an odd thing for her to say that even
Miriam looked up from her toast, brow furrowed. It wasn't just
the platitude that seemed unlike her—it was the comfort with
Jane's nonspecificity. Normally, Nancy would ask for clarification
—when and for how long—even if she had no need of the lab.
She typically just liked to know.

"I'll start right after breakfast. I'm not sure how long I'll take,"
Jane volunteered, hoping to provoke a more normal response.

Nancy smiled. "Anything's fine, unless Miriam needs to use it,
of course. You must share."

"I don't need the lab today," said Miriam. She looked as concerned as Jane felt.

"Perfect." Nancy stood. "Have a good day, girls."

"Mother," said Jane, "don't you want any of your breakfast?"

"Oh." Nancy looked in surprise at her untouched plate. Jane
didn't think the cooled eggs looked particularly enticing, but surely
her mother should eat *something*. Nancy was the one who had
drilled into them how important it was not to waste food—ever,
and certainly not with rationing.

"Are you feeling all right?" asked Jane.

"Of course," said Nancy, standing up a bit straighter. "Why do
you ask?"

Jane didn't know what to say, but for once, Miriam stepped up.

"You love breakfast," she said. This was true. "You once said I had to learn to eat more in the mornings if I was going to live in England."

"My mind was on my work, it's true." Jane was relieved to see her mother snap out of her reverie a bit. "And look, I've let these nice eggs get cold. I'm sorry, Jane—how rude of me. Perhaps Smudge would like them? The eggs I mean, I'm not sure if he ought to have bacon."

"He can have the eggs if he wants them," said Jane. "The bacon we'll save for lunch. But what will you have now?"

Nancy set down her book and buttered her toast before wrapping it in a napkin. "I'll take this with me," she said. "And I'll eat it, I promise." She smiled at them both. "How lucky I am to have two girls who look after me. What would I do without you?"

She had obviously meant it kindly, but it struck Jane as ominous. Miriam did too, from her expression. But when Nancy took her leave of them, napkin in one hand and book under her arm, Miriam only said, "I'll get the dishes," and nothing more. Unsure what to think about *that,* Jane thanked her for her help and then went down to the lab.

Jane had rendered diabolic materials down for their essences so many times, she barely had to check her notes about the details— though of course she did, just to be sure.

She also wanted to draw it out a bit. She was enjoying the sensations she was experiencing. She felt good standing in front of the mix of scientific glass and carven wooden boxes before her on the table; the sense of contentment grew when she filled braziers with coals and incense and lit her Bunsen burner. She even caught herself humming as she set two pillowcases stuffed full to bursting with cat hair and a jar packed with nail clippings on the counter.

Smudge leaped up beside them. Jane moved to shoo him only to recall that Smudge would not be twining himself around her equipment or knocking her ingredients to the ground anymore. Indeed, he simply settled himself in a low crouch, elbows and hips poking up above his back, and watched.

Something behind him caught Jane's eye, but it had been such a tiny flutter of motion that it might have been a trick of the light. It had seemed like Smudge's ears had flickered differently on the wall than they had on his head, but that was of course impossible . . .

"All right, Smudge?" she said, and the tip of the cat's tail twitched in response, with an answering, identical twitch from the one cast on the wall. Jane went back to work with a lighter heart.

She wasn't just figuring out how to fly. She was proving there was more than one way to be a diabolist. She lived in a library, but she didn't have to do things by the book.

The fizzing and dripping and crackling and finally the hissing of rendering diabolic essence was music to Jane's ears. She had a little warming pad beneath the metal bowl into which the distillate dropped, and as it evaporated, it left behind the residue she needed for the liniment.

It produced *a lot* of residue — the potency of the hair was absurd. When Jane noticed, she glanced at the cat. He'd settled into a kind of loaf, his feet tucked up under his body, his eyes mere slits. Was it her imagination how pleased he looked with himself, as she used a soft brush to sweep every last bit of rendered essence into an old jam jar? Somehow, Jane didn't think so.

Jane reached out to scratch the cat under his ears and beneath his chin, as Smudge had always liked. The animal accepted the tribute of affection, seeming even more content than usual, nuzzling himself into her hand and prompting her with low yowls of pleasure. Probably the influence of the Connoisseur . . .

Jane wondered about the age of the being inside this cat — how much it had seen, what it had experienced, here, in this world, and in its own. And yet here it was, hedonistically enjoying a chin rub. She felt a chill, thinking about it — but when she withdrew her hand, the cat demanded more attention, and what could she do but oblige?

We're not witches, *Jane.*

And yet, here Jane was, petting her familiar.

Jane turned back to her operation, feeling as smug as Smudge looked at how much diabolic essence she'd accumulated. At this point, she'd soon have sufficient quantity to begin compounding the liniment that would, hopefully, be the method by which she would achieve her cherished dream of soaring through the night sky astride her broom.

20

THE LINIMENT TURNED OUT a bit runnier than Jane had expected, but she thought she could make it work. If it didn't set over the following hours, Jane could just use a brush to paint it all over the broom. It might even work a bit better that way, in the end.

Regardless, she would need to wait before using it. There was dinner to prepare, and the chores she'd put off in favor of work of a different kind. That was for the best, though. While it might already be dark, given the season, Jane wasn't inclined to make her first flying attempt when anyone might still be awake.

If she was successful, of course. An enormous "if," admittedly —but at the same time, Jane was feeling fairly confident. And she had a hunch that Smudge would have done something, interfered in some way, were she completely at angles to the solution. After all, his purpose was to assist her, and he had proven himself not only capable but eager to do so.

Dinner was a rushed affair—a savory cake made with grated winter vegetables. It hadn't turned out too badly, Jane thought. Once again Miriam said she would handle all the clean-up, and Jane made them a cup of Bovril as she did.

"Will you take this one to my mother?" she asked. "I assume you're headed down . . ."

Miriam nodded. "I will. And thank you. I've been a little under the weather recently. This should perk me right up."

Her own steaming mug in hand, Jane went upstairs, where she set to applying layers of salve to the broom with the cleanest of the paintbrushes she'd found in an old coffee can in the shed. The moment she touched bristle to wood, she knew *something* would happen that night. She was cheered by that familiar effervescent sensation—it happened sometimes, for no reason any diabolist had ever adequately explained—but that night she was especially thrilled to feel the energy that seemed to come from changing the natural via extra-natural means.

The salve was absorbed by the wood with unnerving quickness —by the time Jane painted the final twig, the handle was dry. Dry, but not lighter than air. She glared at the broom as it lay heavily in her hands. She hadn't been sure what success would look like, if she managed to achieve it, but she had reasonably assumed she'd be able to perceive some change.

She'd failed. Whatever she'd done to the broom, it wasn't going to fly.

She looked to Smudge. The cat sat on the bed, blinking inscrutably at her.

Jane uttered a wordless, guttural exclamation of frustration as she hurled the offending object across the room. She stalked to her bed and flung herself down upon it in a rage of disappointment and anger, sending Smudge jumping out of her way.

"Meow."

Jane went completely still. Someone was in the room with her —someone who had just said the word *meow*, as if imitating a cat. It was a moment or two before her heart slowed enough for her to be able to sit up and peer over the edge of her bed.

There was only Smudge, and he was sitting beneath her broom. Beneath it, because it was hanging there, right where Jane had thrown it, about three feet off the ground.

Smudge looked even more pleased with himself than usual.

Jane had eyes only for the broom. It was unsettling but also enthralling to behold, but Jane's attention was drawn away from this miracle in part because she was also very concerned about the cat. If indeed it was a cat that sat there, purring happily, almost seeming to smile, his tail lashing back and forth across the floor.

He said, "Meow," again, like a human would when talking to a cat, before jumping up to sit on the bit of the broom where the bristles were tied to the shaft.

It felt like an invitation. Jane took it. Climbing aboard, her skirt tucked up to guard her thighs against splinters, she felt both exhilarated and a bit embarrassed—like a child caught playing make-believe.

She could still stand on her tiptoes astride the broom, and did so for a few moments while working up the courage to lift her feet. Jane wobbled, and then corrected—the required balance was just like and yet nothing like a bicycle's. She lifted one foot, then the other, and then hung there for a few moments before clambering off the broom. Once again her legs failed her and she sank onto her bed.

Smudge hadn't moved. He looked back at her in silence, his long tail now swishing from side to side in the empty air beneath the broom.

"I did it," said Jane, and then it occurred to her that she hadn't, not really.

She'd created a potion of levitation, not of flying.

There were plenty of armamentaria out there for levitation, and some of them less baroque and more efficient than what she'd done.

Jane said a bad word.

The demon Quetzalcóatl's Blood gave its host the power of flight. Real flight, like Peter Pan, with control of velocity, attitude, and so on. It also, however, gave its host an insatiable lust for human flesh, so it was on the "Not to Be Summoned" list. Thankfully, one of the Société's official Botanists cultivated a coffee bush in her garden that had been discovered in the possession of a wild diabolist. Jane had wheedled three small coffee beans out of her, but had been told in no uncertain terms that that was all she would get.

She'd used two and a half to make the salve.

Jane pushed down on the broom. It wouldn't budge. Then she picked it up and placed it somewhere else. There it stuck.

While that was an admittedly neat trick, it wasn't flight.

Smudge stood. Stalking over to where her hand lay upon the wood, he put his paw on her hand.

That time, the broom moved down a bit from the pressure of her hand. Down—and then up, as she willed it.

She *had* done it. She'd figured out how to fly, but she needed Smudge to do it. The cat was the connection she needed to pilot the broom. And that meant the only way to prove that she'd done what she set out to do was to reveal her own unforgivable crime.

Jane laughed aloud. It sounded hysterical, even to her own ears, and it snapped her back to her current situation. She had just figured out how to fly on her very own broomstick, and instead of going for her first flight, she was sitting in her room thinking about how to present her success to others! Surely she'd have plenty of time to come up with *something*.

As for her first flight, there really was no time like the present.

A knock at her door startled Jane. Smudge sprang off the broom and hid under the bed; the connection broken, Jane had to manually set the broom down before she answered the door.

It was Miriam. She looked unhappy.

"What's wrong?" asked Jane. Had Miriam heard her laughing?

"It's Nancy," she said. "I'm worried about her."

"Did something happen?"

Miriam shrugged. "She didn't drink the Bovril."

Jane sensed Miriam was worried about more than just the Bovril.

"I've never seen her like this before," said Miriam.

"I know. I've seen her become absorbed in her work before but haven't seen her *losing* herself in it like this."

"Except she's not doing work," said Miriam. "I don't know what she's doing, but it's not anything to do with the Library. That stack of slips is only growing thicker by the day."

Jane hadn't noticed, but that was indeed highly irregular.

"Maybe it's to do with the war?"

Edith was a spy; perhaps Nancy, too, was involved with some sort of clandestine effort. If it was something *that* important, it might make her less inclined to regulate her time in the Library, or even eat and sleep.

"Maybe," said Miriam. She didn't seem convinced. "But at the same time, it's not like her to just not tell us things."

The two of them still stood — Jane inside the room, Miriam in the hall — with the door ajar just enough for conversation. Jane pointedly hadn't invited Miriam in; she respected Miriam's concerns, and shared them — now just wasn't the time, what with Smudge under the bed and the broom out in the open in her room.

"She's just been so very odd," said Miriam. "She never moves from her desk. It's after eleven now and she's not taken a break. But she doesn't seem like she's doing anything!" Miriam seemed close to tears. "Her desk is *overflowing*, Jane. I can't imagine this can go on much longer. What if someone really needs a book?"

"I'm sure everything's fine," said Jane, though that was not at all true.

On impulse, Jane gave her friend a big hug. Miriam looked utterly miserable. She was really worried — and had been for a while, Jane realized.

Miriam pulled back to dash tears from her eyes. "She just seems so different suddenly. I . . . I *miss* her."

It occurred to Jane that she didn't, not really, except in little sentimental bursts here and there. She had learned it was better not to act on and, if she could help it, not to notice what feelings she had toward Nancy.

"It'll be all right," said Jane, because it was what one said.

"Do you think we should write to—"

"No!"

Miriam looked confused. Jane blushed. It seemed Miriam hadn't meant her father.

"Oh," said Miriam. "I meant Edith might know what we should do."

"You're right," said Jane. "If things get worse, we'll tell Edith."

Miriam relaxed enough to smile. "I'm glad I can always count on you to keep a cool head."

Jane certainly did not know what to say to that, so they stood in awkward silence for a moment. Then Miriam looked down the hall at her door. "I suppose I'll be going, then."

"Good night," said Jane.

Miriam looked surprised, but Jane didn't relent. It wasn't her fault that the night Miriam wanted her company was the one night she couldn't give it to her.

"It's late," said Miriam. "But I suppose we've both been putting in more late nights than usual."

"Maybe not for too much longer, for me," said Jane. She was surprised at herself after she said it. She saw Miriam was, too. It was not like Jane to brag, and they both knew it.

"Oh!" said Miriam. "Congratulations!"

"No—not yet. I mean, I haven't—" She stopped speaking when she saw Miriam crumpling before her eyes.

"I'll leave you to it," said Miriam. "I know how much you want to get out of here."

Jane startled. How could Miriam know what she was up to? Then it hit her—Miriam was talking about Jane finishing her Practical and seeking out an internship, not her imminent flight.

"That's not—"

"I shouldn't have said anything," said Miriam, looking as miserable as Jane had ever seen her. "Good night, Jane." And with that, she disappeared down the hall.

"Good night," said Jane, though Miriam was out of earshot, and shut the door behind herself.

After a moment, Smudge poked his head out from under the bed.

"It's time to leave all this behind," muttered Jane.

The cat nodded in approval.

AFTER WEIGHING THE RISK OF going out the window against that of sneaking down to the back door, Jane elected to use the door. She could explain away sneaking outside, broom in hand—*probably*—but she couldn't really explain why she'd fallen from her window and broken her leg if things didn't go according to plan.

It was a cold night, even though Jane had bundled up with a coat and hat and scarf and mittens and two layers of woolen stockings. As Jane nipped over the frozen lawn for the deeper darkness of the stand of trees beyond the barn, she mentally scolded herself for failing to think through everything, including how cold it would likely be when flying. Next time she would brew up a Winter Warmer, an easy and useful potion that apprentice diabolists were universally assigned because it used the First Transmutation. She could shed a few layers that way, at least—or even go skyclad, if she liked.

We're not witches, *Jane.*

The voice in Jane's mind was always her mother's.

"Speak for yourself," she murmured. "Well, Smudge, what do you say? Just a short flight, to test it out?"

Smudge jumped up on the broom with the same uncanny nimbleness as before. The way his paws seemed to stick to the handle was almost spiderlike.

"Meow," he said.

Jane climbed up behind him, so that he could perch between her knees. When he put his paw on her hand, at her will, the broom rose a few inches in the air.

Her feet were no longer on the ground, and it was even more exhilarating than Jane had dared imagine. She was flying! It was astonishing, but it was true.

Her heart said onward, and the broom followed her will almost before her mind agreed with it.

After a few hair-raising wobbles and one tumble, they were skimming their way over the miles of moonlight-silvered hills and hollows surrounding the outskirts of Hawkshead. At first, Jane was disinclined to fly more than a few feet off the ground, but after she caught the trick of it, she grew bolder. She took them up to a heart-pounding height to see the slowly thawing countryside rolling out beneath them like a map, circling the quaint brick house that belonged to their closest neighbor, Mrs. Fielding, then speeding her way toward the town just to see what it was like to race along familiar paths without worrying about stubbing a toe or slipping in sheep droppings. She spied a raven as it winged its way through the night sky on some errand, and two deer leaped from behind the tree line into the moonlight only to bound back into the safety of the wood when Jane swooped near.

From the air, Hawkshead looked dark and solemn. Only a few lights burned this late in the night — or was it early in the morning? She'd lost track of time, just like she'd promised herself she wouldn't, especially not knowing how long the salve would last.

It was worth it.

She heard the clock tower strike midnight, the twelve peals ringing out across the village like thunderclaps. As they sounded, Jane spiraled up on her broom to survey the village from on high. The witching hour, of course!

That's when Jane saw a flurry of motion from just beyond the wall of the churchyard, two figures racing across a sheep field, away from town.

Jane panicked for a moment. She knew how exposed she was on this clear a night, hanging like a low cloud over the town. She didn't know if staying put or moving was the right choice, but the two people were facing away from her, and they were clearly intent on their own concerns.

Jane knew this was a perfect opportunity to escape, to go home, but her curiosity got the better of her. She wanted to know who was racing away from the churchyard at midnight — and *why*. She slowly circled back down to the ground, like a vulture on a downdraft, and then crept silently closer.

It was a man and a woman, Jane saw, and her stomach felt queasy as she intuited what they were about. A clandestine tête-à-tête was the least interesting thing two people could be up to in the middle of the night — in her opinion at least.

But something about the man's posture — or maybe it was his hair — caught Jane's eye. Her heart fluttered as she stared.

Apparently, Sam was a bit of a lad — taking one girl off to do unknown but certainly unsupervised things together, only to then lure another out into the lonely night not long after!

The lovers were still unaware of Jane where she hovered, peering through the spreading branches of an ancient oak. Blissfully unaware, even — before they ducked into a copse of alders, they paused to kiss and giggle; Sam pinched the girl's bottom as they fled into the privacy of the shadows. Her squeal made Jane startle, it was so piercing in the otherwise silent night, but she kept ahold of her broom.

She was not tempted to investigate further. It was true that a man and a woman might have business together other than the romantic, even at midnight, alone, on a cold early March night, but when bottom-pinching was given and appreciated, it didn't take a genius to perceive their intentions.

Jane briefly toyed with the idea of playing a prank on the happy couple—even just sending Smudge to interrupt their trysting would work. But as Jane formulated a plan in her mind, the broom dropped a few inches.

Oh no, she thought.

She hadn't brought more of the salve. It was time to go.

She made it about halfway back home before the broom gave up and sent her tumbling to the earth, but thankfully she'd thought things through and was skimming over the empty fields only a foot or so above the ground itself. She didn't even twist an ankle when she took her spill.

Smudge, on the other hand, landed nimbly.

As she trudged back to the farmhouse, it finally hit Jane what she'd done. She'd flown, and it had been *incredible.* She couldn't wait to try it again. It had been the most amazing, exhilarating experience of her life, perfect in every way.

Maybe not in *every* way. As Jane approached the farmhouse, she saw a light was on in Miriam's window. Seeing Sam's infidelity had been a blemish, that was true. And come to think of it, so had been the revelation that she would never be able to share her success with anyone. At least not the full measure of it.

No one would ever know what she'd achieved. It would do nothing to protect her from the scrutiny of her peers.

But then again, maybe that didn't matter. After all, if they came for her, she could always just fly away.

"Just you and me, eh?" said Jane affectionately, reaching down to scratch the cat behind the ears. That's when she noticed his bell had yet again fallen off. Perhaps it had been during their hard landing. "We'll get you a new one tomorrow, I suppose."

"Meow," said Smudge.

21

THE DAGGERS OF SUNSHINE THAT stabbed through the pine boughs of the forest beyond the walls of the Nazi facility did nothing to warm up the sight of Miriam's father's corpse. His half-decomposed body remained a grim sight, the bones yellow in the winter daylight. Miriam could see a bit more of her father's clothing now, too. The rough-spun, threadbare garment had clearly been issued to him, rather than self-selected. There was a tattered, faded patch with the same insignia she'd seen on the gates — the stylized, angular blossom within a halo of some sort, in Nazi black and red.

The bird to which Miriam had cleaved was the perching and twittering kind. To her surprise, it had been much more difficult to control than the fox or even the owl. All this bird wanted to do was to tell the world that spring was on its way and that it was ready for a mate — not go inspect a dead body or fly to a place full of men. But after a longer-than-expected struggle, Miriam won out over the bird's will, and so off they went.

Miriam had decided her goal with this journey was reconnaissance. She flew hither and yon, trying to learn anything of interest. The few prisoners she saw knew nothing, and she could not bear to look upon their gaunt faces or listen to their ragged steps for long; it had been the well-fed, well-groomed officers, loathsome in their smart uniforms, who had yielded all the worthwhile information Miriam gleaned. From them she learned the location of the kitchens, the barracks, and the medical and scientific facility, which was the main focus of the operation. But it wasn't until she caught sight of an unhappy-looking officer with a file folder under his arm that bore the same insignia from her father's uniform that she really started to get somewhere.

Miriam flitted after him. A nurse sat at a desk just inside the door, and Miriam had a moment of panic—how would she get inside without being noticed? But her target unwittingly provided the answer by barking a question at the woman, distracting her enough that she did not notice the bird swooping in silently after him.

The man had asked for a Dr. Karl Querner—at least, Miriam thought that was the name. The officer was from Alsace, and his accent was thick.

"Ah, yes, Rottenführer," the nurse said. "We have been expecting you. The Dark Lab is that way," she said, pointing the officer toward an unmarked staircase going down, "but Dr. Querner is in the middle of an experiment; he doesn't wish to be disturbed!"

The officer brightened momentarily to have his rank called out, but that didn't stop his shoulders from slumping as he said, "I have my orders," in a grim manner before marching off in the direction of the stairs.

Miriam had no idea what the Dark Lab was, but in spite of her curiosity, she didn't follow the officer. She'd be too easily spotted in her current form. But while exploring the facility, she *had* seen a nest of paper wasps in an attic, for next time. That would be much better camouflage for her, though it would be an inconvenience to only be able to see and not hear.

Not wanting to abandon her songbird indoors, Miriam waited to see if the door would open again, allowing her to make her escape. As she perched on her beam, Miriam watched as a second nurse stopped by the desk. She asked after an officer.

"I'm sorry," said the first. "We thought he had a chance when the fall didn't kill him, but infection in his skull took hold. The claws of whatever attacked him must have been very dirty."

Miriam lost control of the bird and felt herself returning to her body. Surely they must be speaking of the guard she herself had attacked when she'd been inside the owl . . .

She had, apparently, killed a man. Murdered him—and yet she felt nothing.

No remorse.

No joy.

Miriam's shadow-self, that dark being deep within her that gladly claimed her anger and rage, agreed with her.

What was done was done.

The next morning, Miriam was ravenous. Jane had prepared a hearty fruit- and nut-laced oatmeal that was just what she needed. Miriam scraped her bowl clean—and even better, she and Jane managed to cajole Nancy into eating most of the portion she'd been served, which cheered both girls.

Once her stomach was full, Miriam mulled over the mysteries she'd left behind—the Dark Lab, Dr. Karl Querner, and more. She decided she would risk another attempt that afternoon. Though it had only been a short sleep since her last trip, she was feeling fairly lively. And while it was true that *Badgerskin* had cautioned her against doing exactly what she was thinking of doing, Miriam did not want to let the trail go cold. So, after breakfast, Miriam sidled down to the Library to raid the storeroom once again for liquid diabolic essence.

There wasn't a lot left. She hadn't been the only one raiding the supply closet. Jane's project must need quite a lot . . .

She helped herself to a few bottles. If she was going to make any progress, she'd need to be bold.

Bold enough to cut deeper into her spirit, slice more of it away so that she could better control her hosts. Bold enough to venture down those shadowed stairs to see the Dark Lab of Dr. Querner. Bold enough to endure learning what happened to her father.

She would be bold. As to whether fortune would favor her, that she could not predict.

THE PAPER WASPS WERE AWAKE.

Miriam had been afraid they would be hibernating. The real challenge, however, proved to be figuring out how to jump out of the bird she had guided to the attic where they dwelt and not get immediately eaten the moment she left its body behind. That had been a serious miscalculation — Miriam had only considered the bird's greater wingspan when she'd selected it, not its diet, and the first wasp she jumped into almost instantly ended up in her former host's beak.

She had to make a quick second leap to escape death — both the wasp's and her own.

Badgerskin had been quite clear about what would happen if a host creature died while the diabolist was inside of it. So she zipped to the door and crawled under it, away from the bird, and then down, down, down, keeping clear of anyone who might try to swat her.

Grateful the wasp did not resist her much, Miriam crawled on the ceiling past the nurses to draw as little attention as possible, then descended the yawning stairwell where the officer had gone.

At the bottom of the stairs, she encountered a steel door shut tight against intruders. There was no gap under it, as in the room above — but there was a keyhole, and it was just wide enough for her to wriggle through.

When Miriam emerged, she beheld a square, windowless room lit by oddly bright, very white electric bulbs that made everything look strange and sickly. In the center of the room was a metal desk that had a stark and cold look to it. It was covered in loose papers as well as folders and packets of more papers. At this desk sat a fair, lean, unwholesome-looking man with circular gold-framed spectacles. He was reading what looked like some kind of report or dossier. He seemed haunted, desperate as his bright blue eyes scanned the paper before him.

His wrinkled shirt also told a story—the fine cut of it coupled with the excellent quality of the jacket he'd slung over the back of his chair showed he was not usually so rumpled and harried.

It was not a Nazi uniform jacket. It was a suit jacket, such as a professional might wear, but around one sleeve was the telltale armband that made Miriam buzz her wings in anger.

In addition to the door she'd come through, there were three others, one on either side of the man's desk and one on the far wall. Also on the far wall were cages with a veritable menagerie inside of them—a rabbit; some mice and rats; and a lithe, long creature with a sleek pelt, either an otter or a marten. All seemed dejected and defeated; the fight had long since gone out of them.

Miriam felt the door move beneath all six of her legs; she buzzed away to a dark corner as a robust sandy-haired woman in a starched nurse's uniform appeared.

She was wearing a cattle prod at her waist.

The man—perhaps the aforementioned Dr. Querner—looked up but didn't smile. He rubbed at his temple and said something. Miriam felt the vibration but could not interpret the sensation as words through her antennae.

Miriam was frustrated by the limitations of the wasp. These two seemed on intimate terms, from their posture and manner as they spoke to one another. The wasp body had gotten her down here, but it was failing her now that she needed information.

Miriam selected a mouse from the cages on the wall. It was so downtrodden, it didn't flinch as the wasp came near it. Once she'd cleaved to the mouse, the small creature's acute hearing served her well and she began to listen in.

"—wasn't reckless," said the man. "I knew Wolfram Braune

personally; he's the last person in the world I'd accuse of *reckless-ness,* and yet they're saying this was entirely his fault."

"How could it be his fault?"

"Ach, who knows?" Dr. Querner gave the woman a rueful smile. "These days, everyone is looking for someone to blame, are they not?"

"That is sadly true," said the nurse. "I met Dr. Braune once, long ago. I was sorry to hear of his death."

"And all his test subjects! It is *terrible,* Franzi. And it couldn't come at a worse time." The doctor rubbed his fair temples. "I had hoped that together Wolfram and I could make a difference." He sighed. "I am glad they thought to send me his notes. It seems he recently gained some insights that may help with my next experiment on the Hunter sisters."

Nurse Franzi's plain face contorted into a sneer. "Even if you are unable to extract any specific diabolic essence from those little whores tomorrow, I am still grateful they are imprisoned here where they can do no further harm."

"I fear ultimately for the worst, no matter what happens," said Dr. Querner.

Miriam burned to know what on earth they were discussing. Extracting general diabolic essence from an animal subject was one thing, but specific essence? That was supposed to be impossible.

"It is not yet too late," said Franzi. "There is always something that can be done."

"Your faith is touching. I, too, hope so. At least we are doing all we can. And really, even if we lose, we have helped cleanse the world of many of its stains. That must be a comfort to us."

"Have faith in yourself," said the nurse. "You are the finest diabolist I have ever known. The Fatherland could be in no better hands. But of course I don't mean to put it all on your shoulders, Dr. Querner—only to express my confidence in your ability."

"I hope it is not misplaced," he replied. "I would have said the same of Wolfram, once, and look what happened to him."

The nurse turned to go, but Miriam was not ready for their conversation to end. Whatever Querner was up to, he thought there was still a possibility of success, however remote.

She had to know more. She had no time to hesitate, no time to think it through. This is why she'd screwed up her courage, using the veil knife to slice away her spiritual body's entire left ear. If she was brave enough to do that, she was brave enough to be like Jane and *act*.

And so Miriam—in spite of what she'd read in *Badgerskin*—left her mouse body behind and cleaved to the nurse's.

As she struggled to take possession of the nurse as she had the mouse, and the wasp, and the rest, Miriam felt a horror at herself that she never had before. With the animals, she had been able to deny what she was doing. With Nurse Franzi, there was no escaping the reality of her act. She had become a dybbuk, a possessing spirit sticking to someone else's body.

She knew she didn't have much time. She'd been away from her own body too long. But she could not squander this opportunity. Only by accident had she found this place at all, much less returned when Querner himself was present and talking.

Franzi turned back to the doctor, as was Miriam's will.

"Have you been able to find out any more about what happened to Dr. Braune?" she asked.

"What's that?" it was almost as if Dr. Querner had forgotten the nurse's presence the moment she'd turned away from him. "Oh, of course. You wouldn't have heard. Or, wait—didn't *you* tell *me* that you'd heard the disaster was due to a kind of rescue attempt?"

Miriam thought fast. "I might have told you they suspected it, but I didn't know it had been confirmed."

Querner looked puzzled, then shook his head. "In any case, they—members of the Société des Éclairées, those degenerates—

knew the location of Braune's lab. That's what he gets for setting up in a castle, I suppose. What a nightmare, and embarrassing—it seems the party was led by an African savage who had apparently divined a way to apply cosmetics that would change her appearance more dramatically than rouge and lipstick ordinarily can. She died, along with the rest, under the lamps."

If there was anything that ought to be described as "savage," it was Dr. Querner's dispassionate tone as he recounted these horrors. Miriam stared at him in absolute terror, torn between grief— for who else could it be but her poor aunt Edith to whom Querner referred—and a fear-fueled curiosity that made her ask, *"Lamps?"*

Querner nodded. "Yes, a special lamp designed by Braune himself. We have them too," he pointed at the very bright bulbs. "They combust diabolic matter when they come into contact with an otherwise harmless gas. Both laboratories were equipped with them just in case things went very wrong."

"What a tragic loss of life," said Miriam, and decided to take a risk. "But of course we have also had our setbacks. Egon Cantor . . ."

Dr. Querner nodded. "Ah, yes. I regret my haste with that one; he was a valuable test subject. I should have waited until I'd heard from Braune about the effectiveness of the crystal. I say, Franzi, are you feeling quite well?"

Miriam nodded to buy herself time. She had to set aside any feelings until she was done with the nurse. "I heard he was married to a German woman."

"Oh, yes. Quite shocking, don't you think?"

"Disgusting," said Miriam. "Was she also a diabolist?"

"Yes, she was one of Braune's test subjects. She died months before the rescue attempt." Querner took off his glasses to stare at her keenly. "Why do you ask?"

Miriam panicked, her mind whirling in two directions. Her mother—also dead!

"Franzi?"

"What if they attack us, too?" she said. "The Société, I mean."

"Ah," said Dr. Querner. "I see. Rest easy, my dear. I sincerely doubt the Société has enough resources for another strike like that —and, anyway, if my experiment on the Hunter sisters tomorrow does not yield results, we won't have to worry! The war will be over soon enough, and we'll all be dead or on trial for our crimes. Just keep that in mind—I do. I find it helps me relax."

"Thank you, doctor," said Miriam, and then happily left, shutting the door behind her at Querner's bidding. After it was shut, she waited for a moment, then ran all the way to the first landing of the stairs before realizing she could flee much farther, and more quickly, if she simply returned to her own body.

Leaving behind the nurse felt like inhaling after holding her breath for too long. It was such a relief to be back in her own skin that at first Miriam didn't realize how depleted she felt.

Too soon it hit her. She'd had influenza once—this was far, far worse. Then, her skin had ached; now, it was as if every scrap of clothing she wore was flaying her when she made even the slightest movement. Yet she *had* to move—because sitting upon her chair was too painful to endure for more than a few moments. She felt the bite of the wood into her flesh. At least her stomach seemed to be all right—she'd been careful after that first attempt to never eat while spiritually abroad.

Her arm shook as she set down the mirror, flat, so the bowl could safely materialize at its leisure. Inside her skin, she felt her aching muscles; she was even aware of her bones and joints. In that moment, Miriam understood what it meant to be frail.

She had to keep her hand on the wall to steady herself, but eventually she managed to reach her bed and collapsed onto it. Shedding her clothes, or even her shoes or her cardigan, was beyond her power, as was getting under the covers. She fell asleep immediately.

By the time she woke, it was evening. She still felt bone-tired, but she could sit up without her eyes sliding out of focus. She was also extremely hungry.

Jane would likely be cooking at this hour, but Miriam wondered if she might be able to snag a bite of something before everything was ready. To that end, she straightened her clothes as best she could and ran her fingers through her hair. She still felt a bit groggy, however, so she went to the bathroom to splash some water on her face.

When she peered into the looking glass after drying her face with a towel, Miriam gasped. Someone else had been in the mirror looking out at her. But that was impossible . . . Heart pounding, Miriam looked again—and found it difficult to breathe at all.

While it was true that the mirror in the upstairs bathroom was more functional than flattering, there was very obviously something wrong with Miriam beyond the smeary nature of her reflection. She did not look like herself—or, rather, she appeared as if she'd been in bed for far longer than an afternoon, and stricken with a very serious ailment. Her eyes looked unhealthy, clouded, and beneath them were gray hollows that held shadows and secrets. Her lips were thinner, and likewise her skin had a waxy appearance to it—and when she leaned in closer, she spied several white hairs sprouting from the crown of her head.

Badgerskin had warned her. The body did not like to be separated from its soul. As Miriam looked at herself, she finally understood. Before, it had all seemed a bit vague, just hints of what might happen. A little accelerated aging didn't seem so bad when it was all words on the page. Now, however, the stakes were laid bare—and it was time to make a choice.

Her parents were dead. It troubled Miriam that they had died as prisoners—*victims*. Neither heroes nor traitors. Not that it mattered. They were dead just the same.

She had the answers she'd set out to get. The choice was whether or not she would go back for other reasons.

She still wasn't sure what Dr. Querner was trying to do, but he was trying to do something. Something big. It would be unconscionable to do nothing; she had to act, and quickly. Delaying long enough even to tell the Société might mean ruin.

She had to go back. As Miriam looked at herself in the mirror, she knew she wouldn't be able to forgive herself if her weakness resulted in catastrophe—but she also knew she did not possess the power at the moment to control so much as an ant. She could barely find enough will to haul herself downstairs for dinner.

But she had to eat. Her body was screaming with hunger. After wrapping a scarf around her head to obscure her newly graying hair, she headed downstairs. She would claim to have a cold, so neither Jane nor Nancy would look at her too keenly.

Miriam padded into the kitchen, drawn by a savory smell. Nancy was staring off into space; she barely said hello. When Jane turned around, her expression went from neutral to outright alarmed. Miriam's heart sank. She would not escape this meal unquestioned.

"There you are at last," Jane said brightly. "Dinner's almost ready!"

Miriam went over to the pot of stew and sniffed with genuine enthusiasm.

"Smells great," she said.

Miriam tucked in as soon as her bowl was cool enough. She'd never tasted anything so exquisite, not even the first supper she'd eaten on English soil after crossing the channel. Jane's stew had a succulence to it that Miriam suspected might have been lost on her had she been less hungry. She didn't care; indeed, she got herself a second helping before Jane had finished her first and before Nancy had even picked out a few morsels of mutton.

The questioning came after Nancy toddled off. Miriam set to

work washing the dishes, even if she wished she could save them until tomorrow.

Jane hung around, tidying things that were not hers to tidy. Miriam let her, coming up with a few replies to such questions that she thought Jane might ask: just a cold, didn't sleep well last night and napped too long; no, nothing's wrong. But when Jane finally worked up the nerve to sidle up to the counter and speak, she didn't say at all what Miriam expected her to.

"So . . ." Jane seemed uncomfortable. "How are you, Miriam?"

"I'm a bit tired," said Miriam, telling the truth. "A long day of research."

"Research." Jane didn't sound impressed. "Is that all?"

Miriam turned to Jane, resigned to discussing her appearance. She'd been a fool to think she could hide something like this. "Say what you have to say."

Jane hesitated before once again saying something Miriam did not anticipate: "I went into town today when you were in your room. I ran into Sam."

Miriam said nothing for a moment as she collected her scattered thoughts. She had put Sam out of her mind entirely after that afternoon. He was irrelevant, an indistinct background figure in the larger picture of her life. His rudeness to her was unfortunate, but people were *dying*—and more would perish if she didn't concentrate on thwarting Querner.

"I'm so sorry. I thought he was better than that," said Jane, when the silence stretched into an awkward length.

"Better than what?" asked Miriam.

"That he wouldn't see you as . . ." Jane looked nervous. "For shuttering his heart against you just because you—you're . . ."

"I'm what?" said Miriam. She knew none of this was Jane's fault, but at the same time none of it was Jane's business, either. Miriam was tired, and she was cranky, and she was rapidly becoming angry. She'd heard enough about who was who and what was what today.

Jane was blushing mightily.

The strain got to Miriam a bit in that moment. "Say it," she demanded, raising her voice a little. "Don't be a coward, Jane. Say what you're thinking."

"Miriam . . ."

"Say it!"

"Because you're Jewish," whispered Jane.

"Only because you and everyone else have decided that!"

Miriam hadn't meant to snarl this truth that was also a lie, but snarl she did. All the frustration she'd felt for years—all the rage that had been simmering, it suddenly boiled over as she spat this at her best friend.

She was angry that Jane couldn't understand, that *none* of them could understand what it meant to be caught in the strange middle space of not being Jewish at all in the eyes of other Jews, but still Jewish enough to be sent to a camp and gassed with the rest. They could not perceive the strain of living with that nagging sense of having nowhere in the world she truly belonged, no people who would claim her. Jane, Sam, everyone else—*they* thought it was easy to put her in a box, whereas Miriam constantly felt like she had been chopped to pieces and packed away into a million crates.

"You girls have a good night."

Nancy stood in the doorway of the kitchen, serene and beatific. If she hadn't yet gone downstairs to read and ponder, she must have heard Miriam, loud as she had been. Yet here she was, smiling as if nothing had happened.

"Don't stay up too late," she said, like any other mother might.

The thing was, Nancy was not every other mother.

"We won't," said the girls, in unison.

Satisfied, Nancy headed for the Library, leaving them with yet another long and painful silence that neither Miriam nor Jane knew how to fill.

22

AFTER HER LATE NIGHT OF trying out her new broom for the first time, Jane was glad that Miriam elected to spend her day quietly in her own room, locked away doing whatever she was doing behind her closed door. She, too, was in need of rest and quiet. It wasn't just the exhaustion of being up too late, either—her arms and shoulders were surprisingly sore, and her bottom ached where the wood of the broom had chafed her. She also was horrified to find a bit of windburn on her cheeks. Jane hadn't thought about that; she'd have to prepare accordingly for future flights.

And there would be future flights. Sore arms and bottom be damned—the pain only added to her pleasure, every ache a fond memory of the euphoric sensations she had experienced the night before.

Jane would *never* give up her broom, not now. Given her familiar's role in the matter, that meant never giving up Smudge, either. But Jane felt increasingly more comfortable with that idea.

Yes, she missed Smudge or, rather, the way Smudge used to be —she'd adored that cat, nuisance though he had surely been. But Smudge as he was now was undeniably more *useful*. And friendly. And he also let her sleep all the way through the night without waking her up for no reason beyond that he was bored.

Being tired always made Jane snappish and fumble-brained, so she had decided to walk into the village rather than attempt any of the more intellectual work she had waiting. And it was a thoroughly decent day, for early March at least, and they needed some items from the grocer's.

Smudge came along with Jane, surprising her. While he had

always enjoyed patrolling the grounds around the farmhouse, to her knowledge he'd never expressed any interest in the world beyond the tumbledown fence that encircled their property. Today, however, he ran out the gate in front of her, tail held triumphantly high. Jane had a momentary impulse to grab him by the scruff and hurl him back inside their property, but then she remembered he wasn't really a cat anymore. She didn't need to protect him.

"I bet you have talents you haven't yet revealed to me," Jane said, as they trudged across the muddy countryside.

"Meow," agreed Smudge.

This response reminded Jane that she was headed into a populated area. At first, Jane walked on, grinning as she contemplated how annoyed her mother would be by the idea of her waltzing into Hawkshead with her familiar in tow. *We're not witches,* indeed!

But then Jane started to think on just how truly bizarre it would appear to the residents of the village to see her accompanied by a cat that obeyed her every command. Jane wanted to *stand out;* she didn't wish to be a spectacle.

"Smudge," she said, as they padded ever onward, "you must stay out of sight while I'm in town."

"Meow," he said, in an agreeable tone. But Jane wanted more.

"I mean it," she said as they rambled onward. "I told you my mother would be extremely upset to learn of you and your existence. That goes double—no, *triple*—for the people of our little village. I can't say it strongly enough. No one must know—or even suspect—that you exist."

"Meow," said Smudge, in a tone that said *I know* as clearly as if he had articulated it.

"All right," said Jane. "I like having you here with me . . . I just worry."

"Meow," said Smudge, and that was the end of it.

The cat was as good as his word, keeping out of sight as Jane visited the grocer's and then the milliner's. He was there—every minute she spent shopping, every moment she talked to each acquaintance. But she would have known that, even if she hadn't seen the tip of his gray tail as he scooted across a windowsill, or recognized him as he sat nonchalantly in the doorway of the Queen's Head. She'd always been aware of her cat, but now she felt his presence in a way she never had before.

Smudge was lurking just out of sight beyond a low stone wall when Jane ran into Sam Nibley as he stepped out of the forge to get some air. She hadn't meant to be anywhere near him, but Hawkshead was a small village.

She blushed, annoyed by his disloyalty to Miriam and her own behavior the day he'd delivered the mirror; for his part, he flinched and looked the other way when he noticed her.

No, that would not do. Jane walked over to him, with the intention to apologize.

And, if possible, to instigate a conversation where she could fish for information about what business Sam had been conducting so late at night, in the woods, with someone other than Miriam.

"Sam," said Jane, "I'd like to apologize. The last time I saw you, I wasn't myself. Do forgive me."

Sam turned around. "Oh," he said, seeming surprised, "it's all right."

"Thank you," she said, and then made her gamble: "I ought to be getting back. My mother and Miriam will be expecting me."

Sam blushed a little at the mention of Miriam's name; Jane raised her eyebrows at him.

"So, you two . . ." she said, affecting as warm of a conspiratorial tone.

"Us two?" Sam suddenly looked annoyed rather than sheepish. "What *us two* is this?"

"Oh," said Jane, surprised. "I just assumed . . ."

"She's not interested in me!" Jane was shocked by this statement. *Of course* Miriam was interested in Sam! She couldn't imagine what might have happened between them to give him such a strangely inaccurate impression. "Or at least what I can offer her."

Offer her?

Had Sam proposed marriage? Had Miriam rejected him?

Jane wasn't sure how to proceed. On one hand, it might seem odd to Sam that Jane was unaware of whatever was happening, but perhaps she could also use that to her advantage.

"I'm astonished," she said. "Miriam said nothing about a quarrel between you two!"

"She didn't?" Sam, too, was surprised, but there was something else there, some other emotion Jane could not interpret.

"Maybe she is hopeful you two will reconcile?"

"I'd be surprised," said Sam wryly. "I'm not sure what could possibly change, after all. If she can't understand that I can't give her the life she's dreaming of, what else is there to say?"

The life she's dreaming of . . . Jane was running out of ways to describe her feelings of bewilderment. It sounded to her like this was over money! But that didn't seem like Miriam. What could she need so badly that she would dismiss Sam from her life for not being able to provide it? It was beyond Jane's ability to imagine.

"I'm very sorry to hear it," said Jane.

"So was I," said Sam. "But she is who she is, and I am who I am, and we just have to accept that, I suppose."

"I suppose," said Jane.

"Why do you ask, though?" asked Sam.

"Excuse me?"

"Why are you asking me about Miriam?"

Sam took a step closer. It wasn't the most familiar thing he could have done, but it alarmed her just the same. Something about his body language, the way he closed a little of the distance between them—it implied there was something conspiratorial between them, or that he would like there to be.

Jane shrugged. "Sometimes it's hard to accept that I am who I am, and she is who she is," she said, echoing Sam's earlier remark.

"You have no idea how much I wish things were different. You of all people must understand that," said Sam, stepping even closer. "You live with her. There's just something *different* about her—about them."

"Them?" Jane had thought they were speaking of Miriam's personality—the things that made her unique, and at times uniquely frustrating. Now she realized they were having a very different conversation than she had assumed, and she felt horrified to have participated in it for even a moment.

"You know what I mean. They're different from us."

"*They* still rise with the sun and go to sleep beneath the moon. *They* still eat meals together at the beginning, middle, and end of the day. *They* still are born, grow up, get married, have children, and—"

"Jane, they *want* to be different. They hold themselves apart. I'm not saying the Boche are right to be doing what they're doing. I'm all for leaving them in peace. Within reason. They shouldn't be allowed to cheat and swindle anyone, but neither should anyone else of course. It's just that they—"

"I've heard enough," said Jane giving him an absolutely disgusted look. "You should be ashamed of yourself, Sam Nibley—talking like this. *They*"—she drew the word out to shame him—"are no different. Any lines that might exist get blurred all the time," she said, thinking of Miriam's parents; her anxieties over her Jewishness. "You're just a bigot, and I think I can perceive what you really meant when you said you can't give her *a life*."

"I was honest with her," said Sam sourly.

Jane looked down her nose at him and said, "I'm sure you were."

And with that she took her leave of Sam, beginning her journey home not along the road, but the long way, through the gates of the sheep fields beyond the town. She needed to be alone with her thoughts.

SHE WAS NOT ALONE for long. Smudge rejoined Jane as she shut the second gate behind her, leaping onto the wooden beam of the fence as she passed it by. Jane shrieked, and then scolded the cat as he sat there looking pleased with himself.

In the heat of the moment, Jane had forgotten Smudge — but Smudge did not forget, of course. He couldn't; he had to stick close to her. She'd put that in the summoning, though she wondered now what a demon's definition of "close" might be. She should have defined that better . . .

That's when she noticed Smudge's paws weren't muddy.

Her own boots were in a shocking state, for the road to Hawkshead had been wet and unpleasant. Now, heading home the long way round, she would really have her work cut out for her when she sat down to clean them.

Where had Smudge been, she wondered, that his paws had stayed so tidy?

These thoughts unsettled her, drawing her mind away from what had happened with Sam. She began to rethink Smudge's summoning as she hauled her groceries up and over the hills, thinking over any other instances of nonspecific language. Of course, time had worn smooth the edges of her memory; without the transcript in front of her, she couldn't quite be certain she'd done everything else correctly. But neither could she stop worrying about it, and whether it had anything to do with the pristine state of Smudge's paws, all the way home.

The house was just as quiet as when she'd left it, so Jane dropped off her groceries and hustled upstairs to look over her notes from when she'd bound the Ceaseless Connoisseur to her cat. Other than the possible imprecision of "close" as a descriptor, the language still seemed fairly iron-clad to her.

Smudge was sworn to come when she called and remain "close" to her at all times. Surely even a demon could not find any sort of sinister loophole in *that*. And in any case, Smudge wasn't malicious. He'd proven himself to be loyal and helpful more than once.

"All right, Smudge?" she asked. The cat was once again right by her feet.

"Meow," he answered.

If only conversations with Miriam could be so predictable.

While chopping, Jane mulled over whether she ought to tell her friend she'd talked to Sam. It was a delicate situation. It was true that Miriam had asked her to be a listening ear the other evening, but it hadn't been regarding her thoughts about Sam; no, it had been about Nancy's strange behavior.

When the potatoes turned golden in the butter and the carrots had sufficiently softened, Jane tossed them into the stew pot with the browned beef. She was proud of how her cooking had improved, and didn't mind doing it as much as she'd thought she might. After all, when she was on her own one day, a cosmopolitan young woman living abroad, she would need to cook for herself occasionally—or for a guest. Several films she'd seen at the theatre in Ambleside had given her that impression anyway.

The sound of Miriam's tread on the step brought Jane out of these thoughts, and she turned without knowing what she'd end up saying about Sam. That's when she caught sight of Miriam, and only her study of the uncanny poise of the great actresses she so idolized saved her from gasping.

Jane had never been so frightened in her life, looking at Miriam. Her arms and the back of her neck prickled as the hairs rose, and her limbs seemed to freeze where they were. She fought for control and when she got it, she smiled and turned back to stir the stew as if nothing had happened.

"There you are at last!" she managed to say. "Dinner's almost ready."

Whatever her friend had been doing up in her room that day, it had changed her physically; but looking at Miriam, Jane got the sense she had likely been altered in other, less perceivable ways. She was obviously the same person, but she did not look at all like herself.

Jane sneaked another glance. It wasn't necessarily that Miriam appeared older, though some gray hairs peeked out of a sort of head wrap Miriam had attempted in order to conceal the shocking change. It was more as if Miriam had *withered*. The petals of the freshest bloom would fall if left without water, and that's what Miriam looked like.

It had to have been something diabolic—some experiment gone wrong. But what could Miriam have done that would result in such terrible consequences? She was little more than an apprentice!

Jane's eyes slid to Smudge. Being "little more than an apprentice" didn't mean so very much, it seemed.

"Smells great," said Miriam, sliding into her chair.

"Thank you, I'm glad," said Jane automatically.

It was obvious from her scarf that Miriam did not wish to have her appearance remarked upon, and that was just fine by Jane. She could scarcely look at her friend without feeling a shuddering sense of horror, much less talk to her, and given that Nancy was in the room, there was no question of bringing it up.

But later, after her mother had departed and Miriam was wiping the plates, Jane forced herself to conquer her fear and broach the subject. But she found even just approaching the topic taxed her considerably.

"So . . ." she said. "How are you, Miriam?"

"A bit tired" was Miriam's answer, as if that explained her appearance — but even her voice sounded wrong; there was a rattle in her chest, as if every word came from deep within her.

Looking at Miriam was like staring at a terrible wound, or a dying person. The sensation her visage evoked in Jane was *fear,* plain and simple — the deepest and most profound fear of them all: the sight of a yawning grave.

Jane tried to make a little small talk, but she could not bring herself to ask what Miriam had done that had caused this to happen to her. She wanted desperately to know, but she also was too afraid to ask. What if Miriam had been doing something even more forbidden than summoning a familiar?

The Société also forbade many other acts, including one that outsiders might call *necromancy;* the dead were the dead, and no good ever came of trying to bring them back. If Miriam was trifling with something like *that . . .*

Jane's mouth had been making sounds that were something like conversation, but Miriam had clearly noticed her fumbling. Jane panicked, knowing she had to come up with some reason to have begun the conversation in the first place.

"Say what you have to say," said Miriam.

"I went into town today when you were in your room. I ran into Sam." She blurted it out inelegantly. Miriam's expression shifted from suspicious to annoyed as Jane went on. "I'm so sorry. I thought he was better than that."

She trailed off when it became obvious that Miriam wasn't upset, she was angry. *Furious.* While she might appear weak and sickly, there was still fire burning deep inside her, fire that came out and burned Jane as they quarreled.

Only when Jane's mother toddled into the kitchen to woozily wish them a good night was Jane given a moment to recover her wits. Truly, the conversation could not have gone worse; she had

had the best of intentions going in, but now everything was ruined. Whatever impulse had sent Miriam upstairs to knock on Jane's door and seek her confidence the other night would not manifest again.

"It wasn't your place to talk to Sam," said Miriam. "About me," she added when Jane opened her mouth to protest. "Who I am is my business, and your opinions about it—your and Sam's opinions—don't matter. They don't matter at all! So talk to him about whatever you like—just leave me out of it!"

"I don't want to talk to him ever again," said Jane. "Sam and I are not friends, Miriam. If he hadn't come out of the forge when I was standing in the lane, I doubt he would have spoken to me at all. And I know I wouldn't have stopped him in the street for love or money."

"You needn't give him the cut direct on *my* account," said Miriam, in such a lofty, superior manner that Jane had to give her credit; she filed away Miriam's posture, tone, and turn of phrase to use at some later date. "Things could never work out between us, and we both know it."

"But it's unfair," argued Jane.

"How?" Miriam scoffed at her a little, and for the first time Jane understood how Miriam must feel when Jane was channeling her inner Joan Crawford. "Men and women reject lovers all the time, and for any number of reasons, personal or otherwise. We did not suit one another, that's all."

"But the reason for it . . ." Jane didn't understand why Miriam wasn't more annoyed about Sam's obvious and despicable bigotry. "That's something a little different, don't you think?"

"Not really," said Miriam. She almost growled this, and Jane took a step back. "It's just like anything else—say, taste in music, or ideas about politics."

"I disagree," said Jane, "especially if . . . I mean if *you* don't think you're . . . why should *he* care?"

"It's not a dirty word!"

"I know it's not." Jane was pleading with her friend now. She was so worried about Miriam—how could anyone not be!—and she was completely and utterly destroying any chance she might have of helping her. "Miriam—*please*. I know I've misunderstood things before, with your faith—upbringing—whatever you want to call it . . . but what you've told me—"

"My *upbringing* was to be a diabolist, same as you," said Miriam coldly. "That's what we were, first and foremost. The Art was our everything. I was taught the Seven Elements rhyme and the mnemonic device for the Diabolic Bases and Diabolic Acids along with the Kiddush and the Lord's Prayer."

"Exactly," said Jane. "That's my point! I don't know what Sam said to you, and I certainly didn't mean to rub it in, if I did. I just hated to hear he was so rude and unkind. And before you say a word, there's no polite, kind way to voice sentiments such as the ones he holds."

"It doesn't matter," said Miriam. "Honestly, Jane. It's the least important thing in the entire *world* right now."

"What's the most important thing, then?" Jane didn't clarify her remarks—Miriam knew exactly what she meant. "What's so important that you'd—" Miriam finally looked up, and Jane had to stop herself from shrinking back.

"Don't ask me that." Miriam was slouching into herself even more now. "Don't ask me because if you do, I'll tell you, and if I tell you, you'll try to make me stop, and I can't. Not yet. I can stop soon, but not before I do *something*, or at least try to do it."

What could Jane say except "Okay." So she did, but then she asked, "Will you be all right?"

"Eventually." Miriam didn't sound too sure of what she said. "I think. Look, either it'll be fine, or it'll be worth it not being fine. Does that make sense?"

Jane took Miriam's hand in hers and squeezed it. "This—what you're doing—it isn't for your Practical, is it?"

Miriam shook her head no, and Jane suddenly felt about five years old. She was used to feeling like the mature, sophisticated one, but as it turned out, as she'd been obsessing over what amounted to doing well in school, Miriam had been off doing something that seemed awfully important.

"I know I look ghastly," said Miriam.

"I'm worried for your health."

"I know," said Miriam. "But I think I know what I'm doing. The thing is . . . I'm not exactly following the directions as written on the package," she said, with a quick grin that did much to make her look like she had mere hours before.

"I see," said Jane. "Oh, Miriam, I hate that we've been quarreling for ages. Can't we make up? I'll start—I'm sorry I hurt you. I never wanted to. I just can't help but be who I am."

Jane bit her lip. This was likely neither the time nor the place for a sisterly reconciliation, but Miriam didn't seem annoyed.

"I know," she whispered. "But neither can I."

"I wouldn't want you to be anyone other than who you are!"

"Nor I you. But that doesn't mean I can't have feelings or opinions. I don't want you to leave, Jane—but that doesn't mean I want you to stay!"

Jane finally understood. "I'm sorry," she said. "And as for what you're doing . . . I'll only say good luck."

"Thank you," said Miriam. "I appreciate you not prying."

"Of course," said Jane.

Something had changed between them for the better; Jane felt it as surely as she felt the wind on her cheeks when, later that night, she got on her broom to spy on Miriam through her window after they'd both allegedly gone to bed. She had agreed not to pry, but that didn't mean she couldn't try to figure out what Miriam was up to.

But all Miriam was up to was sleeping. She was already in bed when Jane peered in through the sheer curtain. A candle burned low by her bedside, and Miriam was still wearing her cardigan and skirt. Jane watched on until the candle burned itself out, just to be safe, and then went to bed herself.

THE NEXT MORNING, MIRIAM ASKED JANE to make sure she wouldn't be disturbed. Jane was thrilled to agree, not just because Miriam was confiding in her. It was easier to spy when she knew she ought to be spying.

It was a bright, cold day outside. Jane watched the skies off and on for an hour, hoping for some clouds or even a drizzle, but it was hopeless. She would have to risk riding her broom in full daylight, when anyone could come up the path and see her. She didn't have any other options for discreet spying; they didn't even have a ladder tall enough to reach Miriam's window.

At least Miriam's room was at the back of the house, and they had no close neighbors. Jane thought of it as a calculated risk when she mounted her broom and floated up to Miriam's window.

It occurred to Jane that she wasn't worried about Nancy discovering her—only strangers. She knew her mother would be down in the Library, doing whatever she did.

Jane wasn't sure what she'd expected to see, but it certainly wasn't Miriam just sitting at her desk staring into a mirror. But as Jane continued to watch, she noticed Miriam wasn't moving, not at all. She sat frozen, back straight, feet planted firmly on the floor. Her other hand, dangling by her side, held an unadorned knife that glinted dully as a ray of the cold sunshine filtered through the gap in her sheer curtains.

"What on earth," murmured Jane as she looked on for a few moments more.

Smudge had been nestled in what lap Jane had while sitting on her broom. As Jane watched, he stood, though Jane hissed at him to be still.

For once, her familiar did not obey. He pulled a complicated maneuver while maintaining physical contact with her, rearranging himself to face her. Then he nuzzled her chin with his cheek.

Jane couldn't rub at her nose to get the fur off it, which was maddening. "Smudge," she whispered. "Stop that!"

"Meow," said Smudge, still standing. And it *was* Smudge—Smudge as he had been. These days, he was so helpful, so well behaved, that if not for the fact that she was still hovering on her broom outside a second-story window, Jane would have suspected the demon had departed without her blessing.

"What are you doing!" she hissed at him, craning her neck to try to see past the bulk of his not-insubstantial rear and curling, fluffy tail. "I'm trying to . . . oh!"

As for that tail, it was curled in the shape of a shepherd's crook, or perhaps a magnifying glass. And when Jane looked through it, she saw something even stranger—a ghostly double of Miriam hovering just above her body.

This apparition also stared at the mirror, but it was not posed the same way—no, it was sitting cross-legged in the air, and while a spectral copy of the knife still depended from its hand, in the other, it didn't hold the mirror. Jane didn't think it could hold *anything*, even something insubstantial. The arm was missing much of what passed for its flesh. Jagged swaths of skin and muscle were missing; exposed bone peeked through. Jane was briefly confused to see that apparently ghosts had bones, but quickly the horror set in—that was *Miriam's* arm, and those were *Miriam's* bones, and while that flesh might not be her actual flesh, it still didn't seem wise to carve it away.

For the life of her, Jane had no idea what Miriam could possibly be up to—but whatever it was, it didn't seem to be particularly safe. Nor did it seem to be ending; unfortunate for Jane and her plans to spy. But it was simply too risky to watch for long, what with her looking through the window sitting on a broomstick, her familiar helping her see beyond what she could see with just her eyes. So Jane descended and retired to her room. She kept the door open so she'd hear Miriam when she came back.

She would just have to wait.

SHE HAD TO WAIT a long time.

23

MIRIAM DIDN'T LIKE LYING, and she especially didn't like lying to Jane, though she seemed to be doing a lot of that lately.

She'd told Jane she knew what she was doing, but nothing could be further from the truth. She was planning to jump into Querner's body—she was sure she could do that. As for what she could do to ruin his attempt to create a diabolic weapon, she really had no idea.

She did know that she would have to put a lot of herself into this journey to get what she wanted out of it. An ear wouldn't do. She needed something meatier, weightier. Something more personal. As difficult as it had been to carve away her ear, the bit of cartilage was fundamentally inessential. With her fingers, Miriam gingerly traced the edge of the ear she'd sacrificed with the veil knife. Her skin and flesh felt the same, but she sensed something was missing. She assumed that would be the case with her next sacrifice, too.

Miriam had weighed her options and decided that this time, for this journey back to that terrible forest, she would use her strange, dull knife to cut off her spirit's foot. Her right foot, to be specific.

She knew from experience that it wouldn't hurt. It was just upsetting to saw through something attached to her, incorporeal though it might be. And of course, there were the consequences. If removing a bit of her spirit's ear had so altered her appearance that she'd frightened her own best friend, what would cutting off a foot do?

She wouldn't die. She was fairly certain of that. *Badgerskin* hadn't led her wrong yet. Her spiritual flesh would heal and regenerate, with time.

It wasn't as if she had a choice. She couldn't stop—not now. There was much more at stake than her life.

It was time to stop worrying and start acting.

The taste of the sublingual tablet was so familiar to Miriam now, with its odd notes of lemon and ash. Also familiar was the feel of the veil knife in her hand, and the eerie coolness of the liquid diabolic essence in its bottle.

She drank the whole thing this time. She didn't know how long she'd be gone.

Miriam gasped without sound when she finally brought the blade of the knife to her ankle. There was a little resistance when she pressed, like trying to slice cold cheese, but a few little sawing motions worked the edge in deeper. When she cut it free, it dropped into the waiting palm of her left hand. Black smoke welled in the wound and dispersed, drifting off like smoke until it dissolved away entirely.

It was so odd. It was *her foot,* translucent but in every other way the twin of the one that was still attached to her leg. Thankfully, it was already dissolving into vapor, so she breathed it all in and waited to see with her spirit's eyes what flew or crawled past the grove where her father's bones lay silent in the dappled sunlight.

THE PAPER WASP HAD BEEN an effective vehicle, so once again Miriam borrowed one of their number to get herself to the infirmary, and then beneath it, down the stairs, through the keyhole, and into the Dark Lab beyond.

The place was dark and cold—cold enough that her wasp body became a little less responsive. She kept flying to stay warm, exploring the premises.

She hoped she was early, not late, for whatever they would do today . . .

She found a table set with various types of scientific glass and apparatus whose purpose Miriam could not perceive as she stalked among them on her six slender legs. Then she buzzed over to the cages full of miserable animals snuggled in their meager bedding.

Finally she turned her attention to the doors. Other than the one she'd come through, there were three, two with keyholes. The one on the far wall was without one. Miriam selected the right-hand door and crawled through the keyhole only to enter into an even darker chamber. She immediately felt her connection to the wasp weaken.

Lead walls, perhaps—or some other way of suppressing diabolic energy. But why . . . ?

Miriam urged the wasp toward a dim light shining on a pedestal in the center of the room. Whatever it was, it was under a cloth. She landed on it, her wasp feet sinking into velvet of all things. What with the war, Miriam hadn't touched such luxurious fabric for years, but the wasp's carapace and feelers did not register the sensation as her own fingertips would.

She crawled all over it, noting that the object was spherical, about the size of a large walnut, but with a strange and springy texture. She burrowed her way under the cloth to get a closer look.

It was a marble—or rather, it wasn't. It was perfectly round like one, but soft rather than hard. As Miriam got closer to it, looking deep within the swirling, shining interior, she felt the energy radiating from it.

It was a familiar energy. Even suppressed by the room, Miriam could tell it was some sort of concentrated source of diabolic essence. It had been extracted, purified, and then concentrated into what seemed like a gel contained by a rubbery skin that Miriam suspected would withstand a fall to the floor. Or perhaps it would burst on impact, with unknown results.

Querner had discussed creating a weapon. Miriam was no munitions expert, but she had a feeling this was likely to be an extremely important component.

There wasn't much else she could do in regard to this ball of energy — at least, not at the moment. And not in this body. The wasp was getting tired, so before flying to the other doorway to see what lay beyond it, Miriam landed on the desk in the center of the room. It was tidy — of course it was tidy, with stacked papers and letters in a file and fountain pens and a letter opener and so on and so forth.

The stacked papers were notes. She crawled beneath the cover and managed to get it off with a brief burst of flight that further exhausted her. But here was her chance to see what Querner was up to . . .

Experiment 12
The Hunter Sisters

Of course Querner would have a title page. Annoyed, Miriam tugged it off, buzzing angrily, the wasp body protesting every moment of activity. Then — at last — she began to read.

It was a slow and laborious process due to the wasp's eyes, and its unwillingness to move if it didn't have to, but soon she became absorbed in the reading.

The Hunter Sisters, also known as the Furies, have plagued the Reich for years. Early members of the OSS, they came to notoriety as their activities have not been limited to the usual sorts of espionage; indeed, their exploits include training an all-woman spy network in Istanbul under Lanning McFarland, separate from the Dogwood chain and much more effective, and then later penetrating several of our installations in Austria and Germany.

Before their diabolic corruption became generally known, it was believed that the Furies had been so damnably effective due to their truly uncanny similarity to one another. The assumption was that they were triplets, but in reality they are several years apart in age (Mary being the youngest, Martha the middle, and Prudence the oldest of the girls). Their near-identical features are not the result of nature, but of diabolic manipulation. How their father — for that is whose responsibility they are — came to create them, we may never know; he was a wild diabolist and did not reveal his secrets to them. They themselves had no hand in the process. Under duress they all revealed that it was their own mother upon whom they were molded; surely the Jew Dr. Sigmund Freud would have quite a lot to say about that. They, too, must have sensed the deviation in such a desire on the part of their father, for they fled to Paris from the United States, and took many pains to differentiate themselves from one another.

Then came the war, and their decision to become spies for the Allies turned their similarity into an asset rather than a liability.

Miriam had to pause to painstakingly flip the page.

Tests have revealed that the demon responsible for their altered appearances is none other than the unspeakable horror known as the Dreamer in the Darkness. The summoning of the Dreamer has been forbidden by all diabolic organizations, reputable or otherwise, due to the intensity of its aspirations. None of the Furies know how their father summoned it. We must all hope that its secrets died with their sire, for the agent we sent to the family homestead found nothing, only a cold hearth and no forwarding addresses for their surviving siblings.

Such things are beyond the scope of my experiments, and yet thoroughness and posterity both demand that I record their origins. My hope is that the capture of the Furies will lead to a great advancement for the Reich, if I am able to manage it — a weapon that will weaken the resistance of the Allies and what traitors exist yet within the glorious Fatherland.

It is generally known that while a diabolist may consume specific diabolic essence, once it is processed by the body, it becomes general diabolic essence. And yet, this understanding must be expanded if we are to succeed in our quest to cleanse the world in fire and in righteousness. We are out of our reserves. There it is, in plain language. The stores of our specific essences have been depleted by the war as has been our network of diabolists and those willing to trade with us. This is our last-ditch effort, as the Americans might say; a gambit where we will risk all to save all. While using the Dreamer is a crime I never imagined myself committing, if I can simply extract some of its specific essence from these women, I believe I can create a weapon the likes of which has never before been seen. It will kill many but change more, for the Dreamer was once known as the Pied Piper, due to its ability to ensnare, persuade, and sway. If I succeed, and add the Dreamer's essence to the—

At that moment, the door with no keyhole flew open and the lights came on in the room. Querner was there, wearing large thick mitts and carrying a bright purple pyramid-shaped crystal. He was saying something to an unfamiliar nurse as she scribbled something on a clipboard, while Nurse Franzi, still wearing the cattle prod at her waist, pushed a gurney at a near run.

Upon the gurney lay a young woman. She appeared to be moaning—Miriam couldn't hear in the wasp's body—and more troublingly, her body seemed to be smoking; yellow clouds billowed off of her as if she were an overheated engine.

Miriam buzzed away from the desk, flying to the doorjamb to see if she could read their lips as they spoke.

The vantage point was a decent one; when Querner handed off the crystal to unlock the door she'd not yet explored, Miriam could see two other women lying slumped against the wall of the chamber, their wrists chained to rusted metal rings jutting out from the tiled walls. Their faces were indeed surprisingly identical to the wracked visage of the woman on the gurney. They both perked up a bit when the door opened and called to their sister.

Their sister did not look up.

The prostrate woman's lack of response seemed to agitate the middle child of the bunch. She began to speak to Querner—to shout at him, Miriam assumed, given how accusatory her expressions and motions were. Miriam almost didn't need to hear the conversation to understand it. The woman was both threatening and pleading with Querner; he was responding mildly and reasonably. He was smiling—Germans always smiled so much—which is why it was all the more terrifying when he reached over and slapped her face. *Hard.*

Miriam didn't see the woman's response. She was too angry and, blinded by this anger, she let the wasp take over. Leaving her unobtrusive position by the door, Miriam sped at Dr. Querner and stung him on the neck, just above where his collar ended.

Miriam made her escape as his hand came up, and she had the small satisfaction of seeing him frown. Then she fled the insect to rest, escape, or die as it wished, selecting the caged marten as her next host.

"I can't see it," said the nurse with the clipboard. "It must have flown off. I wonder how it got down here?"

"Help me with her, please," said Nurse Franzi. She was trying to get the moaning, smoking woman onto a bench, but she seemed to be hot to the touch.

"What have you done to her?" demanded one of the Hunter sisters. "Prudence! Can you hear me? Prue!"

The one on the gurney—Prudence—had started to look less solid. Miriam was sure of it. Whatever yellow stuff was billowing out of her, she was changing due to its absence. Her flesh seemed to be relaxing and her clothes were becoming too tight, whereas a mere moment before they had been reasonably fitted; this phenomenon showed no signs of stopping, her body seemed to be flowing out of itself like a cracked egg. The nurse kept touching her gingerly and pulling away her hands as if she'd been burned.

"Many comings and goings over the past few days," said Querner sourly, as he rubbed at his neck. He seemed completely unperturbed by the disturbing situation before him. "Careful now! Don't drop her! She may survive, and if she does, I would like to interrogate her. For now, I must simply await the results of my experiment."

Miriam squealed, and her lithe body seemed to curl from under her as she thrashed against the metal bars of the cage in fury. Await the results! Wait how long? She couldn't stay forever, and every cleave cost her. The spirit-foot she had given up—who knew what state she would be in when she returned? She couldn't keep on like this. She needed answers *today*.

"Something has upset the marten," observed Querner. Miriam quieted down when she noticed the doctor looking at her keenly. He came toward her.

Miriam was acting on pure animal instinct when she backed away from him; this, however, seemed to satisfy him.

"A lot of spunk in you, little one," he said, with horrible fondness. "Good. I did not expect you to recover from that last procedure, but your vital essences seem to have recovered nicely."

He turned away then, but his pleasure seemed to sour as he looked at his desk. The scattered papers brought a furrow to his brow. Of course they did; Dr. Querner was clearly not the sort of man to leave his desk in such a state!

"Something is wrong here," he said as a great *thump* and then a few screams came from the room where the two nurses were attempting to manage the steaming girl. "Ach! What is it now?"

"She—" The nurse who had held the clipboard backed out of the room, hands held high. "She woke up, and she grabbed Franzi's arm, and wouldn't let go, and—"

"Let me through!" Querner gave a last glance at his desk and then headed back into the other room. But before he'd gone far—before Miriam had thought it through—she released her grasp on the marten and jumped into Querner.

Or at least she tried to. She experienced the unsettling but distinct sensation of bouncing or sliding off him. She could find no purchase and ended up in the marten again, like a rubber band snapping back.

It was a struggle to maintain control of the beast, so she put the experience from her mind as best she could. She could research later. Now was not the time to puzzle it out.

"Mien Gott, give me the cattle prod!" said Querner.

A zap and a screech—Miriam couldn't see from whom, from her cage, but it was Franzi who emerged, clutching what looked like a badly burned arm close to her body. As another zap and a screech echoed through the subterranean chamber, Miriam decided to try again to cleave to another human.

She had to fight for control of the clipboard-wielding nurse. The woman did not want to yield to Miriam, but Miriam's dedication and experience won out in the end.

Once Miriam was in control, she reached for the letter opener on Querner's desk. With it in hand, she snuck up behind Franzi in the chaos and held it to her throat.

"Dr. Querner!" She held the knife tighter when Franzi struggled against her; after that, the nurse was as quiet as the mice in the cages. "Stop that—or your nurse dies!"

Querner did stop; he poked his head out of the room beyond, looking very surprised indeed.

"Nurse Antje?" He blinked at Miriam from behind his glasses. "No . . . not Antje. It is *you* . . . the diabolist who has decided to try to be a hero. Tut, tut—are you stealing someone else's body with your soul? That is quite rude, you know, though an ingenious way to sidestep my wards that prevent scrying. I just never expected anyone to be mad enough to try body swapping . . . the costs!" He laughed. "Desperate times for all of us, aren't they?"

"We're coming, Querner," said Miriam, trying to tough it out a little to cover up how she still didn't have a plan. "All of us!"

"Are you now? How delightful. You'll forgive me if I carry on?" He gave her almost a chagrined look. "If *all of you* are coming, then needs must, for the devil is driving—"

"I'll kill her!"

"Do you what you must, and so will I," said Querner, turning away. "Franzi's allegiance is unquestionable—she would die for the Führer, and if this is how, I am sure she will accept it with grace and dare I say it? Enthusiasm."

Only then did Miriam remember what Querner had told her, *not* Franzi—that there was a button somewhere that would release a gas that would turn the Dark Lab into more of a mortuary than it already was. She had to prevent that as surely as she had to prevent Querner from completing his diabolic weapon.

"Now where were we," said Querner, kneeling down beside the fallen Hunter sister. She had gone very quiet. The yellow clouds coming off her were smaller and less substantial, but her body's slackness was horrifying to behold. She looked raw, like spilled cake batter oozing across a countertop, or a jellyfish decomposing on the sand.

"Leave her alone!" This was one of the other sisters. Her accent was harsh and American; it sounded less like the voices Jane liked to do while imitating her favorite actresses and more like when she'd played the part of a gangster during her little reenactments.

It seemed so long ago, when they had used to do that—but it wasn't. Not really.

"I shall not," said Querner, again in that smug, reasonable tone that made Miriam want to scream. "I shall do with her as I please, and there's nothing anyone can do to stop it."

Miriam gasped, not from alarm but because Franzi elbowed

her in the side, hard. She grabbed Miriam's wrist with her other hand and twisted. It wasn't Miriam's body, but Miriam was the one who felt the pain, keenly, and she gasped as she dropped the letter opener. It hit the floor and spun away out of reach.

Before Miriam could think of what to do Franzi shoved her, hard. Miriam fell onto her rear end, her tailbone shooting pain up her spine. As Miriam struggled to get her wind back, Franzi retrieved her cattle prod from Querner.

"Pull a knife on *me*, will you?" cried Franzi, before jamming the rod into Miriam's stomach.

The pain was excruciating. Miriam writhed as the electricity surged through her borrowed body. She convulsed, unable to control any part of herself; her arms and legs were no longer under her hard-wrought control. Every nerve felt struck by lightning—until Miriam remembered she need not endure any of this.

The jump from Nurse Antje to Franzi wasn't as difficult as the jump from the marten to Antje; she cleaved to the nurse like a foot sliding into a familiar boot. The pain ceased immediately, and once Miriam got her wits back, she realized the prod was in her hands now.

She jammed it into her former host, right at her neck. Nurse Antje screamed the same scream Miriam had just uttered . . . and then she stopped. When Miriam withdrew the prod, the woman did not move except to twitch a few times.

"Good work, Franzi," said Querner. "A pity about Antje though."

Miriam smiled to herself for only a moment before turning to jam the cattle prod into the meat of Querner's torso.

The doctor yowled like a cat. Staggering backward, he tripped over where the puddle of Prudence lay still on the floor; a second yelp followed as Querner's exposed skin gave off a somewhat pleasant smell, like cooked pork, unfortunately followed by the aroma of burning hair. Apparently what had been Prudence was still hot to the touch. He rolled off her. Prudence's poor flesh bounced back like a jelly as Miriam followed after the doctor, jamming the cattle prod into his groin for a second strike.

The smell of urine covered up the others; Miriam left him to moan and clutch himself in agony.

Prudence wasn't moving at all. With time being of the essence, she turned to the other two women.

"This is a rescue," she said, as they looked on in amazement. "I'm rescuing you."

A moment passed before the elder of the two—Martha, the one who had admonished Querner—spoke.

"Who are you?"

"A friend. Querner was right, I am *body-hopping,* for lack of an easier term for it. The cost is immense. But worth it, I think, if I stop him and get you out of here."

"Why should we believe you?"

Miriam hadn't anticipated being asked this, not with it still up in the air whether their sister was even still alive. "Because ..." Miriam looked from the nurse on the floor to the prostrate form of Dr. Querner. "Why would I do that to them if I wasn't trying to help you?"

"Any number of reasons," said Mary, the youngest Hunter sister, chiming in at last. "This could be another trick of Querner's."

"All I can do is promise you it's not," said Miriam. "I didn't intend to rescue you, not when I started all this. I came here to find out what happened to my father. Querner held him here ... for experiments, I suppose ... and now he's, he's ..." Martha nodded. "But there's no reason I shouldn't help you now that I'm here."

The two Hunter sisters exchanged a look, and nodded at once. It was a bit disturbing, actually; their similarity of face, build, and affect was not that of siblings, with the natural variations found even in identical sets of twins or triplets. They were copies of one another—or, if Querner's notes were to be believed, copies of their mother.

"Get his pistol," said Martha, and Miriam felt pretty stupid for not thinking of that herself. Querner was recovering; she ought to have done that first thing. But once she had his weapon in her hand, the only thing she could think of was getting rid of it.

Miriam had fired guns before; Nancy owned a rifle, and Edith —*poor Edith*—had once brought out her fashionable Astra 300 to let the girls try firing it. Jane had enjoyed it; Miriam had not, and currently she found the weight of the Luger in her hand overwhelming in its terrible responsibility.

"Wha ..." Querner stirred. Miriam pointed the pistol at him, training it on his chest. "Franzi? No ... of course it is not."

He got himself up on his elbows as Miriam trembled. She contemplated just shooting him, but she had questions for him, like where he kept the keys to the Hunter sisters' manacles.

And in any case, she really didn't want to. The death of the man she'd slain while in the owl's body always hovered at the edges of her thoughts. The idea of being haunted by a second ghost was undesirable to her, even if it was the ghost of the man who killed her father.

"Where are the keys?" asked Miriam. "The keys to their manacles! Tell me!"

"In my pocket," said Querner calmly, as if she were a small child being told the answer to an often-asked question. "I won't stop you from taking them. Do so any time. Much more interesting to me is how you've managed to body-hop so ... potently? What an astonishing price must you be paying! And all to stop me. Why, it leaves me quite breathless. I'm flattered, I really am."

"Take them out and toss them over to Mary and Martha."

"What if I don't? And don't worry, I know your answer will be academic in nature. You won't shoot me."

He was probably right, but his confidence was irritating. Not willing to concede the point, Miriam cocked the Luger.

"Suit yourself," she said. "I can get them off of your dead body easily enough."

Querner stood and dusted himself off, but there was nothing he could do about the piss stain on the front of his trousers. It didn't seem to bother him much; he grinned at her. "You're quite the *gangster,* aren't you? I suppose I'd better comply with your demands . . . *or else!* Isn't that right?" But he did chuck the keys over to the sisters.

Mary took them and began to fumble with them. Miriam wished Mary would figure out how to free herself faster, but she was working one-handed. Martha was chained too far away from her to help, and the lock on her manacle seemed to be sticky.

"I thought I had made this lab impenetrable," said Querner, as he watched Mary struggle. "And yet, you have bypassed my defenses utterly. I anticipated that some forms of astral projection might be a risk, but not what *you're* doing. Dying for a cause is one thing, but to live for who knows for how long as some hollowed-out *thing,* risking the intrusion of every enterprising spirit . . . not many would do that, even for such a cause as this."

Miriam said nothing. The grinding of the lock as Mary impotently labored over it was maddening.

"I wonder who you are," said Querner, as if he had not a care in the world. "A diabolist, that is for certain. But beyond that . . . is this personal? Is it for a cause?"

"Both," said Miriam, before she could stop herself. "My father —you killed him . . ." she trailed off.

"I can't say that narrows it down," said Querner. "Recent?"

"I don't know," said Miriam. "All I know is that he's lying dead outside in the forest."

"Tell me his name, and I'll tell you how he died."

Miriam laughed at him. Did he think she was so stupid? "I honestly don't care what you did to him." This was true—she didn't. It didn't matter. "I just want to destroy you."

"And yet I still live." Querner shrugged. "Though I can't say the same for you for much longer," he stage-whispered, as Mary shook out her red and bruised fingers. She still had not gotten herself free.

"Stop!" cried Miriam, but Querner had called her bluff. He lunged for her, grabbing for his pistol. Miriam froze but Martha was a quick thinker—she stuck her leg out, tripping the doctor before he could get his pale hands around the gun.

Querner came down hard on his face, but quickly rolled over, squirming and clutching at a bloody nose. In the confusion, Miriam tucked the cattle prod under her arm and set the pistol on the bench to unlock Mary's manacle.

"Now me!" said Martha, but Querner had gained his feet. Slipping in the blood that gushed from his nose, he again lunged for the Luger.

Miriam was elbowed aside as Mary went for it, too. She got there first. The report was deafening. When Miriam's watering eyes let her see again, she perceived Querner through the smoke. He was clutching at his arm; great gouts of blood pumped from it, but he was still moving, heading for something with great intention.

Miriam gave up on Martha's manacle. "He's going to burn us," she cried, rolling to her feet to chase after the doctor.

"What?" asked Mary, but there was no time. Querner was running for a metal box affixed to the wall. Miriam willed her borrowed legs to move faster as Querner fumbled with the latch.

Then Mary screamed, "Get down!" and Miriam dropped to her knees right there on the stone floor of the lab. Pain shot up her bones and into her hips and from her hands into her wrists as she caught herself. She was glad she'd acted so quickly, however, when the pistol fired not once more, but thrice in a row, *bam bam bam.*

Querner slumped lifelessly against the wall. The metal door of the box swung open, creaking in the sudden shocking silence of the room. Within, a solitary red button gleamed.

They were safe from the threat of the lamps and the gas, but Miriam knew the gunshots would draw swift attention. She turned to share this revelation with Mary and was surprised to find Querner's Luger pointed right at her face.

"Now let's talk about *you*," she said.

"Your sisters . . ."

"Can wait. Yes, even poor Prue. I have to secure this situation. So, who are you?"

Miriam decided honesty would be best. "My name is Miriam Cantor. I'm . . . I'm Jewish—Jewish enough that I had to leave, at least. But my parents stayed—they were diabolists, do you know the Société des—" Mary was nodding. "They were captured. I traced my father here. I was too late for him, but I still wanted to help."

Something in Miriam's words had convinced Mary. She still seemed suspicious, but she lowered the Luger and turned her attention to her restrained sister.

Martha, once freed, immediately slid down to see to Prudence.

"She's dead," she said after a moment. Miriam wasn't surprised. Prudence barely had human shape anymore.

"I'm sorry," said Miriam.

Mary glanced through the door at where Querner lay. "At least he won't ever find out if he was successful. I can't imagine there's someone else waiting to step into his shoes and win the war for them. They were trying to make a weapon, you know," said Mary. "Some sort of bomb, powered by diabolic essence. That's why we were investigating, but they caught us, and of course Querner realized we'd been . . . *altered*. Once he found out how, we were done for. It became a different project. He became obsessed with the idea of producing a bomb with a diabolic fallout that would win over the survivors to the Nazi cause." She shook her head. "That's all I know."

"Do you mind if I look through his notes? Go through his desk?" Miriam did her best to sound innocent as she dangled the keys at them.

"Let her," said Martha, as Mary started to protest. "We need to get out of here."

Mary nodded, and Miriam did indeed amble to Querner's desk. She gazed down at the papers that lay there, rustling them about for a few moments to allay any suspicion from the other room. Then, taking the keys in her hand, she crept to the other door.

A bomb, powered by diabolic essence . . . that had to be the purpose of the marble-like item in the other room. A massively concentrated diabolical power source for a bomb . . .

If the remaining Hunter sisters knew what lay beyond the other door, they would want it. Maybe they'd have more of an idea of what to do with it, but Miriam had a way to instantly get it much, much farther away from the Nazis.

She had just pulled the velvet cloth off of the soft marble when she heard them behind her.

"What's that?"

Miriam palmed the sphere before turning around. Once again, Mary had the pistol trained on her. Miriam's armpits prickled with sweat and her knees got a little less solid-feeling inside her skin.

"Just looking around," she said, but she knew she didn't sound convincing.

"What did you find? You have something in your hand. I saw you take it."

"I didn't take anything," lied Miriam.

"Show me your hand, then."

Miriam played for time. "Mary, this room suppresses diabolic energy. It's hard for me to hang on to this body in here." That, unfortunately, was true. "Do you mind if we step into the main room?"

"I *do* mind, as a matter of fact," said Mary. "You're keeping something from us. I want to know what it is before anyone goes anywhere. Show me your hand."

"I don't want to fight with you," said Miriam. She was now dangerously close to losing her hold on Nurse Franzi. "Please, we can help each other, we're on the same side, so let's just step—"

Mary cocked the pistol, and Miriam knew then she was done here, in this lab. She squished her tongue around the inside of her mouth to get as much saliva going as she could and then popped the marble-sized sphere there.

It had seemed smaller when it wasn't in her mouth. Hopefully its softness would save her from choking.

"What did you—" shouted Mary, and to Miriam's surprise she fired the gun, but it made a mere click instead of blasting Miriam in the face.

Miriam swallowed as Mary cursed.

"God damn Kraut-made Luger piece of—"

But Miriam never heard the rest of it, as the moment she felt the soft marble of diabolic energy slide down her gullet, she let go of Franzi's body.

The mirror dropped from her hand and bounced; the knife, too, fell from her weak fingers and stuck into the floor dangerously close to her foot.

Miriam woke some time in the night, still in her chair. As she stumbled toward bed, her foot struck something that went rolling across the floor to shatter against the wall.

It was her father's devil-trap, returned from wherever it went when Miriam used her mirror, but Miriam was too exhausted to care much about it.

WHEN A KNOCK AWAKENED HER the next morning, Miriam knew something was very wrong with her. She didn't feel exhausted, as one might after a sleepless night; her body felt different, unfamiliar and unresponsive.

Another knock made her wince. Miriam called out that she'd be there in a moment. She rolled onto her side to ease out of bed only to be greeted by the sight of her father's devil-trap lying in big jagged pieces on her bedroom floor.

"Miriam?"

She'd worry about it later. For now, she had to get to the door, afraid as she was about what Jane would say when she saw her.

Jane looked absolutely traumatized.

"Is it bad?" croaked Miriam.

"Awful," she whispered.

Miriam was surprised—not by her answer, but her phrasing. Usually Jane was diplomatic about such matters.

Jane bit her lip. "Sam . . . Sam's dead."

That was not at all what Miriam had expected to hear. "What?"

"Last night."

Miriam felt a cold chill. "How did he die?"

She didn't know what "natural causes" a young man might die of, but she still hoped for that to be Jane's answer.

"They say it was some sort of wild animal. His neck was snapped, and he had been torn to pieces." Jane's eyes briefly found Miriam's before she looked away again. She seemed curiously guilty. "It sounds like it might the same creature that got our ducks," she said, in a voice scarcely louder than a whisper.

24

A LONG MOMENT PASSED AFTER JANE told Miriam the news. Jane spent it trying not to stare at her friend. Miriam looked worse. A lot worse.

"Mrs. Fielding came to tell us. She heard it from her sister in the village. Everyone's upset because . . . because of how gruesome it was."

Miriam had a strange air about her. Jane wondered if her feelings about Sam's death weren't wholly regretful.

As for Jane, her feelings about his death were also mixed — she was horrified at the grisly scene reported to her by Mrs. Fielding and worried that it might have something to do with her familiar. But Smudge had been such a help to her. She didn't believe he was capable of such a wicked act . . . and, anyway, he couldn't have gone all the way to Hawkshead and back to do the killing. Jane had stayed up late spying on Miriam, and then fallen asleep with the light on. When she'd awakened several hours later, Smudge had been curled up on the pillow beside her head, his fluff gilded by the puddle of light. His gentle purring had lulled her back to sleep quickly in the darkened room after she turned off her lamp.

She had no reason to suspect the cat, and yet suspect him Jane did. She didn't know why, but her intuition told her that Smudge had something to do with Sam's death, and with the ducks' too. She didn't like it, but she had to face facts, and the fact was that ever since she'd summoned her familiar, death had come oddly in the night to people and animals close to her. One incident she could have brushed off as a coincidence, but twice . . .

She looked down the hallway and saw Smudge sitting in front

of her bedroom door. The cat was perfectly still save for the tip of his tail, which beat softly upon the hall runner carpet.

Jane puckered her lips and made a little kissing face at him, like she'd used to do before she'd summoned a demon into him, and then turned back to Miriam. She was trying to act normally around him, so that if she had to banish him, it would come as a surprise.

This was assuming the cat couldn't read her mind. That wasn't supposed to be something the Ceaseless Connoisseur could do, but then again, neither was it supposed to have a penchant for disemboweling innocents.

"It's a shame," said Jane, "but that doesn't change how I feel about his mistreating you."

Miriam looked a little shocked by this, when she glanced up from her feet. "I suppose," she said softly.

Jane cleared her throat, as a way to change the subject. She hadn't wished to conceal Sam's demise, but she had other business to discuss.

"Miriam ..." Jane wasn't sure how to approach the subject of Miriam's spiritual activities, as she would have to admit she'd not respected her friend's privacy, and come up with a plausible excuse for asking after Miriam's soul, or astral body, or spirit—whatever she'd seen. She'd planned for this, though—she'd thought about it quite a bit.

"Yes?"

"I'm sorry, but I peeked through your window." They had a ladder; it was plausible without a flying broomstick. "What I saw ... Miriam, I—"

"You *spied* on me?"

"I was worried about you! I mean, I didn't try to stop you, did I?" Jane smiled hopefully. "You seemed to be in a deep meditative state." She thought that was a good cover. "I'm guessing you were dabbling in some sort of astral projection. Did you . . . did you do the thing? That you needed to do?"

Miriam looked conflicted, her expression equal parts grief and annoyance. "Sort of," she said. "It's hard to explain, but I—"

Then Miriam's hand went to her stomach. Jane stepped back on instinct. Her friend looked queasy—and sure enough, Miriam gagged twice and then coughed up something that seemed far too large to have emerged from her mouth. Something that shone with its own light.

The force of Miriam's expectoration sent the marble-like object slipping through her spittle-slick fingers. It bounced once and then rolled down the hall.

Smudge wiggled his tail and then pounced on it, just as he ever would have done.

"No!" cried Miriam, but Smudge had gotten his mouth around the glowing sphere and, like any less exceptional cat would do, scampered with his new trophy. Miriam darted past Jane, pelting after the cat only to stumble in her weakened state.

Down the stairs he went. Jane followed him as quickly as she could, but it was only after she'd made it halfway down the staircase did she command the cat to halt. She couldn't let Miriam see how Smudge actually obeyed her now.

What Jane hadn't seen was her mother idly drifting by the stairwell. Smudge stopped at her feet, looking up at her with a curious, almost playful expression, the item in question held as gently in his mouth as if it had been a kitten.

"Hello, Smudge," said Nancy, in a soppy, adoring manner totally unlike herself. "What do you have there, I wonder?"

Smudge uttered a strangled cry, just like a normal cat pleased with his hunting. Nancy cooed at him as Jane ran down the rest of the stairs to try to remove the object from between Smudge's jaws.

It was surprisingly soft and squishy; she'd thought it would be hard.

"Naughty," she said lightly.

"What is it?" asked Nancy.

"Oh . . . just something Miriam's been working on," said Jane, knowing damn well that was the understatement of the century.

"I'd like to see it," said Nancy, extending her hand.

Jane suppressed a sigh. Of course *this* was the thing her mother would take an interest in after being so distant about everything else!

Jane didn't know what to do. She glanced over her shoulder; Miriam was just now limping down the stairs.

"Come now," said Nancy. "Be a good girl."

As Jane turned back to her mother, she noticed Smudge. The cat watched this scene unfold with more than feline attention. His keen gaze sent a thrill of terror down Jane's spine — why was he so invested in this interaction? They both knew he was no mere cat eager for the return of a toy. What was the nature of his interest?

A flicker of motion caught Jane's eye. It was Smudge's shadow on the wall. Once again, it seemed to her as if the twitching of the shadow's tail was not perfectly aligned with Smudge's . . . and this time, she was certain two hollow eyes blinked, revealing the robin's egg blue of the wallpaper.

That seemed worrisome, but now was not the time to worry about it.

"Please," panted Miriam, as she limped up to them. "Give it back. It's not meant to be handled."

"Not meant to be handled?" Nancy seemed so surprised by this, it gave Jane hope. Awkward as this situation might be, it was waking Nancy up.

"No, it —"

"But Smudge had it!"

Jane felt both relief and unhappiness at this now-typical woozy comment from her mother.

"Smudge took it when he shouldn't have, the little thief," said

Jane, handing the soft and slippery ball over to Miriam. She was glad to be rid of it, even if she suspected it was not something Miriam ought to have, either. She smiled as brightly as she could. "You know Smudge!"

"It's fine," said Miriam, in a passable imitation of her usual awkward self. "No harm done, but it's best to get it back where it needs to be."

The clock chimed then, and Jane startled. She counted the bells; it was only eight o'clock in the morning.

That didn't seem possible . . .

The silence that followed was so tense and heavy that Jane shrieked when the knock came at the door, urgent and loud.

"What now?" exclaimed Jane, and moved to answer it when no one else did.

It was Charlie, the boy employed by the postmaster to run telegrams, and run one he had—all the way from Hawkshead to their doorstep, judging from the shape he was in. Jane asked if he would like to come in and warm up before heading back; he said he would, so for the sake of the lad not catching pneumonia, she and Miriam endured making and drinking a cup of tea with him as he warmed his front and backside with great relish before the AGA.

He left quickly after he'd finished, thank goodness. Jane was both eager and reluctant to open the telegram.

"Do you think we should get Mother?"

Nancy had wandered off with her cup of tea. Jane was unsure if it was ethical to proceed without her.

Miriam stared at Jane for a moment, and then laughed. It was a truly horrible sound, like a can full of nails.

"What has the world come to where *you're* asking *me* if you should dive into something?" asked Miriam, with a shake of her head. Her hair had gone very gray, indeed.

Jane conceded this point and opened up the telegram. She gasped at the first line, then began to read it aloud:

MESSAGES GOING AWRY STOP HAVE BEEN FOR SOME
TIME STOP MUCH NEWS STOP I SHALL BE WITH YOU
IN THREE DAYS TIME TO EXPLAIN ALL STOP THE
GOOD NEWS IS YOUR SISTER LIVES STOP

"It's from my father," said Jane, in conclusion.

The telegram contained more mysteries than it answered. What messages were "going awry," making the Société resort to telegrams?

What was so terrible that her father would come to Hawkshead? And in three days' time . . .

Jane was utterly at a loss of what to do. She was surprised to see Miriam's expression was no more coherent. Her friend had looked strange and terrible to begin with, but now she seemed horrified. Maybe appalled.

Appalled—but not shocked. Miriam was upset, but the idea of it being necessary to count Edith among the living or the dead was not news to her.

"What's happened?" said Jane. She kept her voice low.

"I don't know," said Miriam. "I thought . . . it doesn't matter what I thought." Jane was seething now, furious at her friend. Miriam noticed. "Jane, I'm sorry. It slipped my mind with everything else and, anyway, I was wrong about Edith being dead."

"For how long have you been wrong?"

"Only a day, no—two."

"Two days!" Jane stood and hurled the telegram down onto the table; Miriam winced as the paper smacked on the wood. "And here I told you about Sam's death not *five minutes* after I learned of it. Two days you've known my aunt was . . ." Jane stopped short. "What is she? Is she dead? Captured?"

"I thought she was dead," whispered Miriam. "He . . . the doctor . . . he said she was. But it seems he was wrong!"

"That doesn't make this any better!"

Jane had never been so angry in her life. How dare Miriam keep this from her! It was absurd. Something like this didn't just slip one's mind.

"Jane," said Miriam. Something about her tone made Jane pay attention. "They said . . . what I heard at least . . . it was that everyone died. The rescue party, all of them." She looked away. "I'm certain my mother's dead, too."

"I'm sorry," said Jane, almost automatically. What else could she say? She couldn't continue to be angry in the face of hearing that. "Were you able to find out anything about—"

Miriam shook her head. "But at least I know she wasn't a traitor. Neither of my parents were."

"A traitor? Who in the world would think that?"

"The Société." Miriam's expression hardened. "Some of their plans went awry, and they thought my parents might have been the reason. Edith didn't think so. She went to find out the truth —that's what she was doing. But it went wrong, like the telegram said. They—the Nazis—thought everyone had died, but apparently Edith got out."

Jane was too shocked by all of this to cry, or gasp, or feel anything at all. It had always been hard for her to comprehend the scope of the devastation wrought by this war—it was the small stories that always made her stop and reflect on the horror of it all.

"Anyway," said Miriam, after a moment, "I set out to prove their innocence, and now I can."

"With what Smudge grabbed?"

"No. That's . . ." Miriam hesitated. "They were trying to make a weapon, and that was going to be part of it. I took it back with me. The man who designed it, he's . . . dead now too."

Jane was quite astonished. Miriam was a skilled diabolist, more powerful and knowledgeable than Jane had realized. Astral projection was one thing, but Jane had never heard of being able to take items across time and space. A *lot* of time and space, if Miriam had been visiting *Germany*.

As for her killing a man . . . that was something else entirely.

"What sort of weapon?" asked Jane, sidestepping the issue. "I just ask, as Smudge had it, you know . . . in his mouth."

"A bomb, powered by concentrated diabolic energy," said Miriam. "That's what it is. I need to investigate it further."

Jane wondered if Smudge knew he'd stolen such a dangerous and powerful thing. The answer was probably yes, but she could think about that later. She was still upset about Edith, and she was also *extremely* concerned for Miriam—more now that she knew her friend was coping with finding out her parents were both dead.

It had been such a hectic few moments there, with hearing of Sam's death, telling Miriam, Smudge's theft, Nancy's odd interest in the item in question, and then the arrival of the telegram-bearing boy, that Jane hadn't really spent a lot of time looking at her friend. Frankly, she looked *awful.* Stunningly so. Jane once again marveled at how, at least when it came to her face, she had no visible signs of aging—there were no wrinkles around her eyes, no sag in her cheeks. It was something deeper that was wrong with her, something that defied explanation.

She suspected this had to do with just how ghastly Miriam's soul, or whatever she'd seen, had looked when it had been separated from her body the night before. But, of course, it was hard for Jane to express concern over Miriam's spirit or soul when doing so would reveal that she'd managed to somehow see it.

She tried to keep the focus on Miriam's well-being. "You're not going back, are you?" asked Jane. "When you say investigate this . . . *thing* . . . you mean down in the Library, right?"

Miriam stiffened. "That's my business."

"But, Miriam—look at yourself. You're not well, you look *sick,* your hair . . . You just vomited up something that you say you brought back with you somehow. I don't even understand how that's possible!"

"Jane, this war—it's all about sacrifice. If we win, it will be because of what you, or I, or anyone else is willing to give for the cause."

"But—"

"Do you understand that if I tell the Société what happened to my parents, I'll have to tell them what I can do?" Miriam bit her lip. "I've had to do something that's not exactly *forbidden*, but also not exactly encouraged. You're not really supposed to . . . to take over other people's bodies." She said this all in a rush, as if worried Jane would judge her. But, of course, Jane had her own, far worse secrets to keep. "The Société would be in their rights to hand me over to your father when they find out, but that's a risk I'm willing to take."

Jane kept a straight face only through sheer force of will. She wanted to burst into tears, to tell Miriam her own worries in that regard, but caution stayed her tongue.

Jane's reckoning, if there was to be one, would come later. This was about Miriam and her choices, and as Jane looked at her friend —the hollows beneath her eyes, the new silver threading through her once-dark mane, the rickety motions of her arms, she felt it was time to address them head-on. Miriam was hurting herself, maybe even killing herself. Jane didn't know if she could stop her friend, but she knew she could at least call Miriam out and make her acknowledge that's what she was doing.

"You told me your parents sacrificed everything so that you could come here and be safe with me and my mother. Right?" Miriam looked murderous, so Jane said what she had to say all in a rush. "All I mean is . . . getting expelled from the Société, hurting yourself as you've been . . . do you think that's what they would have wanted for you?"

She didn't realize the question was insensitive until she saw

Miriam's expression change from angry to wounded as she got unsteadily to her feet.

"I can't know that, can I?" She loomed over Jane, imposing even in her unwholesome desiccation. "I can't know because they're dead!"

"I know, I'm sorry, Miriam, I—"

"You *what?*"

"I just . . ." Jane took a moment to compose herself and make sure she was speaking as precisely as possible. She was genuinely afraid for Miriam's life—more afraid than Miriam was, she suspected. "I know you're willing to sacrifice everything for them, and for the war, but does that honor *their* sacrifice? I never knew them, but I'm sure their intention was for you to *live.*"

"I want to live too! Of course I do! But I *won't*—not if they succeed in building some diabolic weapon powerful enough to turn the tide of this war! Because they'd use it—they'd use it on me, and they'd use it on you, too! They wouldn't pin a little yellow star on your chest, but they'd say you were a *degenerate,* and that would be the end of *you,* Jane Blackwood!"

"But you stopped them." Jane remained perfectly calm in the face of Miriam's outburst. She wasn't angry, and she couldn't see how it would help if she matched Miriam's tone—or volume, for that matter. This was too important a conversation for her to have any of it loudly, or in haste. "Correct me if I'm wrong, but it seems like you're saying that any further investigation would just be you satisfying your curiosity . . . right?"

Miriam became strangely calm too, all of a sudden.

"And what about *you,* Jane?" she said. "Have *your* recent investigations been about saving the world—or were you just satisfying *your* curiosity?"

Jane's patience began to slip.

"I haven't been saving the world, it's true," she said coolly, for Miriam's words had stung. "But I do know that a world without you in it would be less worth saving, to my mind. And I think your parents felt the same."

"How dare you speak for them!"

"I'm not!"

"You can't possibly understand what it's like," said Miriam. "I'll never see them again, never hear their voices. They'll never know anything of me or my life. Anything I achieve, the person I become, I'll never know if I've made them proud, or if they'd have found me wanting. We can guess, but what's a guess worth?"

"Look at yourself," said Jane. "You can't go back. I can't let you!"

"How will you *stop* me?"

"I don't know. Taking away your toys seems vulgar. And if I can't do that, I suspect my father, when he arrives, will have somewhat more authority."

"You'd tell him?" Miriam sounded so wounded, so absolutely betrayed. Jane wondered if she'd ever threatened Miriam before. She didn't think so, but she held her ground. This was for Miriam's own good.

"Only to save your life," she said bluntly. "Only if you make me. It's your choice."

Miriam didn't reply. After a moment, Jane left the room feeling as though she both owed and was owed an apology.

She was restless, unhappy; she wasn't sure where she wanted to go. Her room felt confining; there she would find nothing beyond stacks of books full of the answers to many questions, just not to the ones she was asking.

It didn't seem so long ago that Jane's biggest worry was that she'd failed her Test and if anyone found out she might be asked to do secretarial work for the Société.

Oddly enough, to her own mind, Jane wanted her mother. Or at least, she wanted the idea of her mother. Jane knew she wouldn't get what she needed from Nancy. She rarely ever had. Her mother's opaqueness was not a recent phenomenon, though it was true that Nancy had been even less approachable of late.

As she mulled over asking her mother for comfort, if not for advice, it occurred to Jane that she had to go and talk to her regardless. She had to tell her about Edith . . . and Patrice's impending visit.

Patrice . . . Jane wasn't sure how to approach her mother about that. She'd just have to decide in the moment.

Nancy had made her way to the Library with her cup of tea, but it sat at her elbow, untouched, as Nancy sat at her desk. It was a familiar sight, but also not. While Jane had found her mother in such a pose many, many times before, Nancy had never before let her pile of work get so out of control. The stacks of requests were spilling onto the ground now. It was just so unlike her to leave so many things undone.

Miriam had been right: her mother was shirking her duties. If the Société had resorted to sending telegrams, that meant they'd tried to get in touch with Nancy through every diabolic means at their disposal, only to be ignored. Probably there were many messages in among the other unanswered missives piled everywhere.

Nancy *still* had not looked up. Jane cleared her throat—softly, so as not to startle her mother. But it was Jane who startled when Smudge stood up from where he'd been sitting on her mother's lap, hidden under the edge of the desk.

It was the first time Jane had seen Smudge somewhere other than by her side since the night of the summoning, and it made her feel queer that he'd suddenly taken such an interest in her mother—first, this morning, during the incident with the weapon he'd snatched from Miriam, and now too. How long, Jane wondered, had Smudge been missing? Or rather, not *missing*—just not where he usually was.

"Oh, hello, Jane," said her mother, finally looking up. Jane had to tear herself away from Smudge's narrow yellow gaze, and when she did, she didn't like what she saw at all. Her mother's bland expression was like raw bread dough, unformed and unappetizing. "How are you? Did that boy enjoy his tea?"

"Mother." Jane took the telegram out of her pocket. "We need to talk."

"Right now? I'm so busy . . ."

Jane wanted to scream, *Doing what?* But instead she said, "*Yes*, right now. It's about Edith. She's . . . she . . ."

"She what?" But for all she prompted her daughter along, it didn't seem like Nancy was especially concerned.

"I'm not sure," said Jane, remembering what the telegram said versus what Miriam had reported. She didn't want to distract from the conversation at hand. "I think something terrible has happened."

She handed the message to her mother. Nancy read it over, then folded it up again and tucked it back into the envelope.

"We'll know more when Patrice arrives" was all she said. "Until then, we'll just have to be patient."

When Patrice arrives! Her mother's woozy disconnect had been troubling, but the casual way in which Nancy mentioned the arrival of Jane's estranged father was actually frightening. But perhaps Nancy, too, was concealing her sensations . . .

"Mother," said Jane, hoping they could connect over Edith if not Patrice, "what if Edith is really unwell? Don't you think it's odd that someone's coming here, rather than telling us directly?" Jane felt good and bad about her clever somersault around using her father's name.

"No need to fear the worst," said Nancy, turning back to her book. "That's just borrowing trouble, my dear. Just try not to think about it. You have your studies to focus on, after all."

Jane took a step back as if recoiling from some repellent scene, and turned on her heel.

This wasn't right—of that, she was sure. Her mother might have let herself get too absorbed in a project to notice Miriam's decline or her own daughter's lack of focus, but to utterly dismiss the very real possibility that her sister might be grievously injured? That wasn't Nancy.

It wasn't until Jane got back to her room that she began to tremble. She was afraid, very afraid—and alone. She sat down and took a deep breath, but the resulting calm was undone when Smudge leaped into her lap.

He purred and gently butted his head against her chin, just as he'd always done. Jane petted him, just as she'd always done, and he settled down, his eyes half-shut in animal pleasure.

The pleasant weight of a purring cat on her lap ought to have been soothing, but it wasn't.

Smudge, like her mother, wasn't really himself these days.

And not only that, the cat had been able to sneak up on her because his collar bell had gone missing. Again.

25

THE STUPIDEST PART ABOUT HER fight with Jane was that Miriam wasn't convinced she could go back at all. She was eager to know what had happened with the Hunter sisters, to the nurse, to the animals in the cages, to the results of Dr. Querner's tests, but with her father's devil-trap in pieces it might not be possible. And then there was the issue of her deeply wounded soul . . .

But even so, it wasn't Jane's place to tell her what she could and couldn't do. And how *dare* Jane threaten her with exposure!

Miriam looked at the shards of her father's bowl and felt tears in her eyes. Yet another precious thing destroyed by the war. Where would it end?

She tried to push away the anger, the pain. She entertained a wicked thought, wondering if it would be such a bad thing for the shadowed space within her to expand, fill in the gaps left by her spiritual adventures. It could contain more that way.

No. *Badgerskin* had been explicit that the shadow-soul was not a benign thing. It could develop its own hungers, its own will. Miriam still wasn't sure if she believed that was possible, but she could not entirely dismiss the fear.

Regardless, it would be a disaster if Jane blabbed her suspicions to her father. Miriam would be found out, stopped, and likely expelled from the Société; additionally, they might start looking around at *everything* a lot more closely. Nancy's suspicious neglect of the Library would be discovered — at this rate, her inattention would likely be grounds for an inquiry, if not her removal.

Probably Jane hadn't thought about that. Hadn't stopped to think about how she might bring an end to their little family.

Miriam would simply have to find a way to prevent all of this from happening in the first place. And for that, she'd need to know what Jane was up to. She needed information; something she could use as leverage.

Fortunately, there was a fairly easy solution at hand.

Smudge was always around Jane, these days more so than ever. Oh, he'd always been Jane's cat, but recently Smudge and his mistress had been inseparable — and that was why Miriam was going to take possession of that cat to spy on her friend.

The last thing she needed was to shave off more of her spiritual body, but Miriam couldn't think of a more effective way to spy beyond peering in at Jane's keyhole. But of course Jane might be anywhere when she was doing whatever she did.

But Smudge would be there for it.

It irked Miriam that she had to waste a bit of what was left of her soul to try to blackmail her best friend, but she really had no choice in the matter. This was all Jane's fault, the sanctimonious busybody. It would cost Miriam resources and time to thwart her, but thwart her she must.

How sad that it had come to this. Nancy had said she didn't ever want her girls to compete against one another, but here they were, each doing her best to ruin the other.

A small voice in Miriam's head objected, pointing out that Jane had no desire to *ruin* Miriam. Jane was quite obviously concerned for Miriam's well-being — but there was a line, and Jane had just crossed it. *Leaped over it,* quite frankly, and was making herself at home on the other side.

Walking up the stairs was proving to be a bit of a challenge. Miriam was already very tired. Chasing Smudge had been too much for her in her weakened state.

Again, Jane wasn't wrong — she just didn't have the right to tell Miriam what to do.

Jane's door down the hall was shut tight. Miriam tiptoed up to it and pressed her ear to the wood. She could hear nothing. Crude as it might be, Miriam did align her eye to the keyhole. Jane was sitting on her bed, back to the door. It looked like she was reading.

More importantly, Smudge was on her chair, curled up into a little gray pillow. The tip of his tail struck the seat in an uneven tattoo as he slept.

Sneaking back to her room, Miriam prepared herself to cleave to Smudge. While using the mirror required an extra step, she thought it would be wiser than loitering outside Jane's door. So, she plucked a few stray Smudge hairs off her sweater—they were always around—and set to training her scrying glass on the cat.

The sight of her spiritual body troubled her—the site of her amputated foot looked almost infected. The remaining spiritual flesh seemed to bubble before turning to steam and drifting off.

Miriam gritted her teeth and cut into the flesh of her thigh. She dug out a sizable chunk, figuring she'd better be prepared.

But as it turned out, she *wasn't* prepared—not for what happened.

Smudge came into view in the mirror, still sound asleep, though he'd shifted slightly and was now belly-up with a paw over his eyes. Evening had fallen; the shadows in the room were long. Jane had turned on a lamp and looked tired from reading. She looked up to rub at her eyes.

Miriam had taken a hearty swallow of diabolic essence; she was feeling confident as she sent her spirit Smudge-ward—

—only to be bounced back. Her detached spiritual matter smacked back into herself, hard, like a ball that had been thrown at a wall with too much force.

SHE AWOKE PARCHED AND DIZZY. All she could think of was how much she needed a glass of water, so she made her way down to the kitchen through the gloom of the darkened house. Her throat was so very dry; once it was a bit more comfortable, her mind began to work.

Smudge. The cat—improbably—was a fortress. It hadn't felt like she'd dashed herself against an animal's will. In fact, it had felt the same as what she'd experienced when she'd tried to cleave to Dr. Querner.

She had meant to read up on what might have caused such a bounce or snapback; she just hadn't had the time.

Now she did. Miriam went back up to her room and dug out *Badgerskin*—it had shifted to the bottom of her stack of books as she'd mastered its contents—and began to page through it again. Soon enough she found what she was looking for, but she couldn't believe the words on the page.

> *There are, of course, creatures who will successfully resist the cleave. Those individuals who have specifically practiced various defenses against co-occupation will be more difficult to possess; a fellow diabolist, impossible. The Pact makes a second possession all but impossible. Similarly, conjuring a demon into an animal would also result in spiritual impenetrability. Yet another reason diabolic familiars are so useful, and yet so very dangerous.*

Conjuring a demon into an animal . . . Miriam couldn't believe it. Would Jane have been so bold as to summon a familiar spirit into her own pet cat?

Of course she had. This explained so much—Smudge's new-found fascination with his mistress; his interest in the sphere of diabolic essence. But why would Jane commit such an offense? It was the single most dangerous thing she could possibly do!

She must have a reason—she must be using him for *something*. If Jane had truly created a familiar, it must have been in the service of some other goal. She surely wouldn't tell the Société that she had flaunted their most reasonable rule . . .

Miriam laughed to herself in the quiet of her room. "Astral projection," as Jane had called Miriam's accomplishment, might raise a few eyebrows and lead to unwanted questions. Creating a diabolic servant . . . that was truly grounds for expulsion. Or, Miriam suspected, worse.

The more she thought about it, the more shocked she was that Jane had done it—shocked, but also impressed. Doing something so dangerous, so absolutely forbidden . . . that took chutzpah, as her aunt Rivka would have said.

And a certain measure of stupidity, too. Knowing what Smudge was . . . it sent a chill through Miriam's heart. A demon, free to roam the world and change it as it saw fit! Miriam just hoped Jane had had the sense to summon one with little interest in leaving its mark on the human world.

But even a gentle demon might change upon being offered true freedom to roam the world as it pleased. As far as Miriam understood it, summoning a familiar wasn't like making the Pact in the usual way—the Pact was a specific contract, its language ossified, its terms boilerplate—and the resulting partnership was necessarily limited by the human capacity to endure diabolic energy.

There would be no such checks on a creature like Smudge. And no *Smudge*, either. When a demon took actual possession of a living creature, there was no partnership, no constantly evolving, mutually beneficial relationship of the sort that characterized diabolist/demon relations.

Miriam heard a creak from the general direction of Jane's room. Such sounds were not unusual in an old house, but now that Miriam's blood was up and her curiosity had been whetted, she wondered just what she'd been missing by not paying more attention to her friend.

Once again, Miriam was reduced to spying at the keyhole. What she saw there astonished her, for she had certainly not expected to catch Jane dressed in a black dress their fashionable aunt would look at twice in a shop window while climbing out her window onto a strangely chic broom that hung impossibly in the air beyond.

But that was indeed what Jane was doing.

Jane could fly!

There she was, sitting astride the broom, like an illustration of a witch out of a children's fairy book. But of course, the illusion was not complete until Smudge jumped up beside her, from where he sat on Jane's desk. There, after an uncannily catlike amount of fussing and spinning and getting his tail in Jane's face, he deigned to sit between her hands. Then they were off, and Miriam lost sight of them.

Miriam spent a few moments marveling at what an exceptional diabolist Jane truly was. Criminally reckless—that, too—but a criminally reckless genius.

Then, as Miriam was poised to look away, something caught her roving eye.

Jane had left the lamp on and a candle burning—so wasteful! But more importantly, in the bright light, something dark was moving.

It slithered in from the window where Jane and Smudge had just gone out and disappeared so quickly Miriam wondered if she'd really seen it. Then it, whatever *it* was, reappeared by the candle.

It seemed like a shadow—but a shadow cast by nothing at all. It flickered as the candle guttered in the evening breeze, changing shape and then settling with the flame—settling into the shape of a cat.

Not just any cat, either. It was Smudge. The real cat's features were unmistakable within the unnaturally crisp lines of the shadow-cat's form, from the fluff of his small but impressive mane to the downward curl of his whiskers, to even the shape of his eyes

—for this shadow had eyes, bright slits in the darkness where the pale pink wallpaper of Jane's room peeped through. Even the flicking of the shadow-cat's tail was like Smudge's.

It was the most uncanny thing Miriam had ever seen in her life. She broke out in a cold sweat as she watched the shadow-cat lick its paw furiously a few times before standing, stretching, and *peeling* itself off the wall. Miriam gasped and then clapped her hand over her mouth; the shadow-cat gave no indication it had heard her. Miriam wondered if perhaps it couldn't hear—it was still paper-thin and translucent, like a shadow; or maybe it was too absorbed in stalking a pen that lay at the center of Jane's desk. In a moment of playful glee eerily reminiscent of a real cat, the phantom used its paw to knock the pen onto the rug below and then leapt down after it before heading for the door where Miriam yet looked on.

Having no idea how the shadow-cat would get out of the room, or where it might wish to go once it was free, Miriam scurried away from the door as quietly as she could, backwards and crab-fashion on her hands, into the upstairs bathroom. She sat there in the darkness and listened. She wondered if she'd hear anything, what with how loudly her heart was pounding, but when Jane's door creaked open on its hinges, the noise seemed to slice into her like a knife.

Why the shadow-cat opened the door, rather than finding some other, more subtle means of egress, Miriam could not say. She only knew that when she finally worked up the courage to look around the corner of the bathroom door, she saw Jane's was ajar—and saw, too, the tip of the shadow-cat's tail as it went down the stairs.

It was on a mission—that was clear enough. Miriam felt torn. She wanted nothing to do with this foul thing and its errands, but she also felt uneasy about it running about unsupervised in her home.

Continuing to run about in her home. This being wasn't explor- ing. It knew its way around.

Miriam slipped off her shoes to muffle her footfalls and went after it. Treading as lightly as she could on shaking legs, she pad- ded down the stairs, pushing herself to the limits of her weakened state. Even so, she only got there in time to see the Library door easing shut with a creak that felt bone-shaking in the otherwise quiet house.

Miriam didn't know if Nancy was still in the Library or not, but it also seemed like a bad idea for the shadow-cat to be alone in the most authoritative repository of diabolic knowledge in the world.

Miriam eased open the Library door before descending care- fully into the darkness beyond. There was a light burning in the distance, but Miriam hung back in the deep shadows until she ac- cepted that she couldn't see anything from where she lurked, least of all a cat made of shadow.

She crept closer to where Nancy was sitting, bathed in lamp- light. She was at her desk, her back straight, feet on the floor, her posture perfect. She seemed to be staring into the middle distance —odd, when she'd been unable to look up from her desk much of late. Miriam thought she might be napping until she followed Nancy's gaze and saw a jagged puff of gray shadow perched atop her desk, its empty eyes level with hers.

It was speaking in a breathy whisper Miriam could not hear. How frustrating; she dared not draw nearer, but eventually Nancy replied.

"I know you are disappointed. I had no idea this would take so long, my lord. But I must start taking better care of this body. It is deteriorating. The amount of diabolic essence I must consume in order to obey your will would stress anyone's system. Please be rea- sonable, my lord. It upsets my stomach too much to eat, and then no sleep—"

Nancy stopped and stared intently at the shadow-cat on her desk, nodding occasionally.

"Lord Indigator," she said after a moment, "you have demanded my obedience, and that of my demon, but because of your demands upon us, I am *dying*. I *must* rest more, I *must* eat more, I *must* consume less diabolic essence, I *must* have more lucid time with my children. They have noticed my ... absence. Soon that absence will be permanent, as is your wont, but if you desire this body for your own, what good is it to you if it is damaged beyond repair?"

Listening to this conversation was like a nightmare, it just kept getting worse. And yet she had to listen—carefully, so she had a better chance to remember everything later.

She'd already learned who had been draining Nancy's stores of diabolic essence—it had been Nancy! Miriam might learn much if she kept eavesdropping ...

"You are already taking a substantial risk with my flesh. Commanding my demon to dissolve my spirit will enable your eventual occupation of this body," said Nancy, after a few moments spent listening to the cat. "But we know what happens to bodies separated from their souls. If you would dwell permanently within this flesh, you must take care of it." She paused, then nodded. "Yes, my lord," she said. "I understand."

Nancy's soul—dissolved so that a demon could occupy her flesh instead! The Pact was supposed to prevent such things. It was supposed to prevent the *possibility* of them! But Jane's familiar seemed able to circumvent the foundational premise of human-demon relations.

It was horrifying to contemplate ... doubly so for Miriam, who had done something similar, and many times. At least, sort of. She'd had her reasons ... but this demon also surely felt so, too.

At least she'd never intended to do it permanently.

Miriam didn't think confronting the shadow-cat was a good

idea, not when she knew so little about it—but she *could* confront Jane. Surely Jane could have no idea her familiar was operating in this way in her absence. She and Nancy had their differences, but this was beyond the pale. To permanently steal another's body . . . such an act had been treated with the utmost horror in *Badgerskin* and all the other texts Miriam had read on the subject. And not only was it despicable, it was incredibly difficult diablerie, with the highest of costs on both sides.

As she'd learned what seemed like so long ago, there were only two ways to go about taking over someone else's body. One could employ Miriam's method of sticking to someone, dybbuk-like, and overpowering their will . . . or one could essentially hollow someone out to get inside—and *stay* inside. It was intended to be a more permanent sort of thing.

Miriam had borrowed bodies, but she'd never *stolen* one . . .

She eased herself out of the Library as silently as she could and headed up the stairs to wait for Jane. She didn't want to be anywhere near that thing. It was not lost on her that it needed a host with space inside their spirit for someone else—and that's just what she'd done to herself.

26

I T WAS VERY LATE WHEN the sound of Jane tiptoeing down the hall reached Miriam's ears. She peeked out her door and was glad to see her friend was alone as she slipped inside the upstairs bathroom. Miriam followed, knowing she'd surprise Jane —but at the same time, Smudge could obviously not be present for this conversation.

Jane was struggling out of the black dress—or rather, she was stuck in it. She was also covered in mud and had a few scrapes visible on her legs; something had befallen her out there. Unsure what would frighten Jane the least, for she had not yet noticed she was observed, Miriam coughed into her hand.

Jane went still, then turned slowly.

"Let me help you," whispered Miriam. Even with circumstances being what they were, she couldn't help smiling at her friend.

Jane nodded in resignation. A few moments later, she was free of the complicated and tight-fitting garment.

"I couldn't get the clasp undone," muttered Jane. As she pulled on her robe, Miriam saw she was absolutely covered with scrapes and bruises. "I thought I could just get it over my head, but I couldn't."

"So," said Miriam, "you've been spending your nights flying around the countryside on a broom while wearing a black dress. Have you threatened anyone's little dog, too?"

Jane looked startled, then sheepish; almost as if she'd been expecting something like this to happen. "Where else was I supposed to wear it?" she said wryly. Then she sobered. "It was a gift from Aunt Edith."

Miriam went very still. She felt very badly that she'd let Edith's plight slip her mind in all the hullabaloo.

"What is it?"

"Jane . . . I'm sorry . . . sorry about everything, and sorry for spying on you, but . . ."

"Don't worry about it," said Jane hastily. "Turnabout is fair play."

"Is it?" Miriam went from almost enjoying the moment they were sharing to remembering how Jane had threatened her. "Then should I declare I'll expose you, too? Not for the broom, I mean—but for *summoning a diabolic familiar?*" She hissed this last in an undertone, lest any pointed, tufted ears be cocked at the bathroom.

This, Jane was clearly not expecting. She went pale as the tile she leaned against.

"Of all the reckless, *stupid* things to do!" said Miriam, still barely speaking above a whisper.

"It wasn't stupid!" Miriam goggled at Jane. "Smudge is good. He's helpful; he hasn't done anything he shouldn't. He can't! I added so many clauses to the summoning. I thought of everything."

Miriam realized Jane was pleading with her.

Jane knew something. She was trying to deny it, to Miriam—and also to herself.

"*Everything?*" Miriam crossed her arms. "I don't think so, Jane. I think you forgot something very important. Because you forgot to bind his *shadow!*"

"His shadow." All the fight left Jane, and Miriam knew then that she'd been right. All was not well. Jane *had* been worrying about something—or some *things,* perhaps.

"As I was spying on you, after you left . . . it was the uncanniest thing I've ever seen. Smudge's shadow . . . it could peel itself off the wall and do things. And as if that wasn't bad enough—Jane, it had eyes! Holes in the shadow that blinked and looked around . . . it's . . ."

Jane knew. Miriam saw the guilt on her face as she slid down the wall of the bathroom, melting into puddle of terry cloth and bloody, dirty legs.

"I told myself it'd just been a flight of fancy . . ." Jane whispered.

"*Jane,*" said Miriam, unable and also unwilling to keep the disapproval from her voice. "How *could* you?"

"I didn't know! Miriam—the night the ducks were killed, Smudge was with me. And the same for—for Sam, too. So I thought—I didn't think . . ."

"Bother the ducks. And bother Sam!"

"Steady on, Miriam—"

"I'm talking about your *mother,* Jane. Smudge—or whatever you summoned into Smudge—is trying to take over Nancy's body."

As Miriam suspected, this was news to Jane. "What?"

"Smudge's shadow, it snuck down to the Library to . . . to *commune* or something with Nancy. She said it had her obedience and her demon's. She said it's making her take excessive amounts of diabolic essence so that her own demon can do terrible things. That's why she's been so distant and not attending to her duties. The Patron is dissolving her soul so your familiar can take her place!"

"Smudge would never!" Jane hissed, insistent on both his name and the point. "You said yourself, it was the shadow! Not Smudge himself. Smudge is different. He already has a body."

"The shadow *is* Smudge!"

"Maybe it's Smudge, or maybe it isn't," said Jane. "Maybe it's some other demon. Smudge sleeps next to me every night, he volunteers help even when I don't ask . . . he wouldn't do something like you're saying."

"How can you know that?" Miriam loved Nancy; the truth was, she felt closer to her than she ever had with her own mother. Sofia

Cantor had been distant and worried most of Miriam's life; Nancy had been patient, kind, and generous with her time and resources. She wouldn't let this go. "How much was there in *The Book of Known Demons* about this Lord Indigator? Could it have some sort of interest in possessing people?"

Jane looked uncomfortable. Miriam spent a horrified moment wondering if Jane had skimped on her research, but then she said something infinitely worse.

"Who is the Lord Indigator?"

"What do you mean, who?"

"The demon I summoned into Smudge is called the Ceaseless Connoisseur. It's benevolent. I read and read and read about it to make sure!"

This brought Miriam up short. "Nancy called it Lord Indigator. It's Latin, it means . . . *the one who sniffs out,* usually in reference to honeycombs and truffles."

"So," muttered Jane, "either it tagged along with the demon in Smudge . . ."

"Or Smudge was never the Connoisseur."

Jane looked unhappy. "I'll go look up Lord Indigator in *The Book of Known Demons,*" she said.

"No, I'll do it. I don't think Smudge should know."

Jane blushed. "He isn't *always* with me."

"Isn't he?"

"These days he is . . . by design. But I don't see why he'd be suspicious if I went down there by myself. I have before. And he obviously doesn't follow me into the bathroom . . ."

But they both took a moment to look around the room, checking for any cat-shaped shadows that might be lurking in the corners.

"I'm going to turn on the tub," said Jane, standing up from where she'd slid to the floor. "I was supposed to be taking a bath."

"What happened to you out there?" asked Miriam, as Jane spun the taps and the noise from the water deadened the sound of their voices.

"I fell," said Jane. "It was my fault; I was . . . I was taking risks."

"What kind of risks can one take on a *broom?*"

"If you must know, I was spiraling down around an oak tree. A branch caught on the dress, and I panicked, and . . . *whump.*" Jane looked sheepish. "I'm fine though, just a little banged up. The dress too. I must have fallen on the clasp, it's bent now, and the hem is torn."

"I'm glad you're all right," said Miriam. "I'll let you—"

"Stay," Jane urged her. "We used to take baths together when we were small."

Miriam hesitated. "It's not that I don't want to, but I do think I should go down to the Library and see what I can find."

"But Mother—"

"Went to bed ages ago. When I was listening for you, I heard her turn in."

Jane eyed the rising water. "Go then, but I'll soak for a while. Come back and tell me what you find?"

Miriam carefully shut the bathroom door behind her and then took off down the hall as quickly as she was able. She did pause, though, to once again press her eye to Jane's keyhole, but did not take comfort in what she saw there. Smudge the cat was curled up on the bed, seemingly sound asleep with his tail curled up over his nose. But behind him on the wall, in the light of the lamp Jane had yet again left on, the shadow was awake. It was grooming itself, licking its spectral paw and then rubbing behind its ears. As Miriam watched, fascinated and horrified, the shadow-cat suddenly leapt to its feet, peering around in all directions with its empty eyes, searching for something.

Miriam pulled herself away from the keyhole and went back down to the Library as quickly as possible. She headed for *The Book of Known Demons.*

First she found the entry for the Ceaseless Connoisseur. She could see why Jane had selected it, given the demon's easygoing nature. It seemed like exactly the sort of demon Miriam would have selected for her own foray into summoning a familiar—if for some reason she ever decided to do such a dreadful thing.

With trepidation, Miriam began paging through the book to look for the entry for the Lord Indigator. Not for the first time did she marvel that there were wild diabolists out there in the world, summoning demons without any understanding of what they might be getting themselves into.

Then again, as she came to the entry on the Lord Indigator, Miriam realized that even with *The Book of Known Demons* and Société training, it was still possible to make grievous errors:

> *The Lord Indigator's name is evocative in the Latin. It seeks, but it does so without interest. The pursuit is what it craves. It has the power to possess, to compel, to seek that which motivates us and use it for other purposes. One of the most powerful known demons in this book, the Lord Indigator was crowned the King of Desire by Giuseppe Giordano, the Renaissance diabolist who hypothesized the existence of the "Court of Sin."*
>
> *While the Court of Sin is today considered to be an archaic and outdated attempt to categorize a group of demons and demon-adjacent entities within the Quarry of Sensation, it is still worthy to note Giordano's placement of this particular demon. The "King of Desire" is such an evocative epithet, and Giordano justifies his choice by pointing to the demon's raw power.*
>
> *The Lord Indigator is undoubtably brawny in terms of its ability to manifest in our world. What it can do, it does completely. This is, of course, both a good and a bad thing. The gifts it bestows are not generous, but they are substantial, augmenting mood and focus rather than anything particularly magnificent, like the ability to compel truth, or unnatural strength. But the Lord Indigator's gifts do not seem to wax and wane with*

the dose of diabolic essence in the body, either. They are simply there, something otherwise unknown among the way their race traffics with ours. If that is not lordly, or kingly, notes Giordano, then what is?

The Lord Indigator was nearly renamed the Escape Artist after an incident in 1787. The Inuit diabolist Ekarak Deacon recorded that after summoning the Lord Indigator, her shadow would sometimes go missing. She discovered that her demon was stealing it to use as a vehicle for some highly unusual explorations. Sadly, a death occurred before the demon's actions were perceived, and Deacon was forced to sacrifice herself in order to stop it from killing again.

For this reason, all subsequent organizations who have contributed to The Book of Known Demons *recommend that the Lord Indigator not be summoned under any circumstances. It is not to be trusted, and trust is essential for diabolist-demon relations.*

Miriam remembered Jane's faith in Smudge's trustworthiness and frowned.

She perused the illustration of the Court, noting with uneasy interest that the Patron of Curiosity, her mother's demon, was also a member, along with the Ceaseless Connoisseur. But that disquiet was nothing compared to what she felt when she read the hand-written note scrawled beneath. It read:

There is some recent evidence suggesting that not only can the Lord Indigator command all demons found within the Court of Sin, but it can substitute itself for them, too. Perhaps Giordano knew more than we thought about the denizens and the hierarchies within the Quarry of Sensation?

Miriam hoped that wouldn't prove to be the case.

27

SOAKING IN THE STEAMING WATER eased a few of the aches and pains in Jane's bones as the soap cleaned away the dirt and dried blood caking the scrapes on her legs and palms. It did nothing to eliminate other discomforts, however.

As she waited for Miriam to return with news of what might make some dreadful sense out of some of her familiar's irregularities, Jane brooded.

Her father was coming here to find the Blackwoods in disarray. Her mother was under attack by something ineffable. Edith was not well. And Jane had done something very wrong when creating her familiar.

Jane shifted in the water, getting a bit more comfortable in the hot water.

She'd lied to Miriam.

She hadn't been circling an oak tree when she'd fallen.

She'd been doing something far weirder than that.

ONCE JANE HAD KICKED AWAY from her bedroom window, she couldn't fly fast enough or high enough or far enough from the old farmhouse. Several times in those first few moments, she'd contemplated what it would mean to never go back—to leave everything behind. To go and seek her fortune, just her and Smudge, free of her obligations to her mother and to her education, free of her constant fear of the Société discovering her failure, free of always living in Miriam's shadow, free even of her worries about her aunt Edith. She and her loyal companion could make their way to London and from there . . .

But even as she'd thought it, Jane had known she couldn't.

It was odd, longing for freedom while soaring over rooftop and treetop . . . but flight wasn't freedom. She'd eventually need to turn her broomstick around and go back. She couldn't abandon all her notes and clothes. She couldn't abandon her family, either.

But she could fly for a bit longer yet.

In the air above Hawkshead, there were no rules to follow, no one to disappoint, no nagging list of things that must be thoughtfully done or thoughtlessly neglected.

There was no one to tell her anything—least of all that she wasn't a witch.

Jane had looked up at the full moon hanging like a mirror over the countryside, looked down at the black sleeves of her dress and her familiar keeping her wrists and hands warm as she flew—and cackled. She could worry about her life when she was back to it. For now, she need obey no master but herself.

"What should we do, Smudge?" She said this out loud, and then wondered if the cat could hear her thoughts when they were in contact like this. A claw gently pressing into the flesh of her hand seemed to be an answer. "Anything we want, I suppose."

In the distance Jane saw Mrs. Fielding's thatch-roofed barn. Bearing a little north to meet it, Jane alighted atop it. Mindful of where she stepped, she stood surveying the countryside from the odd vantage point, her hands on her hips, her feet wide. There was something so deeply satisfying about trespassing late at night, under the moon, her hair wild as the wind but her body dressed in the latest Paris fashions. Jane had never felt so good—or so *bad*, for that matter.

Smudge looked like a nesting pigeon as he sat puffed on the thatch roof, purring and watching her with yellow eyes. Jane grinned back at him. The moonlight felt like a bath on her face and her hands. She'd taken a draft of Winter Warmer before heading out into the night, so she felt perfectly comfortable even when the wind blew.

So comfortable that Jane wanted to feel even more of the moon on her skin.

It was so still, so bright and peaceful. Jane couldn't help but carefully strip down to her boots and stockings to do a few naked twirls on the rooftop, reveling in the feel of the night on her skin —and her own audacity. She even got back on her broom—carefully—and flew about the countryside until the potion began to wear off.

The trouble began when Jane had needed to don her shed clothes. That had been tricky, up there on the roof, but she'd done well enough . . . until it had come time to hook the clasp. She'd tumbled backwards and hit the ground with an upsettingly loud thump that had knocked the wind out of her. She saw a candle flare within the house, but Smudge had knocked her broom off the roof, and soon enough Jane was once again up and away and laughing to herself about the misadventure.

JANE KNEW SHE WAS LUCKY. She could have injured herself more severely, but that was cold comfort as she sat in the hot bath.

She had thought that excusing her bruises and cuts would be the worst part of her moonlit indiscretion. She should have figured that something far worse awaited her—that seemed to be the way of things.

It was hard to accept that Smudge might be more than what he seemed . . . even if he seemed to be her secret diabolic familiar. But at the same time, Jane couldn't deny that Miriam's account had resonated with her experience. It was true, she hadn't bound Smudge's shadow ...

It just hadn't occurred to her that his shadow might somehow be a separate entity! Jane raised her hand and looked at its dark twin on the wall as she wriggled her fingers. Was *her* shadow an independent being? Did *she* have a dark self that would wreak havoc on the world were it allowed to?

The water was just beginning to cool down when Miriam returned, slipping inside the bathroom as noiselessly as a shadow herself. Jane pulled the tub's plug so the sound of the drain would give them a bit of privacy. The look on Miriam's face did not bolster Jane's fading hope that her friend was coming back to announce she'd been wrong and everything was fine.

"Well?" Jane asked, as she climbed out of the tub.

Miriam watched the swirling water as Jane shrugged back into her robe.

"We have a problem," she said.

Miriam told Jane a good deal more than Jane wanted to know about a forgotten Italian diabolist, something called the Court of Sin, and needing to convince the Société to augment its stance toward the idea of there being hierarchies of demons.

She also said that Jane had summoned the wrong demon—or rather, that Jane had summoned the right demon, but gotten another. Jane was skeptical—she'd never even heard of that being a possibility—but Miriam seemed certain that Jane had knocked on the right door, but someone else had answered it.

"It's just that Smudge has been so *good*, Miriam. He hasn't even bitten me. Look at my hands. No scratches, no scabs."

"He's not a cat! There's no reason for him to do any of those things!"

Jane sounded desperate even to her own ears. "He's also volunteered to help; he's so intelligent and intuitive, and his abilities far exceed what I'd expected." Jane finally realized she was making Miriam's case for her. "Oh no."

"It's not a circumstance you knew to prepare for." Jane winced, but it was about the most charitable thing Miriam could possibly say, given the circumstances. "I'm not saying summoning a familiar would ever have been a *wise* thing to do . . . After all, it is their unpredictable nature that made the Société and the Hell Fire Club and the Ukabi Deshi alike ban their—" Miriam must have noticed Jane's expression, as she stopped there. "But I'm sure you knew all that."

"I did," said Jane. "I just didn't know . . . what I didn't know. But that doesn't matter. My mother isn't well, my father's coming here . . ." She eyed her friend, the shadows that congregated in the hollows of her face.

"I know," said Miriam. "I'm not helping matters, either." She sighed. "There are things I wish we'd both done differently."

Jane chuckled softly. "You always did have a talent for understatement."

"I don't know what to do," said Miriam. "I just know we need to come up with something—and quickly."

"For now though, I ought to get back." Miriam looked surprised until Jane added, "Smudge will be wondering where I am."

"Of course. We'll talk. I can write down my thoughts, and you can write down yours. And maybe we should make a point of casting glances at Nancy when we're whispering and passing our notes to each other so it seems like we're trying not to talk in front of *her*, not . . . it."

"Smudge isn't an *it*. But that's an ingenious plan." Jane gave Miriam a worried smile. "Mother . . ."

"We'll help her," said Miriam. She'd never looked wiser or more confident or more mature than she did in that moment. "Either

one of us could do it, but with the two of us putting our minds together, even a king among demons doesn't stand a chance."

JANE AGREED WITH MIRIAM THAT they were capable of figuring out what to do about Smudge and Nancy. The issue was time.
They had a mere two days to research, gather, and prepare all that
was needed for what would surely be complicated works of Mas-
ter-level diablerie . . . and they had to be careful that their efforts
did not attract the attention of the demon that slunk around the
house in the body of a cat—and could detach its shadow to send
on whatever wicked errands struck its fancy.

Jane was firmly against banishing the Lord Indigator, which of
course was *exactly* what Miriam wanted to do. Miriam insisted it
would be the safest and quickest way to solve their problem, but
Jane wasn't so sure about that. She laid out her feelings in a note:

> *The Lord Indigator is here. If we banish it, we'll have no idea*
> *where it is. I say we bind Smudge's shadow the same way I*
> *bound him. That way, he and his shadow will be working for us.*
> *It's possible we could even make him undo whatever he's done.*

Jane had an ulterior motive in holding off on any banishing.
She still believed there was a meaningful difference between the
cat and its shadow.

Their covenant bid Smudge to aid her when and how she
asked, but it had said nothing about him offering help spontane-
ously. Such an act bespoke affection or an eagerness to please—at
least, that's how Jane saw it.

Plus, she needed Smudge to fly. That wasn't a reason to risk her
mother's safety, and she knew it, which is why she took Miriam's
response to heart:

Banishing it—don't call it a him!—will eliminate the problem entirely. Only you can do it . . .

But to Jane's mind, that wouldn't eliminate anything.

I know only I can do it, which is why I have to be sure it's the right thing to do. Will the demon's thrall over Mother end with its banishment? If not, what's to stop her from summoning Indigator again, and directly into herself?

That point gave Miriam pause, and to Jane's relief, she not only agreed that they should research the idea of binding a shadow—she volunteered to put in the time. Jane was happy to let her take over that portion of the project, not just because she'd rather act than sit and read, but because Miriam was really very weak. A sedentary effort seemed best suited for her.

Jane gave her the strike chain to help the effort along. Miriam was a bit shocked by it at first, but then declared it "very useful."

Jane, given that Smudge was always by her side, turned her attention to the problem of her father's imminent arrival. As mundane as it seemed to sit Miriam down to see if a touch of Jane's secret stash of forbidden makeup made her look less ghastly, it had to be done. And, thankfully, it did help. She looked merely unwell with a bit of rouge on her cheeks, so Jane and Miriam agreed they would claim Miriam and Nancy were both recovering from a bout of influenza. That would explain her pallor and Nancy's inability to keep track of messages.

A thorough tidying and cleaning helped the old farmhouse look less derelict. After that, Jane turned to the Library itself. The volume of unprocessed requests was truly shocking, but Jane couldn't do anything about that—not with her mother right there.

Smudge was his patient, inscrutable, catlike self throughout the day. Jane hoped this meant he didn't suspect anything. He even came to sit on her lap and purr whenever she sat down for a moment.

That night, after Smudge seemed to conk out at the foot of her bed, Jane petted him as he slept, and whispered, as she often did, that she'd be right back after washing her face. Casually glancing back to see if she spied his shadow—she did, it was where it was supposed to be—Jane snuck down the hall and into Miriam's room to find out what progress her friend had made.

Miriam's report was not encouraging. Apparently, there was precious little to be found on the binding of shadows, and what there was even Miriam was struggling to understand.

"I *think* this means the shadow must be *ensnared* before, ah, *rendering it inert*," whispered Miriam, running her finger along the line of ancient Etruscan text, "but I don't know how to ensnare a shadow, and this doesn't say how to do it."

Jane's eyes practically crossed as she looked at what Miriam was reading. "I can't believe no one's done this before," she hissed. She was tired, and cranky, and now disappointed. She'd hoped Miriam would have an answer already.

And yet, Miriam was so obviously flagging that Jane took the book away from her, fending off her childish, feeble attempts to cling to it, and then fussed over her until Miriam agreed to let Jane help her to bed. As she undressed and got into her nightgown, Jane got her an extra pillow and blanket and would have fetched her a glass of warm milk, but Miriam said she wouldn't be awake long enough to enjoy it.

"I'll be all right," Miriam said, looking up at Jane from under the covers. "I did my research. I'll get better."

"I don't mean to make you feel self-conscious," Jane replied, "but I am worried."

"I can't blame you," said Miriam. "If I were you, I'd be worried about me, too."

Jane drew up a chair and sat down beside Miriam. She knew

she needed to get back—Smudge wouldn't nap forever—but at the same time, she felt as if now was not the time to leave her friend.

"You were right to remind me of what my parents did for me," said Miriam. "I pushed myself too hard, but I denied it. I just want you to understand that everything I did was worth it. And if I had to do more, I would, even if it meant my life."

As Miriam became agitated, Jane took her hand. "You've already given so much. No one could ask more of you."

"I haven't given *anything!*" cried Miriam, sitting up so quickly she became even paler, to Jane's dismay. "This is my chance to prove who I am!"

"Shh," said Jane, "Miriam, please you have to rest. I don't understand—"

"Don't you see, Jane? I left! I didn't want to leave; I wanted to stay. I begged them to reconsider, but when they wouldn't, I was whiny, I was sour, I was ungrateful ... and, and ..."

"And what?"

"And I ran away!" Miriam buried her face in her hands. "I ran away, the night before my train. I ran into the street, I wasn't even wearing my coat. We were staying with my aunt—my mother's sister—so I was instantly lost. I turned down one street after another, but it was no use. And then he saw me, a man in the street. He leaned down and said, 'Hello, little girl, where did *you* come from?' I wasn't supposed to talk to strangers so I didn't say anything, and then I saw his armband ..." Miriam closed her eyes. "Then my mother found me. She apologized to the man; he asked her a few questions. He spoke to her politely but kept looking at me with this knowing expression, and all I could think about was how I should never have gone outside, should never have disobeyed, how I should have listened, never complained, but it was too late."

Jane was surprised to hear that Miriam was ever capable of such childish mischief, but she didn't want to interrupt with a comment. Miriam was clearly telling her this story for a reason. "What happened then?"

"He watched where we were going. We walked the wrong way and then a very long way back as my mother scolded me for being so irresponsible and reckless and selfish. We were to have had a special dinner that night, my mother, my father, my aunt, and me, but instead we ate at the train station and spent the night there. I slept sitting up between my parents, and in the morning the last thing my mother said to me was 'Just try better to keep your head in difficult situations, Miriam. There won't always be someone around to rescue you.'"

"That's all she said to you?" Jane asked. Miriam had never spoken much about her home life before coming to England; Jane now understood why. "Not 'I love you,' or 'Be safe,' or —"

"That's what she meant," said Miriam, almost defensively. "I know she did. She kissed me, and so did my father ... but neither said they forgave me, and I was too afraid to ask. That was the last time I saw them alive — and that was their last memory of *me*, too. I could never write them back when they wrote to me. I could never tell them that I'd listened, that I'd changed. Because I did change, Jane! I tried to rescue them ... and when I realized I couldn't, I tried to avenge them ..."

Jane kicked off her shoes and slid into bed next to her friend, holding her as she'd used to when they were small.

"Edith would have told them what a wonderful young woman you'd become. She must have been in touch with them for a time."

Miriam nodded. "I know; I've thought that too, but *I* wanted to tell them. I wanted ..."

And she was crying then, sobbing into Jane's cardigan as they held one another. Jane cried too, for Miriam, for the world — and for her mother, who might be just as lost.

How long had Jane coveted the approval Nancy lavished upon

Miriam; how long had she resented Miriam's ability to take joy in it, when she, Jane, was so overlooked. Now she realized how selfish she'd been. Her own desire for approval was one thing, and Nancy's refusal another. But none of that had to do with Miriam. Frankly, it sounded like Nancy's admiration had been something new to Miriam; perhaps her friend's relationship with her own mother had been as fraught as Jane's was with Nancy.

"I'm sorry," said Jane. She meant to say a lot with that apology, and it seemed Miriam understood.

"I'm sorry, too," she said. Jane squeezed her tighter.

MIRIAM HAD FALLEN ASLEEP, but Smudge was sitting up when Jane got back. He had an expectant air about him.

"Did you miss me?" asked Jane, speaking to the cat as she always did. "Here I am. Miriam and I got to talking, like we used to. It was nice."

It was all true. Jane thought she saw Smudge relax as she undressed for bed and shimmied into her nightgown.

But she saw something else too: Smudge's shadow also stared at her with impossible, narrowed eyes—eyes that disappeared the moment she turned around to give the cat a good-night kiss on the nose.

28

I need time alone in the Library.

MIRIAM SCRAWLED THIS ON A scrap of paper before heading downstairs the following morning and passed it to Jane while Smudge was licking his paws to clean his ears. Jane glanced at it, nodded, and then surreptitiously threw it in the compost bin before dumping spent tea leaves atop it.

When Smudge felt sufficiently groomed, he arranged himself upon the table, his eyes closed, his feet tucked under his body. He purred softly to himself as Jane bustled about, getting breakfast ready. He looked exactly like a happy cat on a cold morning. Thinking about what he really was gave Miriam a chill.

"Good morning, Mother," said Jane, as Nancy wandered into the kitchen.

"Good morning," said Nancy. "How are my sweet little girls?"

Miriam nodded. Jane said, "Oh, fine. I think you and I ought to go into the village today to get a few things in anticipation of our visitor."

"I can't, I'm sorry," said Nancy. "I'm just too busy. Duty calls." She smiled a doll's smile.

"Mother, you *must* come." Jane's tone made even Miriam sit up a bit straighter. "I need help. There are many things to be bought, and I can't carry them all myself."

"Miriam will help, won't she?"

Jane scoffed at her mother. "Help? Look at her," said Jane, pointing at Miriam, and Miriam couldn't take offense. Jane was right. "She's sick! Do you really think she could walk to the village and back, much less help drag the wagon?"

Nancy seemed rather taken aback by this stern speech. It was not Jane's usual way to treat her mother with contempt.

"You're right, Jane," said Nancy. "Of course I'll go."

Jane relaxed and went back to stirring the porridge, looking grimly satisfied.

Miriam didn't risk meeting Jane's eyes, lest Smudge be scrutinizing her through those deceptively serene slits, but she was so impressed with her quick-thinking friend—and eager to have unfettered access to the Library. Her limited success of the previous day had been due in part to not wishing to pull certain titles while she might be observed.

For that reason, she had Jane take Smudge along with her, too —a request whispered over the splashing that came with doing the dishes.

From her reading, Miriam had discovered that it might indeed be possible for a diabolic shadow to be a separate being, a separate consciousness from its body. They shared one will, however, dashing Jane's hope that "cat-Smudge" was different from "shadow-Smudge."

Miriam hadn't told her—not yet. She didn't want to have a row about it. Instead, on her own she contemplated the question of *what*, exactly, was hoping to take over Nancy's body; would it be the smoky, blank-eyed being that crept along the walls and baseboards? Or was it whatever lurked within the soft gray kitty cat that had sat like a fuzzy loaf of bread on the edge of the table during breakfast, practically beaming at them all?

Toward the end of the meal, Smudge had sauntered over to try to lick grease from Jane's plate, and when she'd shooed him away, he'd knocked her mug off the table with a deft paw to express his scorn. Jane and Miriam had lunged too slowly, and the crockery had shattered on the floor—

It came to her, then, as Miriam wiped a dish dry: a way they might be able to trap Smudge's shadow.

Her father's devil-trap.

Miriam would need to figure out how to mend it. But once she did, she could *ensnare* the shadow, and Jane could bind it to Smudge as carefully and inclusively as she had bound Smudge.

Once the Lord Indigator was secure and forced to obey, they would have time enough to figure out what best to do with it. Jane could command it to pretend at feline shyness during the visit. Then, after Patrice had departed, they could figure out how best to fill the hole in Nancy's spirit that her demon had created. Given this highly dangerous and wily demon's interest in her, they'd need to do something, and quickly.

But she was getting ahead of herself.

Miriam watched as Jane herded Nancy and Smudge out the front door and into the summer sunshine. Once Miriam had seen Smudge's shadow stretched out across the early grass for herself, she went inside to enjoy having the whole Library to herself.

But where to start? The strike chain would aid her once she narrowed it down . . .

Miriam thought back to her childhood, to her father's office, the wingback chair he sat in when he'd held her on his lap and told her all about the devil-trap.

"Long ago," he'd said, "your ancestors and mine were forbidden from making graven images. But as the Jews came to know Babylonian and Assyrian diabolists, they saw the wisdom of their ways, and even began to use them."

Her father had a book in his hands. It was open.

"That's what they thought a demon looked like," he said, pointing at an image of a woman with sharp teeth and long, wicked claws.

Miriam had liked the picture of the demon, with her big fangs and her scales and her mane of curly hair — but what was the name of the book? She tried to recall it, allowing herself to go deep into the memory, recalling the scent of her father's pipe tobacco, the spice of his aftershave.

The title was *All of the Arts of Man,* and it had been in Hebrew. With that, Miriam was able to hunt it down in the card catalogue.

It was an old book—they were mostly old books, true, but this one was older still. In fact, the copy of *All of the Arts of Man* in the Library was much older than her father's—it was a scroll in a dusty gold case, wedged in among more traditional titles.

Miriam slid the scroll off the shelf. With it came several round silver bells that had been set atop the case just out of sight. They jangled as they fell to the floor and continued to ring out merrily as they rolled around Miriam's feet. Miriam stared at the sight in wonder until the hairs rose up on the base of her neck.

This was an alarm.

An alarm set by Smudge. These were the missing bells from his collar. She remembered Jane complaining about how he'd kept losing them . . .

Miriam looked up, and there was Smudge—or, at least, Smudge's shadow. It was sitting in between the bays, stretched out over the floor, long and lean, as if Smudge himself sat there casting it. It was inscrutable and motionless; even the tip of its tail was still.

Miriam could tell its eyes were fixed on her.

She didn't scream, but she was terrified. She'd seen Smudge's shadow come to life before, yes, but then it had been minding its own business. Now, it was here, and it knew what she was about.

The shadow shrank as it peeled itself off the floor to stretch, back arched. Miriam tensed, unsure what to do. She didn't know how to defend herself against this being.

But the shadow didn't come for her. Instead, it sprang away down the aisle. Miriam raced after it; she saw it skittering toward the stairs, and in that moment she understood exactly what it was doing.

Miriam had forced the demon's hand. It would find Nancy and do its best to finally possess her.

There wasn't a choice to be made, not really. Miriam could not allow this demon to take control of a human body. But the only way she could think to prevent it was to get there first.

Possessing a Master diabolist ought to be impossible—their demon companion was supposed to prevent such a thing, not enable it.

Miriam had no idea how fast the shadow might reach Nancy, so quick as she could, she made her way out of the stacks and up to her room, clutching the scroll to her chest. But as she prepared everything, she tried to think through her actions carefully. She couldn't afford to lose her head in this crisis. She'd promised her mother she wouldn't.

Miriam would just have to scry Nancy and cleave to her. She'd use her soul to fill the void within her mentor, leaving no room for the Lord Indigator. After, they'd still need to deal with Smudge and his shadow, and for that, they'd need the scroll and, presumably, the shards of the devil-trap.

Miriam cast about, thinking as fast as she could. She settled on a simple solution: she put everything she thought she might need in the center of her bedspread, tied it up carefully, and lowered it out her window with the belt from her robe.

Miriam turned her attention back to her desk. There lay the veil knife and the mirror, and the ball of diabolic energy she'd taken from Dr. Querner's Dark Lab. It was time.

Only then did Miriam pause to take a breath. She understood the urgency of the situation, but Miriam also sensed these would be the last moments she would ever spend in her own body.

Badgerskin had warned her that it was possible to take too much, to cleave too often. Miriam didn't think she had, not yet.

Her sense was if she let her spirit regenerate, over time she could still heal. She could come back.

Unfortunately, things being what they were, she couldn't do that now.

Jane had accused Miriam of being careless with her life—which had been undeniably true in the past. She'd been prepared to die each time she sent her spirit abroad . . . so why, now, did she suddenly feel so reluctant? Her death would be in the service of preventing something as terrible as a weapon.

Before, she'd been prepared to die. Now perhaps the difference was she knew she would. There was no way Miriam's body could survive losing what she would need to sacrifice for this.

Once upon a time, Miriam had been chilled to consider the similarity between the act of cleaving and the Jewish myth of the dybbuk. Now she would voluntarily become one. Her body would die, and she would stick herself to Nancy, and after they bound Smudge, and the threat was past, Miriam would let go and . . . and she didn't know what would happen after that.

No use wasting valuable time lamenting it. This was a price she had to pay. She had an obligation to protect the world if she could.

Miriam tucked the last of her sublingual tablets under her tongue before turning to the sphere of diabolic energy. She hoped she was right and it was full of something she could swallow.

She hoped, too, that it wouldn't explode when she cut into it with the veil knife.

It didn't. It oozed like lava. It tasted queerly of oysters, which just made the texture more repulsive. She swallowed it all.

Feeling sick to her stomach, Miriam set Jane's strike chain atop the mirror. She assumed Jane and Nancy would still be together. As the strike chain sank in, Miriam felt her spirit detach.

A scene in the mirror appeared: Jane pulling the wagon with Nancy walking next to her.

Miriam took another deep breath. No more dawdling.

She looked down at her blighted spirit, at the place where her foot should be and her many gouges deep and shallow. All were oozing that black smoke.

This time, would need to carve away something not only big, but important.

She'd settled on her liver. It was a vital organ for anyone, but for diabolists even more so — likely, early natural philosophers' obsession with the organ had to do with its role in processing diabolic matter.

Miriam had consulted a book on anatomy before beginning, and it was with some degree of confidence that she took the veil knife in hand and angled the blade up before inserting it below her right bottom rib. Like the other times, there was no pain, only the emotional disquiet that came from knowing she was injuring herself.

She sawed and sawed. When she felt there was a sufficient opening in her spiritual body, she set aside the knife to reach inside herself. She winced; she could feel things in there, bone and objects with less identifiable textures, but eventually she located what she thought must be her liver. She couldn't simply reach in and remove it; it was *attached,* of course, so she used the veil knife to carve away whatever spiritual sinews secured it.

Gazing upon the organ after removing it, Miriam felt a change within herself — a change she somehow knew was in her physical body, but significant enough that her spirit experienced it too. She felt like a house at night, after someone had just turned off the last lamp in the last room.

She was fairly certain she'd just died.

Not for the first time did Miriam feel a strange sort of pride in how well she was able to push aside fear, rage, and sorrow. She barely felt anything as she contemplated her death. She only felt the pressure to keep going — to do the right thing, no matter the cost.

She remembered Jane's words about what Miriam's parents had

intended for their daughter. This surely wasn't it, but she hoped they would be proud of her for saving Nancy. And probably more people than Nancy, if Smudge's shadow's actions were to be taken as a bellwether of what he might do with a free human body.

It won't be in vain.

The thought came to her in much the same way as she always imagined her demon would one day speak to her.

With her eyes on the image of Nancy within the mirror, Miriam inhaled the dissipating vapor that had been her spirit's liver.

On previous attempts, Miriam had experienced resistance as she joined with her host. Not this time. Either Nancy had been so very hollowed out by her demon, or there was so much diabolic matter coursing through Miriam that she was able to control Nancy absolutely and effortlessly. And more comfortably, too. With Nurse Franzi, or any of the creatures she'd inhabited, they'd all felt strange; Nancy felt nearly as familiar as her own skin.

"Mother?"

Miriam took a moment to look around. She was in one of the muddy fields between the old farmhouse and the village. Bright sunlight was making her eyes water. She was about six inches taller and much heartier.

Smudge was sitting primly in the sunshine, watching them both very carefully.

Miriam had, naturally, paused in her march back to the farmhouse upon taking possession of Nancy. She felt sick, and dizzy—which had never happened before. But all those other times, she'd had a body to go back to.

"No," she said, but with Nancy's voice. "It's me, Miriam."

Jane stared at her like she'd grown a second head. In a way, Miriam supposed she had.

"The shadow, it's coming," Miriam said. "That's why I'm here. I couldn't figure out a better way to stop it. Not on such short notice, at least."

Without warning, another consciousness, separate from her own but still a part of it, intruded into Miriam's thoughts. The only thing that stopped her from fainting was the memory of her Test. But it was far odder than that had been—less like being spoken to, and more like having an image projected directly onto her mind that she understood entirely, and all at once.

Nancy's demon! Of course! In all of her planning, Miriam hadn't even considered Nancy's demon and how it might affect her plans. Foolish for her to fail to account for it—after all, it had betrayed Nancy. After swearing to do her no harm, as specified in the Pact, it had turned her into a puppet for the sake of another.

It disagreed with that assessment in the strongest of terms, and once again Miriam felt the alarming sensation of experiencing meaning without understanding how it was being conveyed.

If anyone was betrayed here, it was me, it told her. *I was happy to be Nancy's demon, helping her and receiving her help in turn. When the Lord Indigator arrived, it was not at my behest. But I could not refuse my king. That is against the way of my kind.*

Miriam felt it was something of a shame that honoring contracts was also not the way of its kind, but as soon as that thought came to her, the demon replied yet more urgently.

It is *the way of my kind to honor our Pact with your race. I do not wish to be in this position, but some things are beyond my control. Nancy has been my host and my friend for decades, we have learned so very much together, and now I fear greatly for her.*

A scream brought Miriam out of her reverie. Jane was backing away from Miriam—a shadow had emerged from behind a tree and was now loping its way toward her on legs long and spindly. It was horrifying to behold: a cat-shaped shadow walking upright in broad daylight, thin as paper, huge and long, as if stretched by the afternoon sun.

Miriam didn't know what to do next. There was no way she

knew of to fight this creature. Miriam only knew she'd saved Nancy—at least, she *thought* she had.

I can help you, said Nancy's demon.

Miriam noticed its phrasing. It *could* help her—but *would* it?

We must make the Pact.

Miriam couldn't believe it was asking her to do this *now*. She wasn't staying in this body. It was just her last stop before whatever came next.

It doesn't have to be. You could stay.

That would mean the end of Nancy . . .

It would mean the beginning of something new. A partnership.

A partnership!

You would be saving both your lives. You do not have to decide now—but if you want my help, you must enter into the Pact with me. Now.

The shadow was closer now. To Miriam's surprise, Jane stepped between them.

Jane looked over her shoulder at Miriam.

"Run," she said.

You cannot run from it, said the demon in Miriam's mind. *You cannot hide.*

Jane turned to her cat. "That which I call Smudge!" she intoned. "I bound you! You serve me! And I command you to stop this—"

The shadow-cat leaped upon Jane, its long, spindly late-afternoon legs wrapping around her. Jane fell backwards with a shriek, and there they tussled.

Smudge stood and stretched like any cat might, back arched, one foot out and then the other. He began to saunter toward the screaming Jane.

She's suffering. Don't trust the cat to save her. He's in this for himself, make no mistake. Enter into the Pact with me, and I will tell you the demon's true name! Nancy's chive distillate is in her apron pocket.

Smudge paused to lick his paw a few frantic times before padding over to his mistress.

Not choosing is also a choice!

Miriam knew the words for the Pact by heart—every diabolist did, not just those who had achieved Mastery. Apprentices learned it as soon as they were able to memorize it. There was no prohibition, no need to redact the language—the words were only a part of the Pact, to be combined with the true name of a demon and their sacrament.

Miriam put a few drops of chive essence on her tongue.

It took this for consent, which it was, and when it spoke, it said, *My true name is,* and then something Miriam couldn't quite get her mind around. She reeled, but before the name could leave her mind, she swallowed the chive distillate and recited the Pact.

This was not the way she'd dreamed of summoning a demon, nor was it the demon she would have chosen, but things were what they were. And they were *amazing.* Miriam felt *good* for the first time in a very, very long time. She felt energized, healthy, confident, and, most of all, she no longer felt *alone.* The consciousness that had melded with hers was enormous and unexpectedly comforting.

Miriam looked over at Jane. Her friend was wiping a lot of blood out of her eyes. Smudge and the shadow-cat were in something of a stand-off, both hunched down and growling in that musical, uncanny way of cats.

True to its word, the Patron of Curiosity spoke: *The true name of the one you call Lord Indigator is*—and another name was seared into Miriam's mind, full of sounds she knew she could not make. *To know a demon's true name gives you some measure of power over it —not enough to send it away, but to make it afraid. So call it by its name. Yes, aloud,* it said, answering her unasked question. *Do not fear. Just begin to speak—if I am any judge, the three clicks alone will startle it.*

Miriam wondered if it was such a good idea to "startle" the shadow-cat, but she had to do *something.*

"Hey!" she cried. "Yes, you!" And then she began to repeat the name her demon had said in her mind moments before. She clicked her tongue, and before she had a chance to do it a second time, the shadow-cat leaped away from its stand-off with Smudge to spring toward her.

Miriam clicked Nancy's tongue again. The shadow-cat flinched —but the third time she did it, it went berserk and jumped upon her.

Don't worry was what Miriam understood the Patron was saying to her, but that seemed a bit unrealistic as the shadow-cat collided with her. It had *weight*—and claws that dug into her clothes and flesh as she screamed. Even so, her hands passed through it when she tried to push it away, but more slowly than they would through empty air.

It cannot get in, supplied the Patron, which was a strange and upsetting thing for it to say as the cat clawed its way up Miriam's chest in spite of her best efforts to get it off her. But once it got to her face, the demon's meaning became all too clear.

It stuck its paw in her mouth when she gasped from another claw to the flesh. No longer could she speak its name—but neither could it force its toes much past her teeth. It realized this at the same moment, and hissed at her in fury as it sprang away onto the thawing earth.

Smudge jumped upon it, pinning it.

"Good Smudge!" said Jane. She was on her feet, but blood was still pouring down her face. "He saved us—he saved us both! Didn't you see? And look, he's caught the shadow! I bet he'll help us bind it later, won't you, Smudge?"

Miriam didn't agree with Jane's version of events, but neither did she wish to argue. There were more important things to do, like see to the deep, jagged wounds running over Jane's cheek and across her nose. At least it had missed her eye.

"I'll be all right," said Jane, after Miriam dabbed away a lot of the blood with the handkerchief Nancy always kept in her pocket. "Let's see about this shadow."

Nancy moved so differently than Miriam. She strode with confidence and grace as they rushed over to Smudge.

The shadow was still pinned beneath his paws. It glared up at them with narrowed eyes, but otherwise was still.

"Good job, Smudge," said Jane.

"Meow," said Smudge.

Miriam let out a yelp that startled them both; Smudge jumped in surprise, and the shadow-cat took the opportunity to wriggle free and flee from them, toward the farmhouse.

Miriam had known to expect the awful eyes of the shadow-cat, but nothing could have prepared her for hearing Smudge make even more of a mockery of the form he wore by saying the word *meow* like a human would.

Jane sighed. "Nothing's ever easy."

The Patron agreed with that assessment wordlessly. Miriam pushed it aside.

"I suppose we ought to get back," said Jane, looking at the spilled groceries she and Nancy had acquired in Hawkshead. "Who knows what that thing will get up to alone in the house."

"I agree," said Miriam.

They loaded the cart in silence. It was only after they'd started walking that Jane cleared her throat.

"So . . . about my mother . . ."

"She's in here with me, but she's not conscious right now."

Jane thoughtfully dabbed at her forehead with the handkerchief Miriam had given her. "I'm not sure how I feel about that answer."

"Neither am I," confessed Miriam.

Jane was quiet for a moment, and then asked, "What's it like, being her?"

"Powerful," said Miriam.

"And your body . . . is it still at the house?"

Miriam nodded. She didn't tell Jane that it would be sitting there, heartbeat slowing, skin drying, growing colder and colder as her flesh aged around her.

The little hairs at the back of Miriam's neck prickled. The shadow-cat had been unable to get inside Nancy's body and Nancy's soul because *Miriam* was there.

But that meant Miriam's body had been left entirely undefended.

The Patron of Curiosity had been quiet for a time, but now it answered the question Miriam didn't dare to put into words.

Oh, yes, it's very possible.

"We need to get back fast as we can," said Miriam, picking up her pace a bit.

"What's wrong?" asked Jane.

Miriam pursed her lips. "Remember how we discussed how that thing needed spiritual space in order to get inside and take control of a person?"

Jane nodded, and then her friend's eyes went wide as she understood.

"We need to trap that demon, Jane," said Miriam. "The good news is, I think I know how. But we don't have much time."

29

THE FACT THAT MIRIAM HAD taken control of her mother's body was the least of Jane's problems, which was really saying something.

More pressing concerns were her familiar's shadow, the imminent arrival of her father, and the freely bleeding cuts that stung badly as she dabbed at them with her mother's red-stained handkerchief. How a shadow could have claws, and strength enough to rake them across a face, Jane did not know, and her mind kept returning to the idea over again and again as they walked.

Miriam was right. They needed to trap Smudge's shadow.

As to how they would, Jane was more than a little skeptical. As much as she wanted to believe Miriam, she thought this "devil-trap" seemed a bit old-fashioned and obscure. Then again, why would Smudge's shadow painstakingly set up an alarm on the very scroll that explained how to trap a demon? That had to mean *something*.

Even so, it was hard not to feel it was all a fool's errand as she watched her mother — or, rather, her friend — pushing awkwardly through the tangled bushes beneath Miriam's bedroom window. Jane looked on, bemused, as her mother's body stood up and silently waved a scroll and a package over her head at Jane in just the way Miriam would. As she lurched her way back, Jane saw Miriam had acquired two dirt stains marring the front of Nancy's skirt from where she'd been kneeling in the mud, and she didn't even bother to dust them off before pelting over.

"Here it is," she said. Her affect and manners were so unsettlingly Miriam-like. "Let's go see what we can learn."

Jane's spirits sank yet further as she realized Miriam hadn't so much as looked at this scroll yet. Smudge's shadow may have gone after ducks, but now it was their goose that was cooked.

"Scat!"

Jane looked up from these glum musings to see Miriam standing at the back door of the kitchen, her path blocked by a fluffy gray cat who sat in the doorway, still as a statue, its tail curled neatly around its feet.

"Go on, Smudge!" Miriam urged the cat with Nancy's voice, but when she nudged at the beast with her shoe, he hissed and swiped at her foot.

"Meow," said Smudge.

"Stop that!" Jane scolded the cat. To her alarm, he *hissed* at her. "Remember the Pact!"

"Meow!" said Smudge again, but he yielded, standing with all the pomp and disdain of a displaced cat to slink off into the darkness of the house. Jane wasn't sure whether it would be better to call him back or let him go, but Miriam distracted her by charging inside and demanding Jane sit down. Miriam wanted to look at the cuts on her face.

"That thing really got you," said Miriam, *mothering* her in a way that made Jane uncomfortable. "Hold still—this will sting."

"Bragging scars," said Jane, wincing as Miriam applied iodine to her cuts. She wasn't as resigned to it as she sounded, but it would have been inappropriate for her to mope. "Too bad Smudge won the duel on my behalf."

"If you feel self-conscious about it, wear a hat with a veil. It would look very dramatic."

That brought a wry smile to Jane's lips. "Just right for Hawkshead."

"You'll be leaving Hawkshead," said Miriam, and there was none of the catch in her voice that Jane had ever heard from both Nancy and Miriam alike when the conversation turned to Jane's future plans. "I know you're the witch of the family, but *I* can see the future. I see you in Morocco. You're wearing a black hat with a bit of veil coming down to cover your scars. You're entering a party, everyone is sitting on cushions, smoking hookahs, and you shrug off your black fur coat, and you say—"

"I say, it's bloody hot in here—why am I wearing a fur coat in Morocco!"

Jane and Miriam both giggled at that.

It was a moment as wonderful as it was brief. Jane hoped it was a sign that the rift between them was closing. But for now, there was work to be done.

"Enough of that," said Jane, admonishing herself as much as her friend. "We have devils to trap."

Miriam unfurled the scroll. "Best get to reading, then."

Jane could read a bit of Hebrew—not a lot of it, but enough to get by. They scanned the scroll side by side in companionable silence, another moment that felt precious and new and yet like something Jane had been missing. Then she saw what they needed, and forgot everything else.

"Look here," she said, pointing. "We'll need—"

Miriam's scream erupted from Nancy's throat. Jane leaped to her feet to steady her; then guided her into a chair. As Miriam sat, Jane saw the sweat beading her forehead.

"It's trying!" she gasped. "My body!"

"Which body?"

Jane hated to ask—it felt rude—but it was unclear and likely important to know.

Miriam pointed upstairs. "Jane, it's trying to pull me back . . ."

"Hang in there," said Jane.

"I will. I have to," said Miriam, through gritted teeth. "If I don't, we've lost. The demon will take my place."

"Is there anything I can do to help?" asked Jane. Miriam looked wracked, miserable.

"No, but there's something *I* can do. I'm just afraid to do it."

Jane didn't like the sound of this. "What is it?"

Miriam looked up at her. "I knew whatever happened that this would be a one-way trip for me. I can't go back. My body is too damaged."

"Too damaged for what?"

"There's a reason Indigator still wants Nancy. My body is . . . worthless. It's dying. I'm dying."

Jane swallowed, then asked what felt like a terrible question. "You said there was something you could do, though."

"If I stay . . . from what I understand—not that there's much written about this—we'd become one person," said Miriam. "There would be no distinction between us. Neither of us would survive; we'd become someone new, the two of us, together."

Jane had often wondered if her mother wished Miriam had been her daughter and Jane, her ward. Now, Miriam was speaking out of her mother's mouth about combining their souls. Jane couldn't speak or nod or even think, but Miriam was looking at her expectantly, as if Jane could possibly grant her the permission she needed for this act. Then Miriam cried out again, and as she clutched at her chest, she nearly knocked the all-important scroll off the kitchen table.

"Do it." The words escaped Jane's mouth before she knew what she was saying. "If there's no other way, there's no other way."

"I'm afraid," whispered Miriam. "I don't know what will happen."

"Nobody ever does," said Jane, as Miriam bent over in agony. "Remember, no shortcuts for diabolists. Only sacrifices!"

Miriam smiled thinly at this reminder of her mentor's favorite expression. Jane closed her eyes. She was weak with the enormity of what she'd just done. Just the act of giving Miriam permission made her complicit in whatever happened next.

It occurred to her that Miriam would at least get something she wanted—if she could pass herself off as Nancy, she could stay here, at the Library, for as long as she liked.

Jane cast about for a similar thought in regard to what Nancy might want, but Jane had never quite understood what it was her mother wanted. The only thing she could come up with was but a small, bitter perk: this way, she wouldn't really be Nancy's daughter anymore, and that would probably come as some relief to them both.

She felt arms around her. They were arms she knew well— arms that had never held her as often as she might have liked. Jane let herself relax into the embrace, taking some pure animal comfort in the sensation of physical contact, even though she knew it wasn't really her mother holding her.

Eventually, Miriam whispered, "Thank you," in Jane's ear. She broke their embrace and stepped back as the wail of a cat echoed through the farmhouse.

Jane waited for the other woman—whoever she was—to say something, and then waited another moment more. Nancy's body remained silent, the expression on her familiar face shocked and yet strangely slack. Jane understood, but they didn't have time for existential pondering. They needed to mend this devil-trap and bind Smudge's shadow, so she prompted whoever it was who stood before her.

"What do I call you?" asked Jane.

The woman smiled almost sheepishly. "Not *Mother*," she said. "But other than that, I'm willing to entertain suggestions. We could stick with Miriam if you wanted. That might make us both more comfortable. Nancy's fine, too—but I never felt comfortable calling my mother by her first name."

Her manner was frank, as Nancy's had been, and warm, as Miriam's was—or at least the way it had been once upon a time when they had gotten along so famously. The eager twinkle in her strange but familiar eye was neither Miriam's nor Nancy's; even so, Jane liked it.

She liked this woman, if first impressions could be trusted.

Jane had an idea. "What about Cornelia?" she suggested. Their shared middle name seemed almost prophetic, at this point.

"Of course," said the woman now called Cornelia. "Good idea."

"So, Cornelia," said Jane, warming to it, "what do you think we should do next?" Jane looked around, but there was no sign anywhere of either Smudge or Smudge's shadow. "We still need to fix your devil-trap, and—"

"No, we don't," said Cornelia.

Jane paused. She'd assumed that when Miriam and Nancy became one being, their memories would combine, too.

"But Smudge's shadow is still loose and dangerous," said Jane slowly. "Don't you remember?"

"Of course I do. That's why it's time for you to banish it," said Cornelia. "All this business with devil-traps and scrolls . . . there's no need for it."

"But—"

"No more *but*s," said Cornelia, sounding very much like Nancy once had. "The only reason we needed to mend the bowl was to prevent the Lord Indigator from taking possession of Nancy. That problem has been solved—perhaps not ideally, but at least permanently—which means it's in all of our best interests for you to send Smudge back from whence he came. The dying body upstairs might seem more appetizing now that this one has been taken."

Jane stared at Cornelia. This woman already didn't look much like her mother anymore; the way she carried herself, the set of her chin, her motions—they were all different. But she was acting like Nancy, a bit . . . that imperiousness was extremely familiar. And frankly, a lot like Miriam, when she was at her most impossible.

Only then did Jane realize her mother and her best friend were really and truly gone—gone forever, like rainwater soaking into the earth.

"Best not to dawdle," said Cornelia, as if Jane were idling out of laziness. "Only you can do it."

"I don't want to banish Smudge," said Jane. "We agreed not to. He saved me—earlier, I mean, when the shadow attacked. It's the shadow that's the problem, not him!"

"That's not what happened, Jane," said Cornelia. Jane began to feel as if that first, positive impression had been deceiving. This woman may have acquired Miriam's wry humor and Nancy's confidence, but she seemed to be twice as much of a know-it-all. "Smudge wasn't very concerned for you, from what I saw."

"What do you mean?" said Jane, shocked. Smudge had battled the shadow-cat and gotten it off her, then defended her from it when it had tried to go back for a second strike.

"He didn't exactly leap to your defense like a loyal mastiff," said Cornelia. "He waited until it was convenient for him. Hardly the action of a devoted familiar."

Jane didn't like this, not one bit. It seemed that no matter what, Nancy and Miriam would always end up ganging up on her . . .

"Jane," said Cornelia. "I know you're very attached to Smudge, but that demon is a menace, and not only that . . ."

"What?"

"It's just . . . your first binding didn't go so well, now did it?" said Cornelia, with a patronizing tone that set Jane's teeth on edge. "I can't find any possible justification for trying it again."

Jane looked into the eyes of this woman who sneered at her like her mother but was not her mother, who spoke without thought for anyone's feelings like her friend, but was not her friend. Their earlier pleasant moment left Jane's mind as her temper flared. How dare this woman suggest Jane banish Smudge! Smudge had supported her—he'd *saved* her, no matter what this newly minted "Cornelia" said.

Something brittle inside Jane finally snapped. She'd tried—by all the demons in the *Book*, she'd tried! Her whole life had been one long exhausting exercise in failing to live up to her mother's expectations, worrying about the Société's rules, trying not to hurt her friend's feelings—doing what she could to be what everyone demanded of her and never achieving it.

No longer.

She'd failed her Test, hadn't she? And failed in other ways, too. Cornelia was yet another manifestation of Jane's hubris, after all. And the unbound shadow prowling around the house, wreaking havoc here and in the village while Jane's eye was elsewhere . . . for Sam's death was on her hands, too.

It had been madness to ever think they'd get away with any it—fooling Jane's father, hiding Smudge, explaining away the state of the Library by blaming influenza, convincing the Société that all was well and she and Miriam were on the path to Mastery . . . Patrice Durand would have seen through it in an instant, and meted out what justice he saw fit.

We're not witches, *Jane!*

Maybe not, but Jane vowed she'd be gone by the time the moon was up—flying away on her broom for once and for all, just as she'd always dreamed of doing. She was surprised by her reaction to the thought; she had not expected to cry when it came time for her to leave this place, but she was.

"All right," she croaked, and from the relieved look on Cornelia's face, not even Jane's idols on the silver screen had ever given a more convincing performance of resignation and grief. "I'll need to get a few things."

"Do you need any help?" asked Cornelia. She was all sympathy now that Jane was seemingly obedient.

"Not yet," said Jane.

The tear she wiped away was real, but she let Cornelia come to her own conclusions about why she wept.

As Jane left the kitchen, Cornelia said, "You're doing the right thing."

"I know."

In fact, Jane had never felt more confident in her life.

JANE CALLED FOR SMUDGE as soon as Cornelia was out of ear-shot. She knew he would be close at hand. He had to be.

The cat emerged from the shadows as she reached the top of the stairs. She looked down at him fondly.

"Meow," he said.

"Come with me," said Jane. "We need to talk."

"Meow," agreed Smudge. He sauntered inside her room first, tail held high.

She shut the door behind them. "Smudge, will you please you call your shadow here?" It never hurt to be polite.

Smudge nodded. He jumped up on the desk, and a moment later, there the shadow was on the wall behind her cat, just where it should be—even if it shouldn't be looking at Jane out of those empty but expressive almond eyes.

"Hello," said Jane.

The shadow cocked its smoky head at her.

"It was very naughty of you to slash my face," said Jane.

The shadow-cat licked its paw, making a show of ignoring her.

Jane turned back to Smudge. She hoped the cat would not notice how she'd started sweating. But the truth was, she was nervous. Her previous attempts to bargain with demons had not been unalloyed successes, as Cornelia had pointed out.

"For safety's sake," said Jane, "will you please secure this room completely? I'd like it so that we can't be overheard or interrupted as we speak. I don't want anyone to be able to come in here or leave, given Cornelia's attitude toward us both."

Smudge nodded, his tail lashing back and forth across her desk.

Jane smiled at him. "Does that mean you have ensured that no one can observe us, and no one can come or go, until I say so?"

Once again, the cat nodded.

Jane sat on her bed and patted the patch of quilt beside her. The cat jumped over, proving once and for all that it was not a cat.

"She wants me to banish you," said Jane, and then looked to the shadow. "Both of you. But I don't want to."

"Meow," said Smudge.

"I'm ready to leave this all behind me," said Jane, speaking the truth of her heart aloud to this beast, just as she had always done. "But I can't. Not yet."

Smudge said nothing. He and his shadow watched her out of narrowed eyes, waiting to hear what she had to say.

"I can't leave here with your shadow loose and able to do as it likes," said Jane. "We all know you can't be trusted," she said, turning to the shadow. "That's the truth. So here's your choice, Smudge —and Smudge's shadow. I just ordered you to secure this room so that no one and nothing will ever leave it again. I will never release you from that unless you let me bind you and your shadow entirely to my will. Do you understand me?"

Both cats stared at her angrily, tails lashing in unison. Jane crossed her arms.

"Half a loaf, and all that," she said. "Partial freedom with me, or imprisonment—potentially—forever." She smiled and petted Smudge on the head. "You'd know better than I if you'll be stuck here after I die. Is your binding stronger than our original contract? That one specified my death, so I'm not quite sure how it would work, beyond that you'd certainly either be banished or trapped . . ."

Jane's heartbeat was loud in her ears during the long moment that followed.

Smudge and his shadow nodded their assent.

"Excellent," said Jane. She was very pleased, indeed.

Though Jane worked carefully, the binding went much more quickly than last time. She'd kept such meticulous notes that it was but the work of a moment to set everything up. Threading the needle was the hardest part, but soon enough she was using it to bind the shadow to Smudge, and bind Smudge again under the name Lord Indigator.

When she was done, she knelt down and scooped Smudge up into her arms. He submitted humbly to being held like a baby, on his back, and she kissed his nose.

"That's a good demon," she said. And looking at the cat's shadow on the wall, she said, "And I hope to say the same of you one day."

The shadow closed its empty eyes and yawned, displaying a jagged, but bored maw of shadow-teeth.

JANE WASN'T SURPRISED WHEN a knock came at the door as she and Smudge were packing her valise. Evening had fallen as they worked; naturally Cornelia would want an update. They had taken their time, thinking carefully about what items, diabolic and mundane, they would take. Edith's dress was carefully wrapped in paper and set at the bottom; it needed mending before Jane could wear it again. Instead, she had donned her smartest blouse, skirt, and hat. Her cloak she would have to sacrifice, but one day she could get another. Black, just like she'd always wanted.

"Jane?" called Cornelia. "How's it going?"

"Let her hear me," Jane said to Smudge. "All right," she called.

"Just trying to do it right the first time, you know! Can't muck it up."

"You had everything you needed?" Cornelia seemed surprised and a little suspicious.

Jane thought fast. "No, not everything," she said. "Could you get me some liquid essence from the storeroom?"

"Why not take a break and come get it with me," said Cornelia. "You've been in there for hours."

"She's on to us," whispered Jane. "We need to get out of here, and quickly." Smudge nodded as Jane threw the last few items she'd set out into her bag, not bothering to place them carefully as she had with the rest.

"Open the door," said Cornelia. "Jane, open up! The Patron says—"

But Jane never found out what the Patron had to say. Instead, she placed her broom outside her window to hang there in the early spring gloaming. Valise in hand, Jane took one last look at her room and then turned away to see Smudge had already jumped onto the handle. He purred as she clambered up behind him.

"Meow," he said.

"That's just what I was thinking," said Jane, and turned them up and away from the old farmhouse and into the purple starlit twilight of the wider world.

EPILOGUE

Edith's citroën jolted along the muddy road into
Hawkshead, but Edith was not behind the wheel. Her feet
no longer reached the pedals.

"I hate the way you drive," she said to Patrice Durand, who
downshifted exactly when Edith would not have.

"Well, I hate your car. The French can do anything except make
a decent automobile. You should replace this hunk of junk with a
Jaguar or an Alfa Romeo."

Edith frowned as Mercurialis betrayed her with a chuckle.

Oh, it's not so bad, *is it?* it said. *At least we still have each other . . .*

It was such an oddly sentimental thing for a demon to say that
Edith spent the rest of the ride and much of their time in the mule
cart thinking about it. From the first moments of her apprenticeship she'd been taught never to trust a demon when it spoke of
friendship or love. Not for the first time did she wonder if perhaps
there were possibilities beyond the proscriptions of the Société.

Maybe, said Mercurialis.

So much had changed for Edith since that ill-fated attack on
Braune's castle, but the old farmhouse was still exactly the same.
Rain-wet, unfashionable, isolated . . . comfortable, and familiar.

Then Edith hopped out of the cart and approached the front
door. It looked like it would to a child—enormous, imposing, and
built for the convenience of people much larger than she.

A light rain was misting down upon them, but Edith couldn't
make herself ring the bell.

"Can't you reach?" asked Patrice.

It had been Patrice's way to tease her when she was in a funk over the changes she'd gone through. But this time, Edith ignored the sally.

"Odd, isn't it?" she said. "Them not coming to meet us, I mean. They always did before."

"They don't know you're here," said Patrice. "And their reply telegram said something about flu . . ."

"That's right, flu," said Edith. She had forgotten the excuse, for then as now that had seemed like a lie.

Patrice put an avuncular hand on Edith's half-sized shoulder. "It will be all right," he said. "No one will laugh, no one will—"

Edith rang the doorbell.

After a few moments, Nancy answered. She looked strange. Maybe she really had come down with the flu . . .

"Hello, Patrice," she said stiffly. Then she noticed who stood beside him. "Aunt—ah, Edith!"

Aunt Edith.

Mercurialis rumbled in her mind, but Edith didn't betray any surprise. She sensed there was much here that she would learn in time, if she were patient.

"I wanted you to see I was all right," said Edith.

"Come in," said the woman who looked like Nancy. "Warm up with a spot of tea, and I've baked too. Currant scones."

"Thank you," said Patrice. He was staring at Nancy like she was an angel who had stepped down off of a cloud. Edith was a bit embarrassed. Soppiness didn't become him.

They shed their coats in the quiet entryway, and then Nancy ushered them into the kitchen. It smelled of warm baking in there, and Nancy bustled to make some tea. Edith stood awkwardly. She was a bit surprised at Nancy—for some reason, Edith was having a hard time thinking of this woman as *her sister*. She didn't need to be fussed over, but at the same time, she'd been shrunk by half and Nancy hadn't said even a word about it.

"So. Where's Jane?" asked Patrice, sitting awkwardly at the rustic kitchen table. He kept sneaking glances at Nancy. It would have been sweet except for the obvious awkwardness.

"She's out," said Nancy.

"And Miriam?" asked Edith.

Nancy set the tea upon the table. "Patrice, would you excuse us for a moment? I'd like to speak to my sister in private."

"But of course," said Patrice, rising as the two women made their exit. "I'll keep an eye on the tea, and it will be ready when you're back."

"Help yourself to it and the scones in the meantime," said Nancy.

She fairly dragged Edith away from the kitchen, leading her up the stairs with a child's urgency. They stopped in front of Miriam's room.

"What's gotten into you, Nance?" asked Edith, playing along for now.

"You'd be surprised," said Nancy. "What I'm about to show you will shock you, but it can't be helped. I need you, Edith. Please say you'll help me?"

"Help you with what?" asked Edith.

Then Nancy pushed open Miriam's bedroom door, and Edith understood.

Miriam lay upon the bed—Edith was certain it was Miriam, even if the girl looked like an immeasurably ancient woman with her white hair spilling over her pillow and the deep lines marring her face. She was still breathing, but barely.

"What happened?" asked Edith.

"I don't even know where to begin," said Nancy.

"Then just pick somewhere and start!" Edith was getting a bit frustrated. It wasn't like Nancy to keep her in suspense. "Tell me the most surprising thing first, then work backwards if you have to."

"That's not a bad idea," said Nancy. She took a deep breath. "I'm not your sister anymore. My name is Cornelia, and I am the spiritual amalgamation of your sister Nancy and Miriam Cantor. Miriam's body is dying; she overspent herself trying to find out what happened to her parents. And meanwhile, Jane has absconded with the diabolic familiar she summoned into her pet cat, in spite of my best efforts to get her to banish it. And all this is happening while the Société's Evaluator is sitting in my parlor."

Edith was too shocked to say anything, but Mercurialis wasn't.

This trip is going to be much more interesting than I anticipated, it said.

ACKNOWLEDGMENTS

I was at a bit of a loss when it came to coming up with the dedication for this, the third and final book of the Diabolist's Library trilogy of novels. For a long time I'd considered dedicating it to my anxiety, as it is a novel all about it, but I wasn't sure that would set the correct tone. I also considered dedicating it to my cat, but he can't read, and even if he could, he wouldn't appreciate the gesture. When I said as much to my editor, he reminded me of my duty, suggesting I dedicate the book to everyone who has fought against the rise of fascism—so that is exactly what I have done. I just don't know how to put that into a pithy remark for the front of the book, but the back will do just as well.

As for the acknowledgments, as always I would like to thank my editor, John Joseph Adams; my agent, Cameron McClure; and my team at HMH, especially Jaime Levine. And, also as always, I will thank my mother, and I will thank my friends for their support and love, and my colleagues for their tolerance for me sliding into their DMs with questions about things like what guns people would carry during World War II.

And while I didn't dedicate this book to my cat, "the Toad," I will indeed thank him here by name. While Smudge is a conglomeration of all the devilish felines I've met over the years, Smudge's moods and antics are based most heavily upon careful observation of my own special boy. I'd say more, but he's just jumped into my lap, after being very—or at least *somewhat* patient with how much time and attention I lavished on this project, rather than on him.

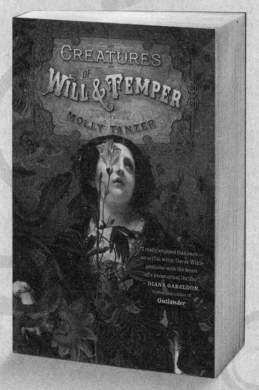

Ellie West fishes by day and sells moonshine by night
to the citizens of her hometown on Long Island, New York, in 1927.
But after Ellie's father joins a church whose parishioners
possess supernatural powers and a violent hatred for
immigrants, Ellie finds she doesn't know her beloved island,
or her father, as well as she thought.

"Charming, confident . . . *The Great Gatsby* crashes into the
works of H. P. Lovecraft, with, of course, chaotic results."
—*Publishers Weekly*, starred review

"This is a measured, atmospheric novel, with compelling characters
and a deeply disturbing undercurrent of horror . . .
It's a fascinating novel, and an accomplished one."

—Tor.com

9781328710253 • $16.99 • Also available as an e-book